Tree-House Comix Proudly Presents

DOG MAN
BRAWL of The WILD

WRITTEN AND ILLUSTRATED BY DAV PILKEY
AS GEORGE BEARD AND HAROLD HUTCHINS
WITH COLOR BY JOSE GARIBALDI

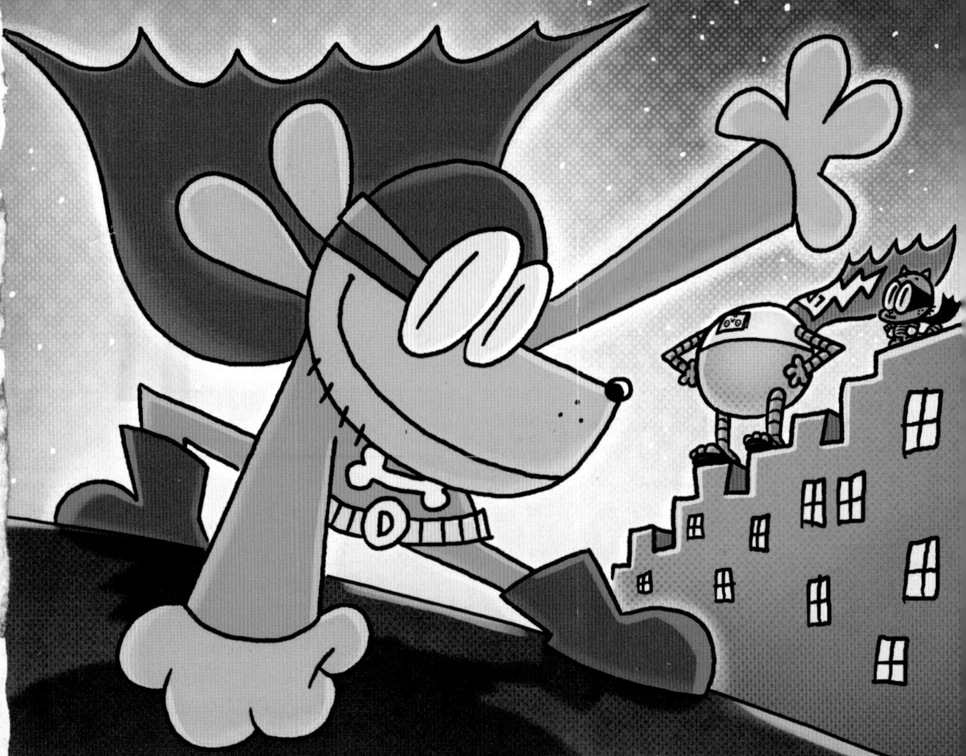

graphix
AN IMPRINT OF
SCHOLASTIC

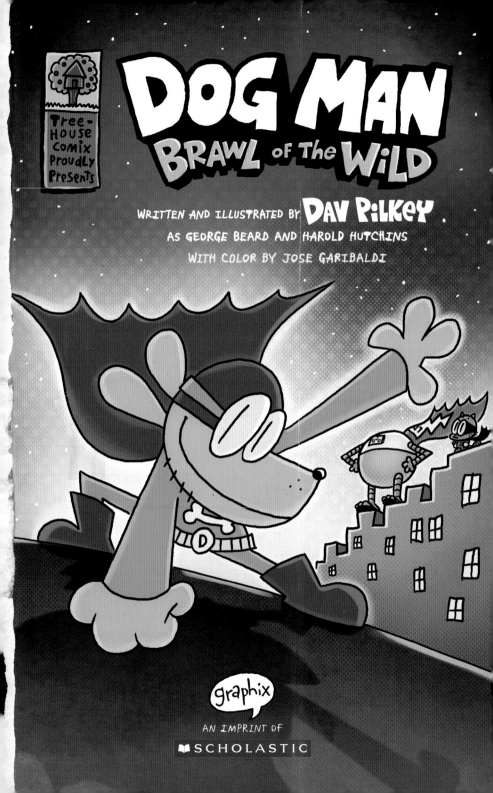

FOR LIZETTE SERRANO
THANK YOU FOR YOUR STRENGTH,
COMPASSION, AND DEVOTION
TO LIBRARIES AND KIDS

Library of Congress Control Number 2018945989

978-1-338-74108-7 (POB)
978-1-338-29092-9 (Library)

10 9 8 7 6 5 4   21 22 23 24 25

Printed in China   62
This edition first printing, August 2021

Edited by Ken Geist
Book design by Dav Pilkey and Phil Falco
Color by Jose Garibaldi
Color flatting by Aaron Polk
Creative Director: Phil Falco
Publisher: David Saylor

CHAPTERS

WITHDRAWN

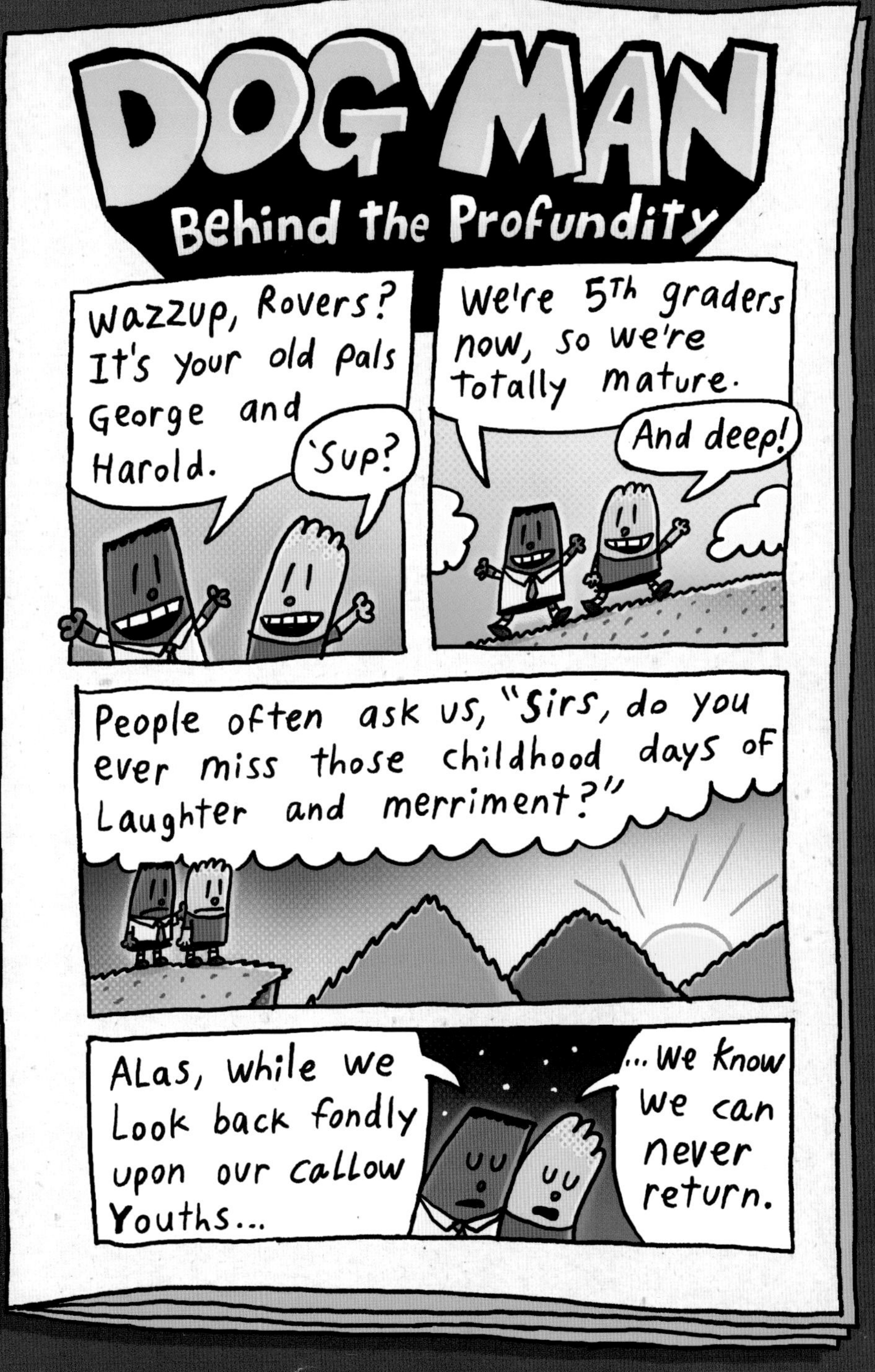
DOG MAN
Behind the Profundity
Wazzup, Rovers? It's your old pals George and Harold.
'Sup?
We're 5th graders now, so we're totally mature.
And deep!
People often ask us, "Sirs, do you ever miss those childhood days of Laughter and merriment?"
ALas, while we Look back fondly upon our calLow Youths...
...We know we can never return.

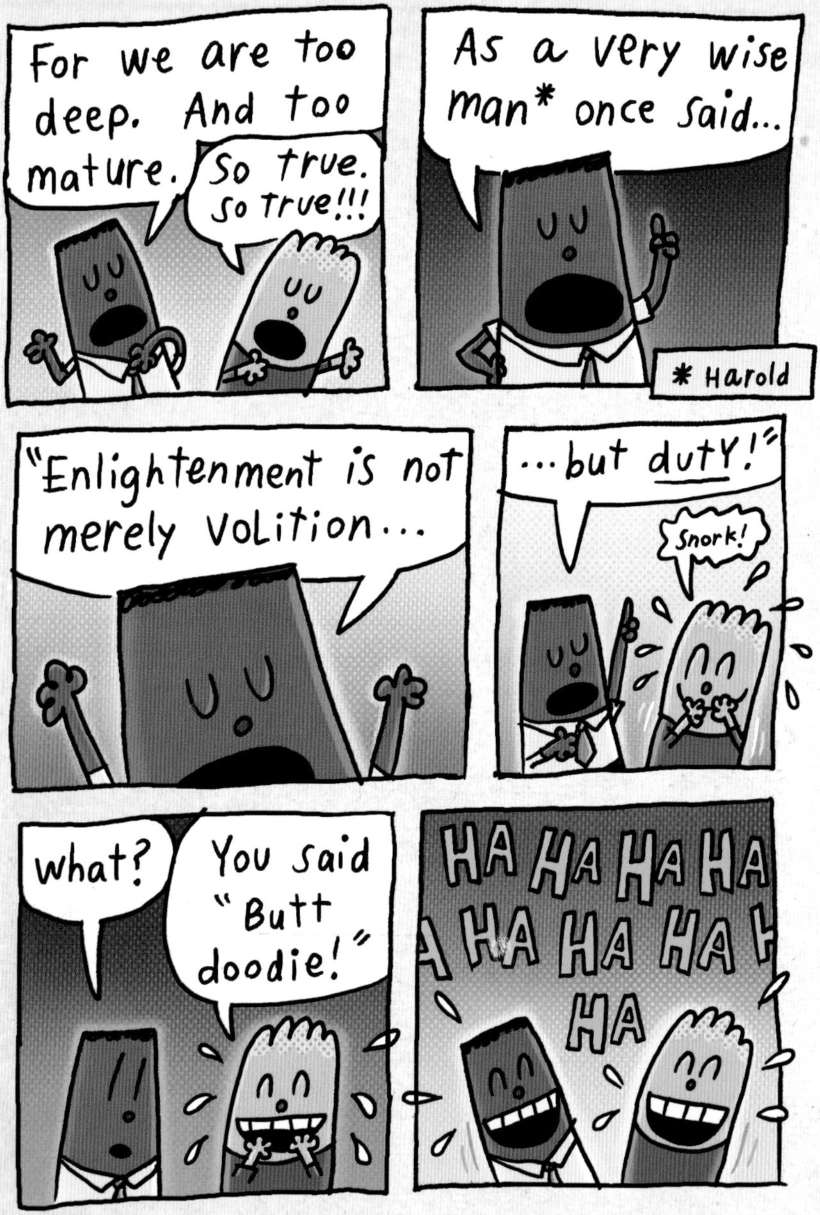
For we are too deep. And too mature.
So true. So true!!!
As a very wise man* once said...
* Harold
"Enlightenment is not merely volition...
...but duty!"
Snork!
What?
You said "Butt doodie!"
HA HA HA HA
HA HA HA HA
HA

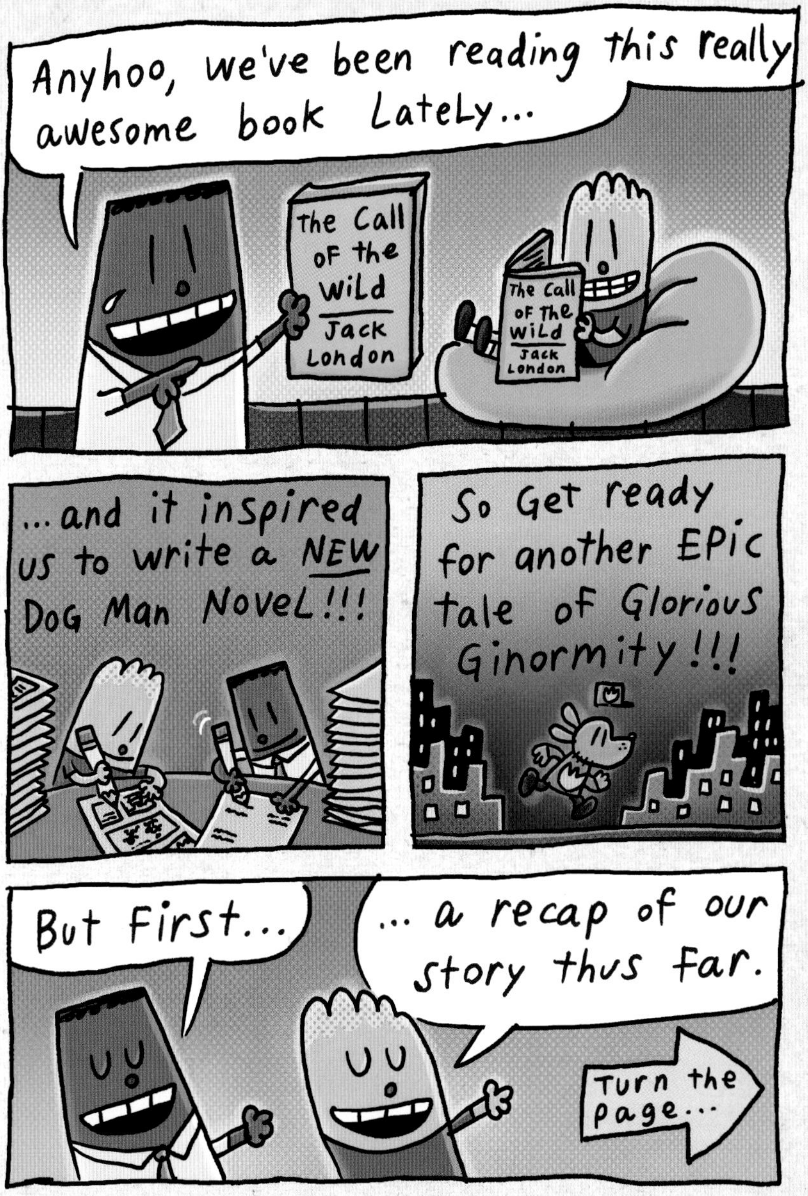

Anyhoo, we've been reading this really awesome book LateLy...
The Call of the WiLd Jack London
The Call of The WiLd Jack London
...and it inspired us to write a NEW Dog Man NoveL!!!
So Get ready for another EPic tale of Glorious Ginormity!!!
But First...
...a recap of our story thus far.
Turn the page...

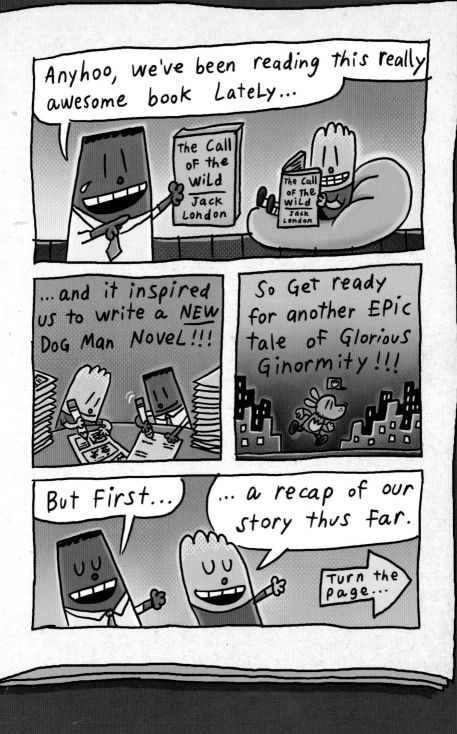

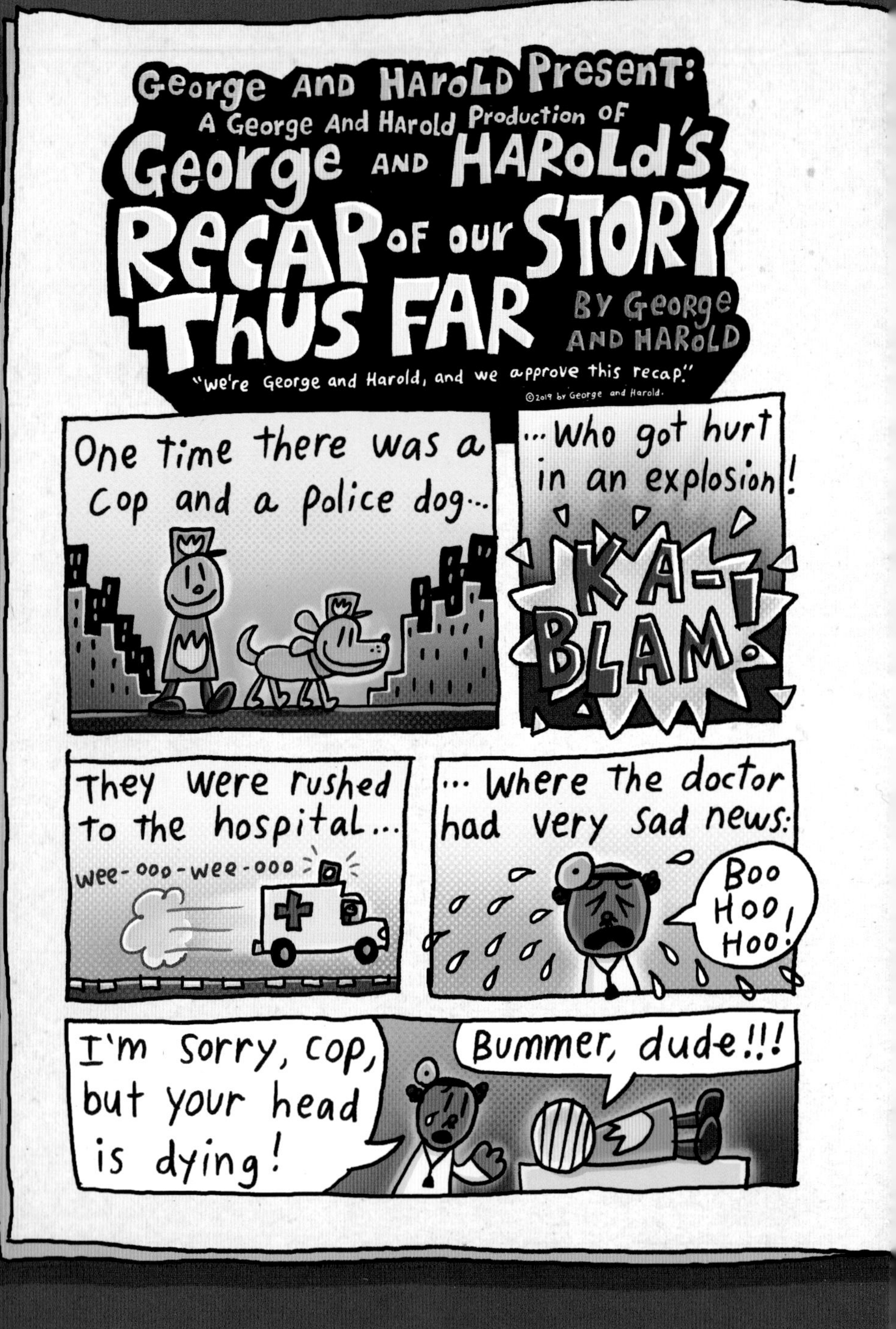
George and Harold Present:
A George And Harold Production of
George and Harold's
Recap of our Story Thus Far
By George and Harold
"We're George and Harold, and we approve this recap."
©2019 by George and Harold.
One time there was a cop and a police dog...
...Who got hurt in an explosion!
KA-BLAM!
They were rushed to the hospital...
wee-ooo-wee-ooo
...Where the doctor had very sad news:
Boo Hoo Hoo!
I'm sorry, cop, but your head is dying!
Bummer, dude!!!

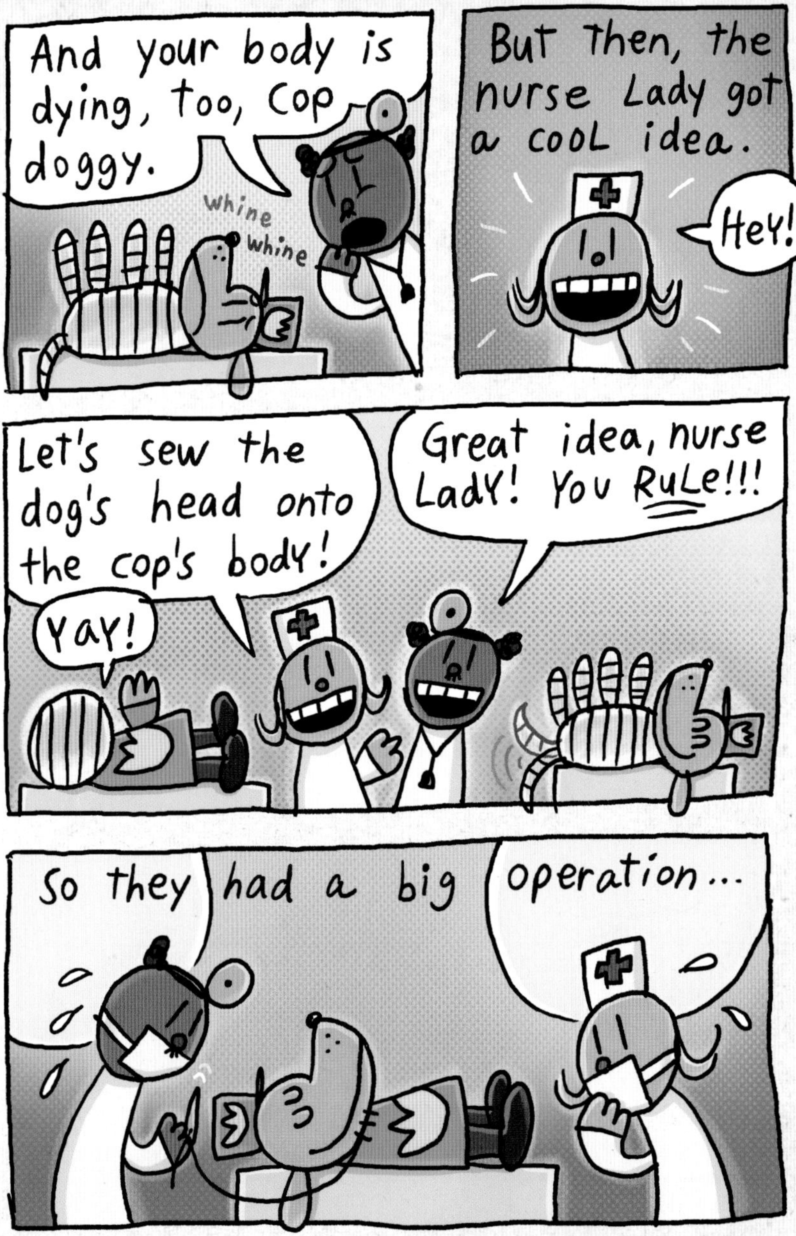
And your body is dying, too, Cop doggy.
whine whine
But Then, the nurse Lady got a cooL idea.
Hey!
Let's sew the dog's head onto the cop's body!
Great idea, nurse Lady! You RuLe!!!
Yay!
So they had a big operation...

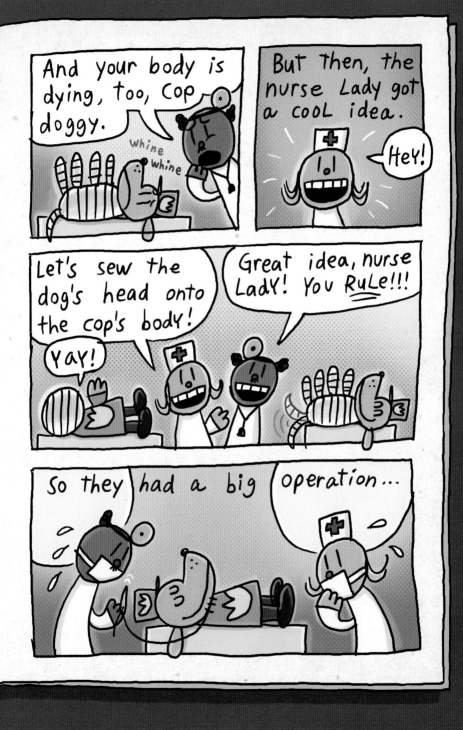

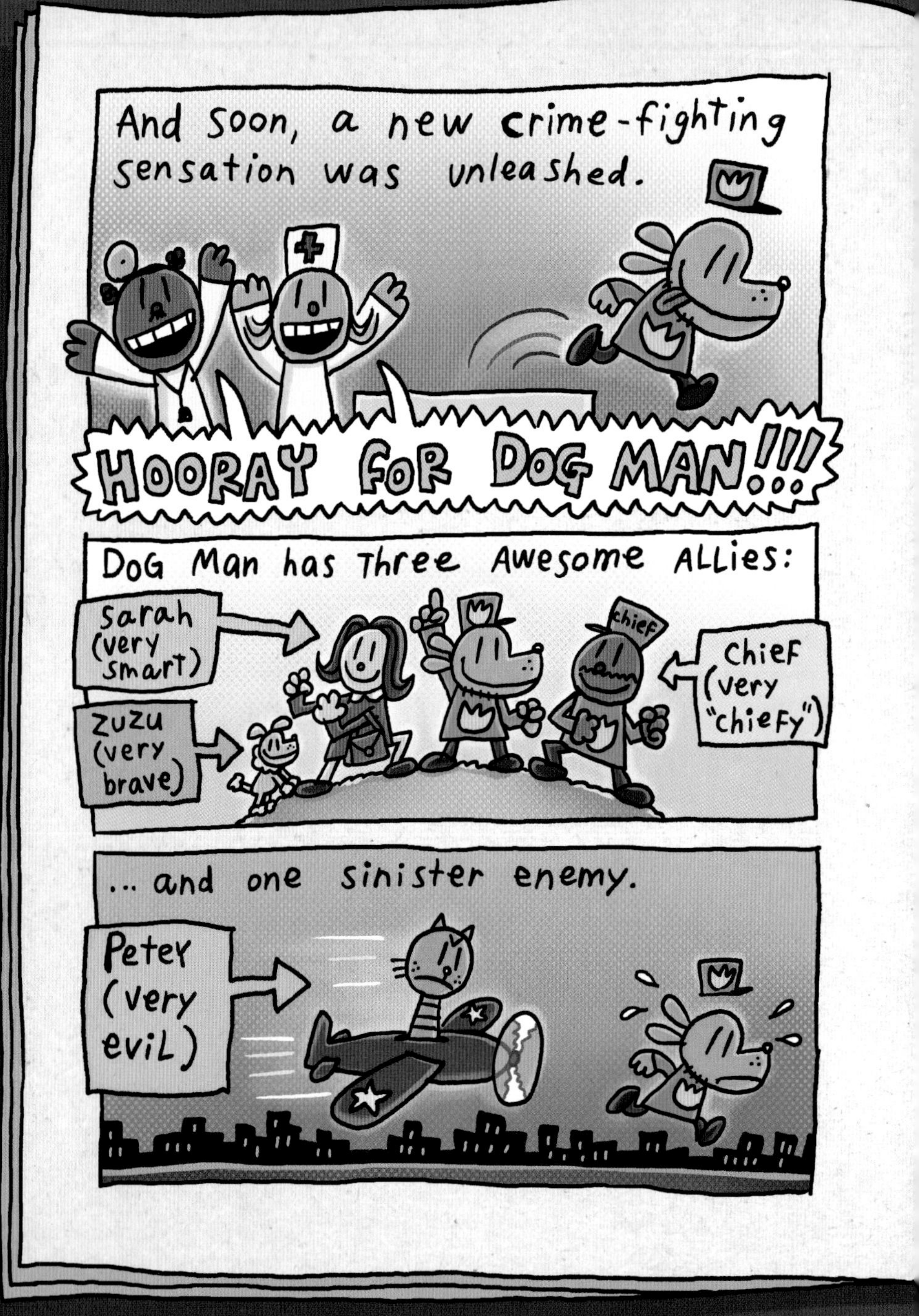

And soon, a new crime-fighting sensation was unleashed.
HOORAY FOR DOG MAN!!!
DOG Man has Three Awesome ALLies:
Sarah (very smart)
Zuzu (very brave)
Chief
Chief (very "chiefy")
... and one sinister enemy.
Peter (very evil)

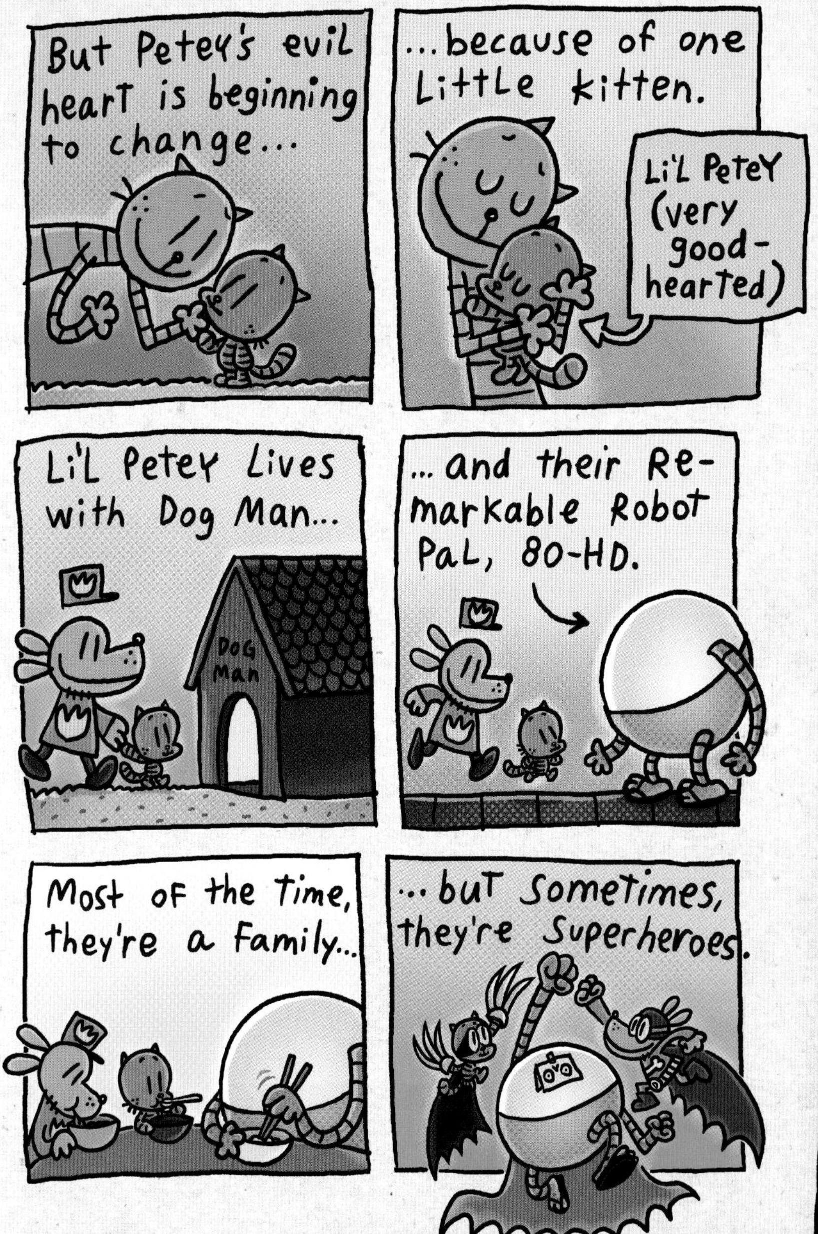

But Petey's evil heart is beginning to change...
...because of one little kitten.
Li'l Petey (very good-hearted)
Li'l Petey lives with Dog Man...
DOG MAN
...and their Re-markable Robot Pal, 80-HD.
Most of the time, they're a Family...
...but Sometimes, they're Superheroes.

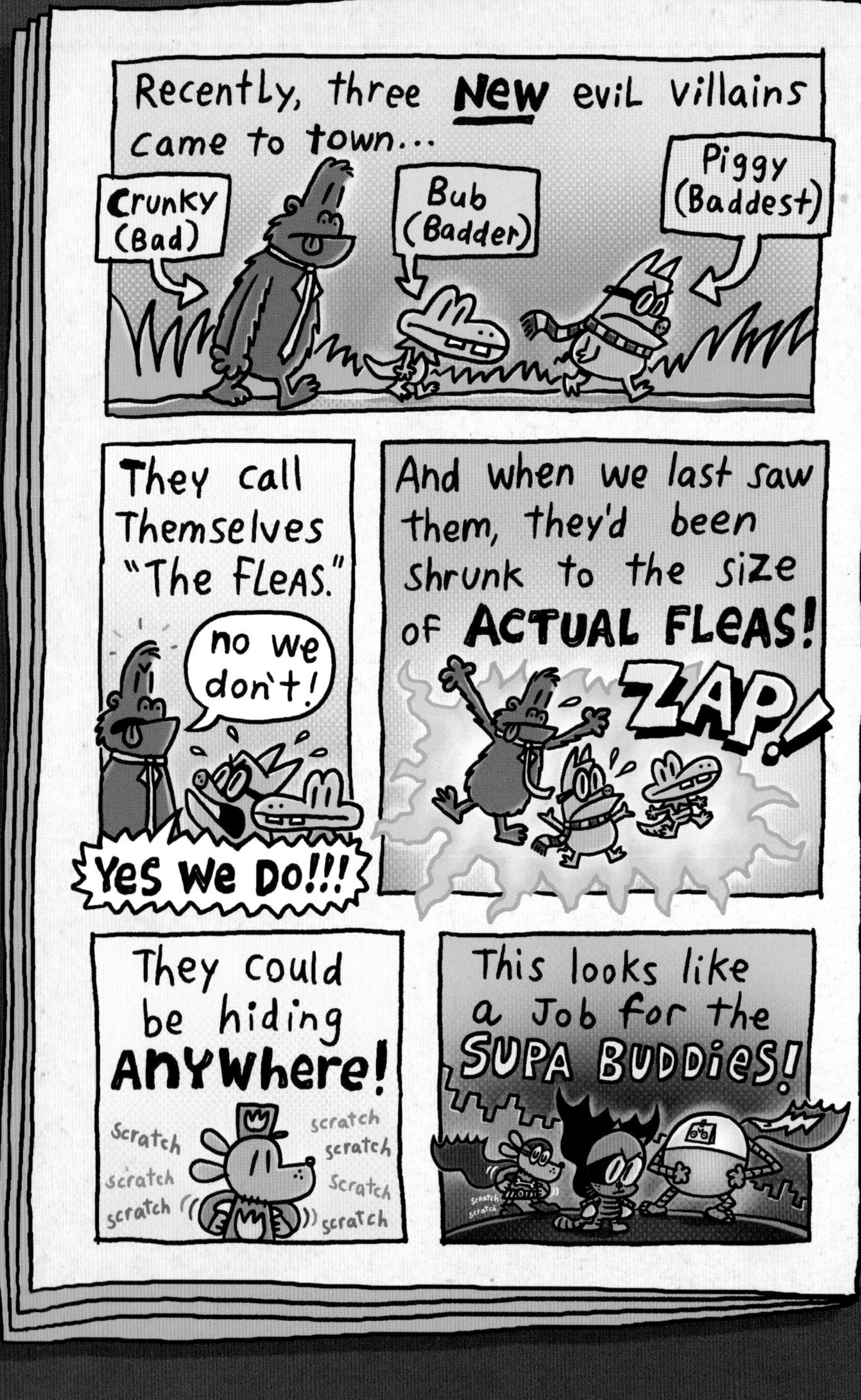

Recently, three NEW eviL villains came to town...
Crunky (Bad)
Bub (Badder)
Piggy (Baddest)
They call Themselves "The FLeAS."
no we don't!
YES WE DO!!!
And when we last saw them, they'd been shrunk to the size of ACTUAL FLEAS!
ZAP!
They could be hiding ANYWhere!
scratch
scratch
scratch
scratch
scratch
scratch
scratch
scratch
This looks like a Job for the SUPA BUDDIES!

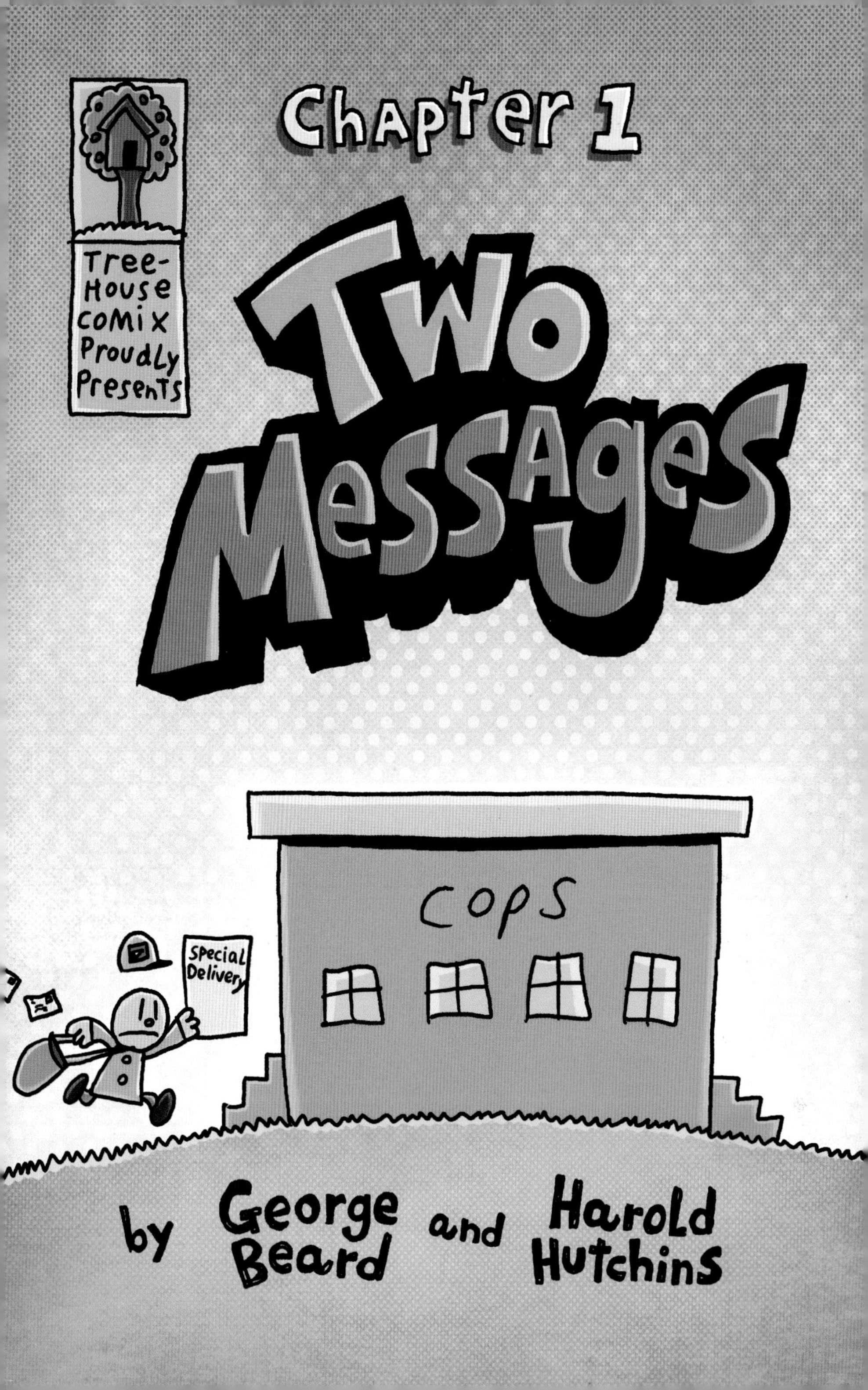
Chapter 1
Tree-House Comix Proudly Presents
Two Messages
Special Delivery
COPS
by George Beard and Harold Hutchins

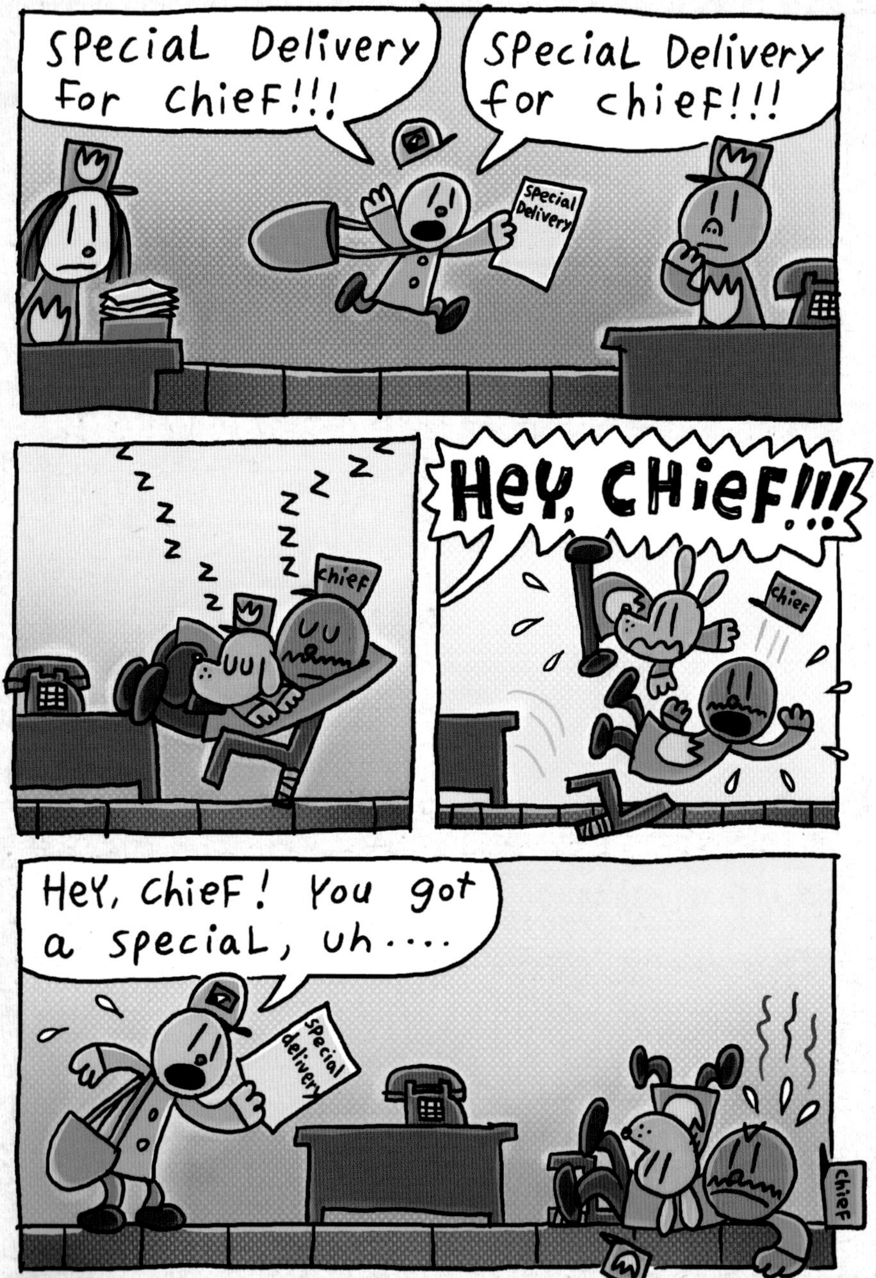
Special Delivery for Chief!!!
Special Delivery for chief!!!
Special Delivery
chief
HEY, CHIEF!!!
chief
Hey, Chief! You got a special, uh....
Special delivery
chief

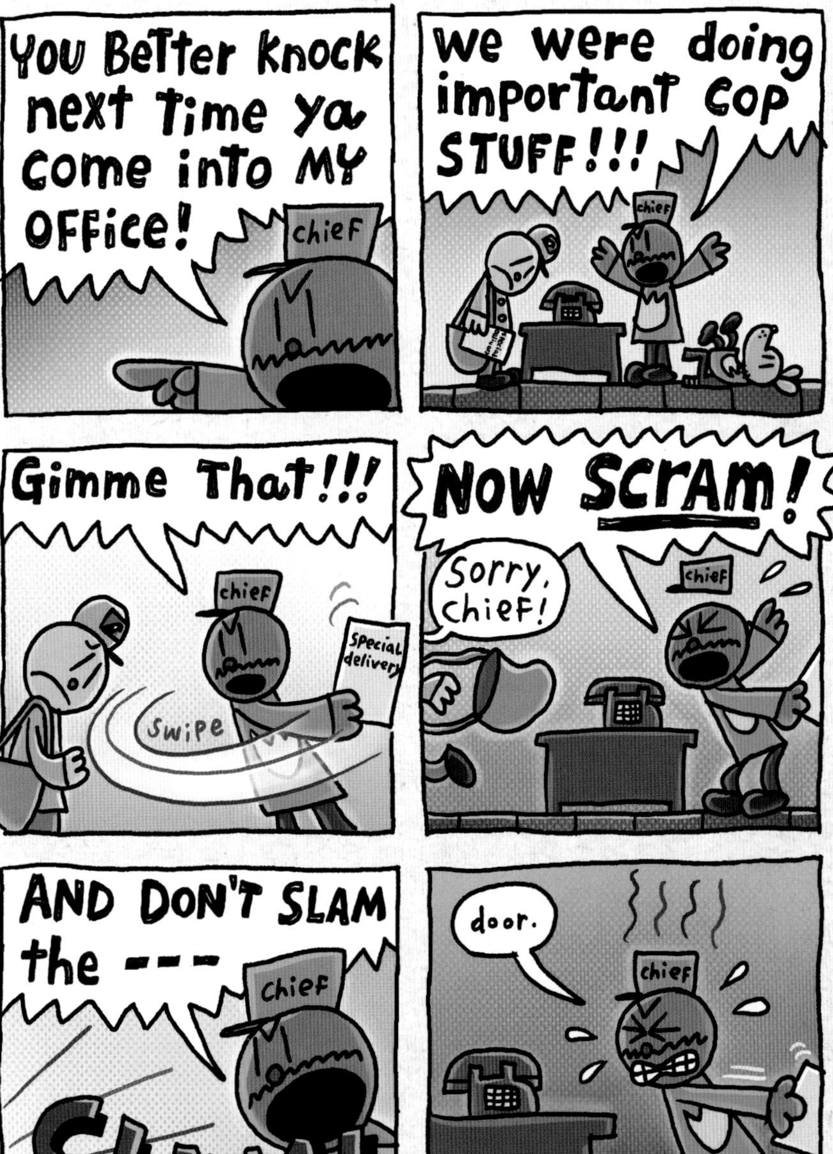

YOU BeTTer Knock next Time ya come into MY OFFice!
chieF
We were doing important cop STUFF!!!
chieF
Gimme That!!!
chieF
Special delivery
swipe
NOW SCRAM!
Sorry, chieF!
chieF
AND DON'T SLAM the ---
chieF
SLAM!
door.
chieF

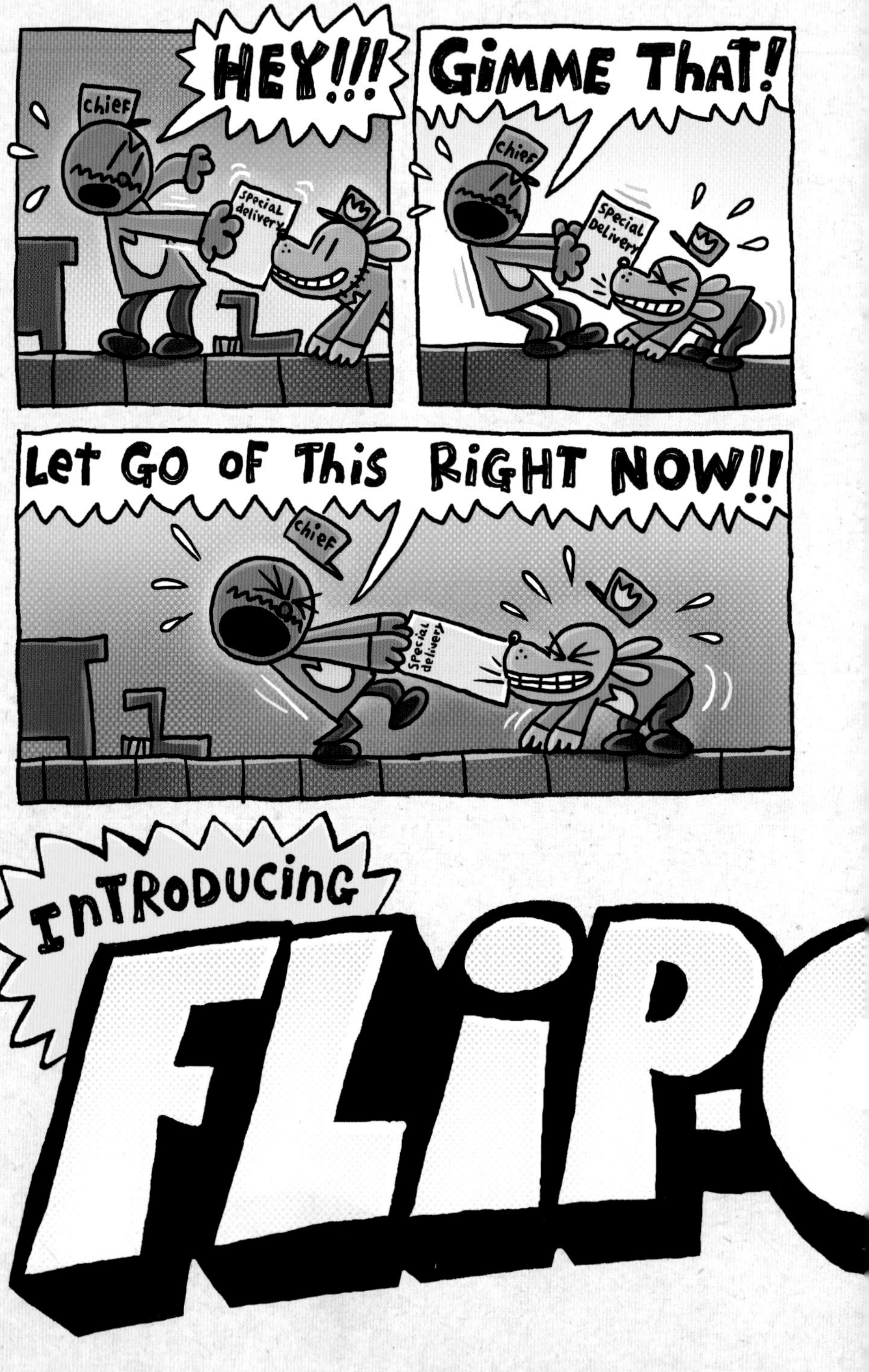
HEY!!!
chief
special delivery
GiMME THAT!
chief
Special Delivery
LET GO OF THIS RIGHT NOW!!
chief
special delivery
INTRODUCING
FLIP

STEP 1.
First, Place your Left hand inside the dotted Lines marked "Left hand here." HoLd The book open *FLAT*!

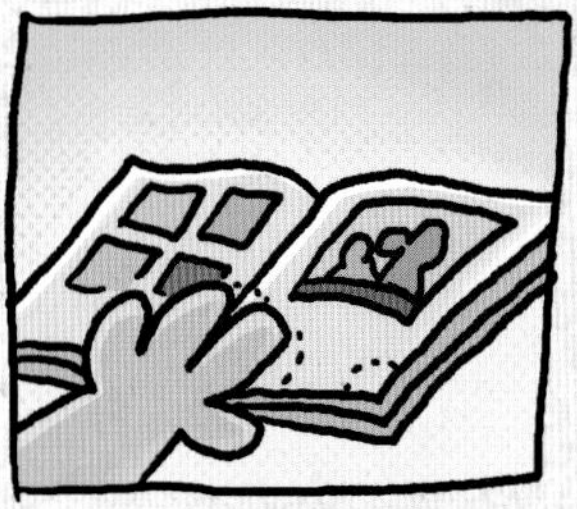

STEP 2:
Grasp the right-hand Page with your Thumb and index finger (inside the dotted Lines marked "Right Thumb Here").

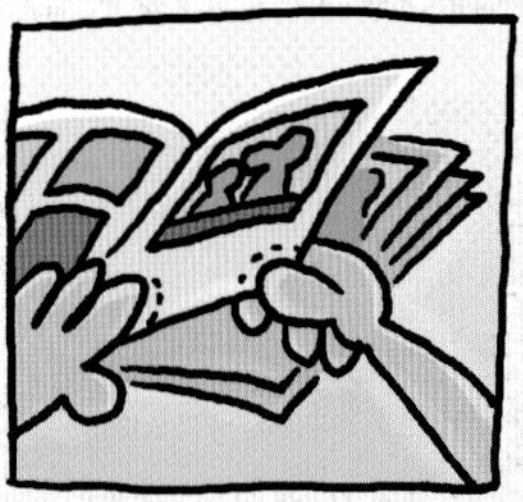

STEP 3:
Now *QUICKLY* fLip the right-hand Page back and forth until the Picture appears to be *Animated*.

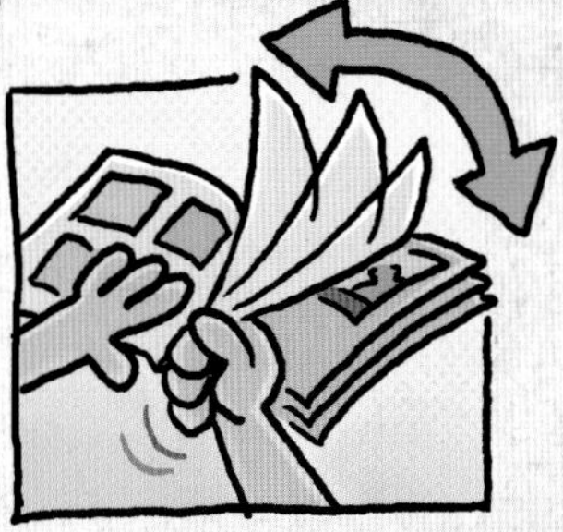

(for extra fun, try adding your own sound-effects!)

RAMA

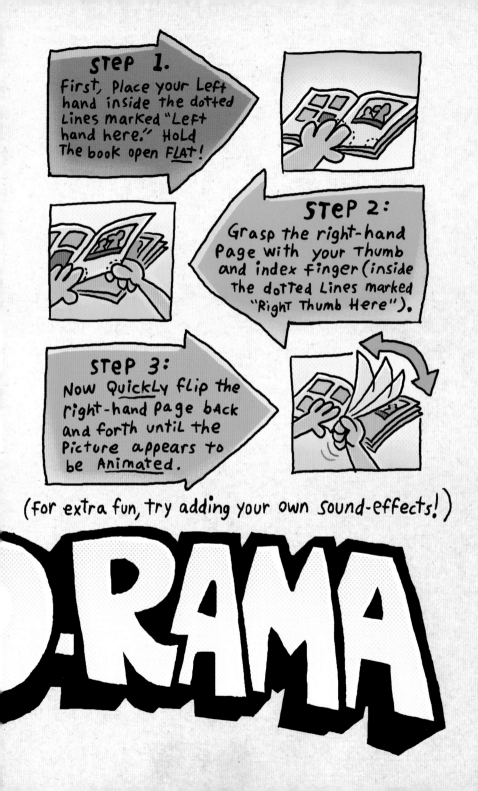

Remember,

while you are flipping,
be sure you can see
the image on page 19
AND the image on page 21.

If you flip quickly,
the two pictures will
start to look like
one **Animated** cartoon!

Don't forget to
add your own
sound-effects!

Left
hand here.

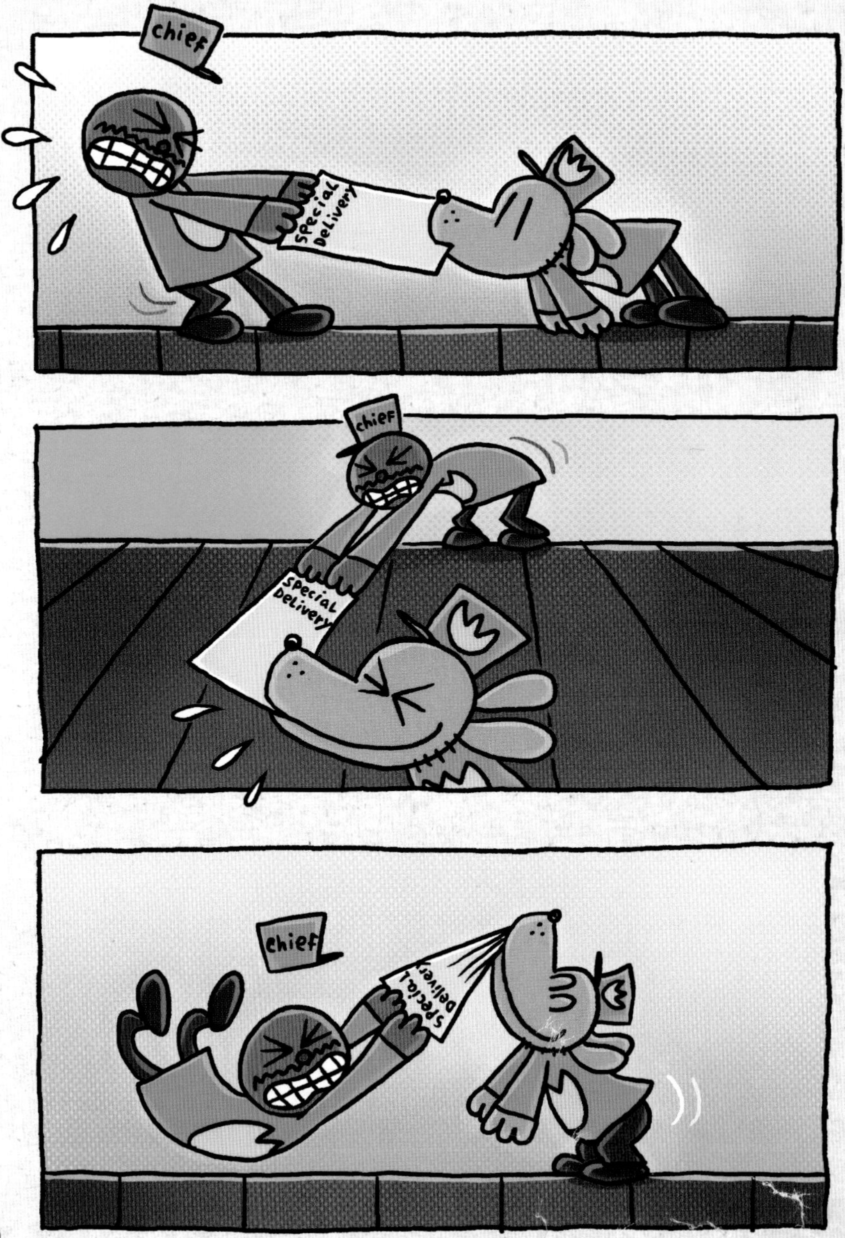
chief
Special Delivery
chief
Special Delivery
chief
Special Delivery

Right Thumb here.

21

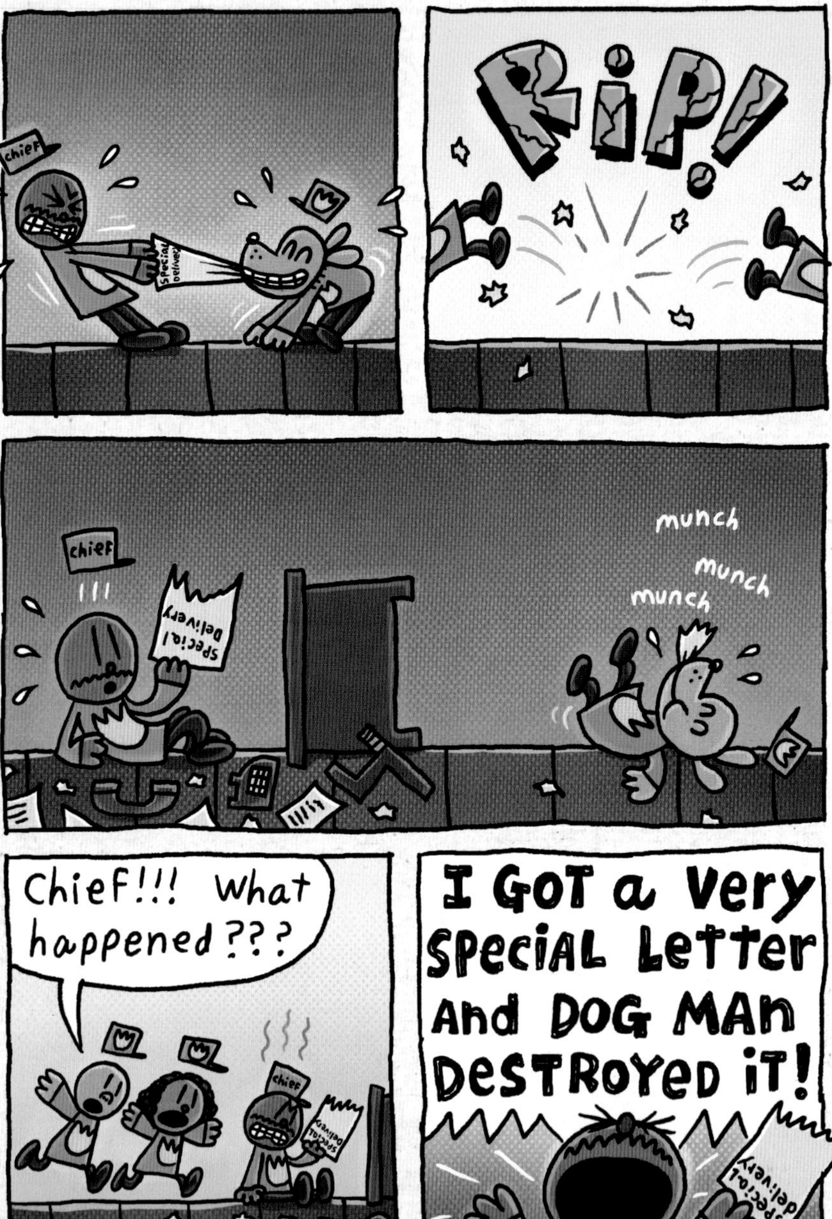
chief
Special Delivery
RiP!
chief
Special Delivery
munch
munch
munch
Chief!!! What happened???
chief
Special Delivery
I GOT a Very SPECiAL Letter And DOG MAN DESTROYED iT!
Special delivery

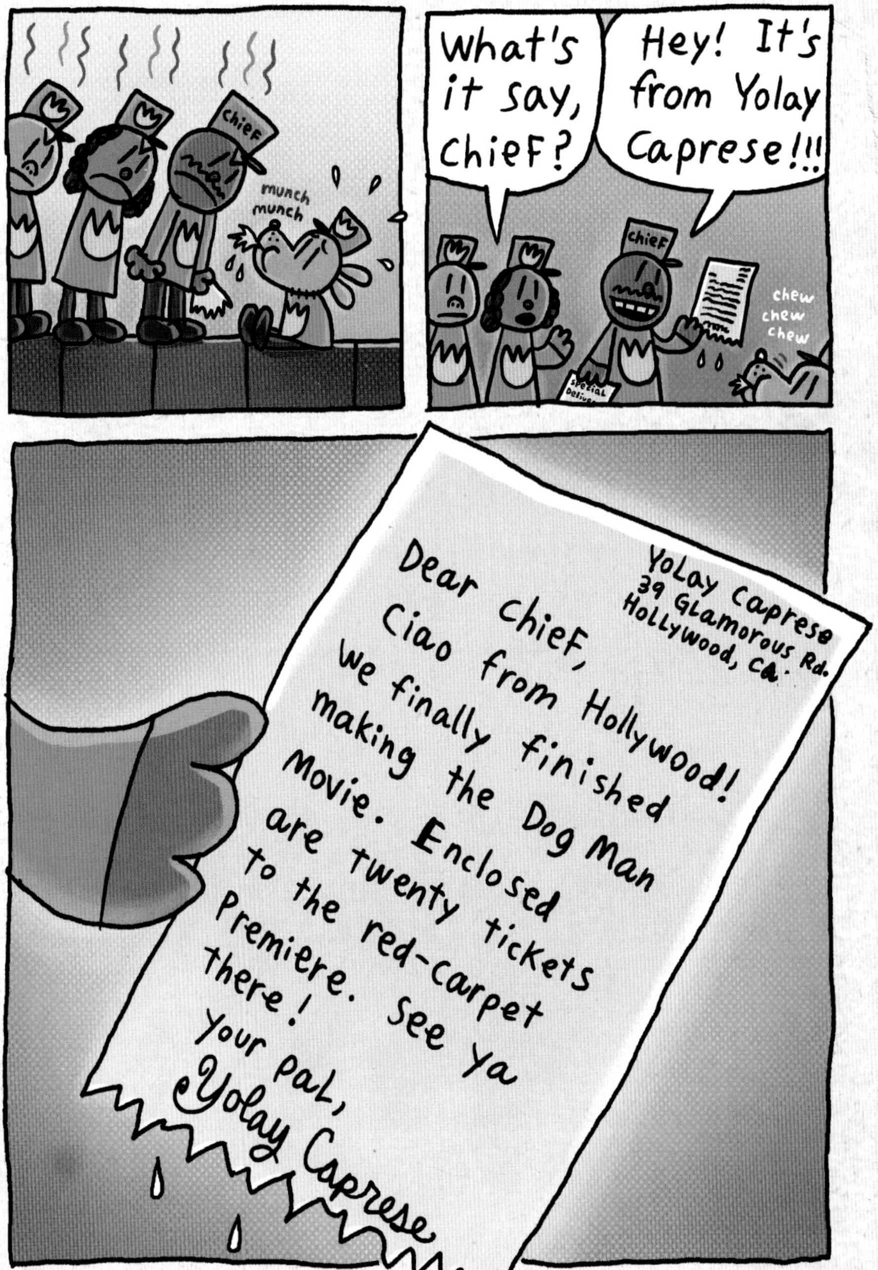
munch munch
What's it say, Chief?
Hey! It's from Yolay Caprese!!!
Chief
Special Delivery
chew chew chew
Yolay Caprese
39 Glamorous Rd.
Hollywood, CA
Dear Chief,
Ciao from Hollywood!
We finally finished making the Dog Man Movie. Enclosed are twenty tickets to the red-carpet Premiere. See ya there!
Your pal,
Yolay Caprese

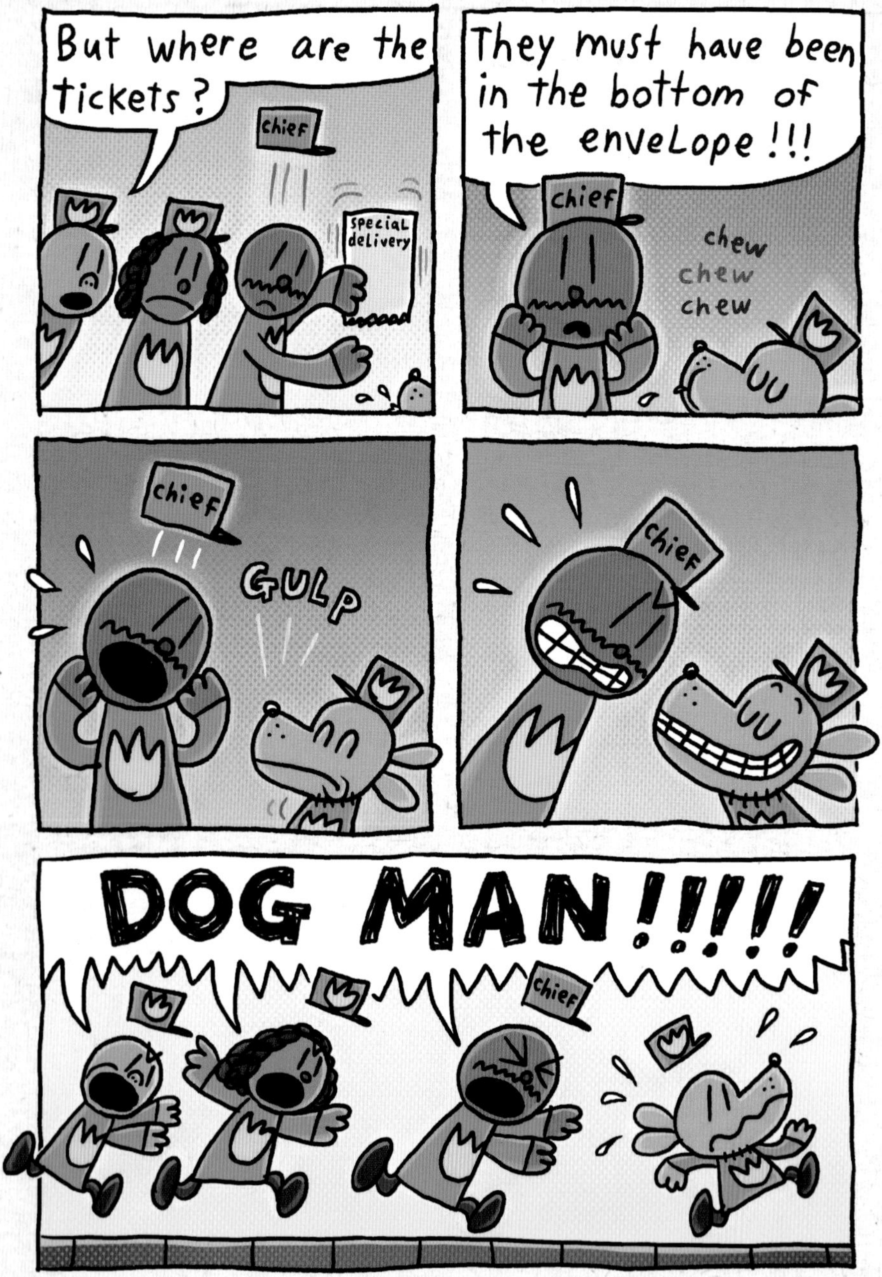

But where are the tickets?
chief
special delivery
They must have been in the bottom of the envelope!!!
chief
chew chew chew
chief
GULP
chief
DOG MAN!!!!!
chief

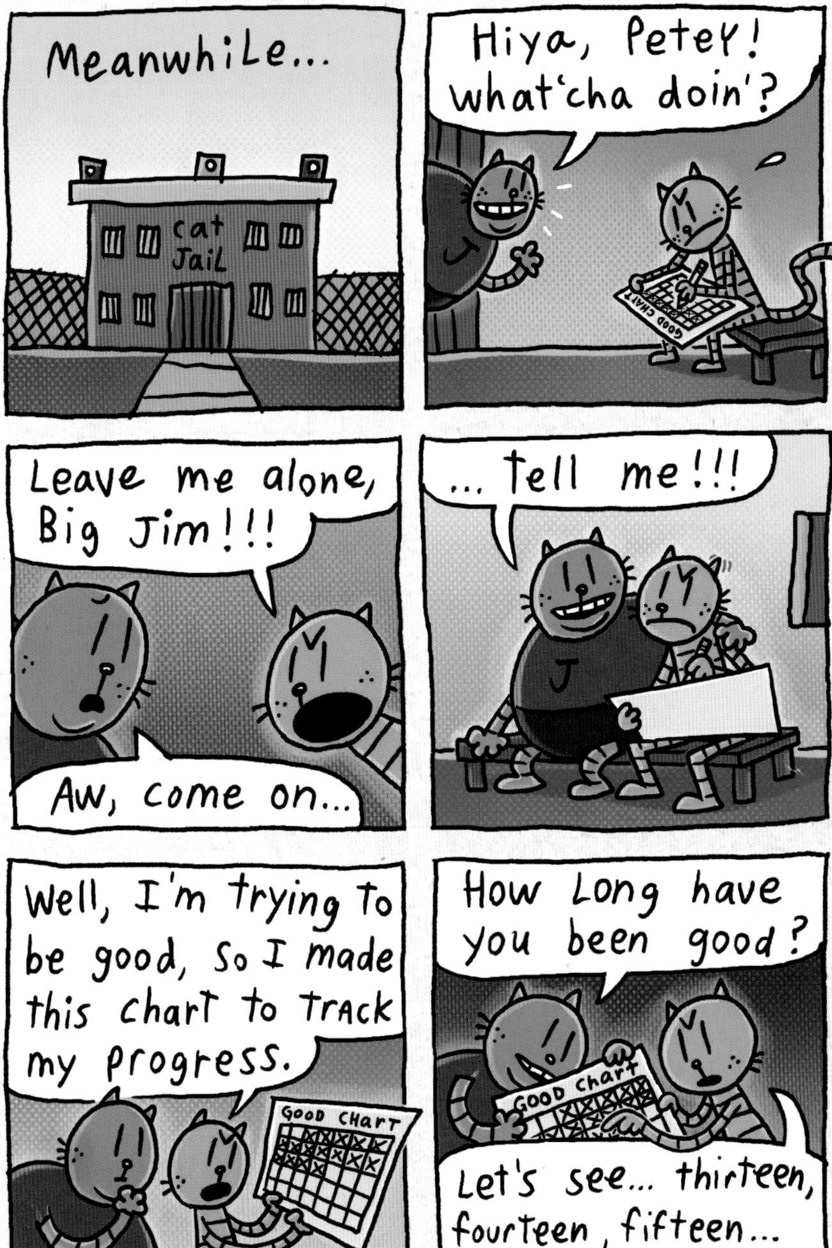
Meanwhile...
Cat Jail
Hiya, Petey! what'cha doin'?
GOOD CHART
Leave me alone, Big Jim!!!
Aw, come on...
... Tell me!!!
Well, I'm trying to be good, so I made this chart to track my progress.
GOOD CHART
How long have you been good?
GOOD CHART
Let's see... thirteen, fourteen, fifteen...

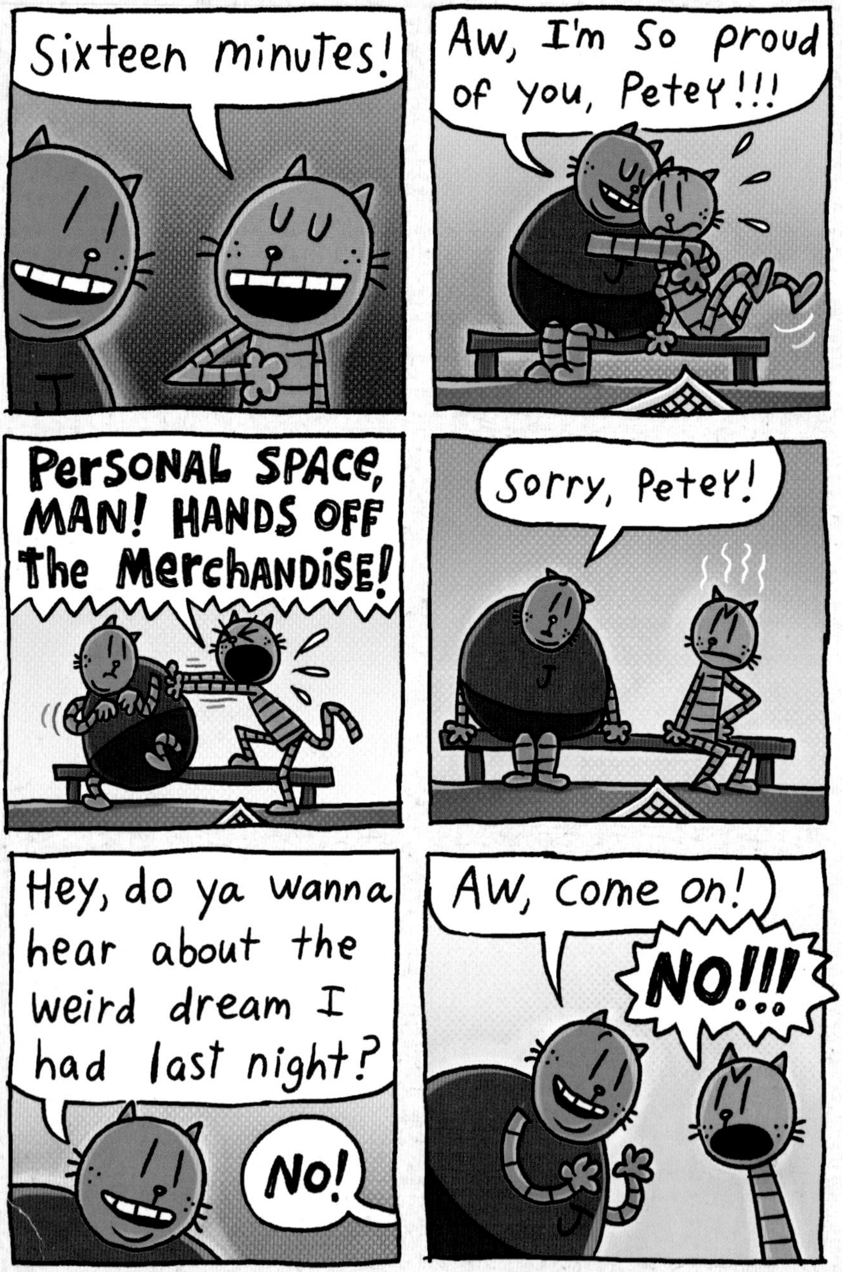
Sixteen minutes!
Aw, I'm so proud of you, Petey!!!
PERSONAL SPACE, MAN! HANDS OFF the MERCHANDISE!
Sorry, Petey!
Hey, do ya wanna hear about the weird dream I had last night?
NO!
Aw, come on!
NO!!!

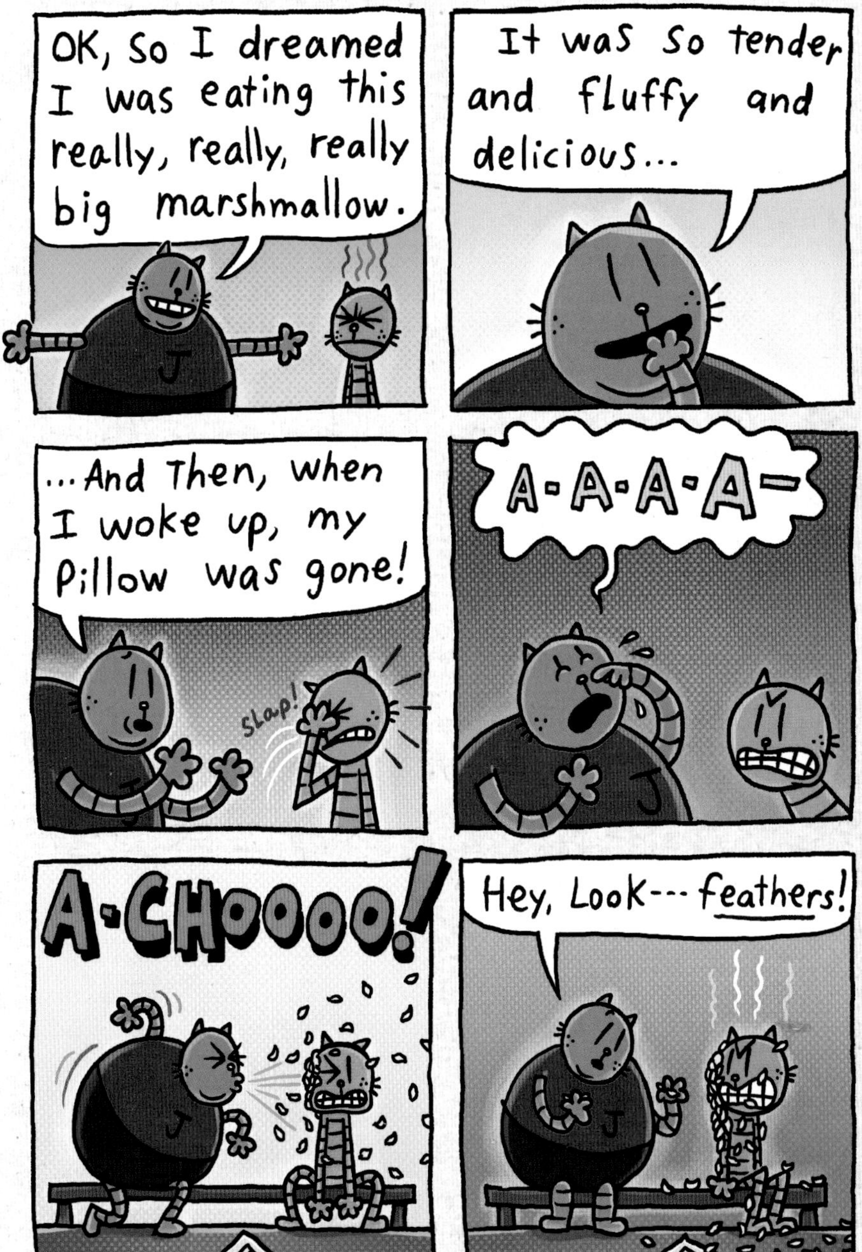
OK, So I dreamed I was eating this really, really, really big marshmallow.
It was so tender and fluffy and delicious...
...And Then, when I woke up, my pillow was gone!
SLAP!
A-A-A-A-
A-CHOOOO!
Hey, Look--- feathers!

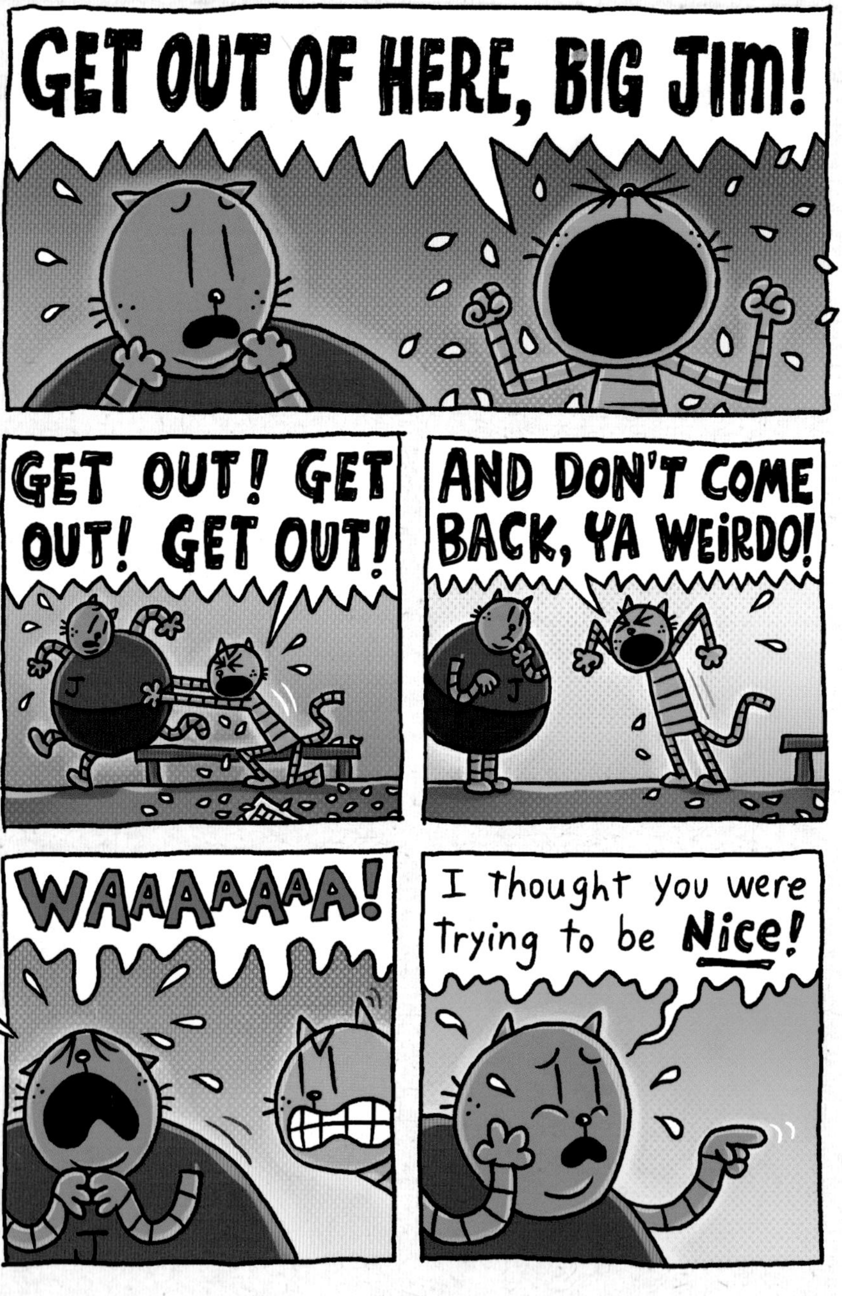
GET OUT OF HERE, BIG JIM!
GET OUT! GET OUT! GET OUT!
AND DON'T COME BACK, YA WEIRDO!
WAAAAAAA!
I thought you were trying to be Nice!

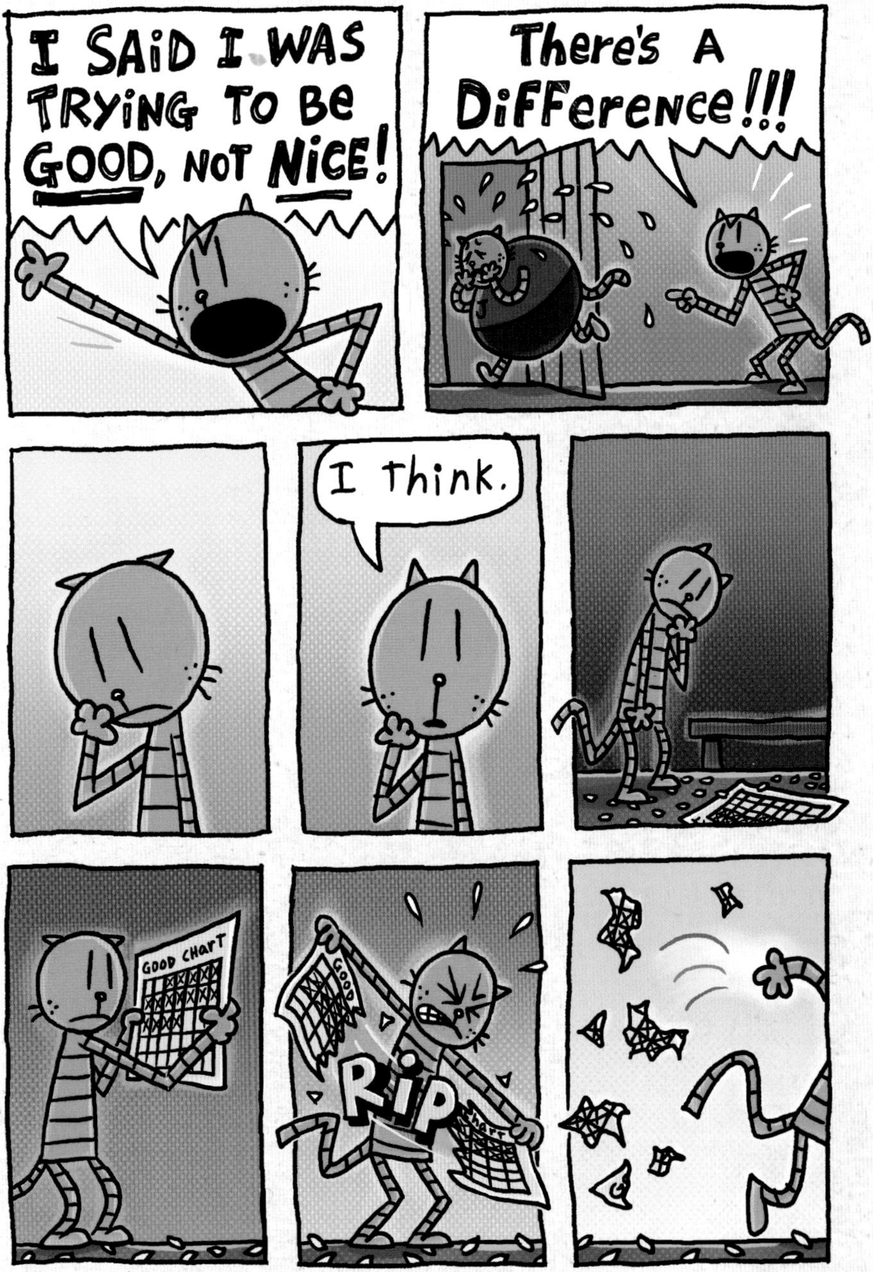
I SAID I WAS TRYING TO BE GOOD, NOT NICE!
There's A DiFFerence!!!
I think.
GOOD CHART
RIP

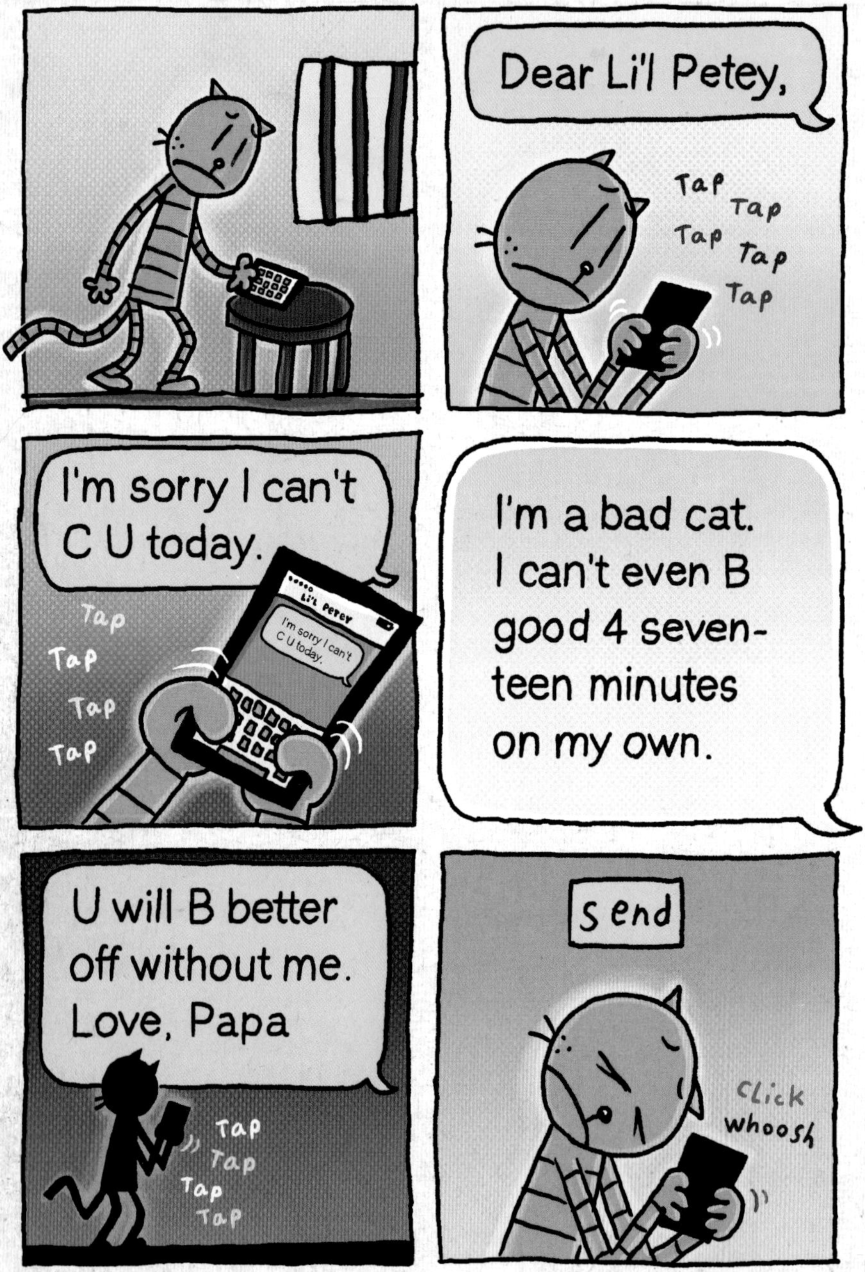
Dear Li'l Petey,
Tap Tap Tap Tap Tap
I'm sorry I can't C U today.
Tap Tap Tap Tap
Li'l Petey
I'm sorry I can't C U today.
I'm a bad cat. I can't even B good 4 seven-teen minutes on my own.
U will B better off without me. Love, Papa
Tap Tap Tap Tap
Send
Click whoosh

Chapter 2

The Sad Guys

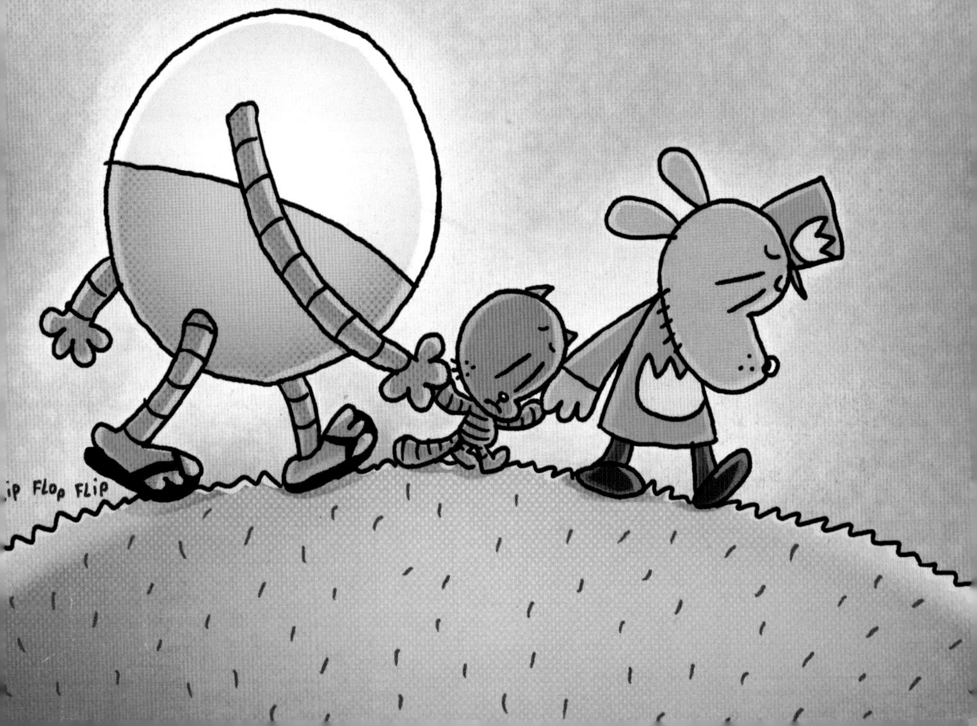
ip FLOP FLIP

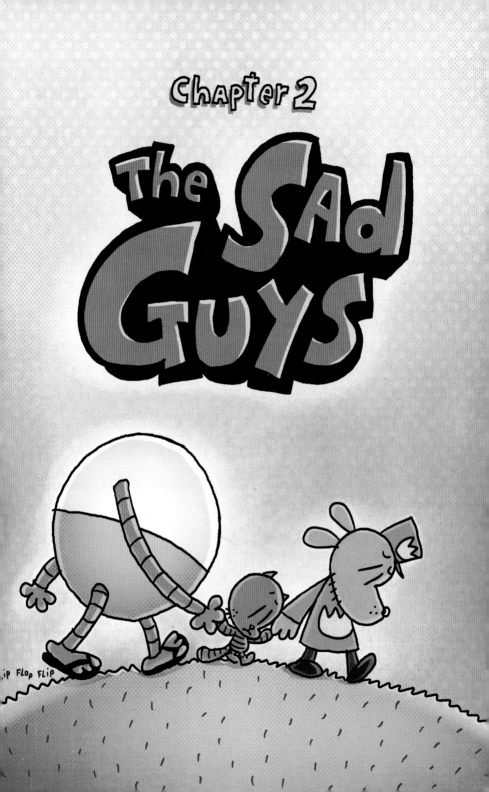

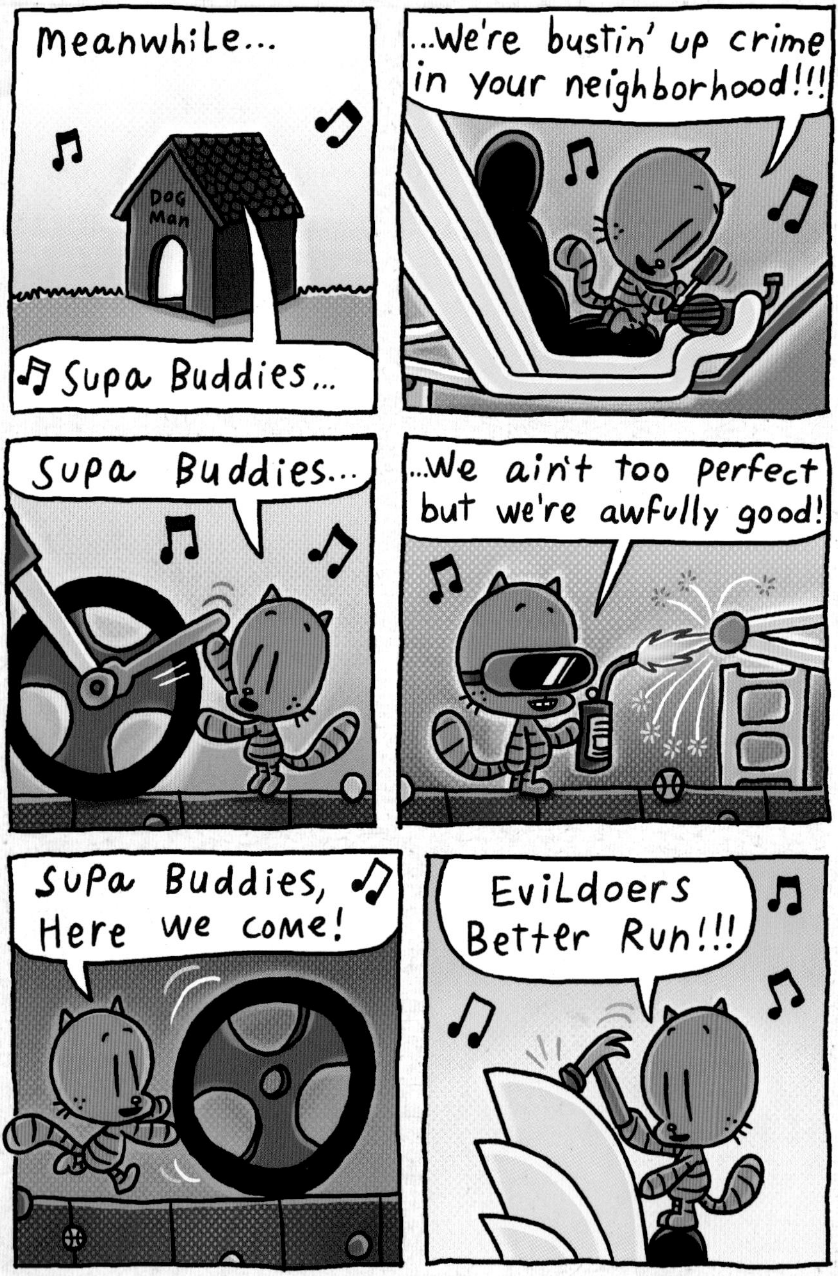
Meanwhile...
DOG Man
♫ Supa Buddies...
...We're bustin' up crime in your neighborhood!!!
Supa Buddies...
...We ain't too perfect but we're awfully good!
Supa Buddies, ♫ Here we come!
EviLdoers Better Run!!!

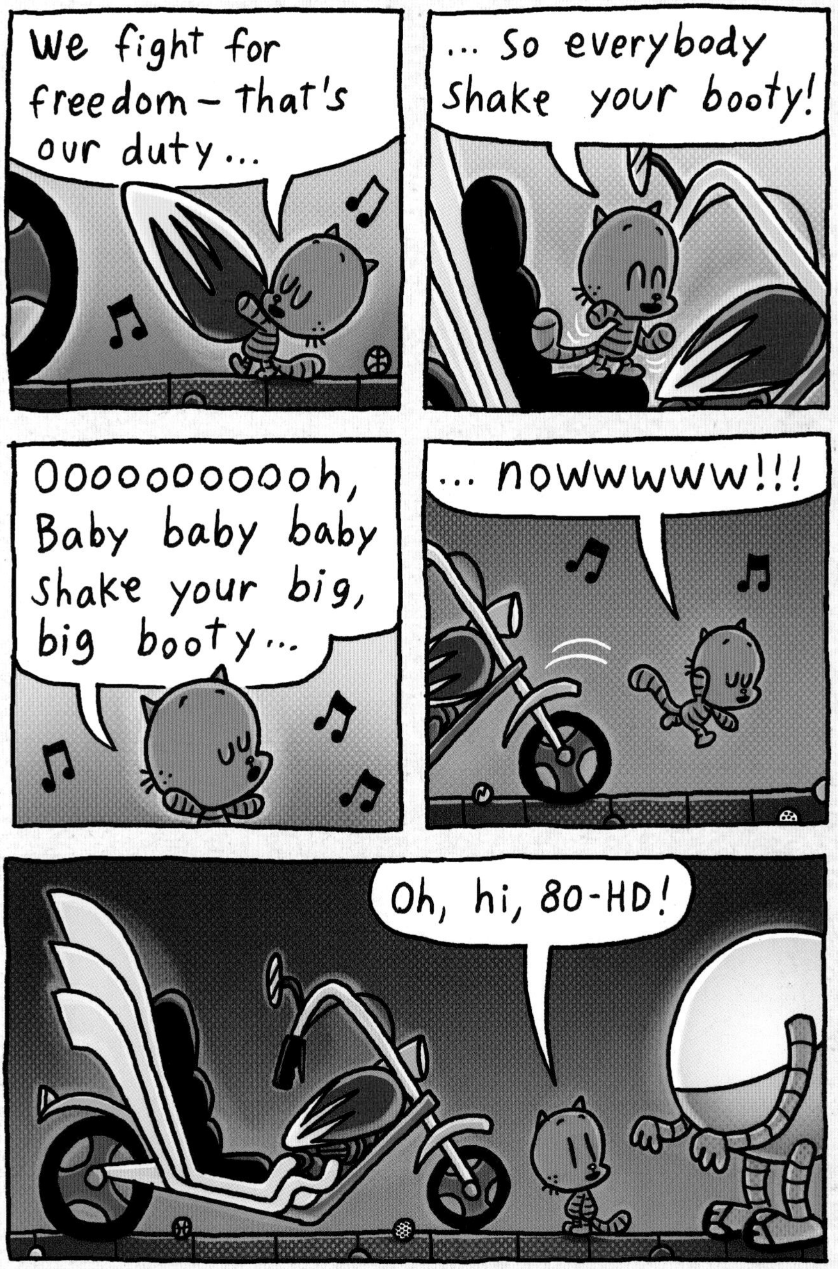
We fight for freedom – that's our duty...
... So everybody shake your booty!
Ooooooooooh, Baby baby baby shake your big, big booty...
... nowwwww!!!
Oh, hi, 80-HD!

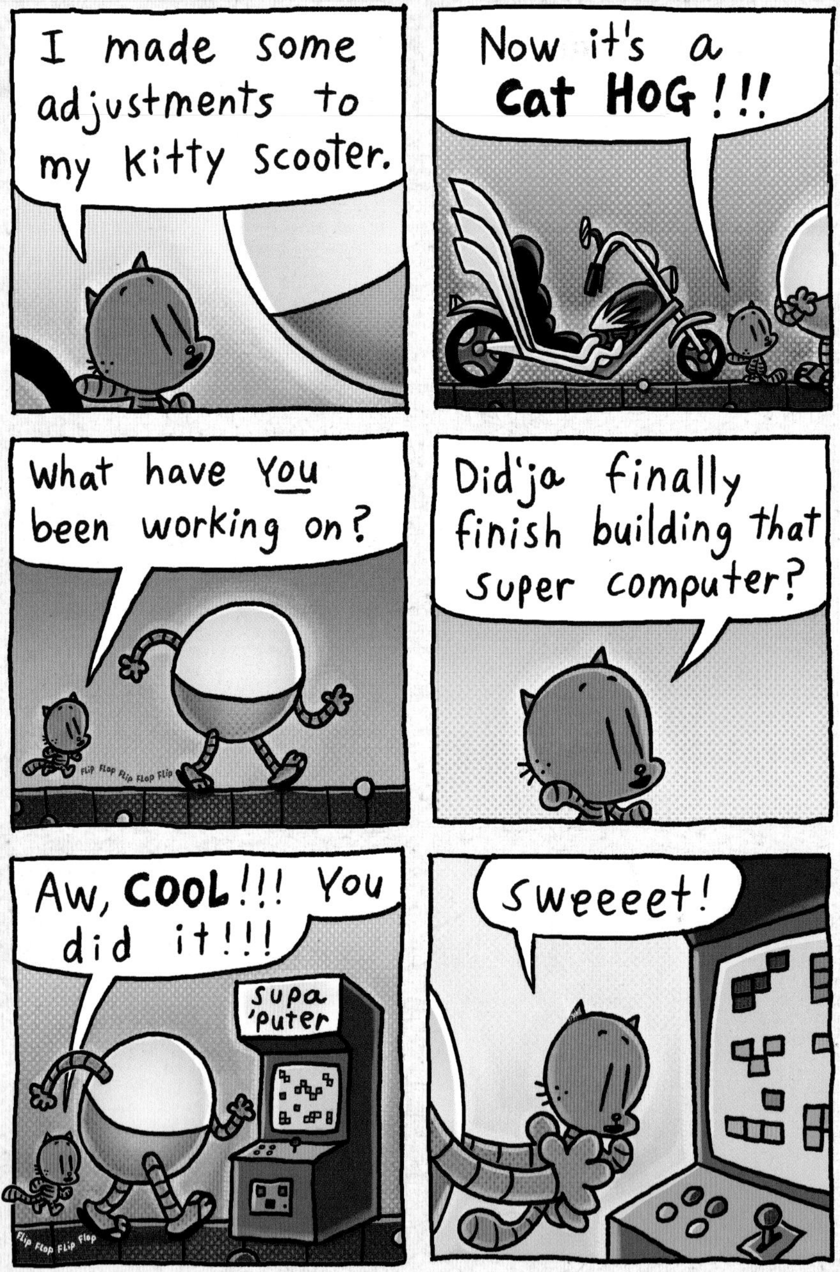
I made some adjustments to my kitty scooter.
Now it's a Cat HOG!!!
What have YOU been working on?
FLIP FLOP FLIP FLOP FLIP
Did'ja finally finish building that super computer?
Aw, COOL!!! You did it!!!
Supa 'puter
Flip Flop Flip Flop
Sweeeet!

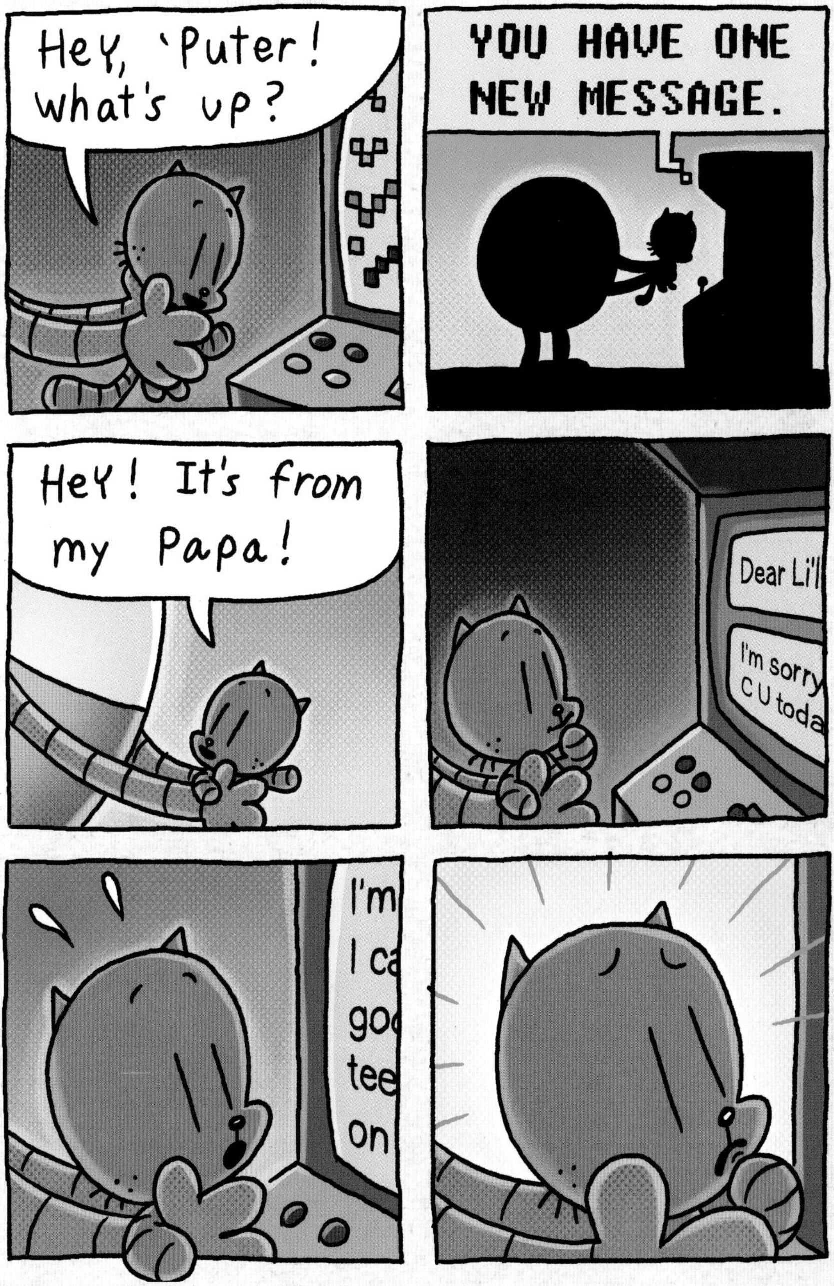
Hey, 'Puter! what's up?
YOU HAVE ONE NEW MESSAGE.
Hey! It's from my Papa!
Dear Li'l
I'm sorry
C U toda
I'm
I ca
goo
tee
on

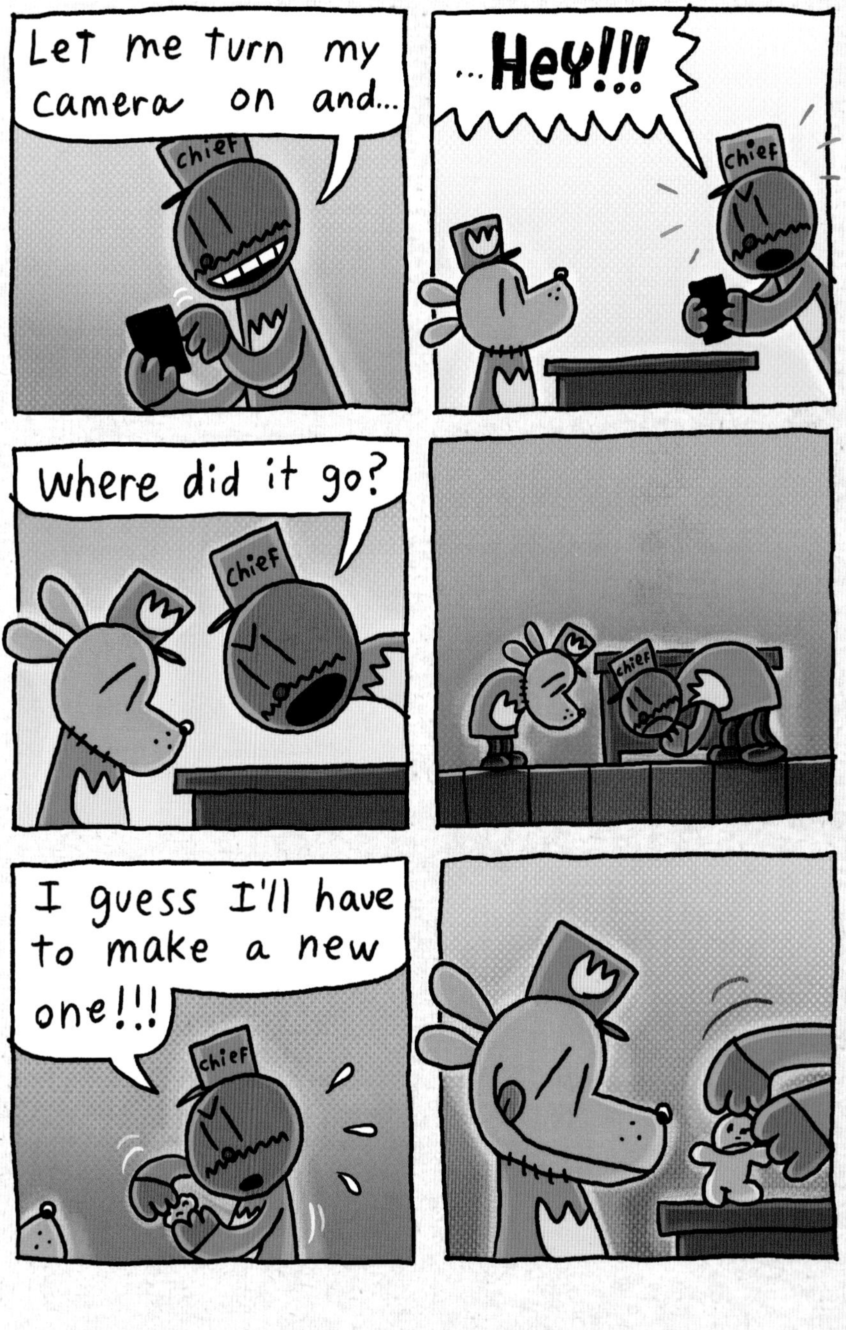
Let me turn my camera on and...
chief
...Hey!!!
chief
Where did it go?
chief
chief
I guess I'll have to make a new one!!!
chief

41

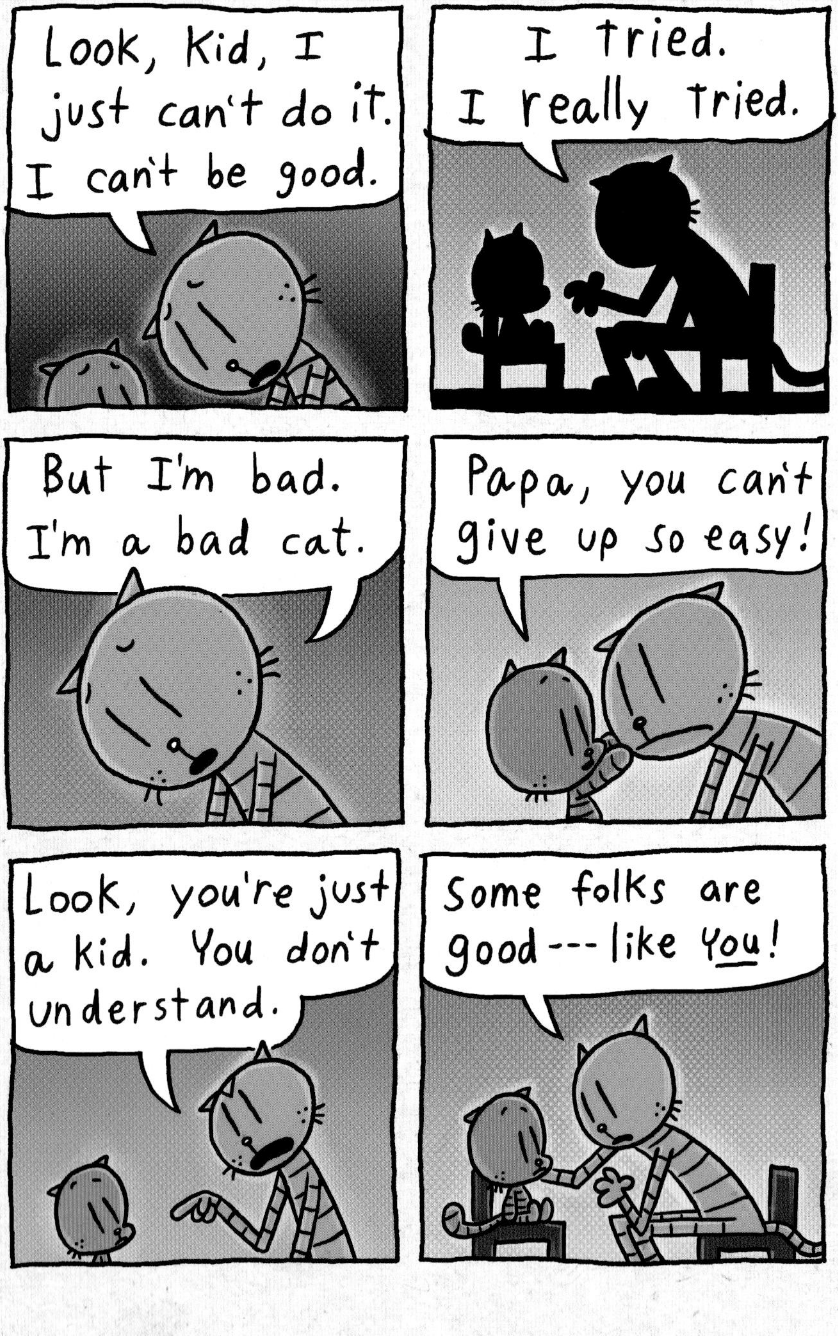
Look, Kid, I just can't do it. I can't be good.
I tried. I really tried.
But I'm bad. I'm a bad cat.
Papa, you can't give up so easy!
Look, you're just a kid. You don't understand.
Some folks are good --- like You!

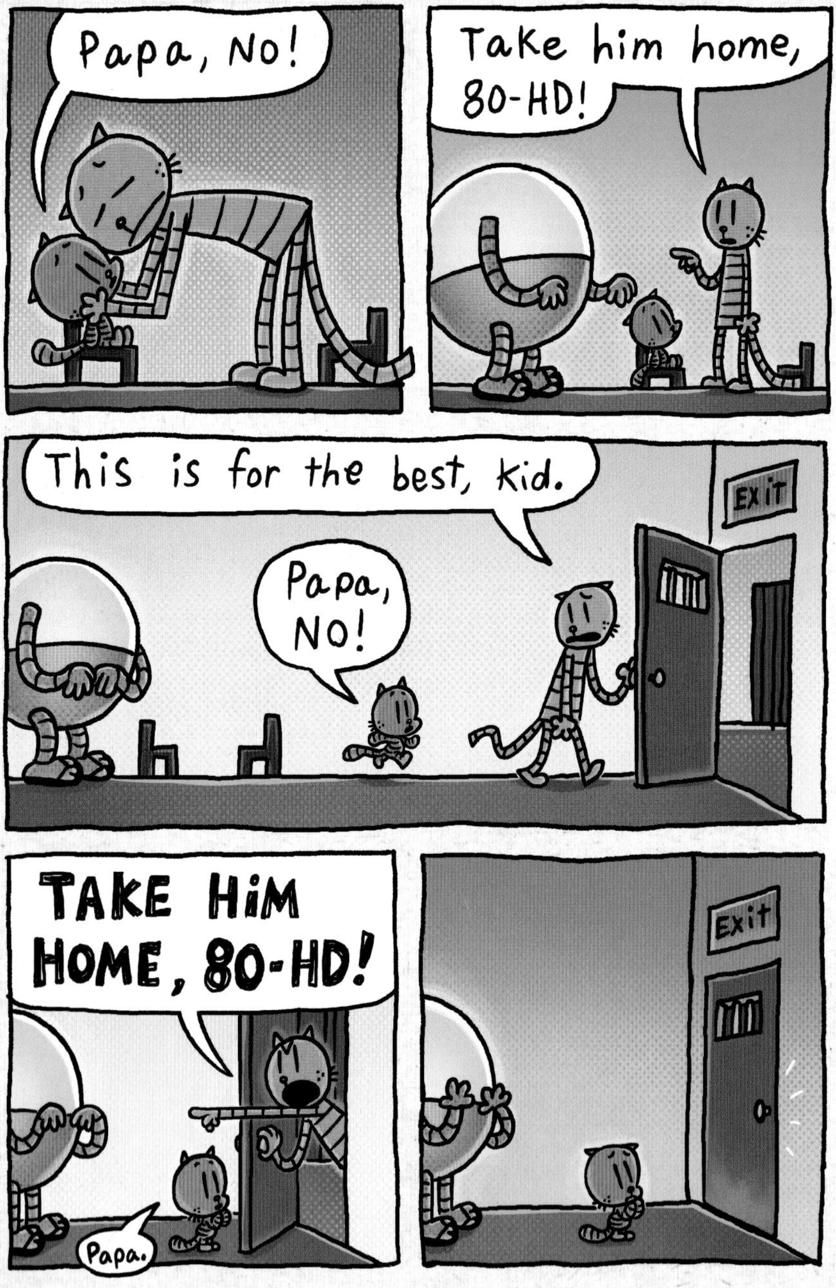
Papa, No!
Take him home, 80-HD!
This is for the best, kid.
EXIT
Papa, NO!
TAKE HIM HOME, 80-HD!
Papa.
Exit

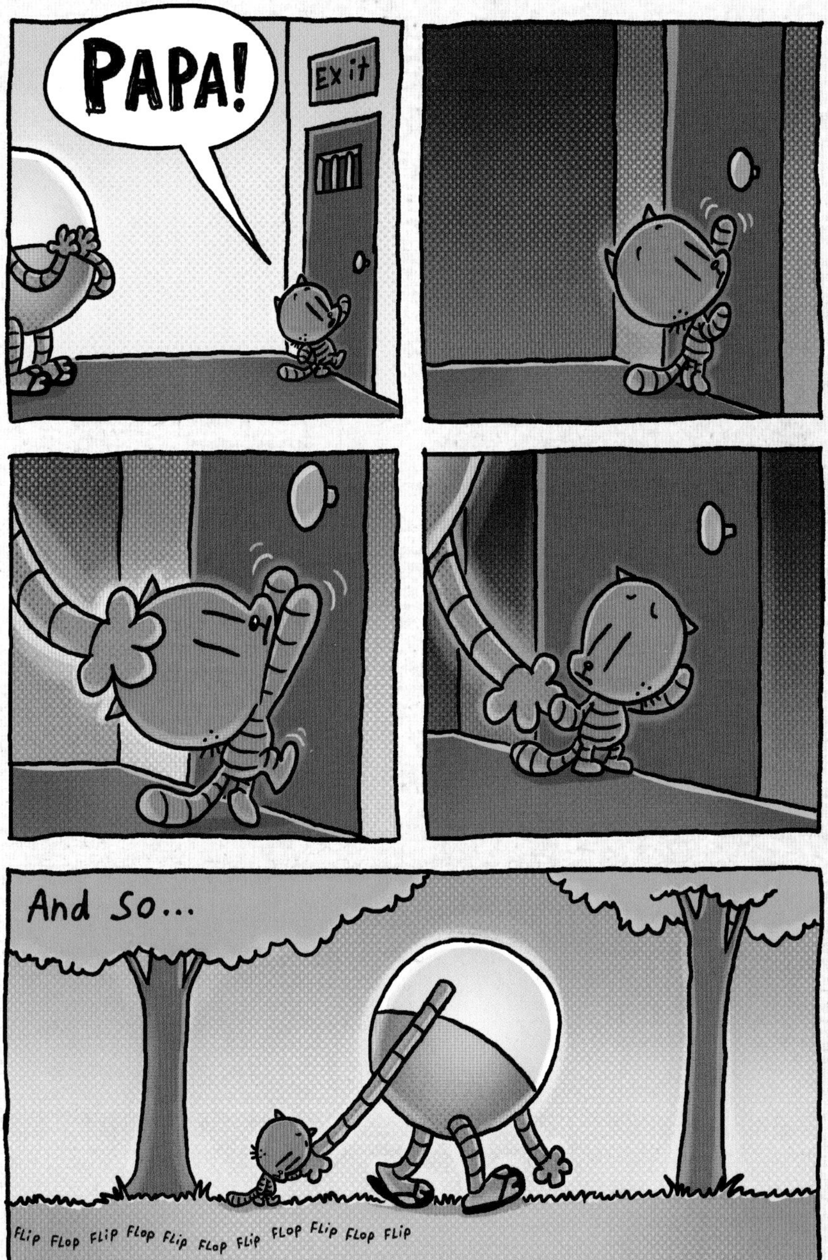
PAPA!
Exit
And so...
FLip FLop FLip FLop FLip FLop FLip FLop FLip FLop FLip

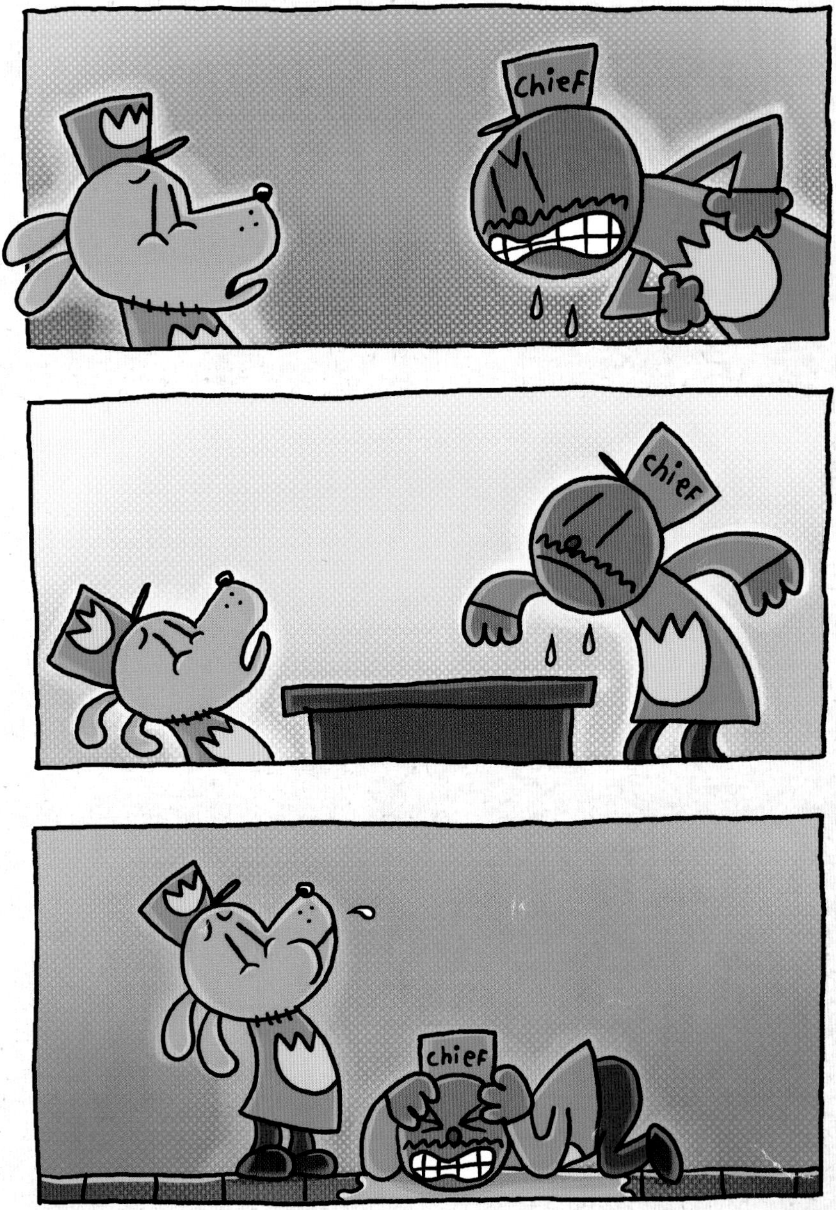
Chief
chief
chief

Right Thumb here.

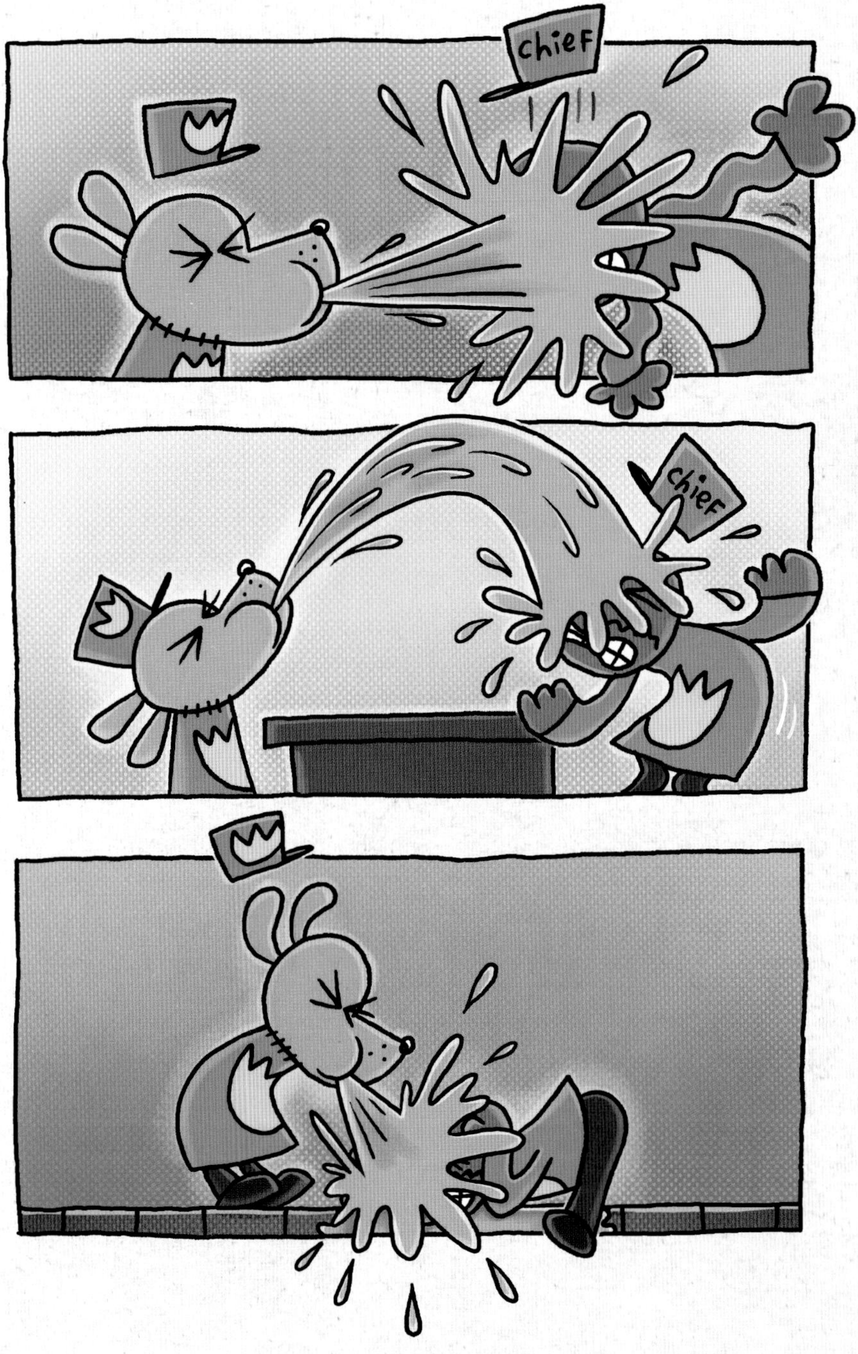
chief
chief

GET OUT OF HERE NOW!

COPS

52

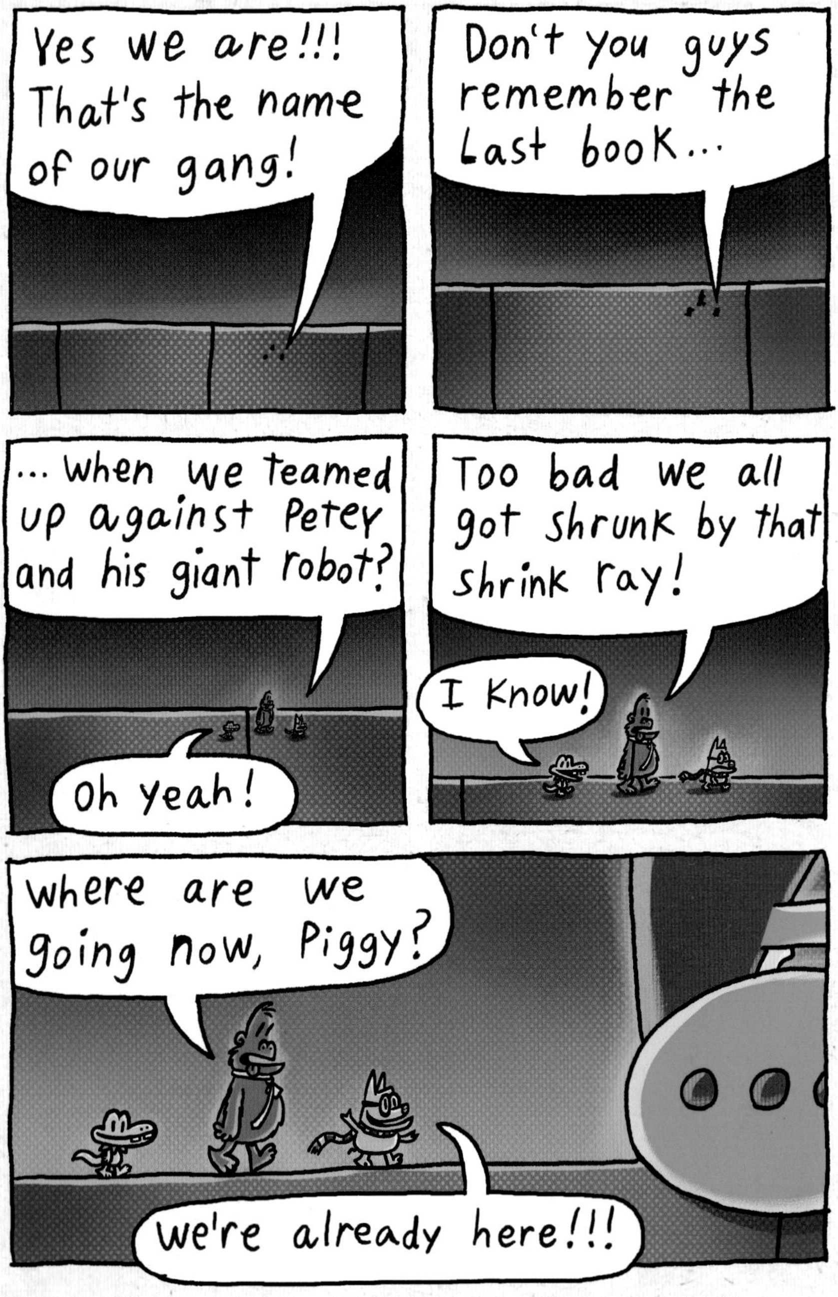
Yes we are!!! That's the name of our gang!
Don't you guys remember the Last book...
... when we teamed up against Petey and his giant robot?
Oh yeah!
Too bad we all got shrunk by that shrink ray!
I Know!
where are we going now, Piggy?
we're already here!!!

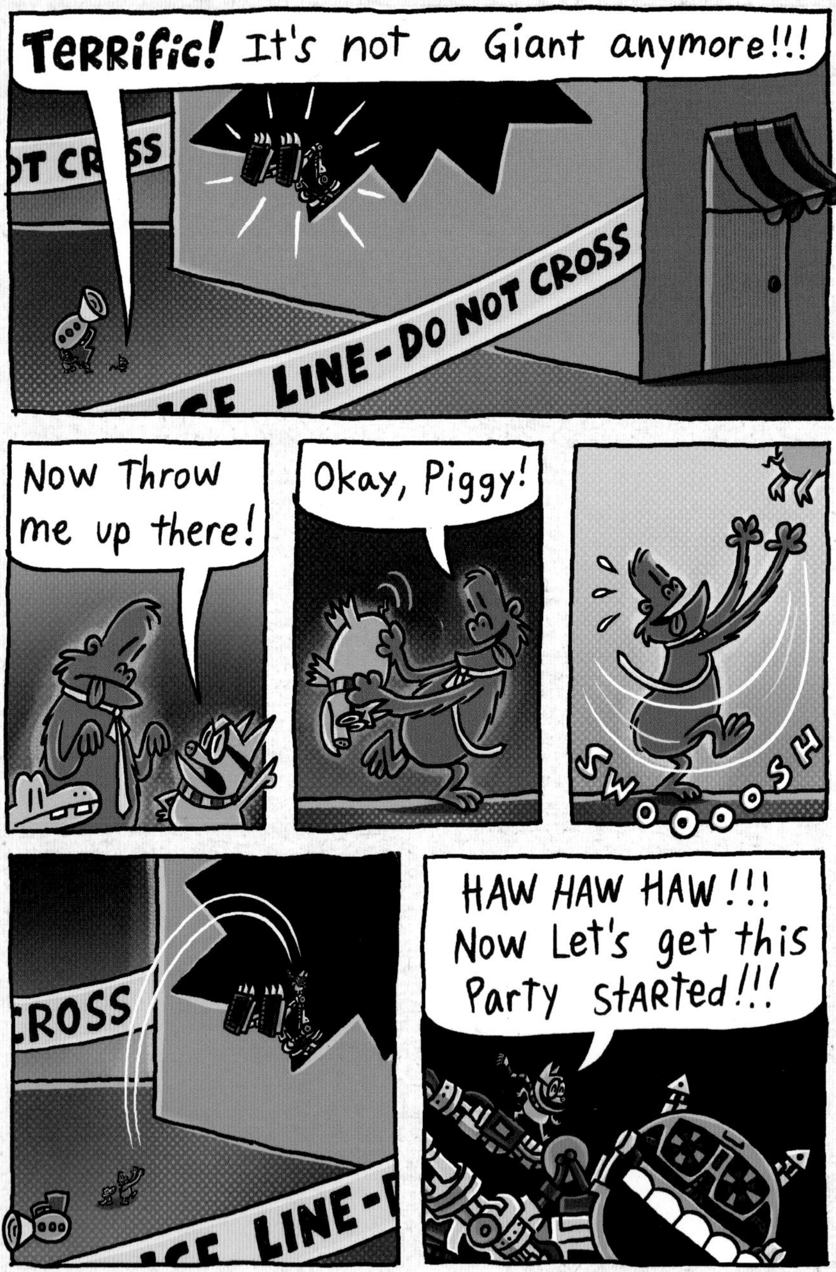
TERRIFIC! It's not a Giant anymore!!!
OT CROSS
LINE-DO NOT CROSS
Now Throw me up there!
Okay, Piggy!
SWOOOOOSH
CROSS
LINE-
HAW HAW HAW!!! Now Let's get this Party STARTED!!!

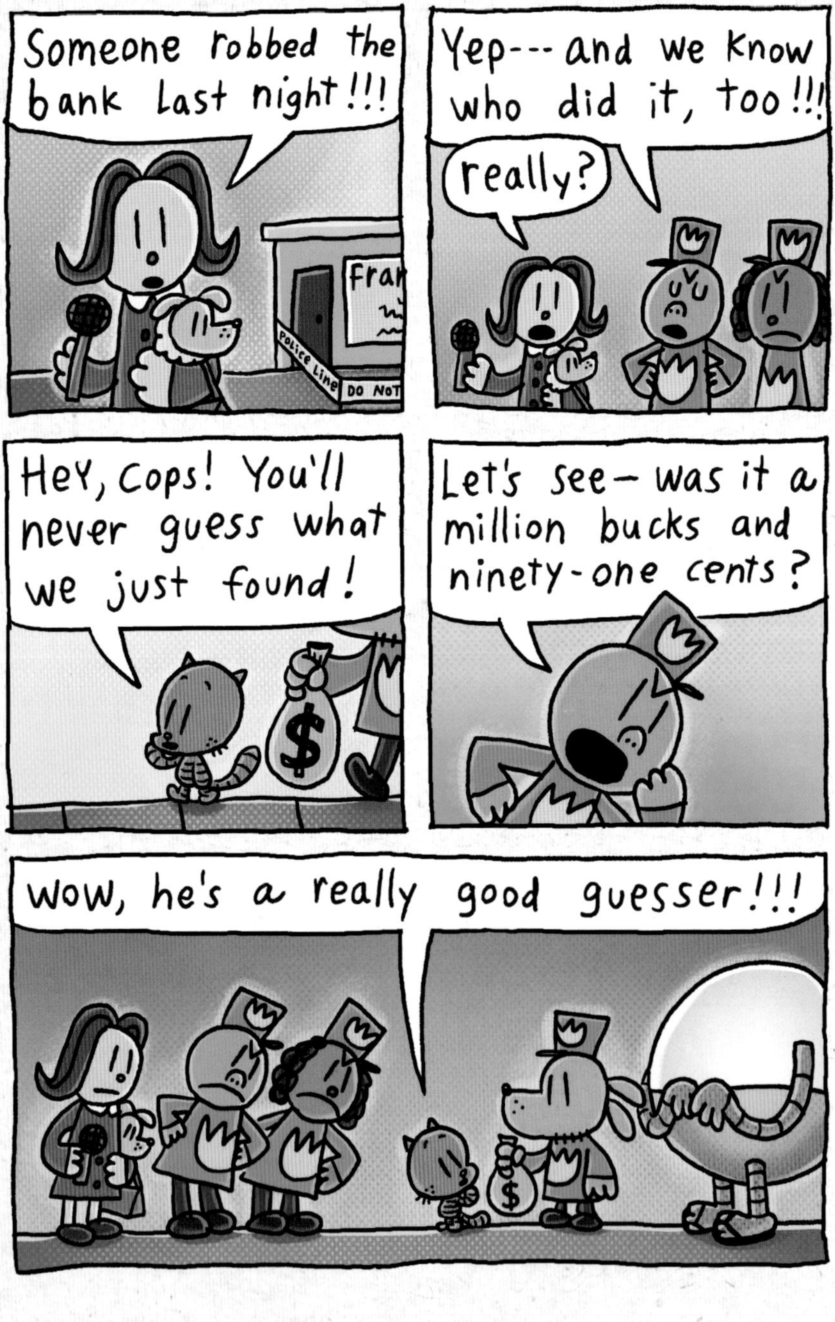
Someone robbed the bank last night!!!
Fran
POLICE LINE DO NOT
Yep---and we know who did it, too!!!
really?
Hey, Cops! You'll never guess what we just found!
Let's see—was it a million bucks and ninety-one cents?
wow, he's a really good guesser!!!

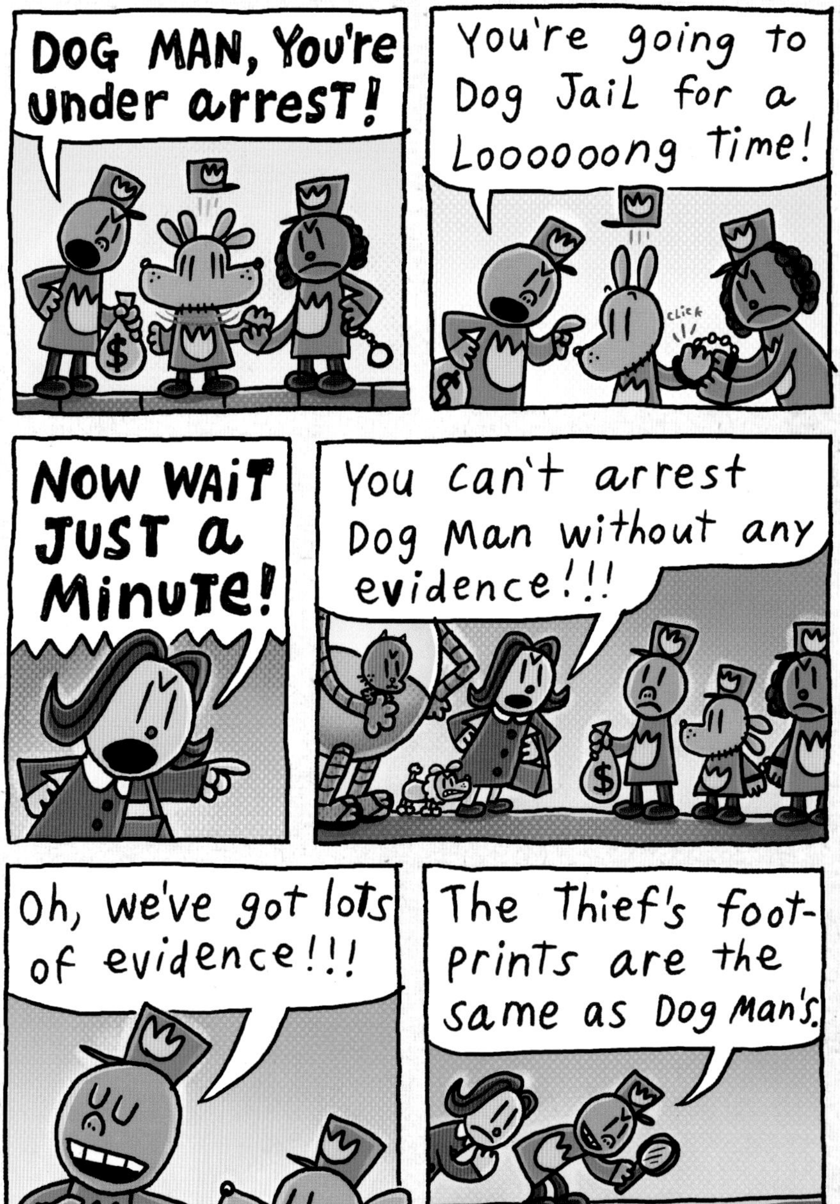
DOG MAN, You're under arrest!
You're going to Dog Jail for a Loooooong time!
click
NOW WAIT JUST a Minute!
You can't arrest Dog Man without any evidence!!!
Oh, we've got lots of evidence!!!
The Thief's foot-prints are the same as Dog Man's.

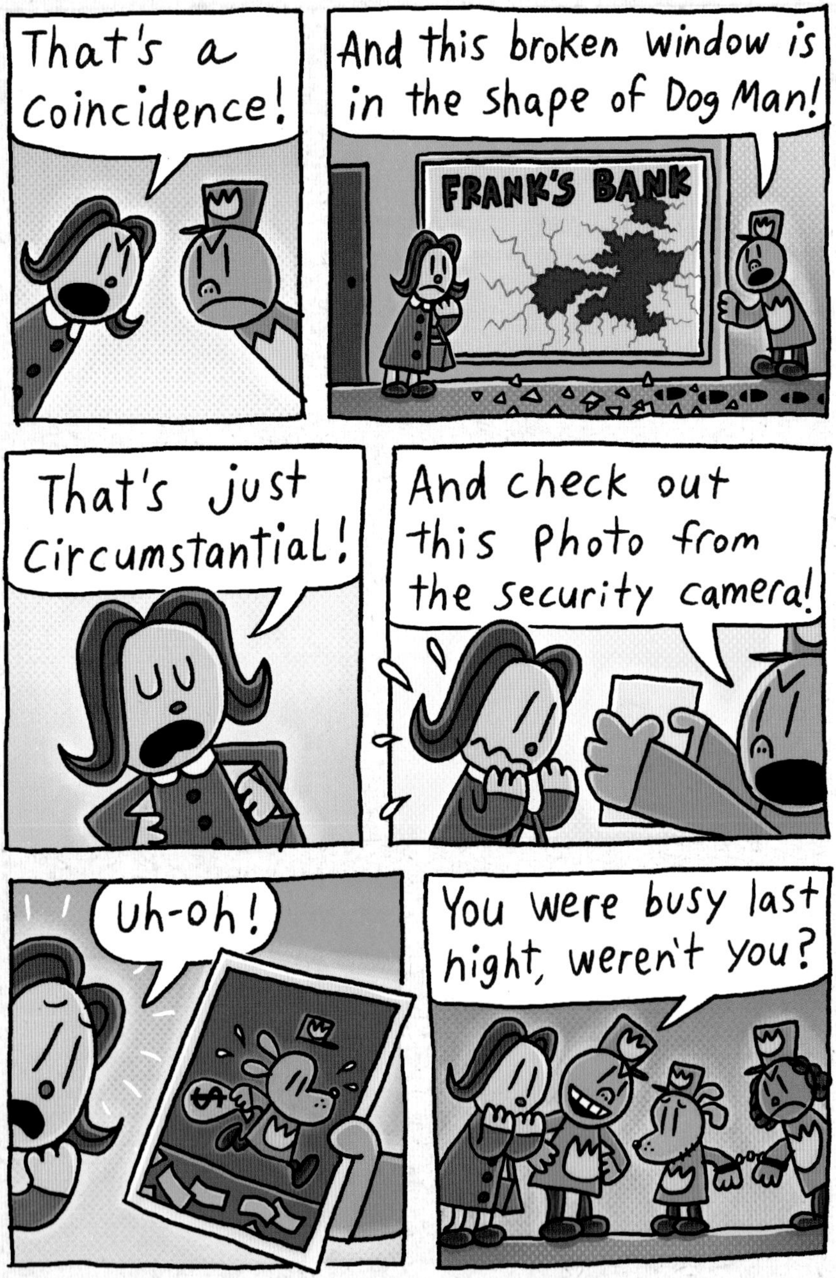

That's a Coincidence!
And this broken window is in the shape of Dog Man!
FRANK'S BANK
That's just Circumstantial!
And check out this photo from the security camera!
Uh-oh!
You were busy last night, weren't you?

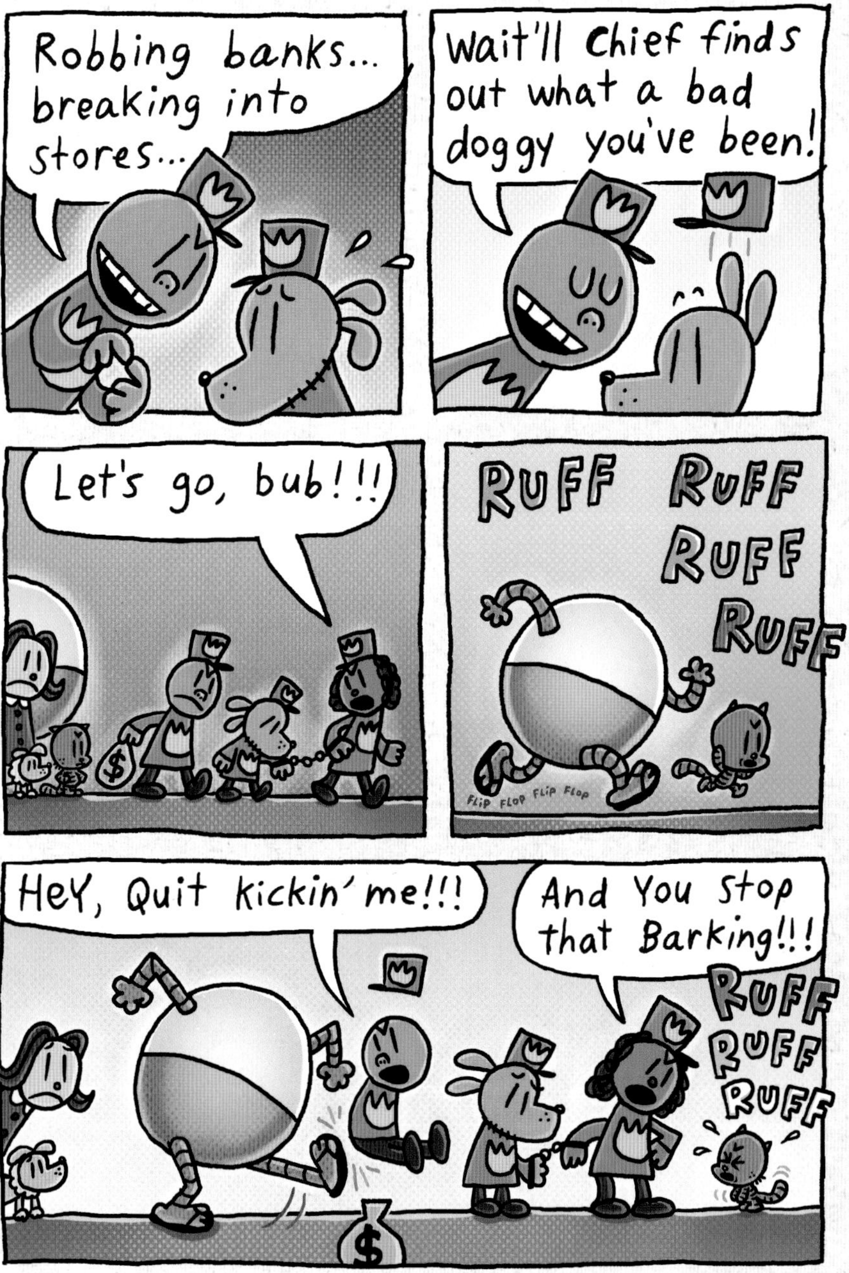
Robbing banks... breaking into stores...
Wait'll Chief finds out what a bad doggy you've been!
Let's go, bub!!!
RUFF RUFF RUFF RUFF
FLIP FLOP FLIP FLOP
HEY, Quit kickin' me!!!
And You stop that Barking!!!
RUFF RUFF RUFF

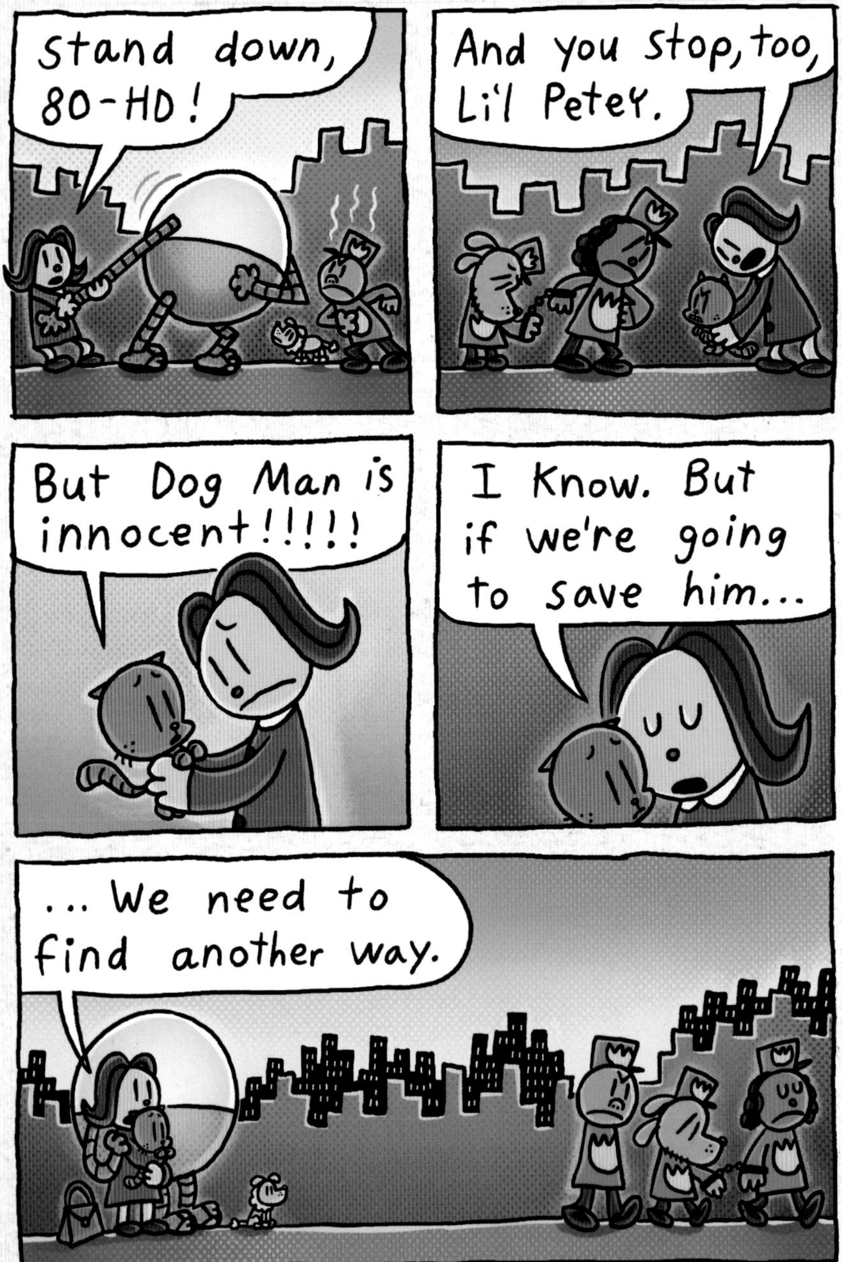
Stand down, 80-HD!
And you stop, too, Li'l Petey.
But Dog Man is innocent!!!!!
I know. But if we're going to save him...
...We need to find another way.

CHAPTER 4

A Buncha Stuff That Happened Next

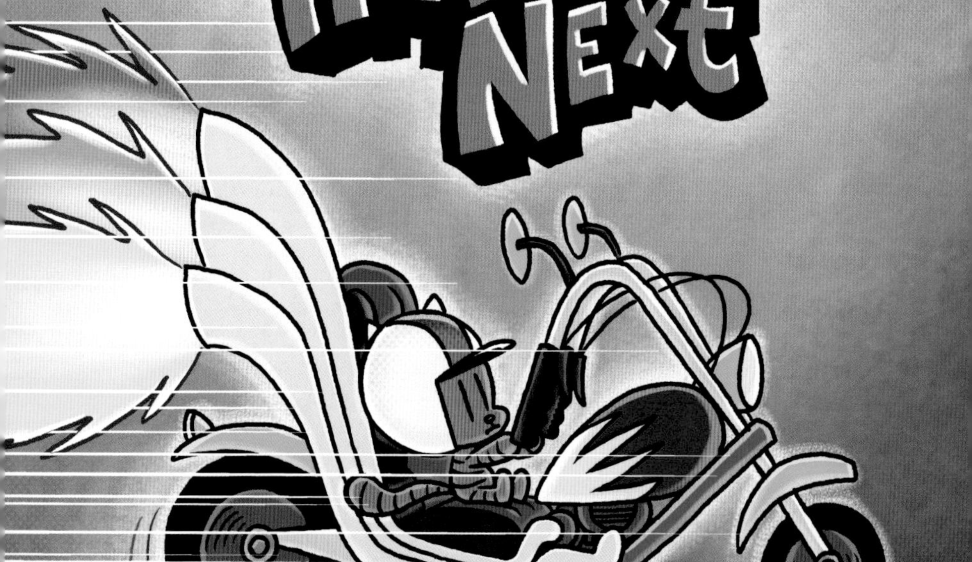

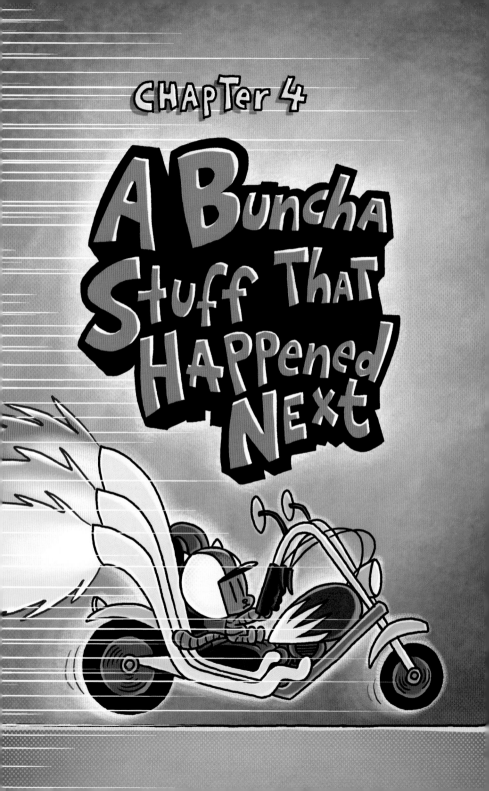

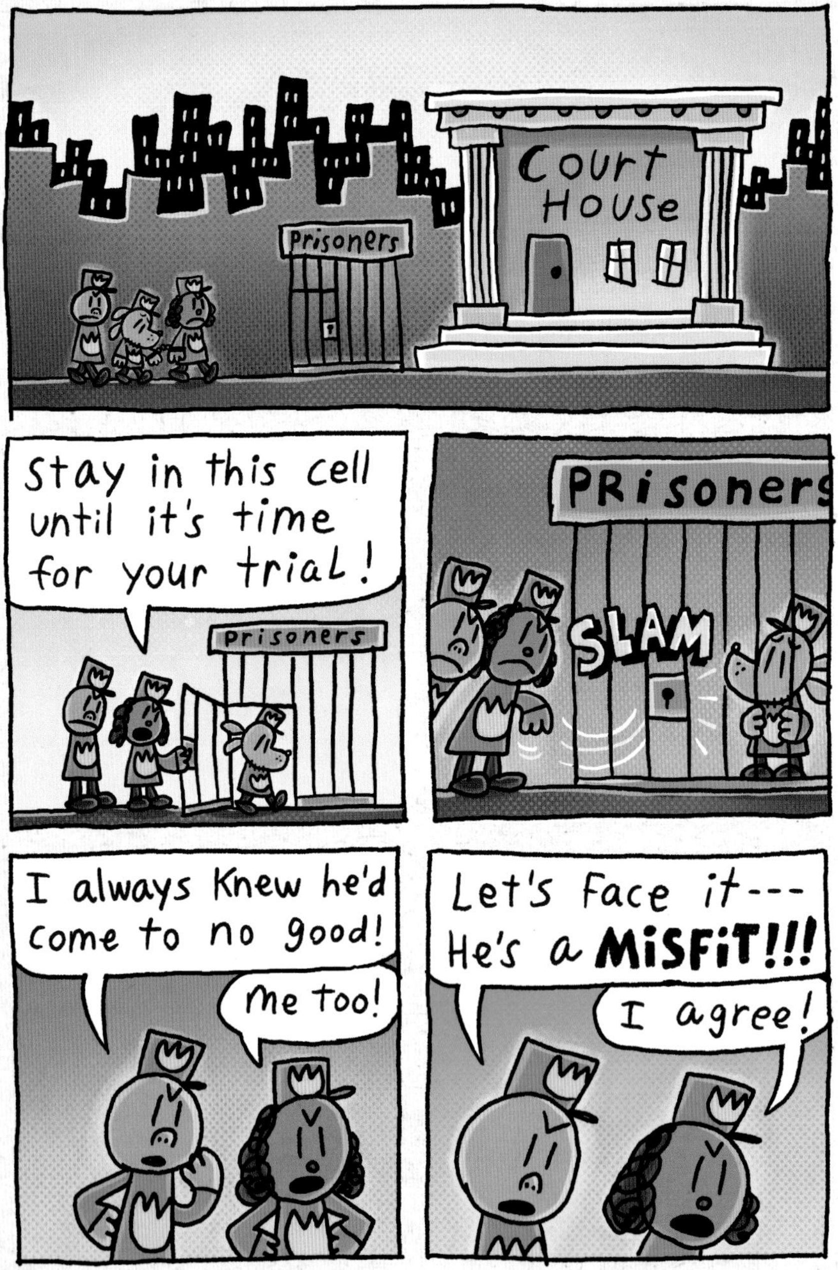
Court House
Prisoners
Stay in this cell until it's time for your trial!
Prisoners
PRisoners
SLAM
I always Knew he'd come to no good!
Me too!
Let's Face it--- He's a MiSFiT!!!
I agree!

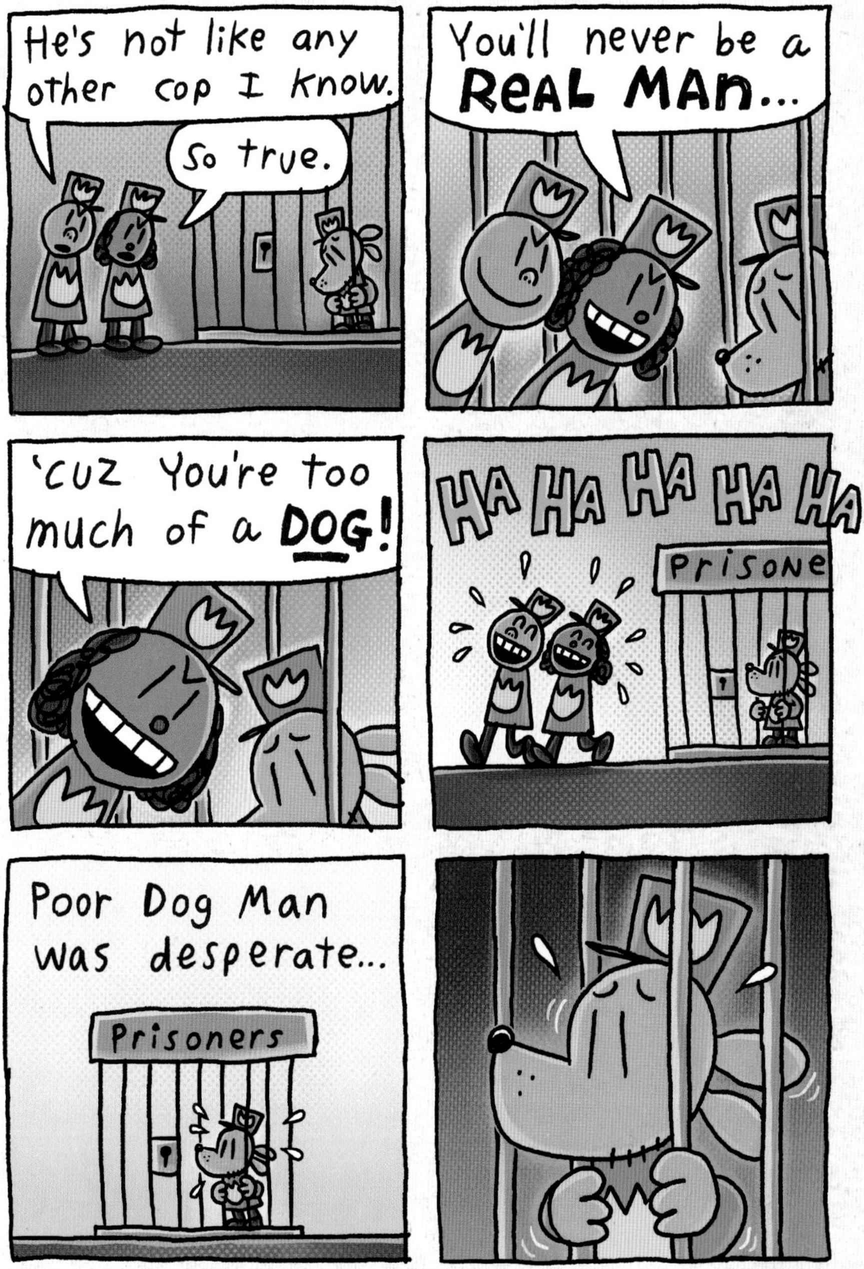
He's not like any other cop I know.
So true.
You'll never be a REAL MAN...
'cuz You're too much of a DOG!
HA HA HA HA HA
Prisone
Poor Dog Man was desperate...
Prisoners

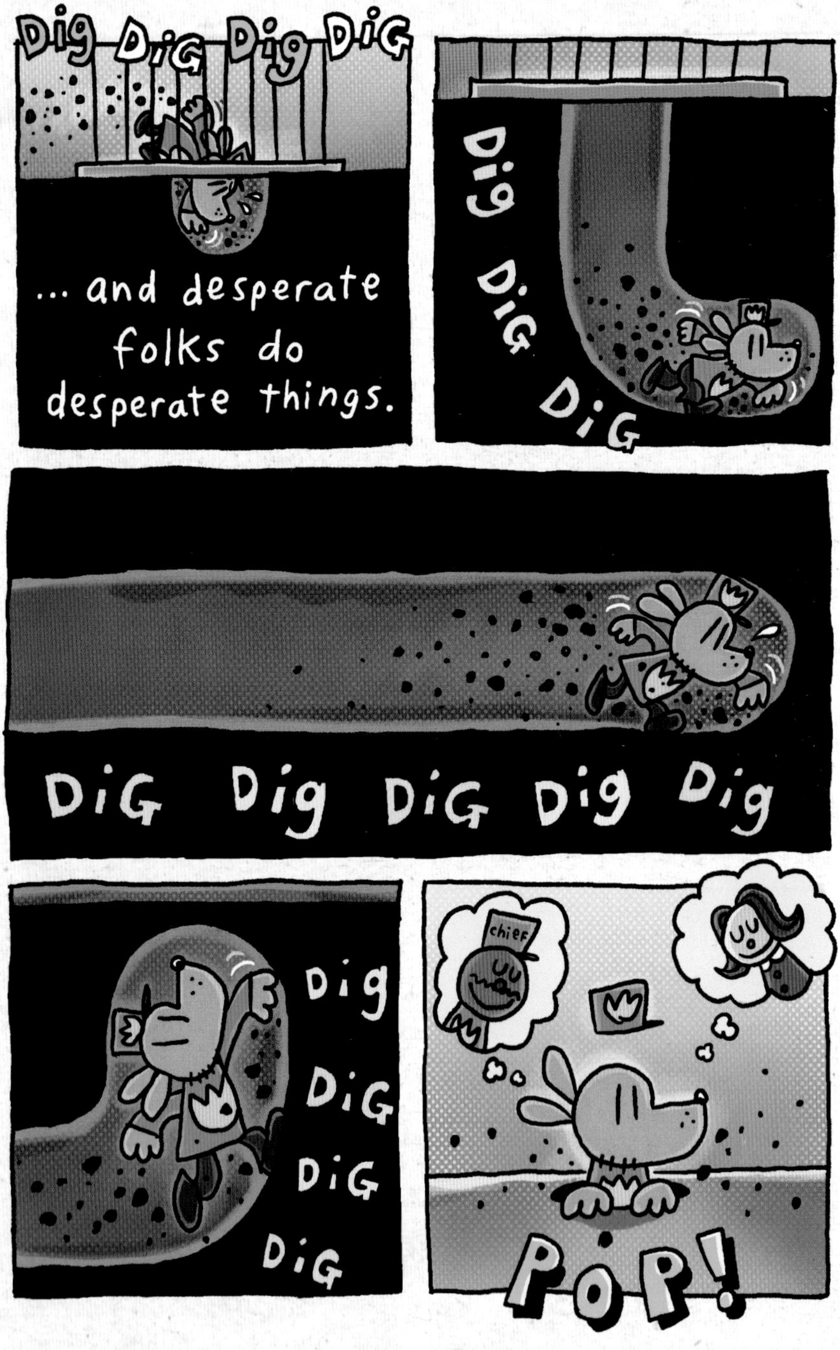

Dig DiG Dig DiG
... and desperate folks do desperate things.
Dig DiG DiG
DiG Dig DiG Dig Dig
Dig DiG DiG DiG
chief
POP!

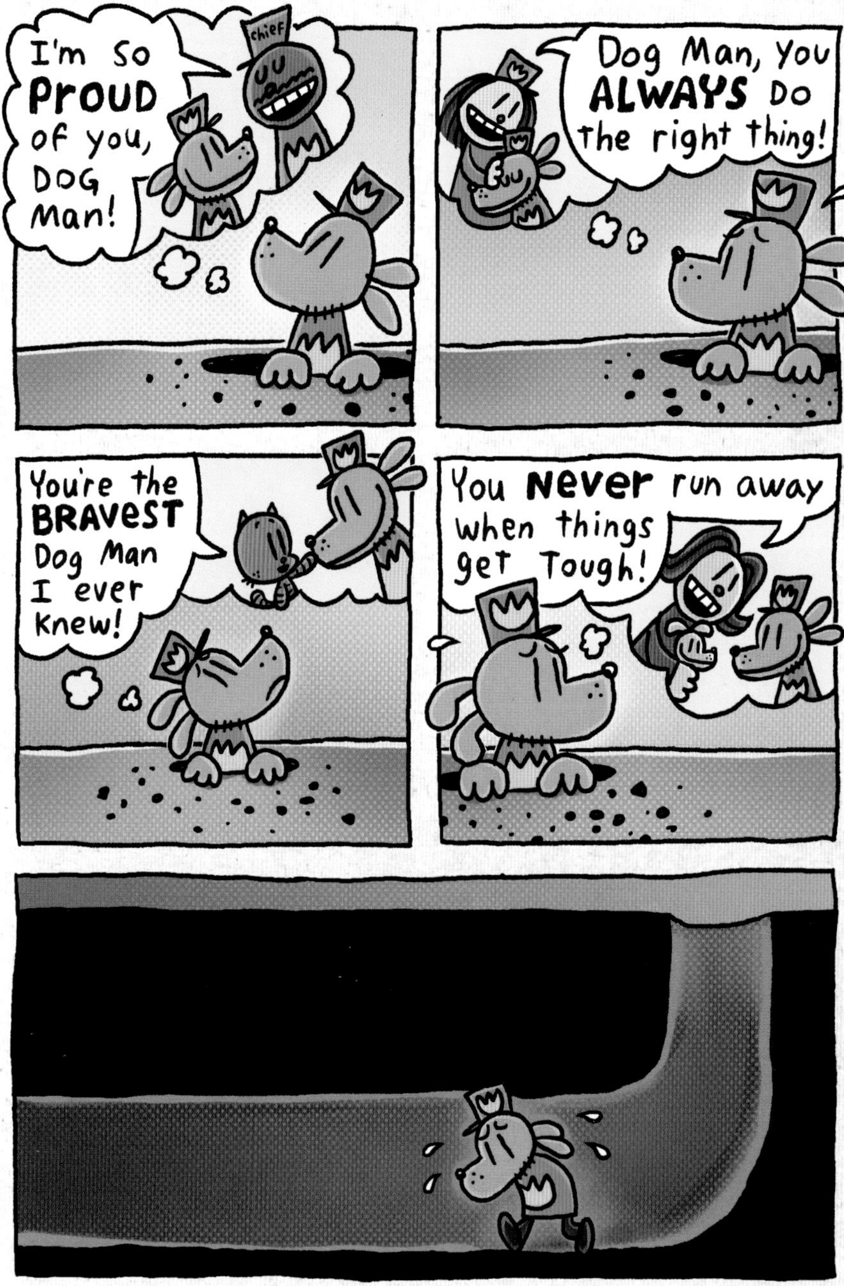
I'm so PROUD of you, DOG Man!
Chief
Dog Man, you ALWAYS do the right thing!
You're the BRAVEST Dog Man I ever knew!
You NEVER run away when things get Tough!

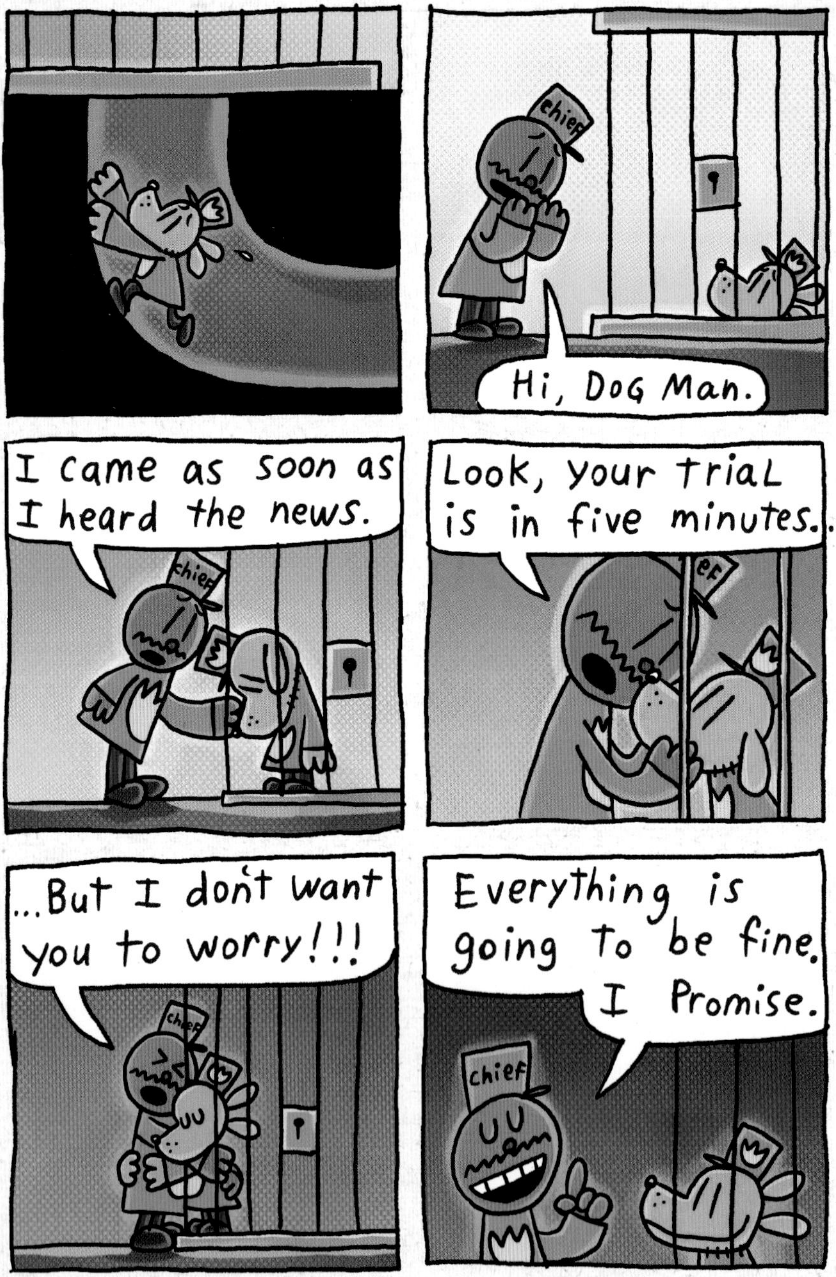
Hi, DOG Man.
I came as soon as I heard the news.
Look, your trial is in five minutes...
...But I don't want you to worry!!!
Everything is going to be fine. I Promise.

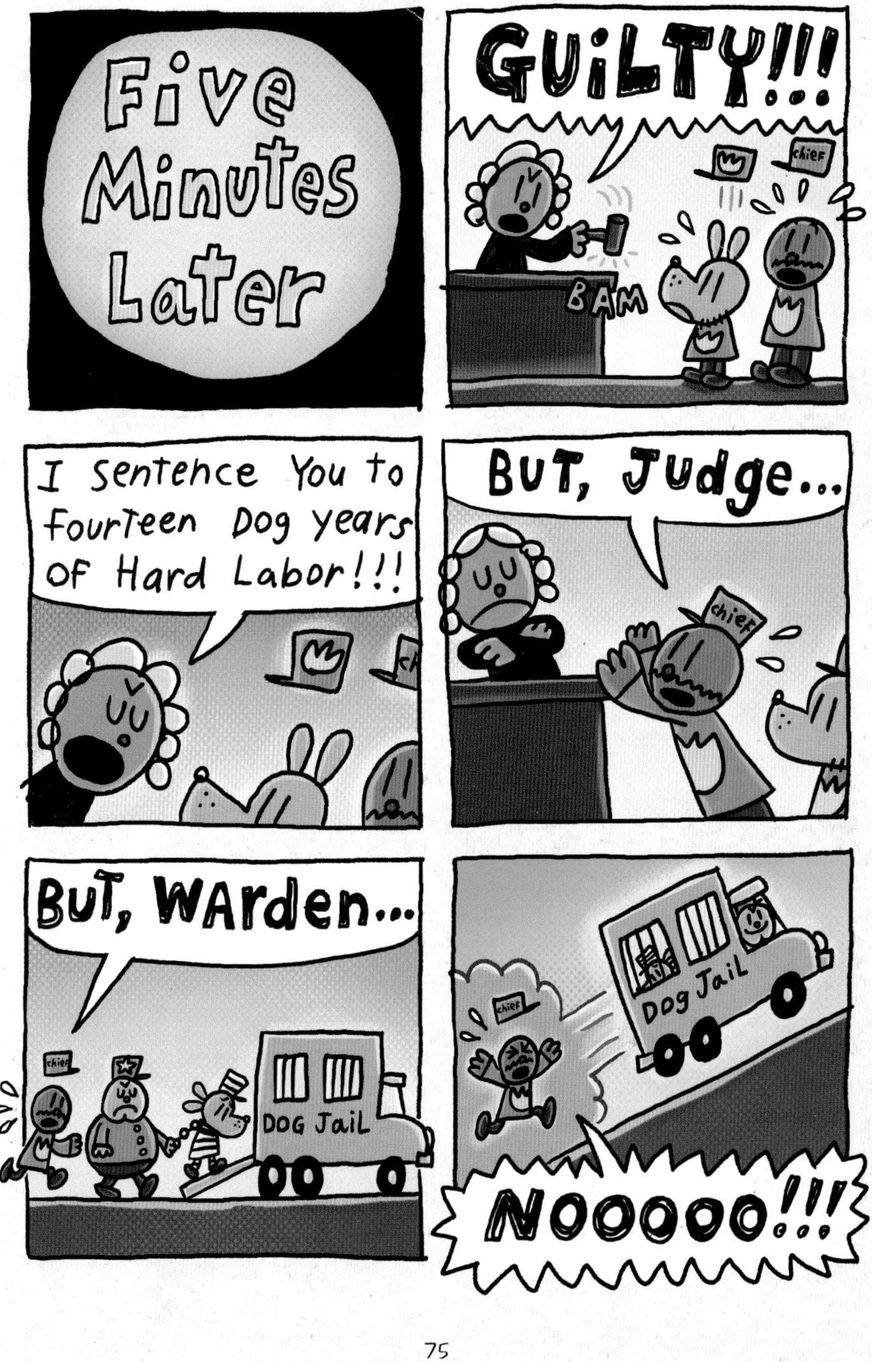
Five Minutes Later
GUILTY!!!
BAM
chief
I sentence You to fourteen Dog years of Hard Labor!!!
BUT, Judge...
chief
BUT, WArden...
chief
DOG JaiL
chief
Dog JaiL
NOOOOO!!!

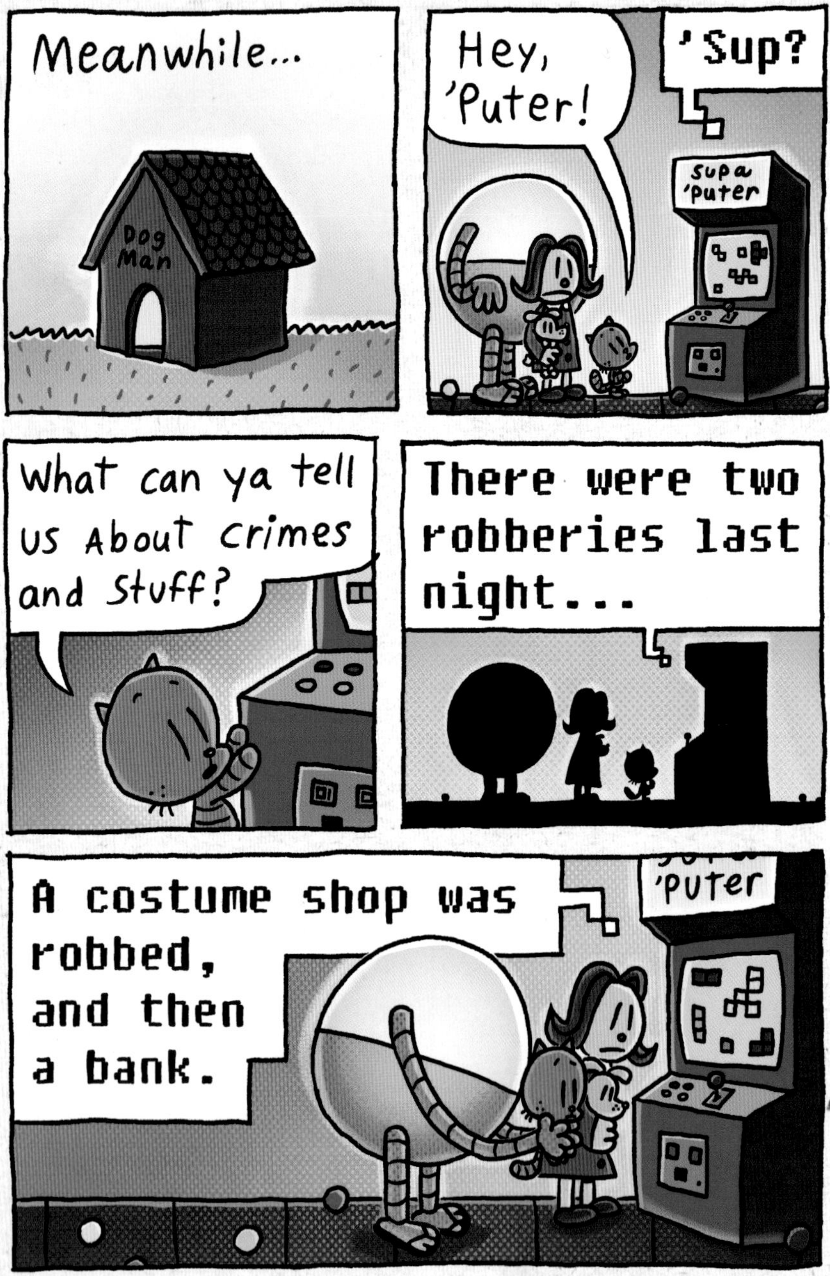
Meanwhile...
Dog Man
Hey, 'Puter!
'Sup?
Supa 'puter
What can ya tell us About Crimes and Stuff?
There were two robberies last night...
A costume shop was robbed, and then a bank.
'Puter

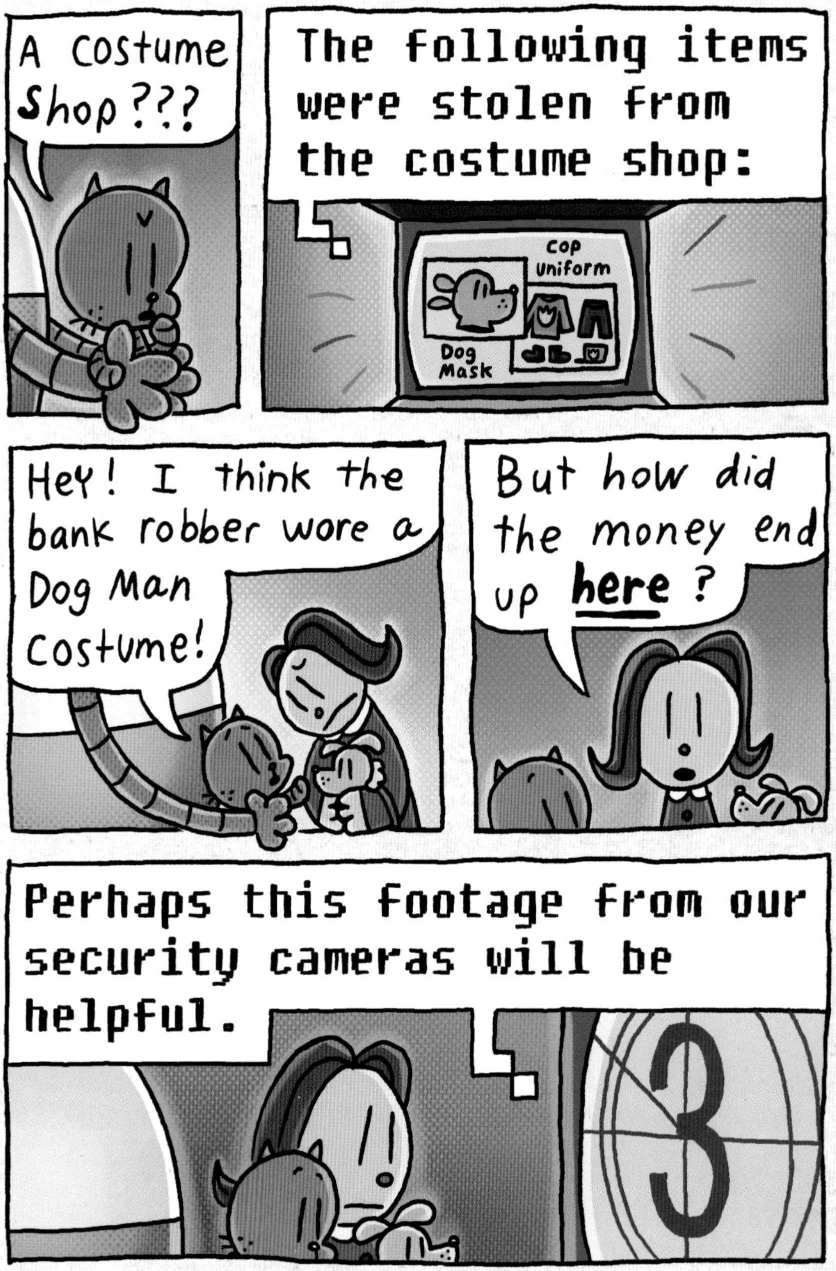
A costume Shop???
The following items were stolen from the costume shop:
Cop Uniform
Dog Mask
Hey! I think the bank robber wore a Dog Man costume!
But how did the money end up here?
Perhaps this footage from our security cameras will be helpful.
3

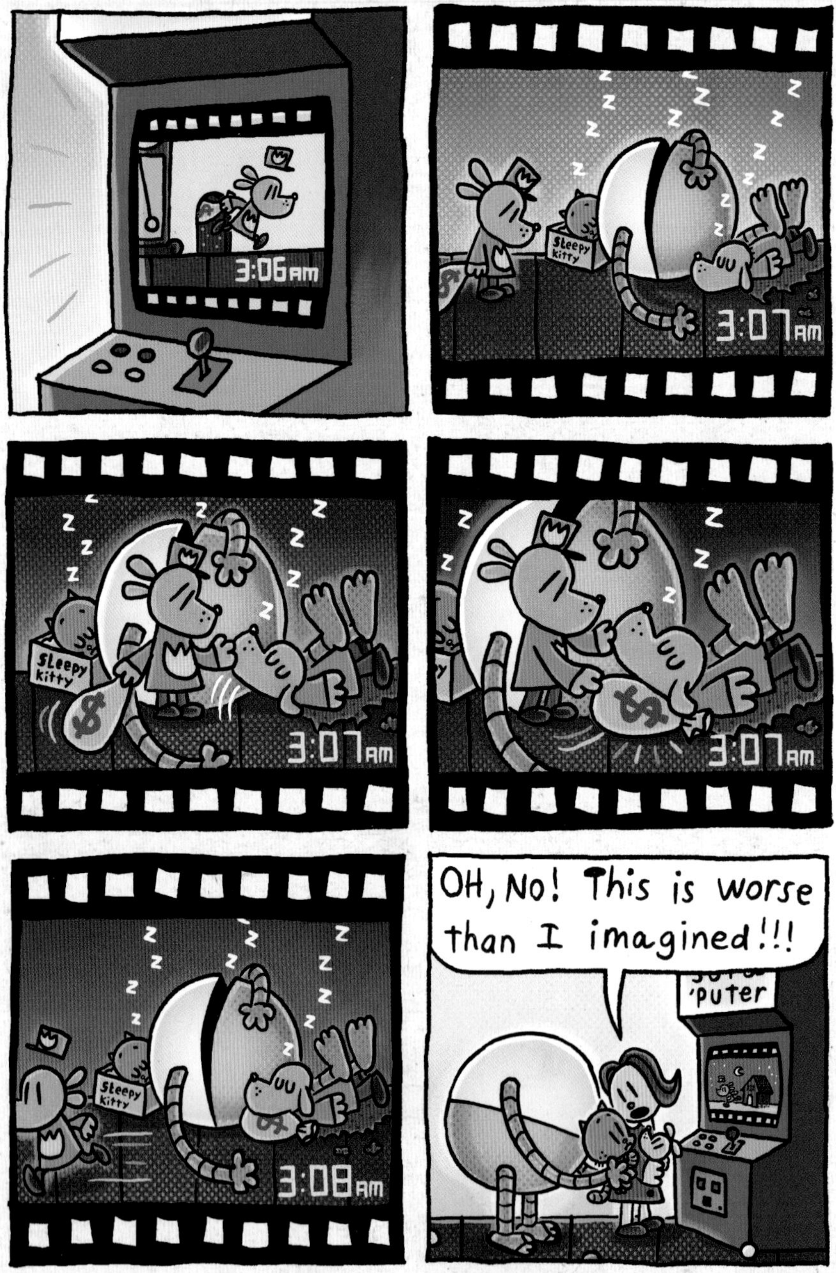
3:06AM
Sleepy kitty
3:07AM
Sleepy kitty
3:07AM
3:07AM
Sleepy kitty
3:08AM
OH, No! This is worse than I imagined!!!
'puter

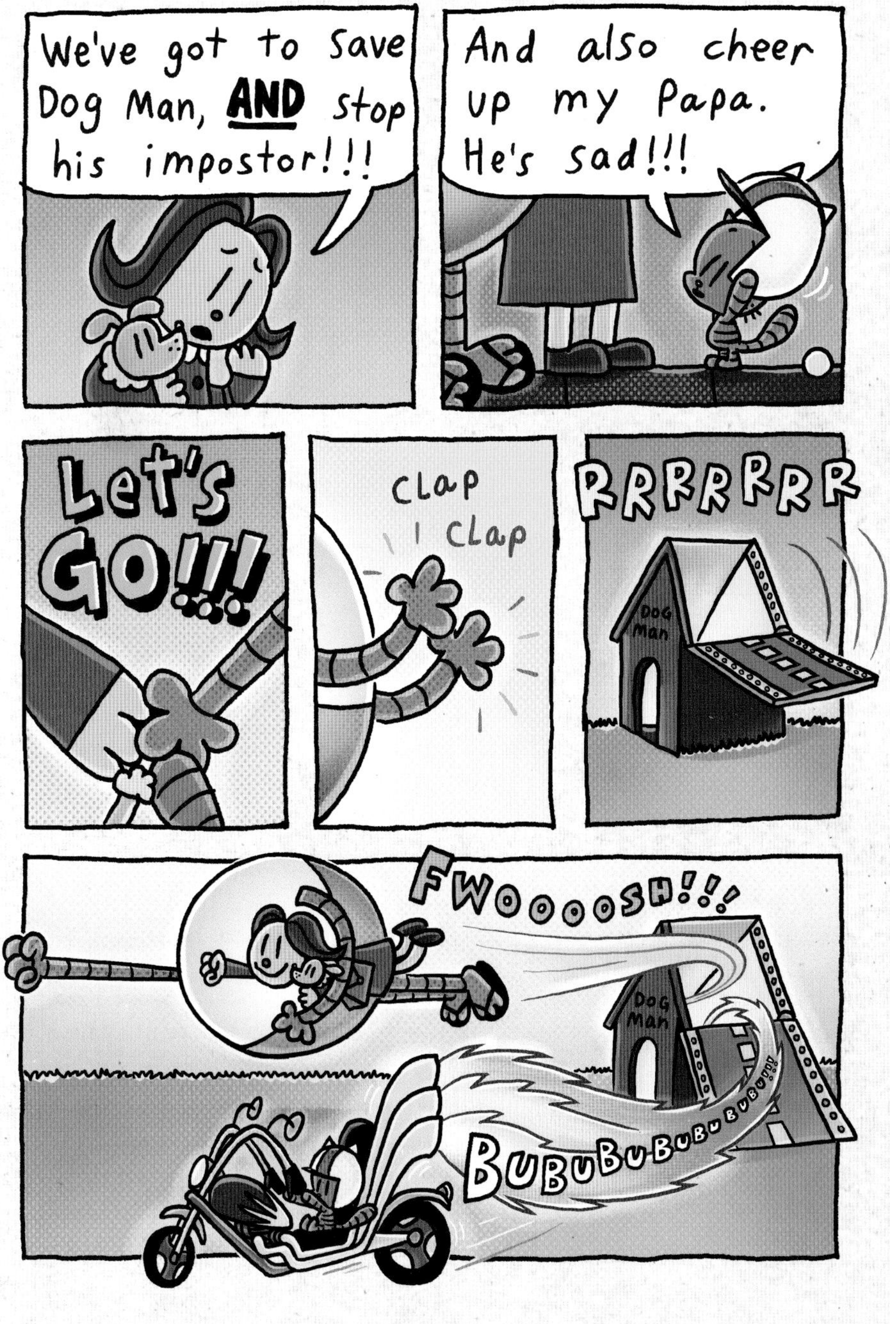
We've got to save Dog Man, AND stop his impostor!!!
And also cheer up my Papa. He's sad!!!
Let's GO!!!
CLAP
CLAP
RRRRRRR
DOG Man
FWOOOOOSH!!!
DOG Man
BUBUBUBUBUBUBUBUBU!!!

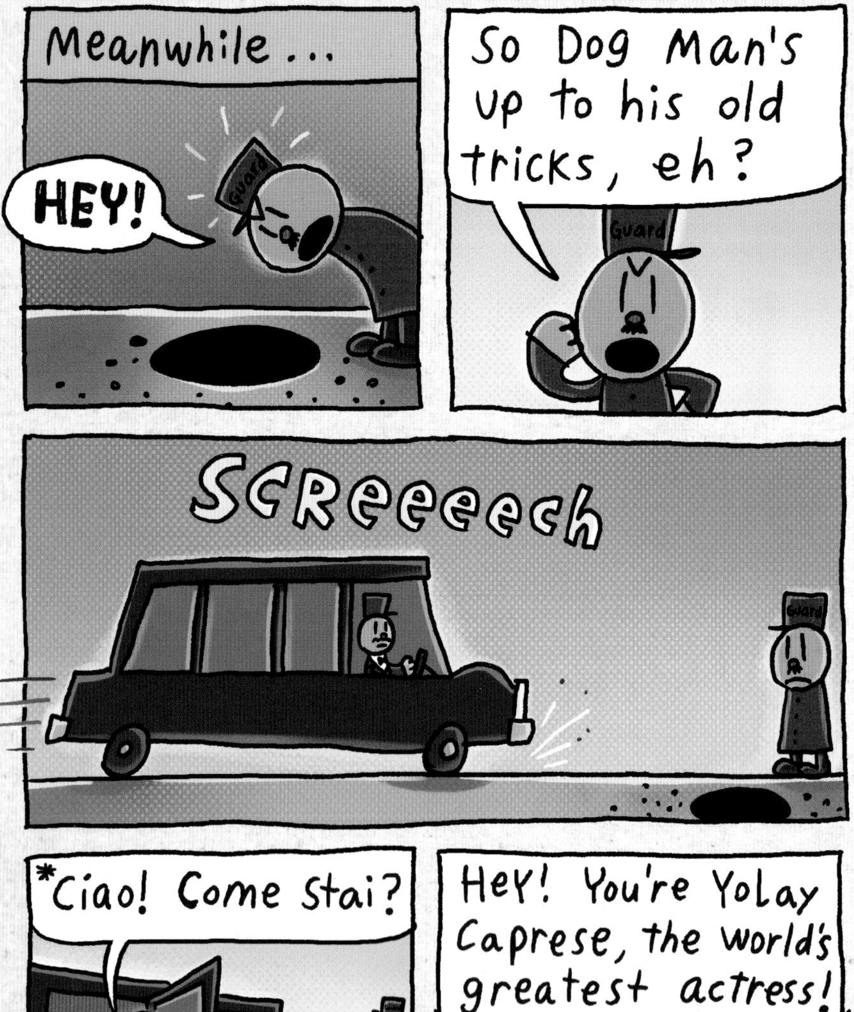
Meanwhile...
HEY!
Guard
So Dog Man's up to his old tricks, eh?
Guard
SCREEEECH
*Ciao! Come Stai?
Hey! You're Yolay Caprese, the world's greatest actress!
Guard
Sì*

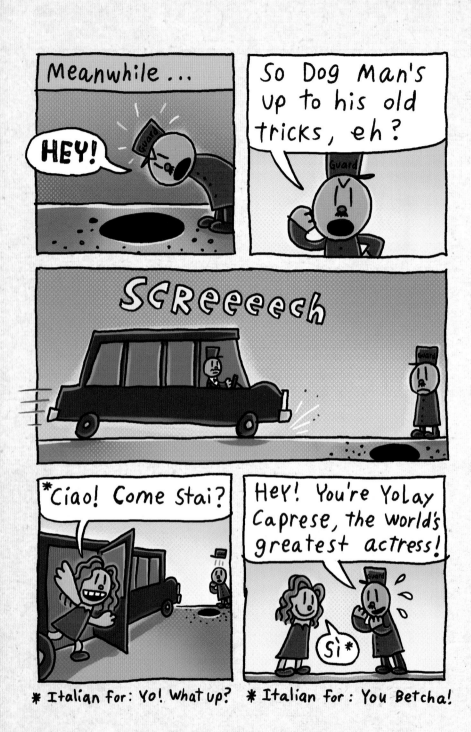

* Italian for: Yo! What up?

* Italian for: You Betcha!

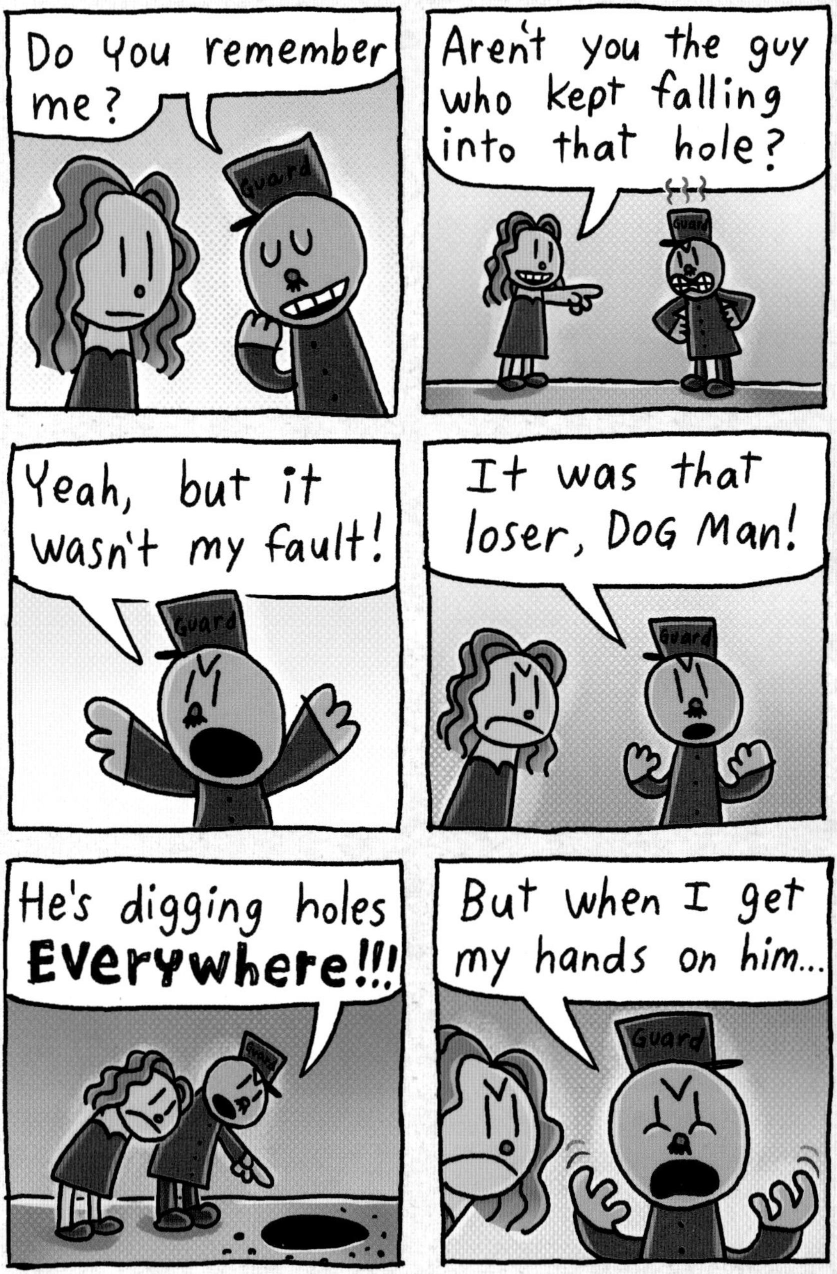
Do you remember me?
Aren't you the guy who kept falling into that hole?
Guard
Yeah, but it wasn't my fault!
It was that loser, DOG MAN!
He's digging holes **EVERYWHERE!!!**
But when I get my hands on him...
Guard

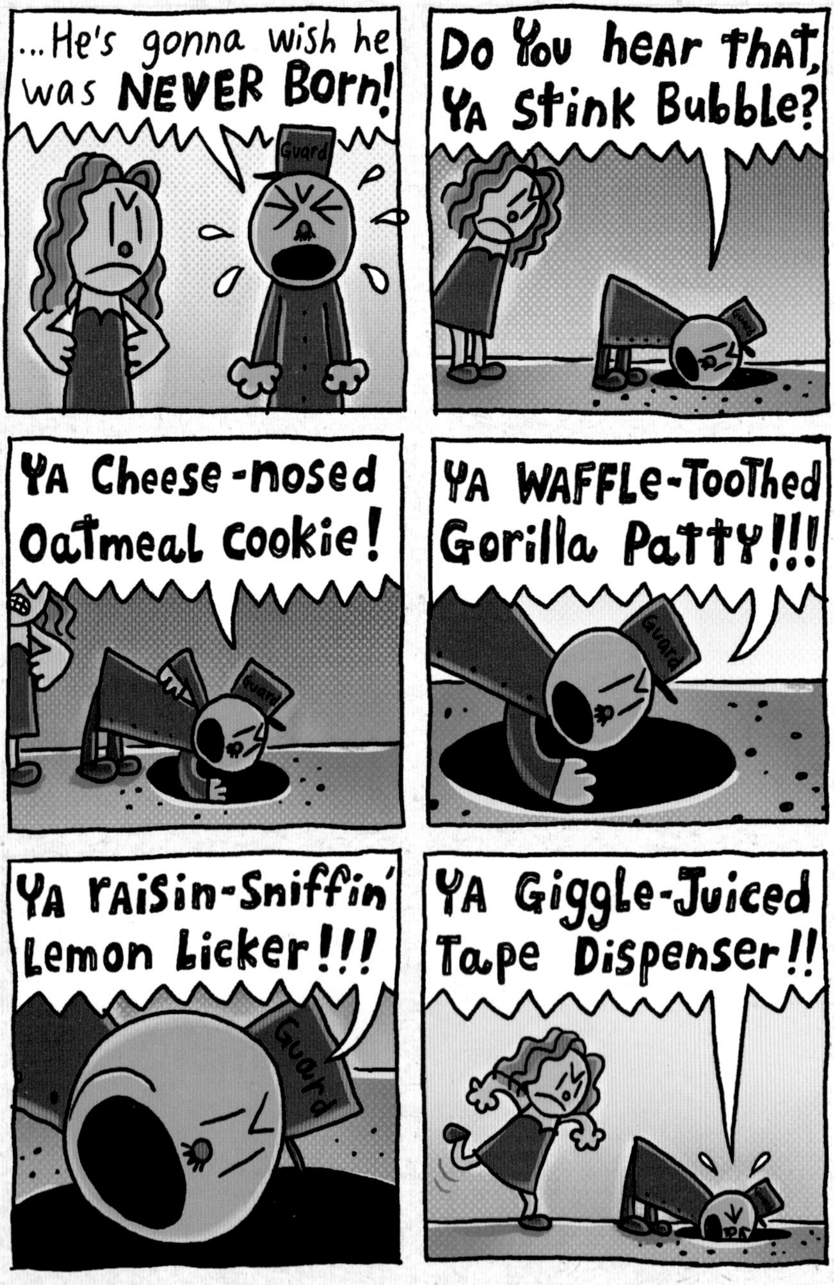
...He's gonna wish he was NEVER Born!
Guard
Do You hear THAT, YA Stink Bubble?
Guard
YA Cheese-nosed Oatmeal Cookie!
Guard
YA WAFFLE-TooThed Gorilla Patty!!!
Guard
YA rAiSin-Sniffin' Lemon Licker!!!
Guard
YA Giggle-Juiced Tape Dispenser!!

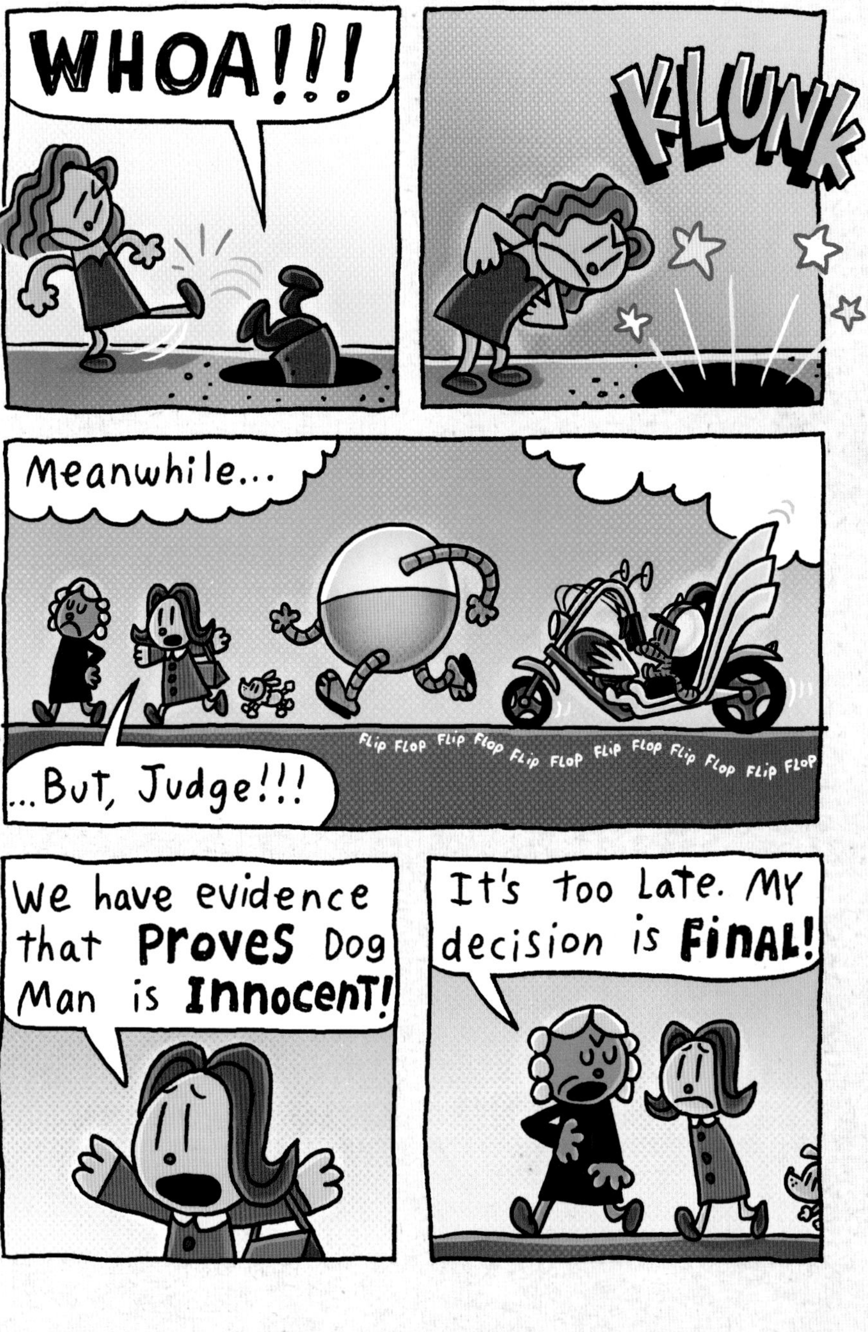
WHOA!!!
KLUNK
Meanwhile...
...But, Judge!!!
FLIP FLOP FLIP FLOP FLIP FLOP FLIP FLOP FLIP FLOP FLIP FLOP
We have evidence that PROVES Dog Man is INNOCENT!
It's too Late. MY decision is FINAL!

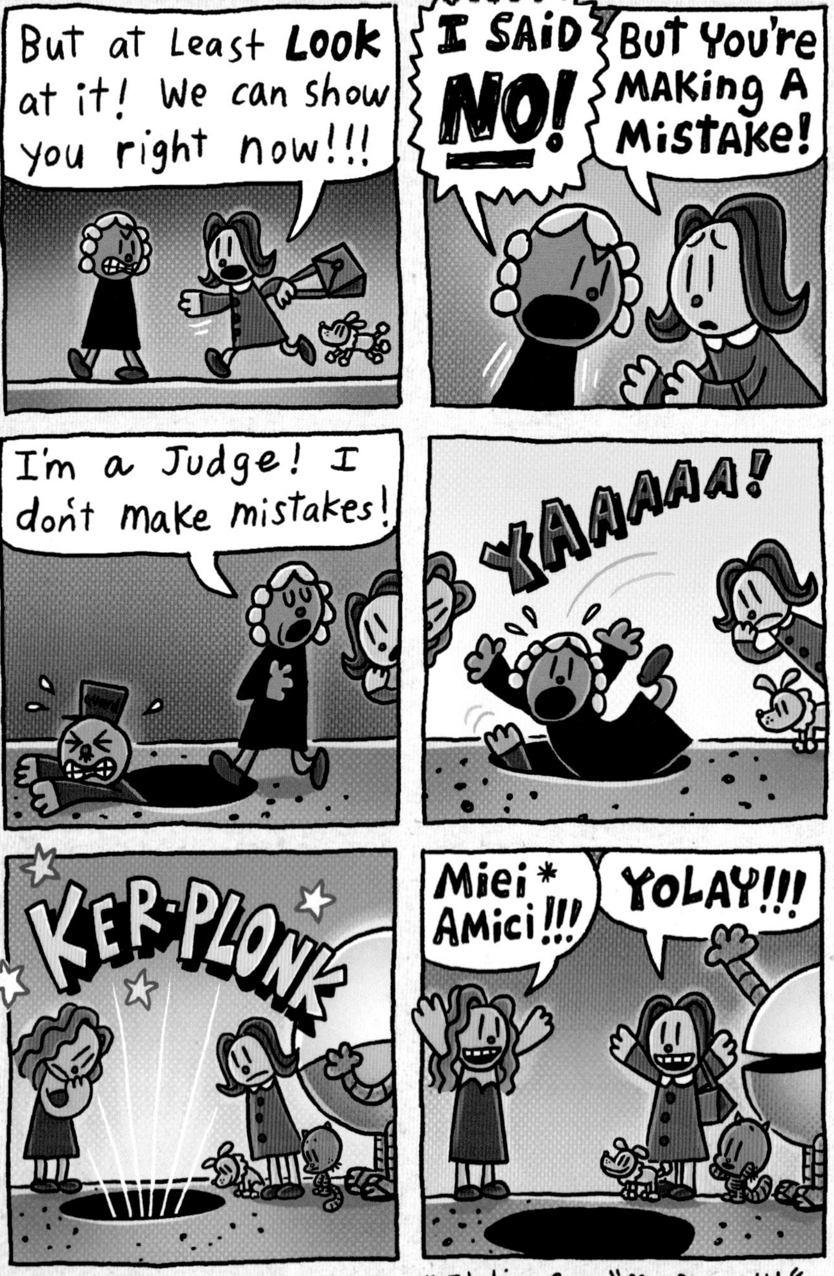
But at Least LOOK at it! We can show you right now!!!
I SAID NO!
But You're MAKing A MisTAKe!
I'm a Judge! I don't make mistakes!
YAAAAAA!
KER-PLONK
Miei* AMici!!!
YOLAY!!!
* Italian for: "My Peeps!!!"

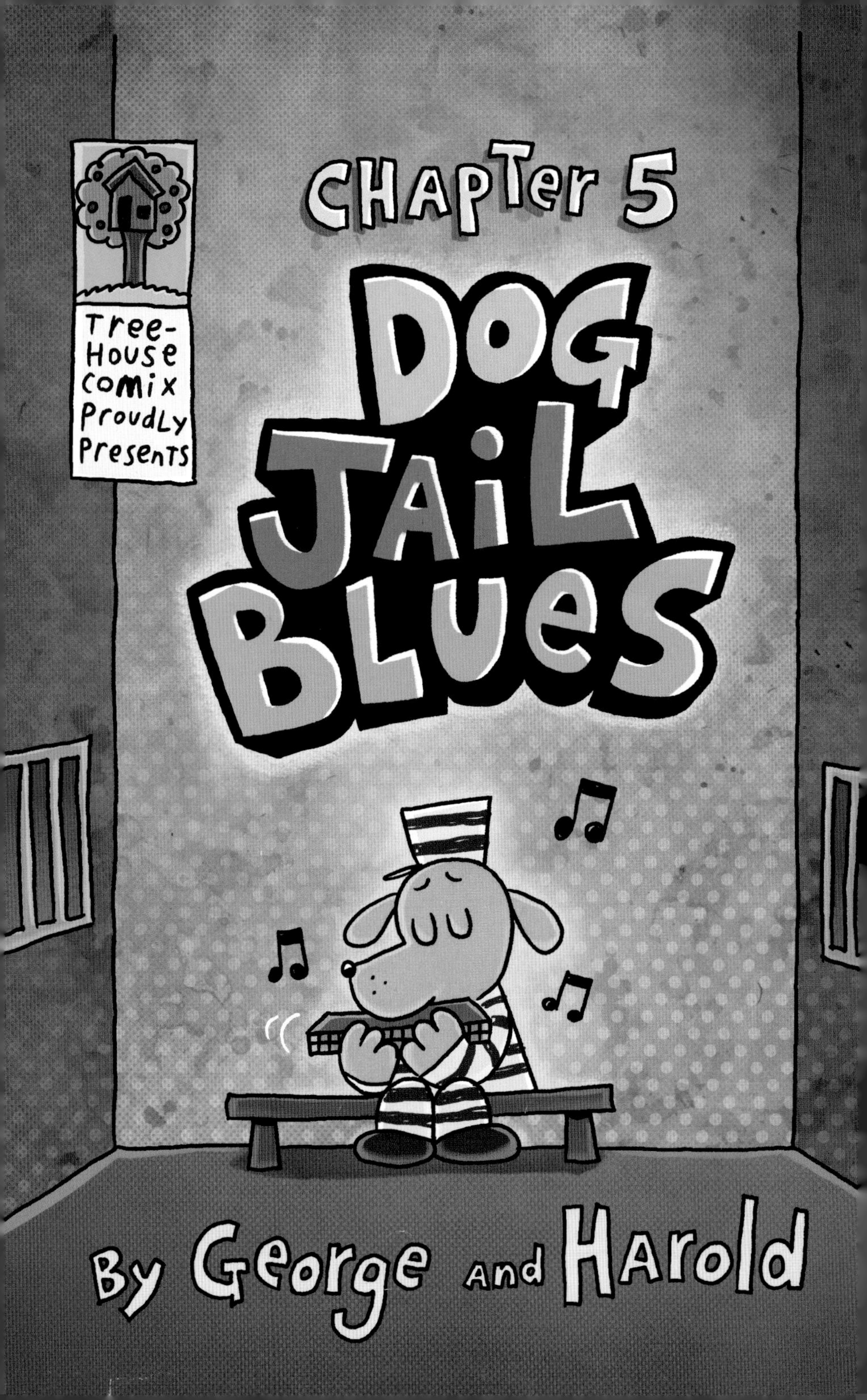
Tree-House Comix Proudly Presents
CHAPTER 5
DOG JAIL BLUES
By George and Harold

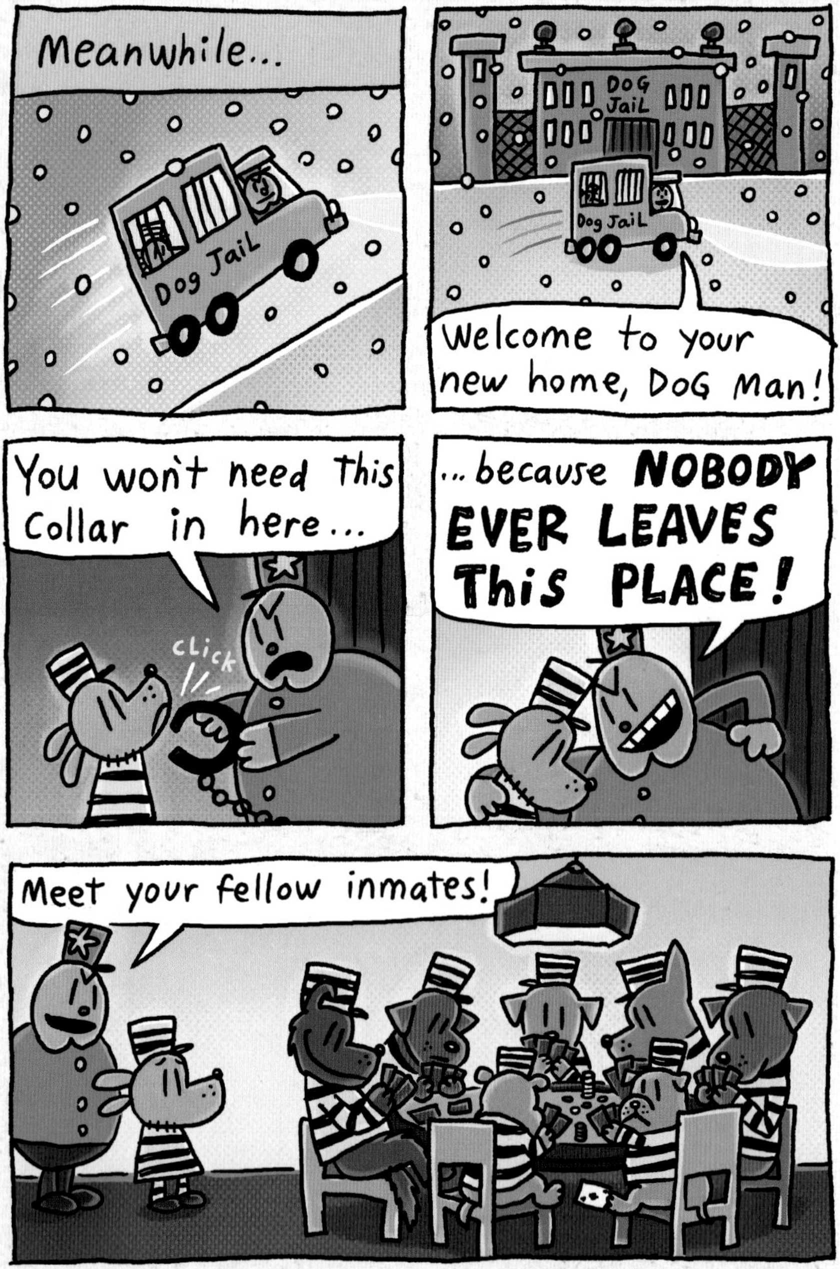
Meanwhile...
Dog Jail
DOG JaiL
Dog JaiL
Welcome to your new home, DoG Man!
You won't need this collar in here...
CLick
...because NOBODY EVER LEAVES This PLACE!
Meet your fellow inmates!

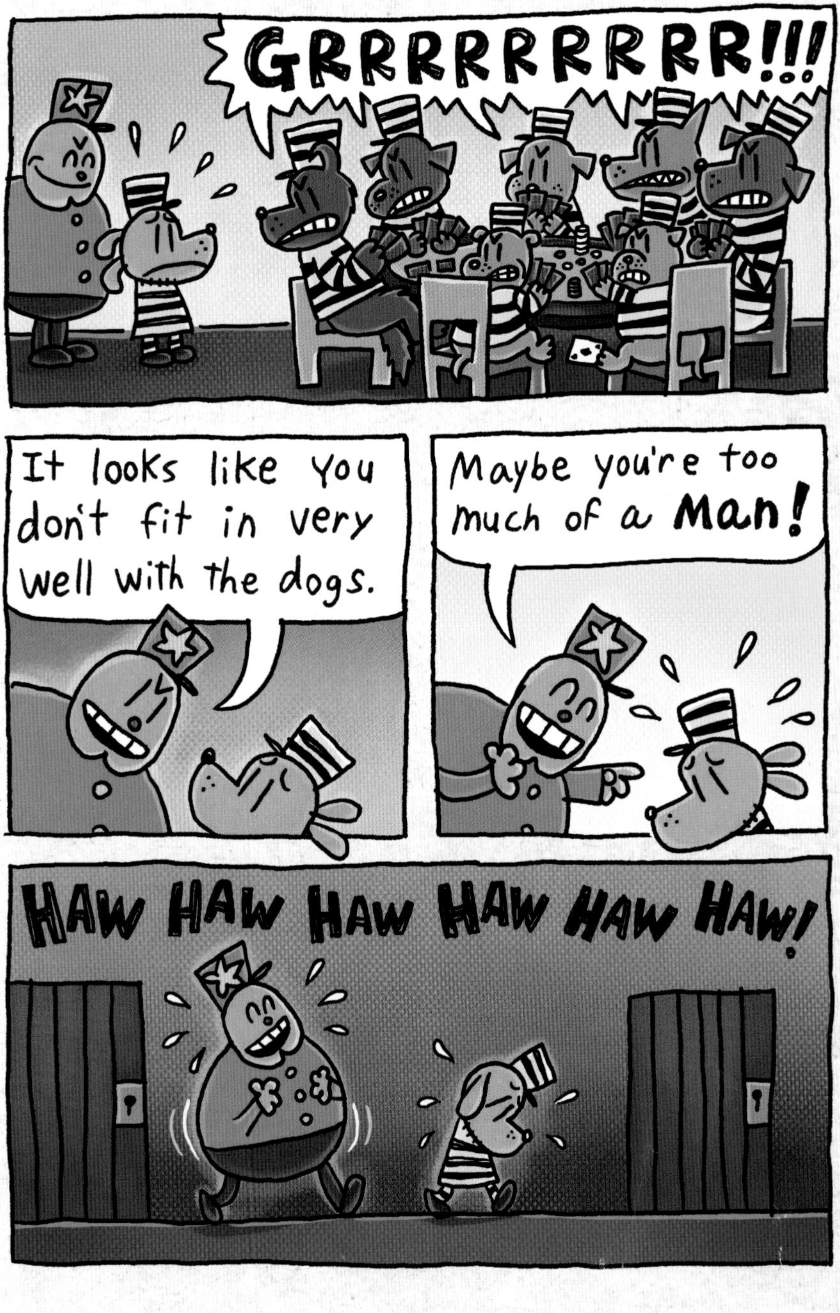
GRRRRRRRRR!!!
It looks like you don't fit in very well with the dogs.
Maybe you're too much of a Man!
HAW HAW HAW HAW HAW HAW!

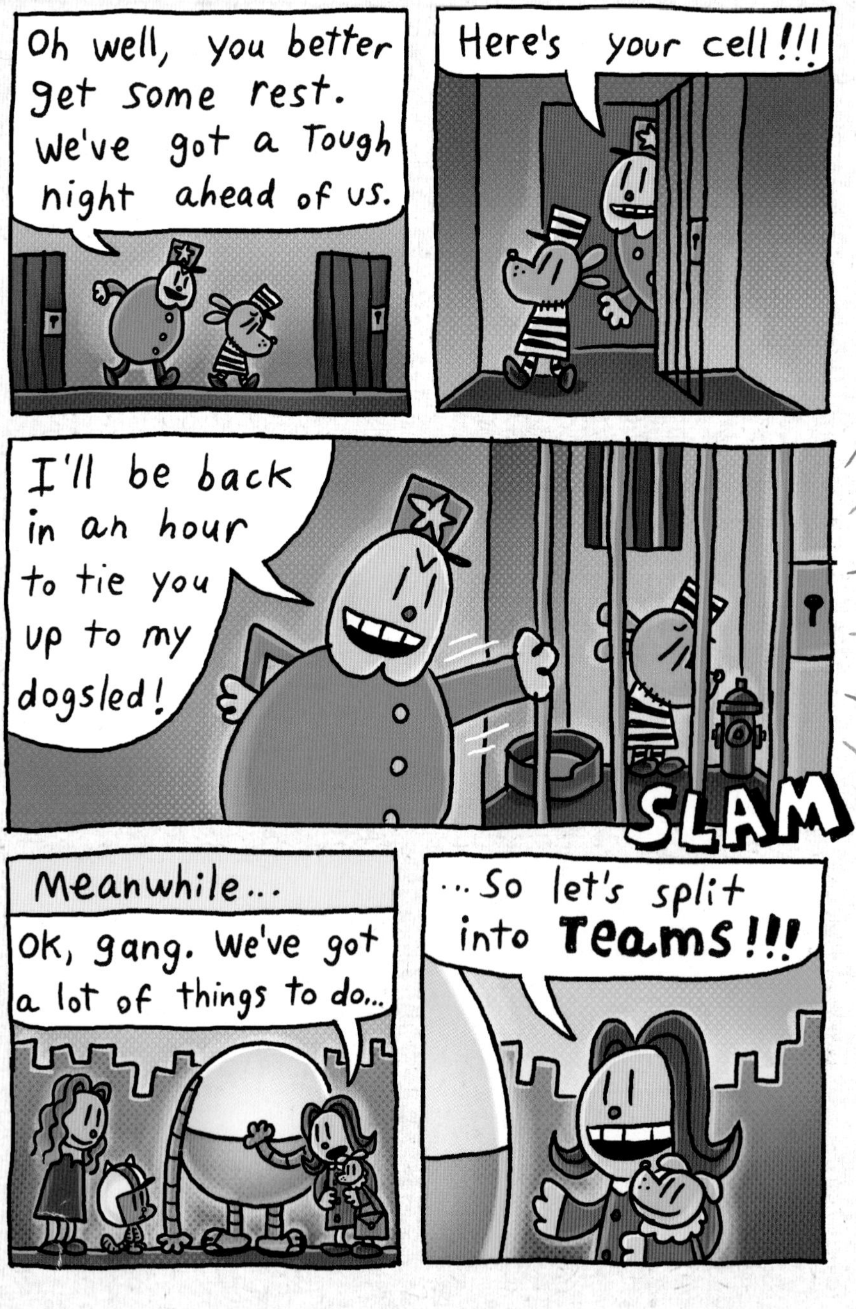
Oh well, you better get some rest. We've got a Tough night ahead of us.
Here's your cell!!!
I'll be back in an hour to tie you up to my dogsled!
SLAM
Meanwhile...
Ok, gang. We've got a lot of things to do...
...So let's split into Teams!!!

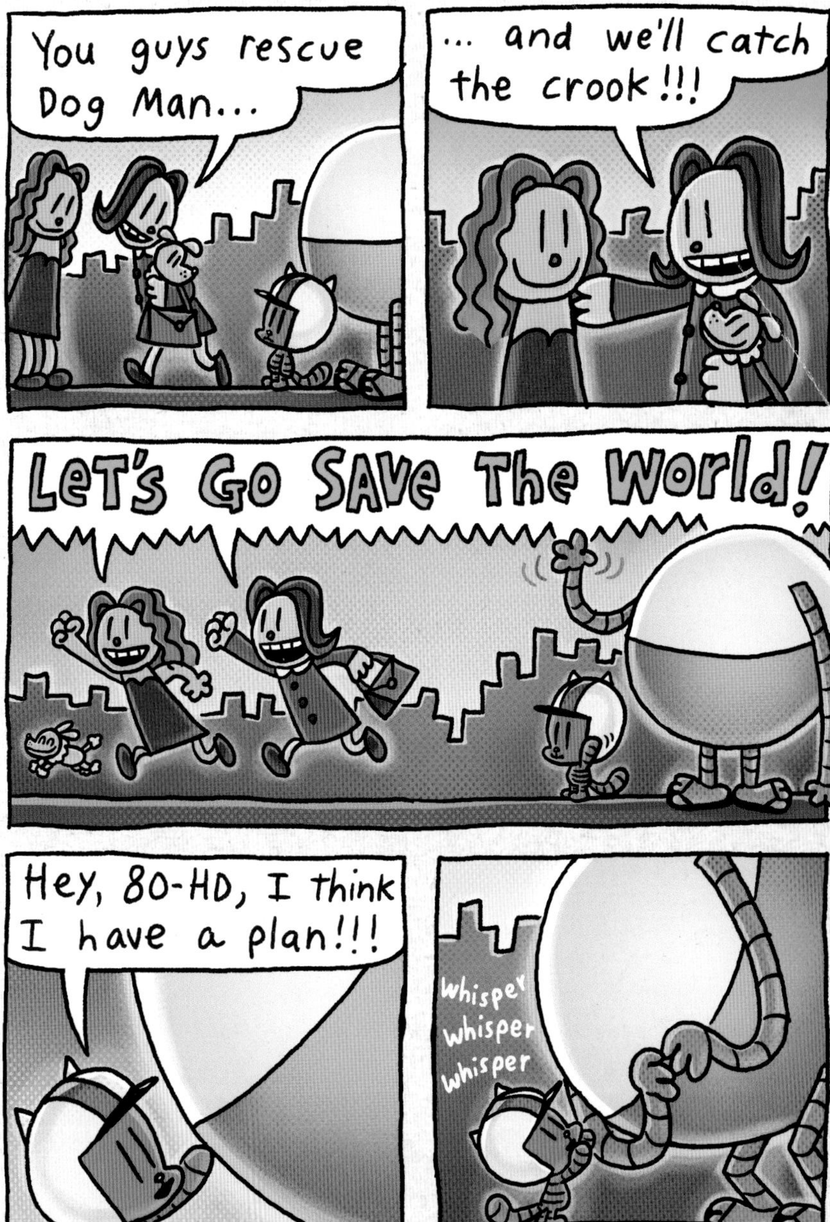
You guys rescue Dog Man...
... and we'll catch the crook!!!
LET'S GO SAVE THE WORLD!
Hey, 80-HD, I think I have a plan!!!
whisper
whisper
whisper

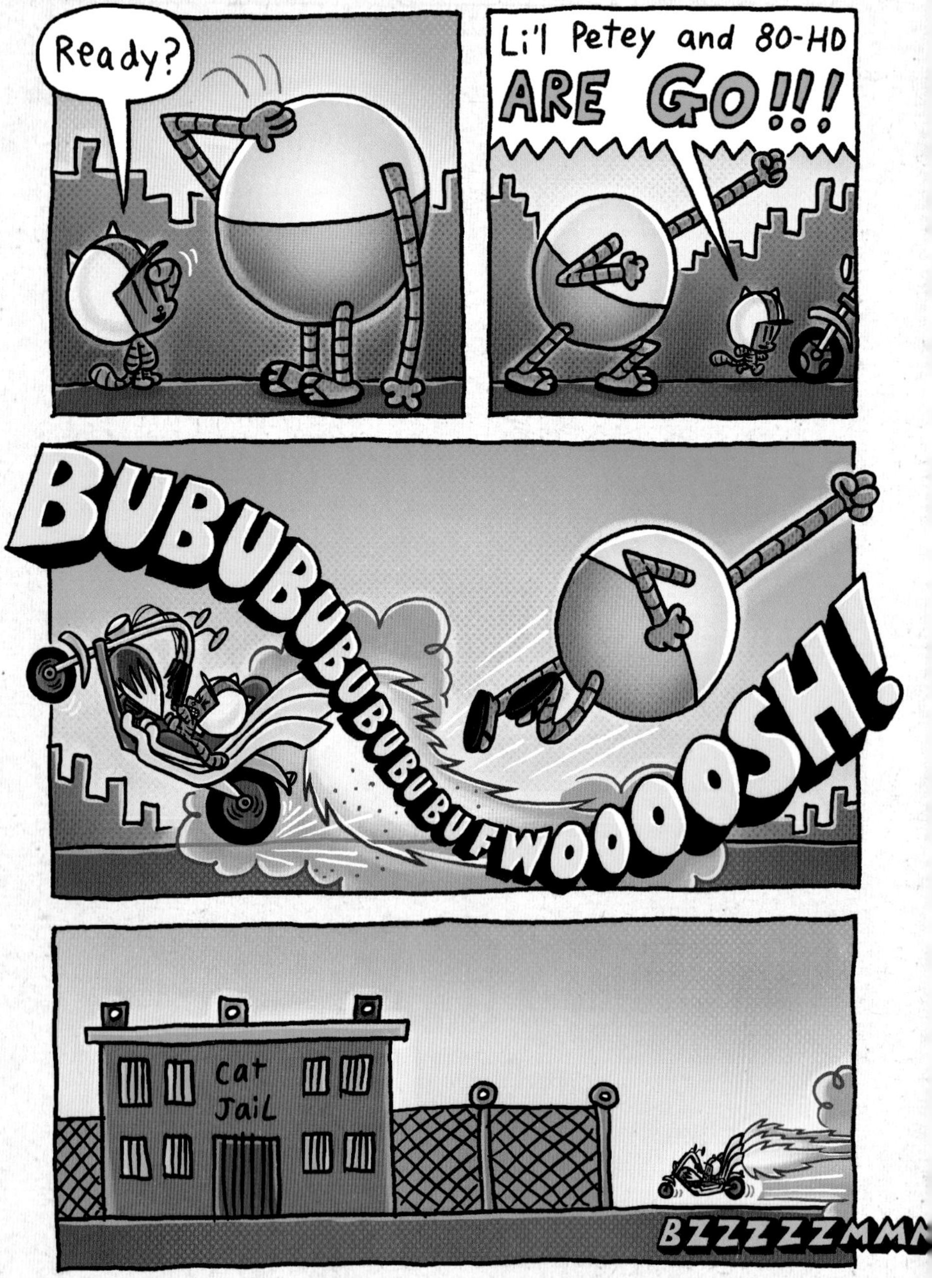
Ready?
Li'l Petey and 80-HD ARE GO!!!
BUBUBUBUBUBUBUBUFWOOOOOSH!
Cat Jail
BZZZZZMMM

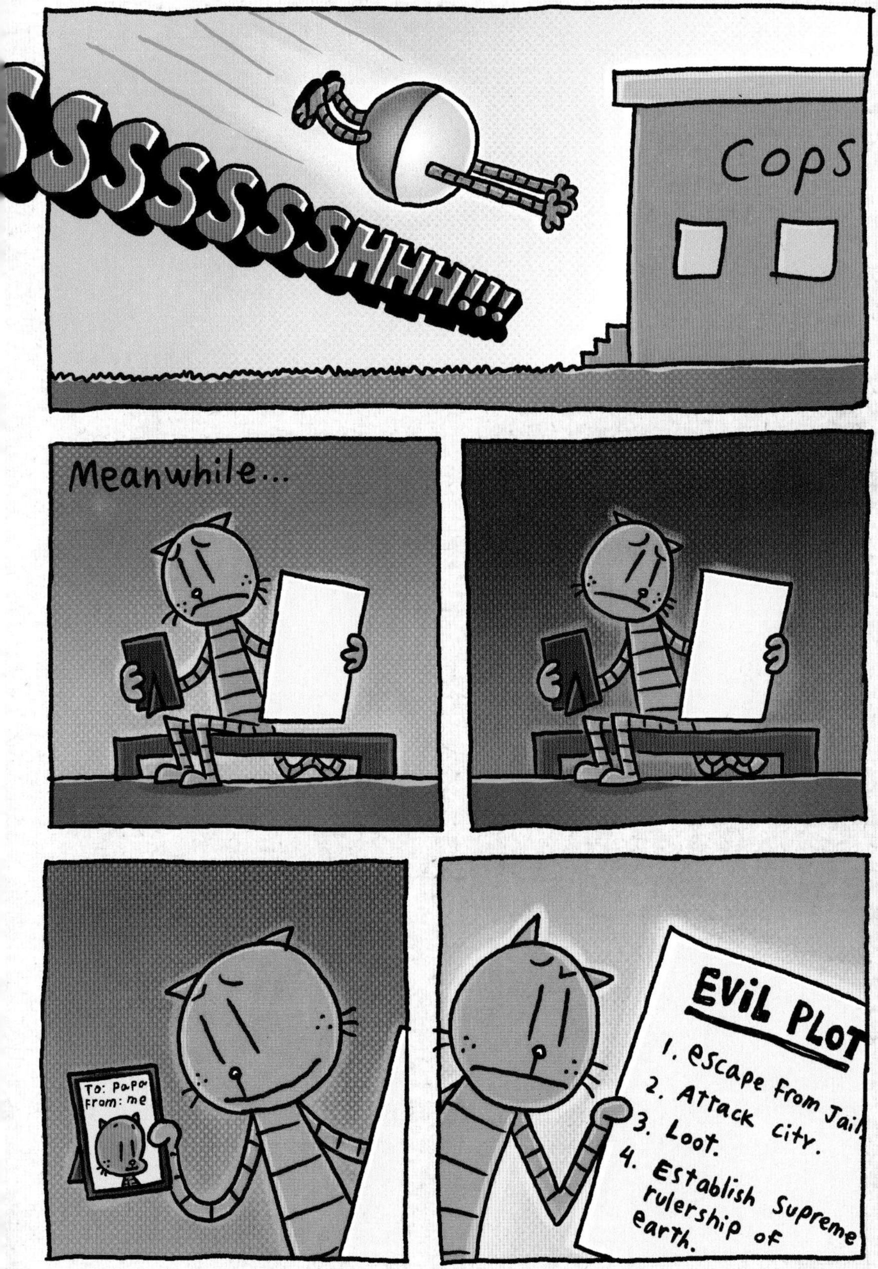

SSSSSSSSHHH!!!
COPS
Meanwhile...
To: Papa
From: me
EVIL PLOT
1. Escape From Jail.
2. Attack city.
3. Loot.
4. Establish Supreme rulership of earth.

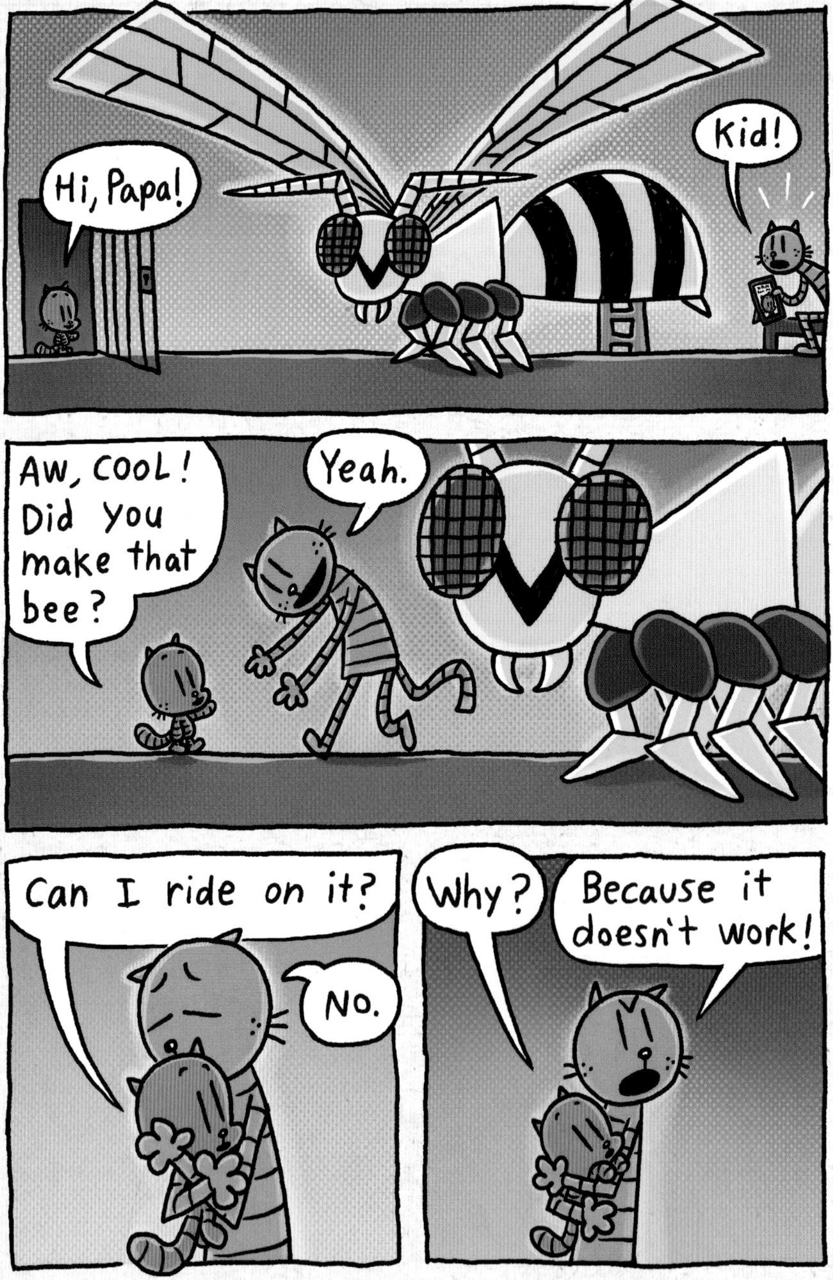
Hi, Papa!
Kid!
AW, COOL! Did you make that bee?
Yeah.
Can I ride on it?
No.
Why?
Because it doesn't work!

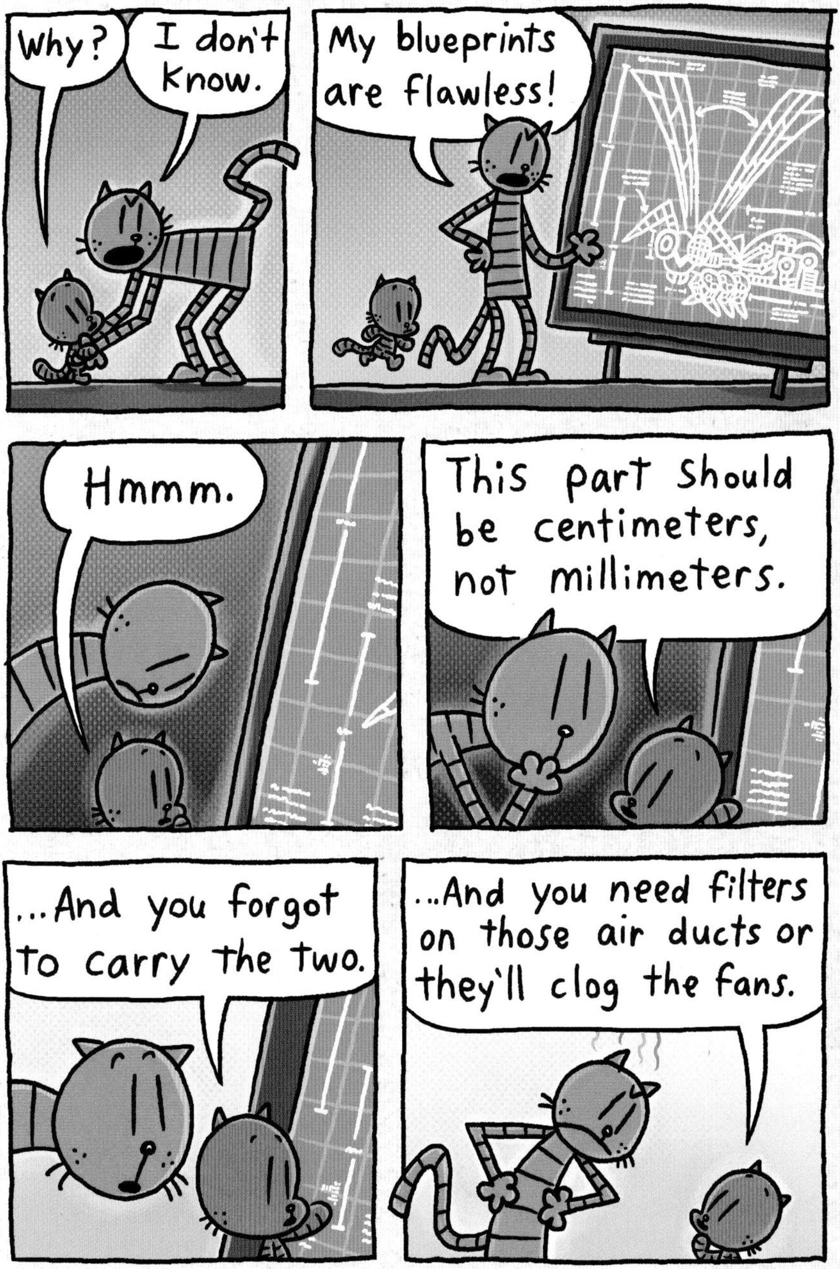
Why?
I don't know.
My blueprints are flawless!
Hmmm.
This part Should be centimeters, not millimeters.
...And you forgot to carry the two.
...And you need filters on those air ducts or they'll clog the fans.

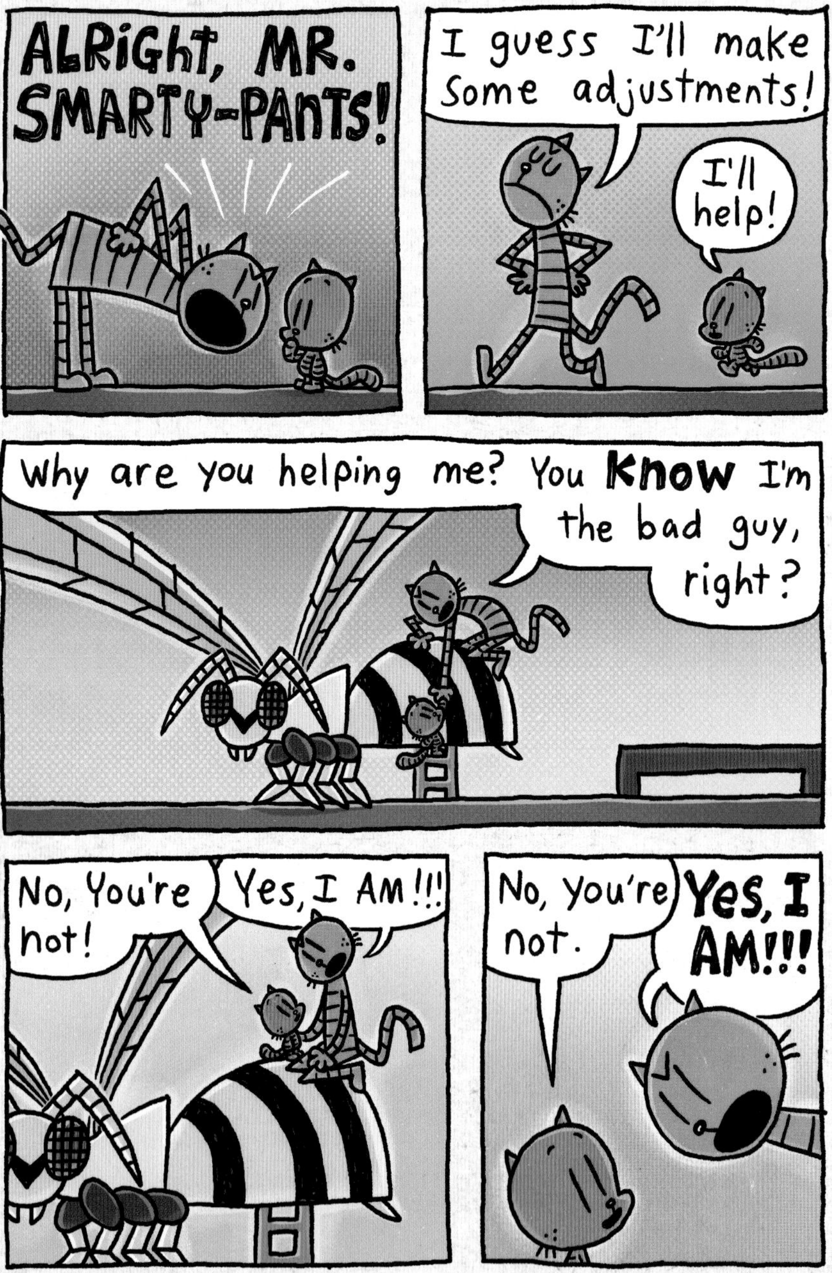
ALRIGHT, MR. SMARTY-PANTS!
I guess I'll make some adjustments!
I'll help!
Why are you helping me? You KNOW I'm the bad guy, right?
No, You're not!
Yes, I AM!!!
No, you're not.
Yes, I AM!!!

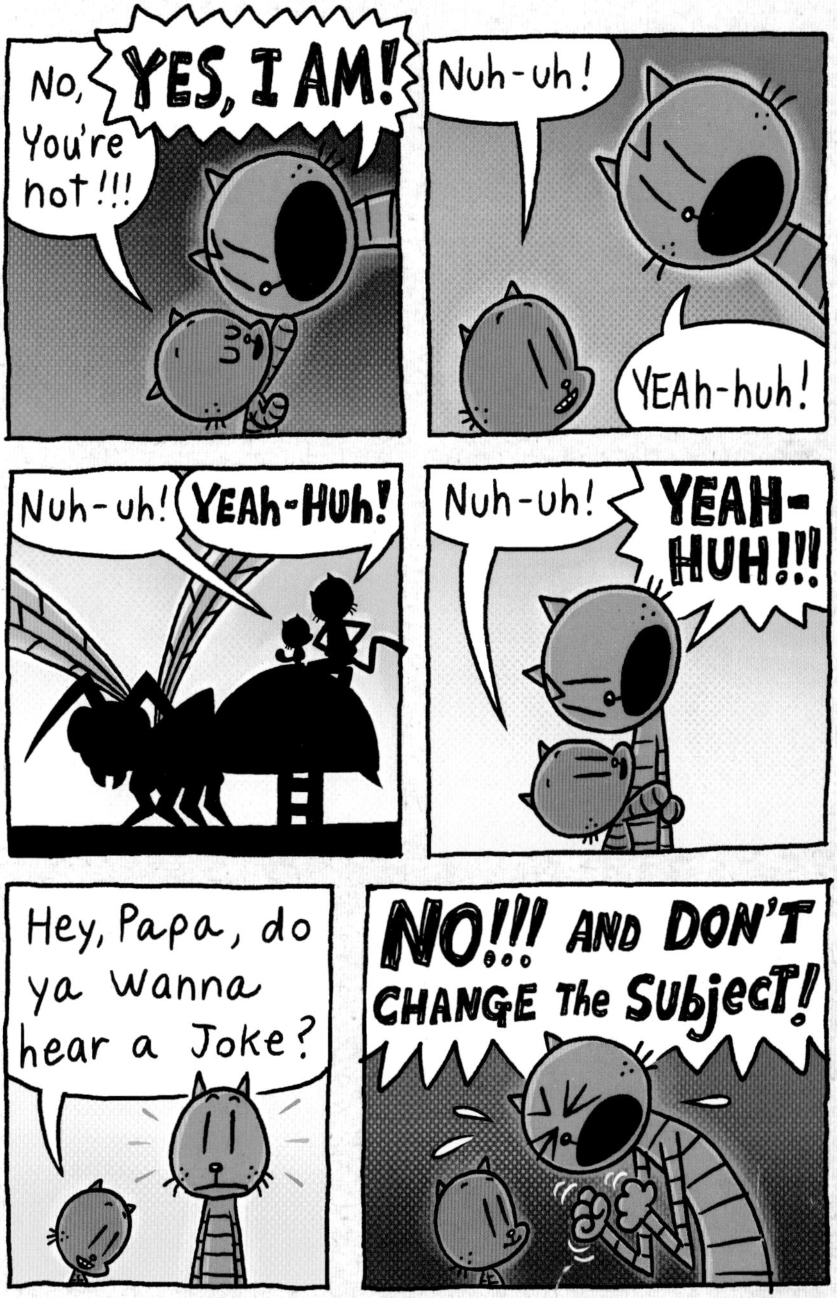
No, You're not!!!
YES, I AM!
Nuh-uh!
YEAh-huh!
Nuh-uh!
YEAh-HUh!
Nuh-uh!
YEAH-HUH!!!
Hey, Papa, do ya wanna hear a Joke?
NO!!! AND DON'T CHANGE The SubjecT!

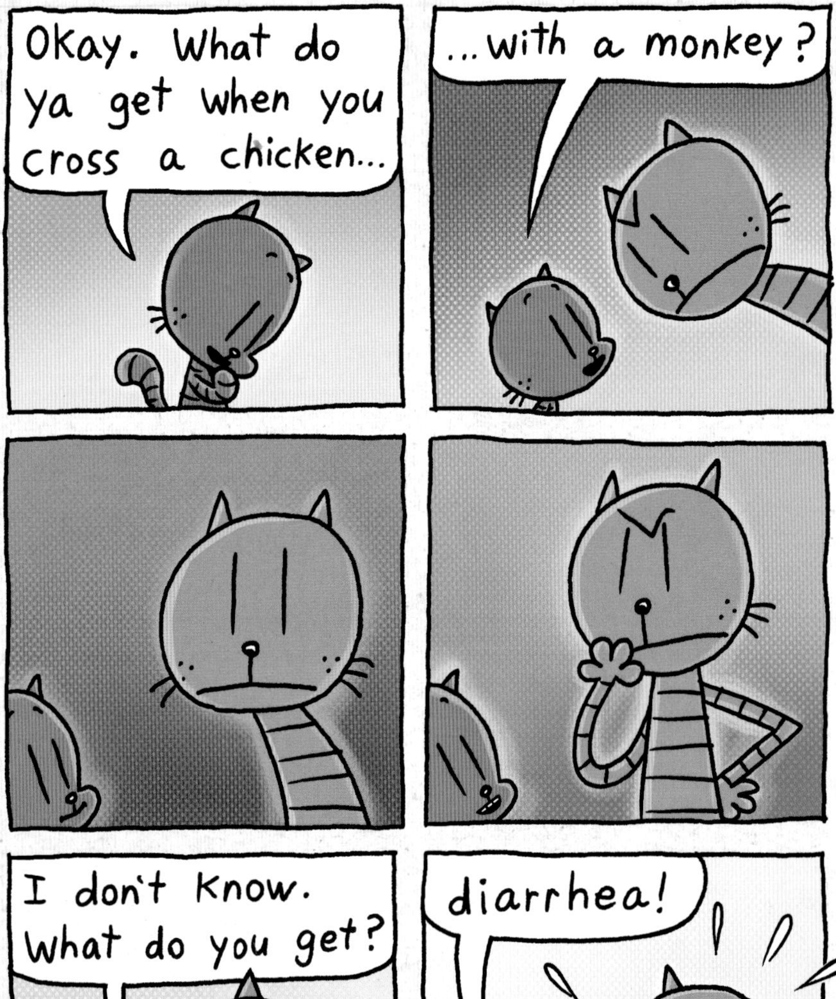
Okay. What do ya get when you cross a chicken...
...with a monkey?
I don't know. What do you get?
diarrhea!

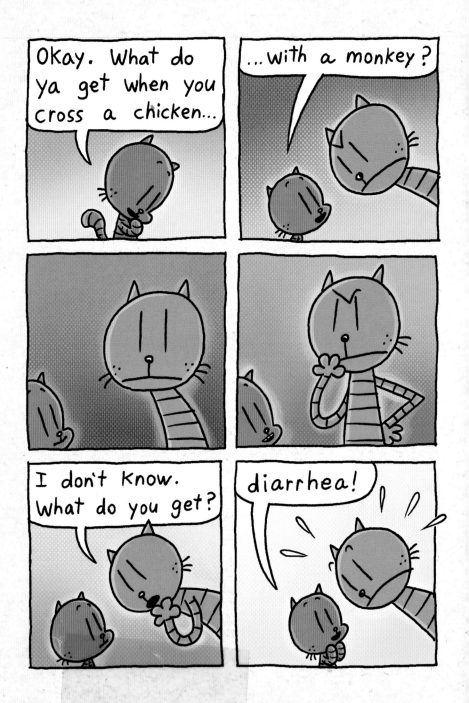

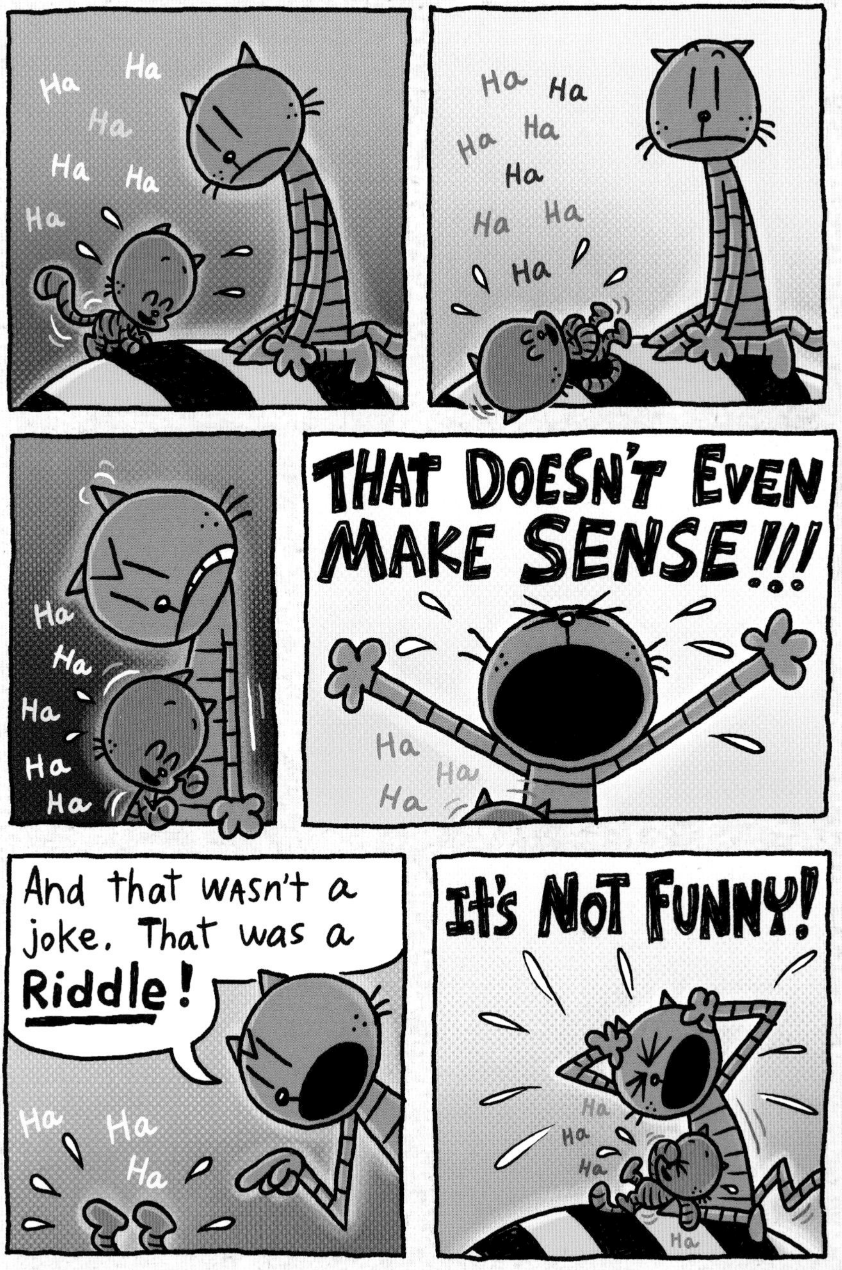
Ha Ha Ha Ha Ha Ha
Ha Ha Ha Ha Ha Ha Ha
Ha Ha Ha Ha Ha
THAT DOESN'T EVEN MAKE SENSE!!!
Ha Ha Ha
And that WASN'T a joke. That was a Riddle!
Ha Ha Ha
IT'S NOT FUNNY!
Ha Ha Ha Ha

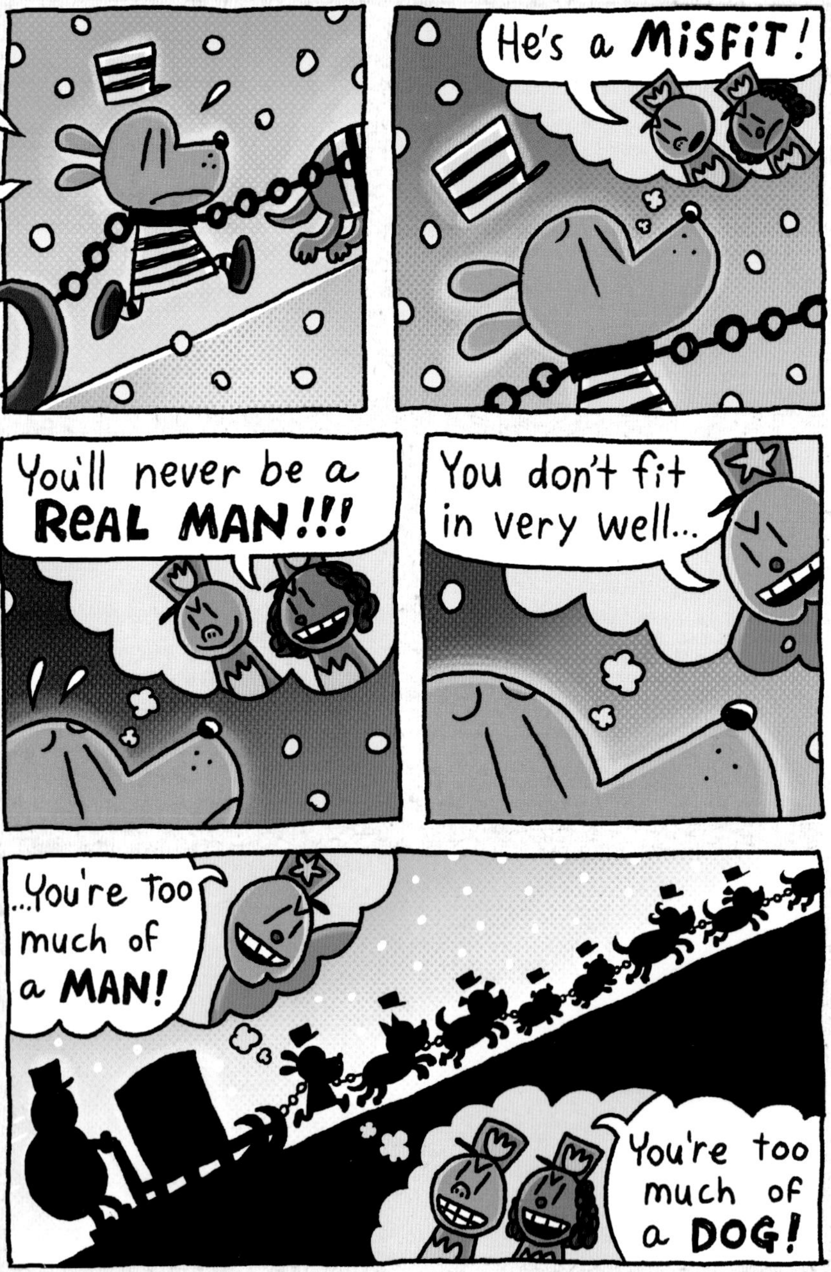
He's a MISFIT!
You'll never be a REAL MAN!!!
You don't fit in very well...
...You're too much of a MAN!
You're too much of a DOG!

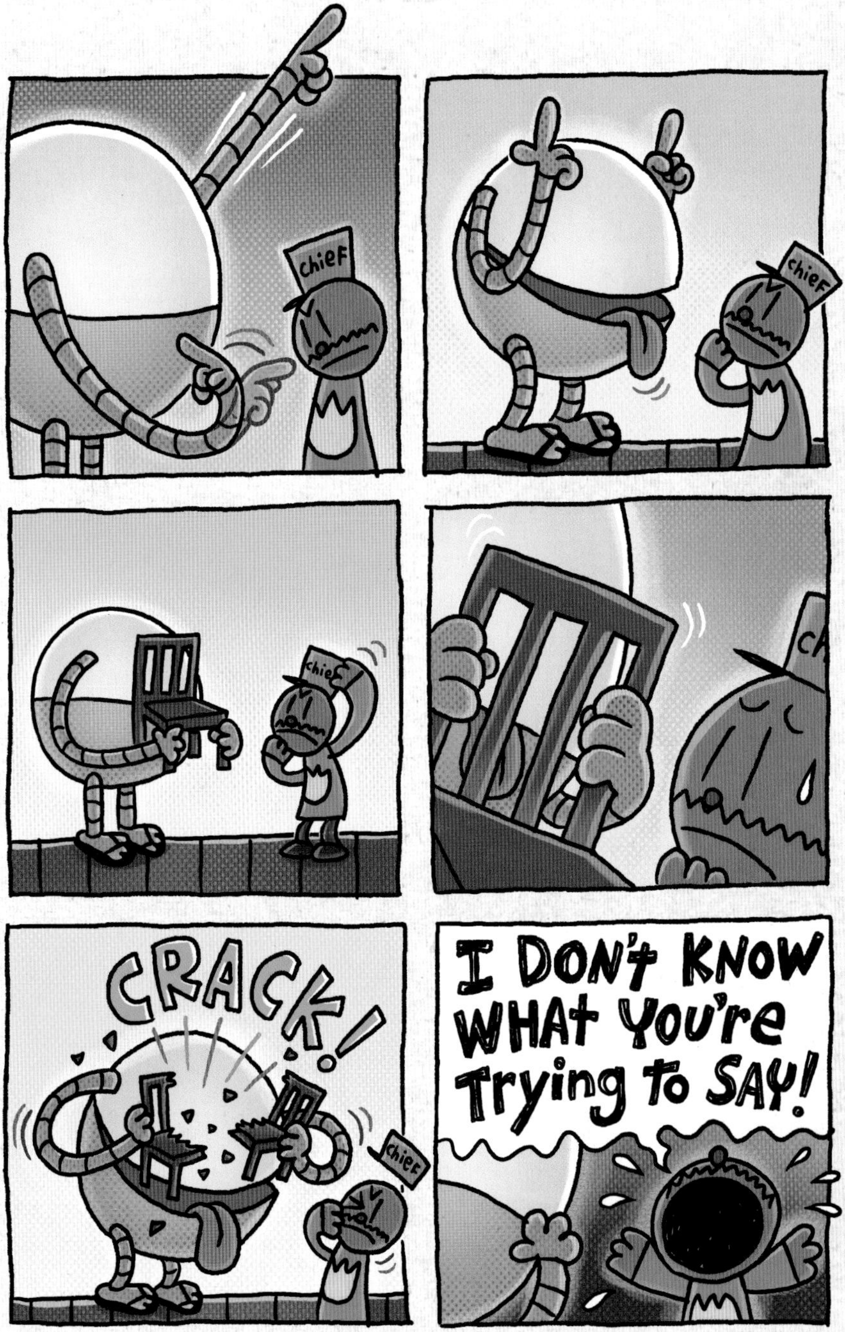
chief
chief
chief
CH
CRACK!
chief
I DON'T KNOW WHAT YOU'RE TRYING TO SAY!

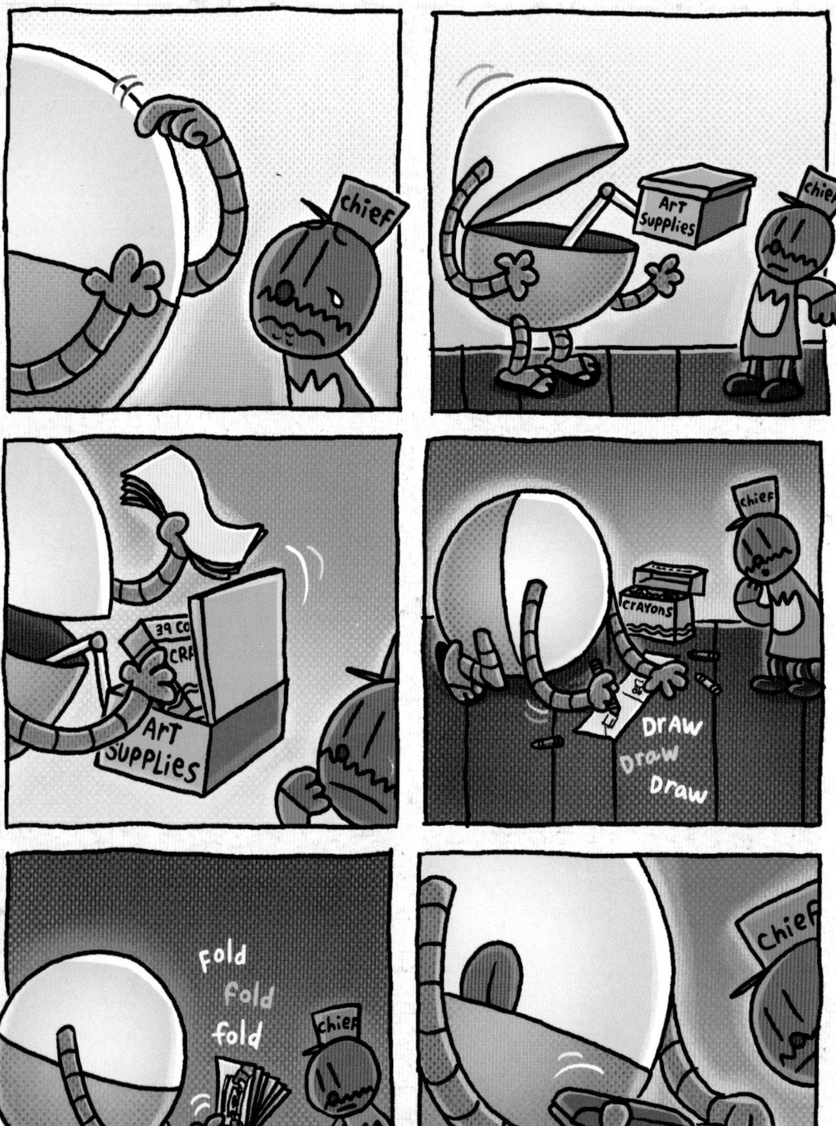
chief
ART
Supplies
chief
ART
SUPPLIES
chief
CRAYONS
DRAW
Draw
Draw
Fold
fold
fold
chief
chief
staple
Staple
staple

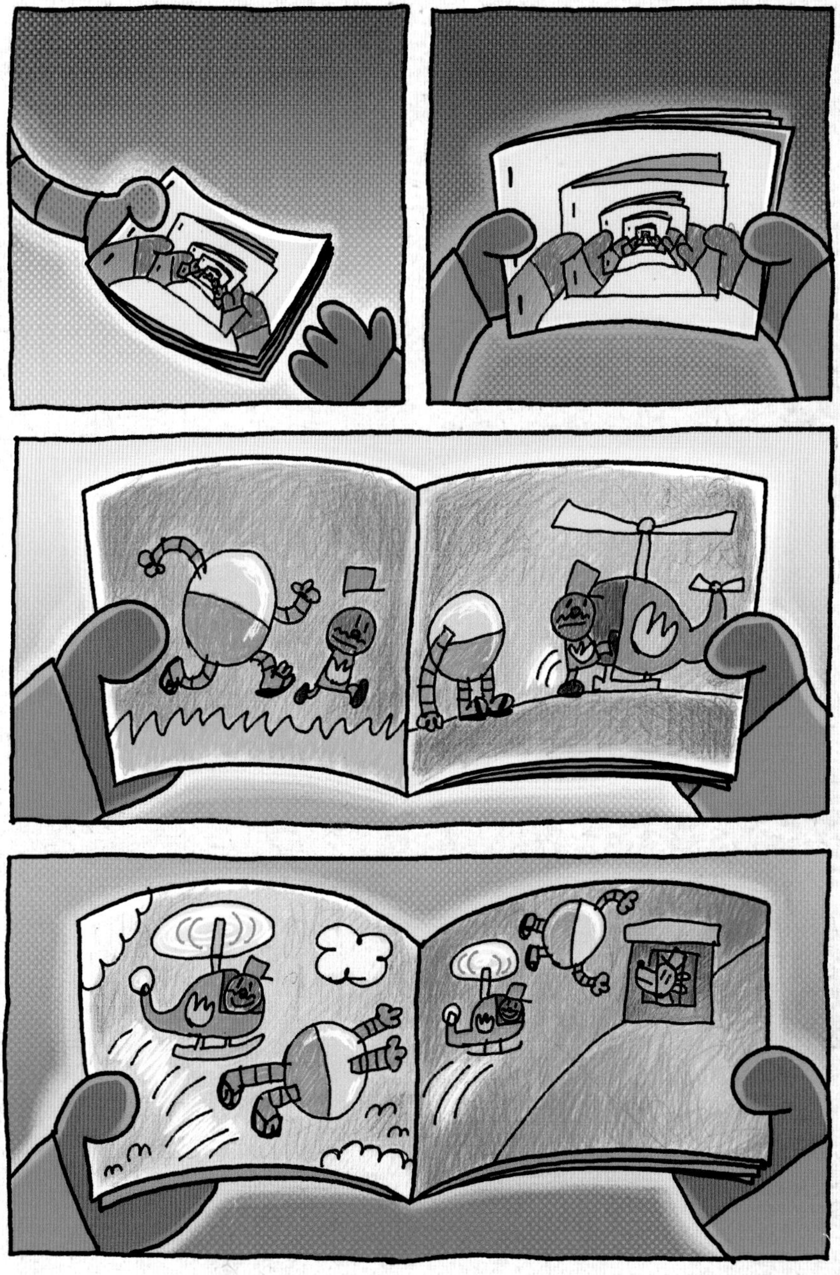

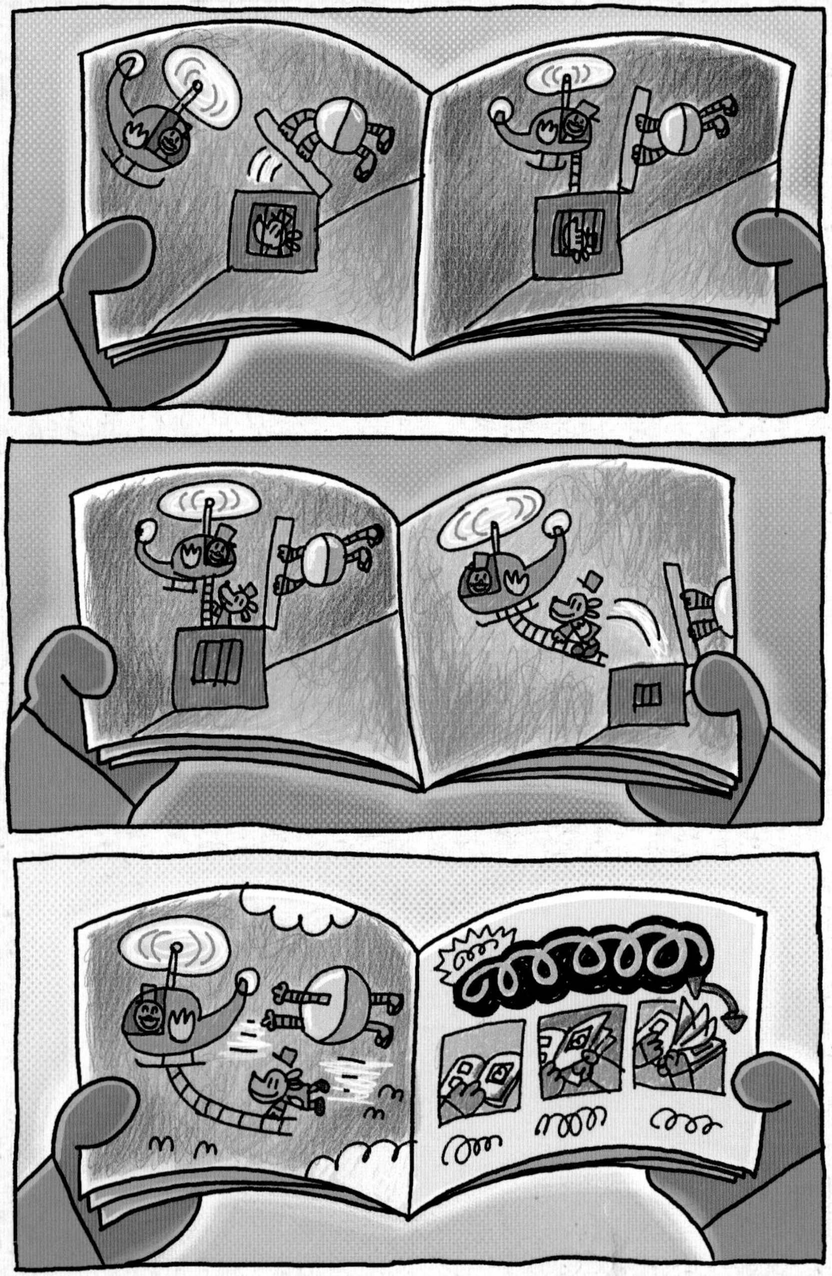

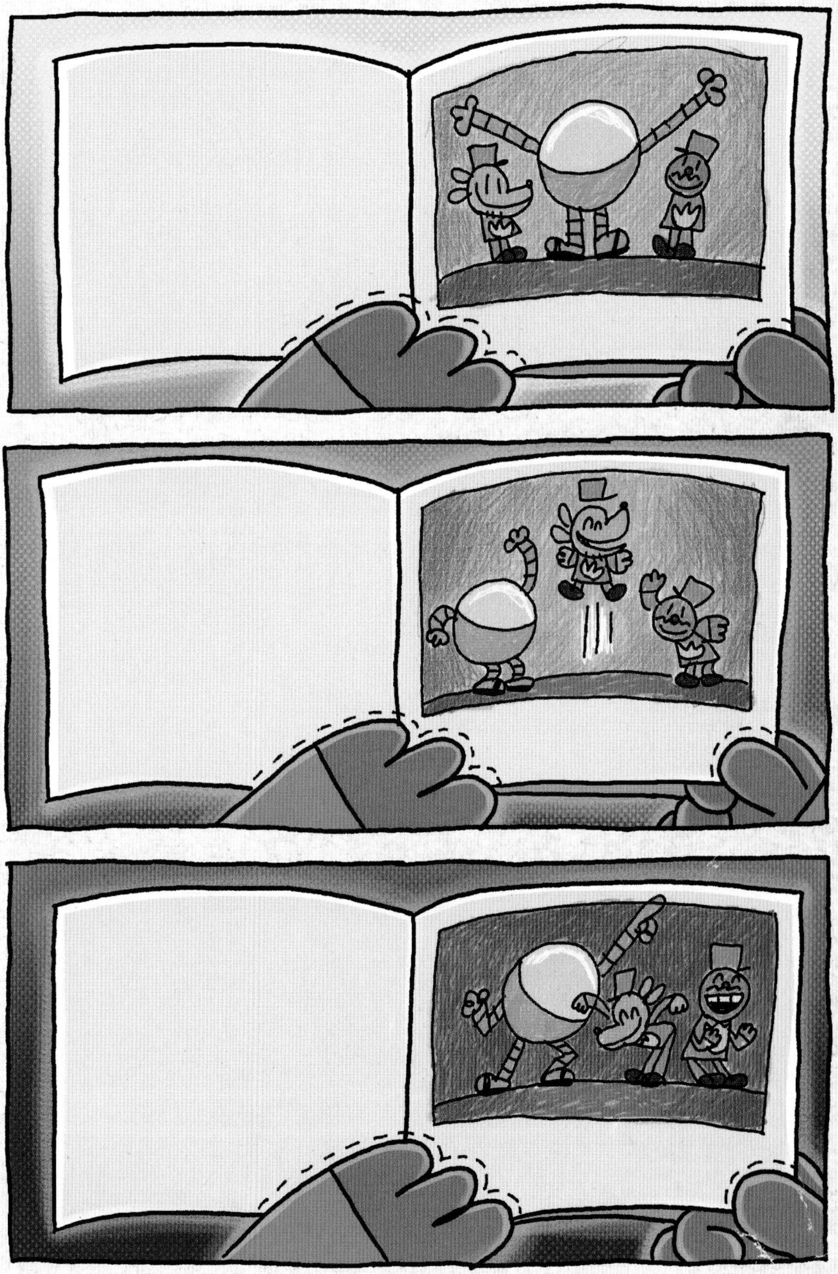

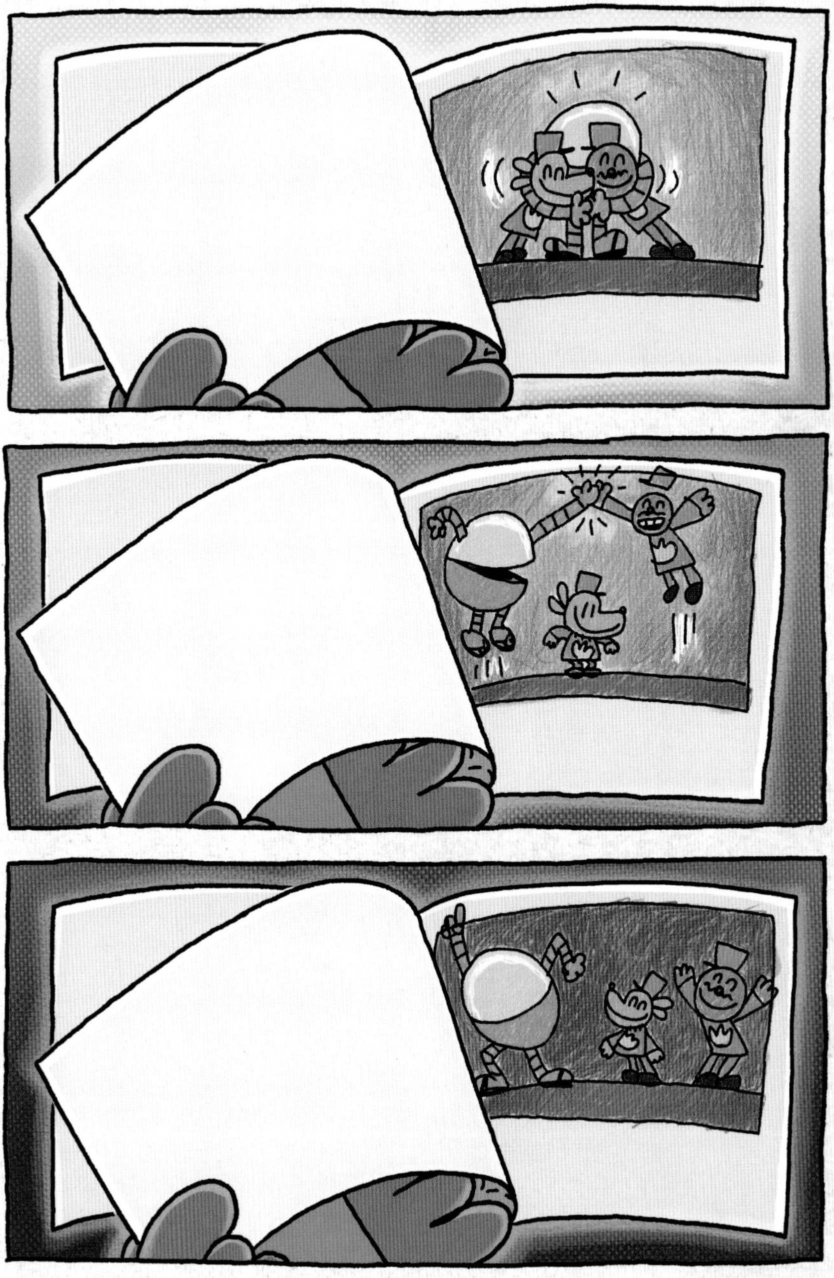

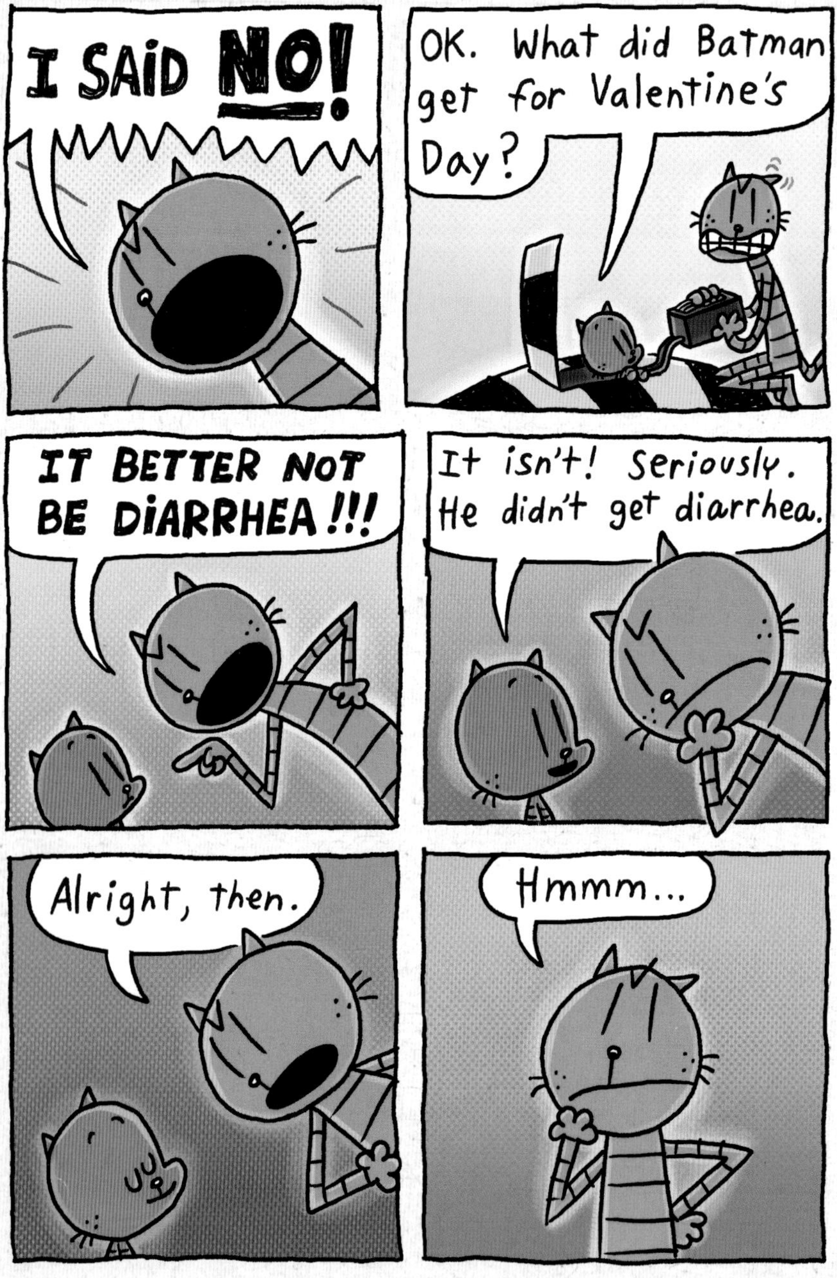
I SAID NO!
OK. What did Batman get for Valentine's Day?
IT BETTER NOT BE DIARRHEA!!!
It isn't! Seriously. He didn't get diarrhea.
Alright, then.
Hmmm...

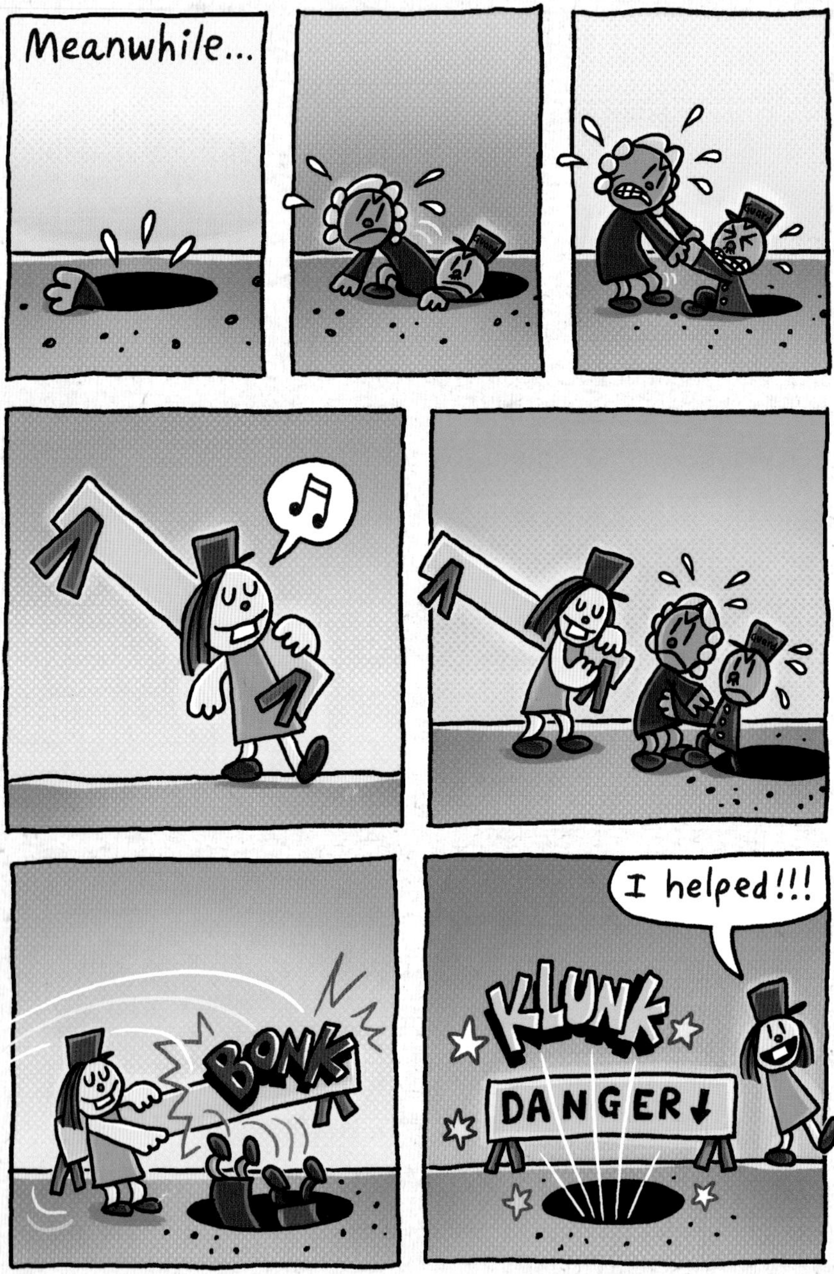
Meanwhile...
Guard
Guard
Guard
BONK
KLUNK
DANGER↓
I helped!!!

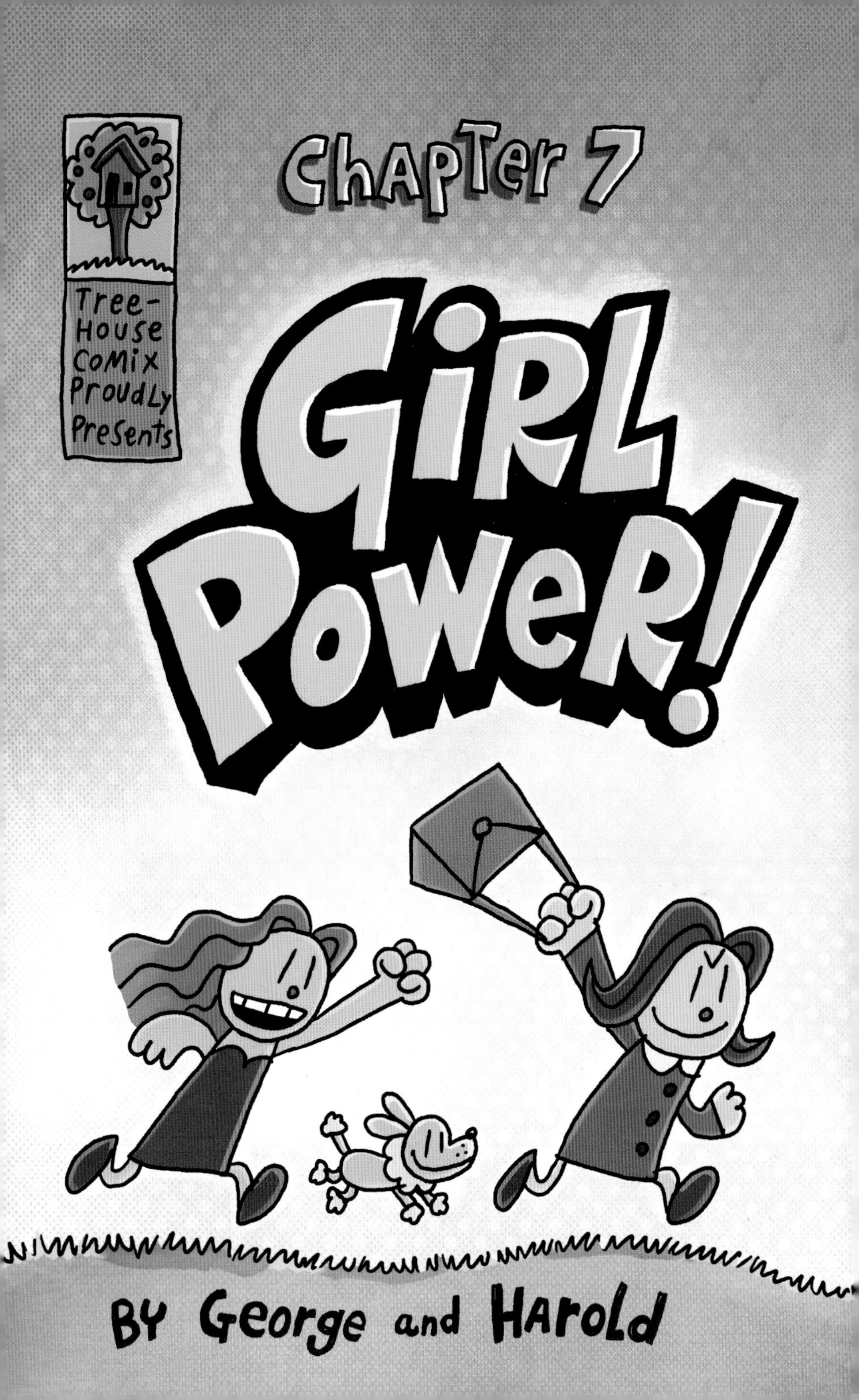

Tree-House Comix Proudly Presents
Chapter 7
Girl Power!
By George and Harold

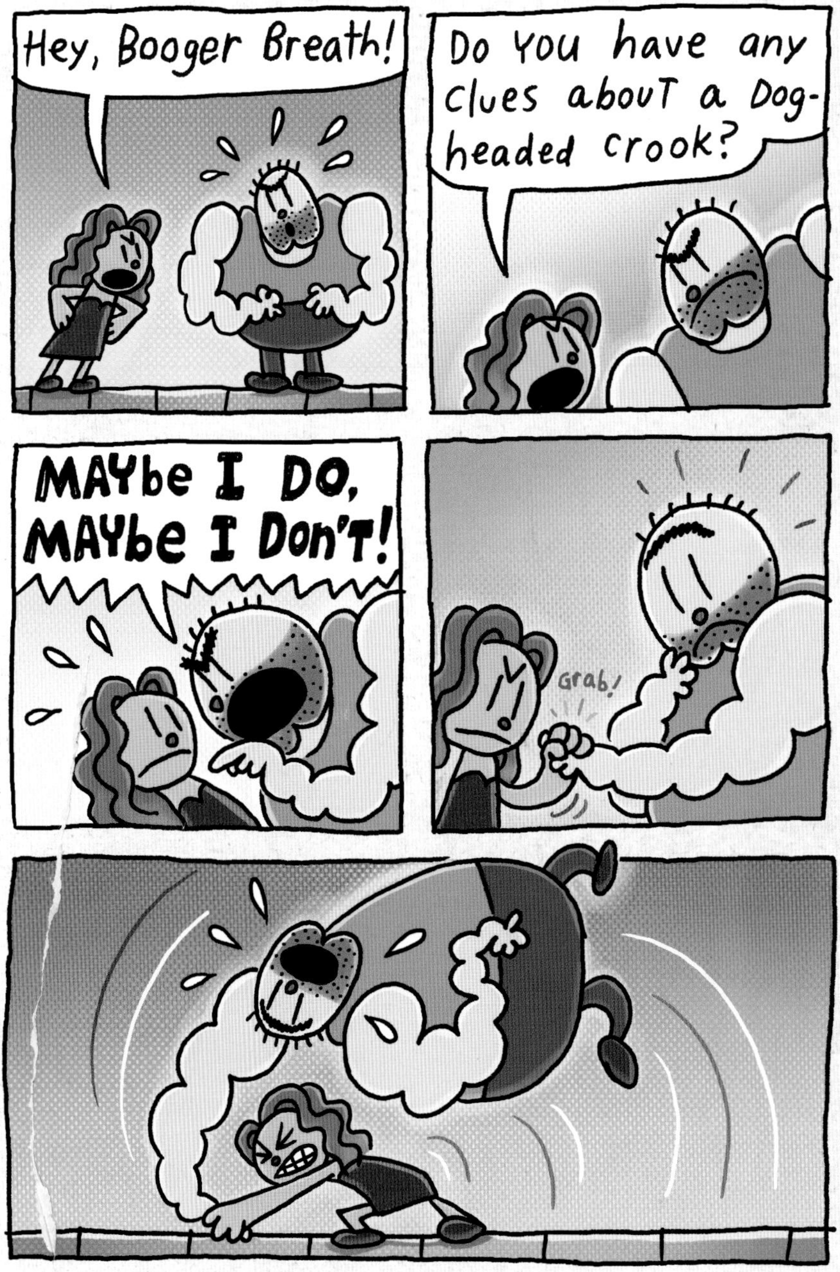
Hey, Booger Breath!
Do you have any clues about a Dog-headed crook?
MAYbe I DO, MAYbe I Don'T!
Grab!

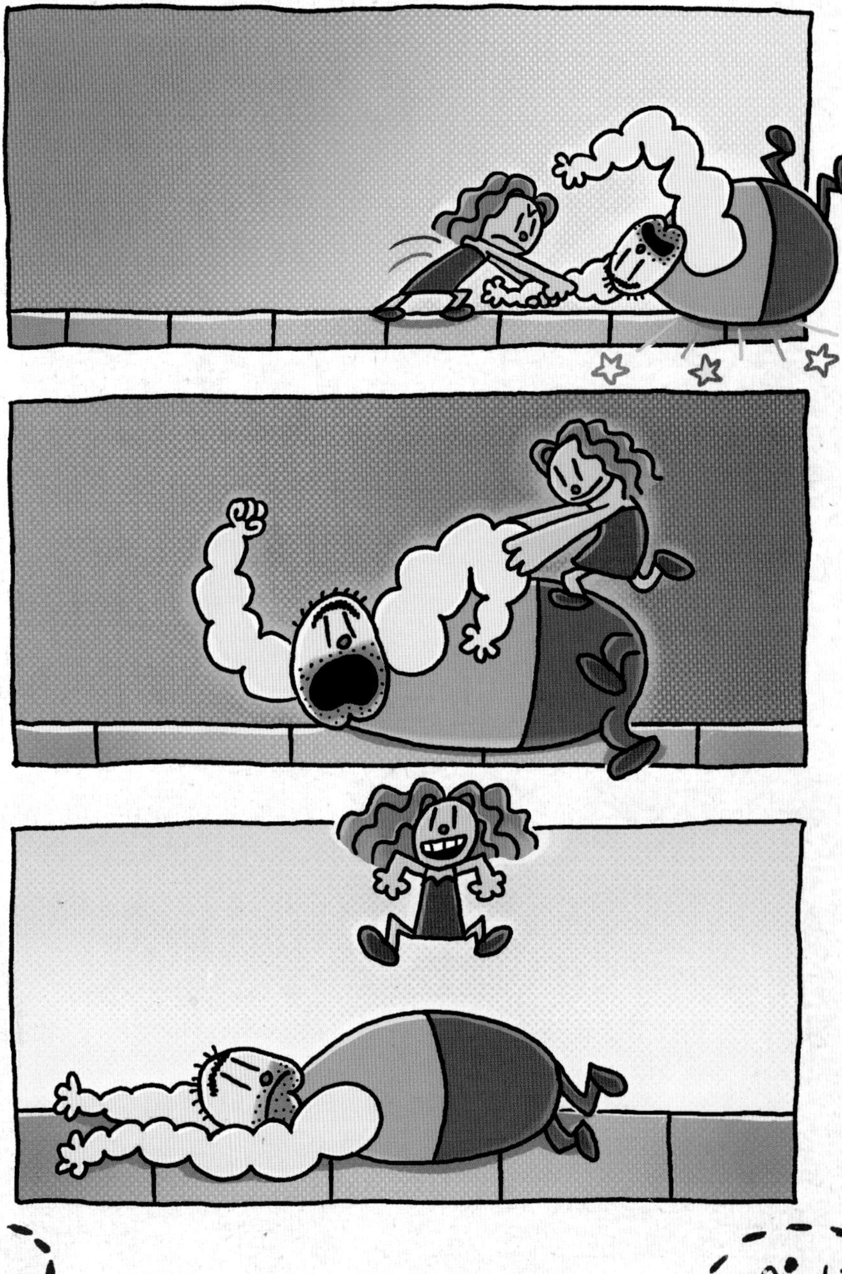

Right Thumb here.

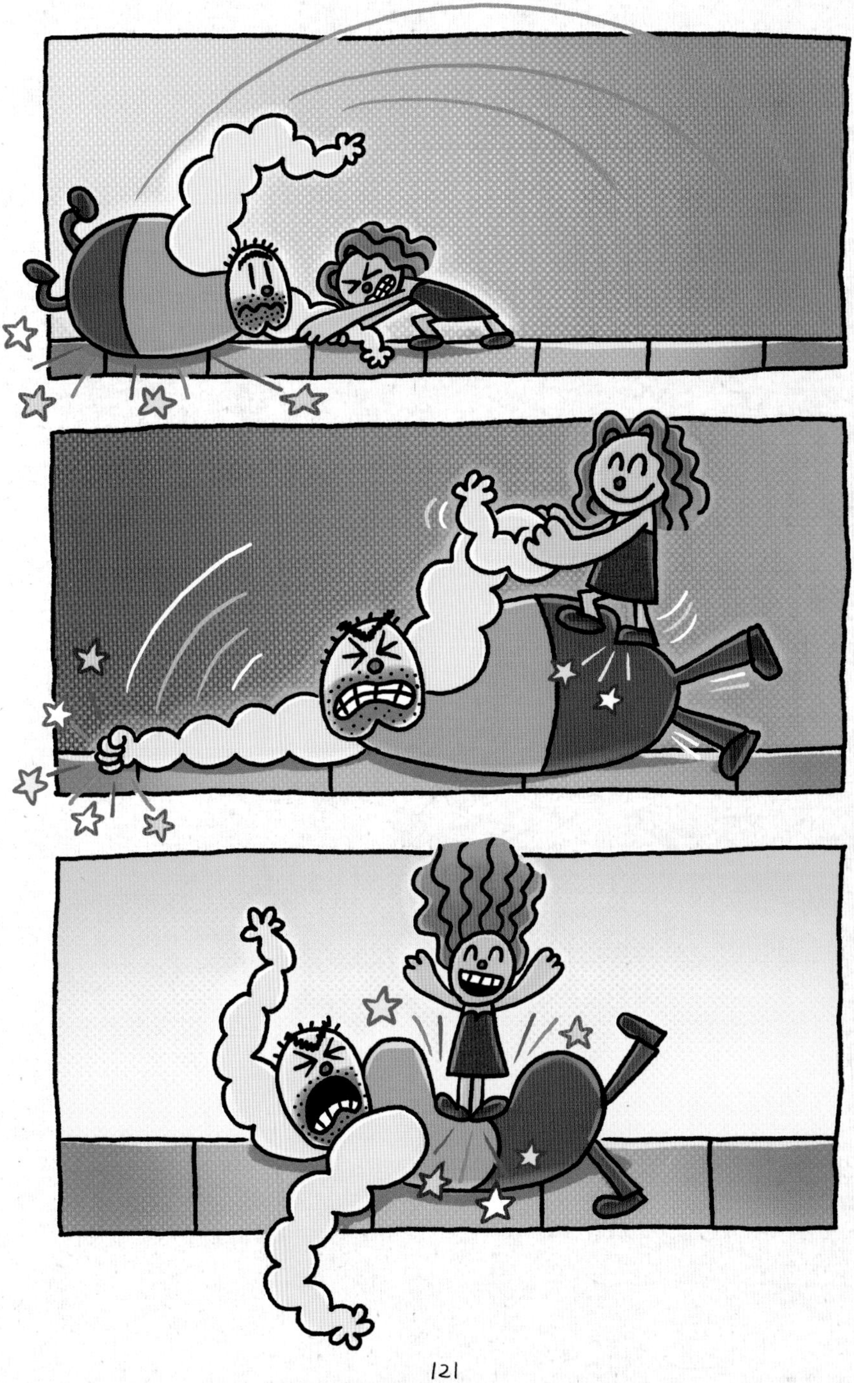

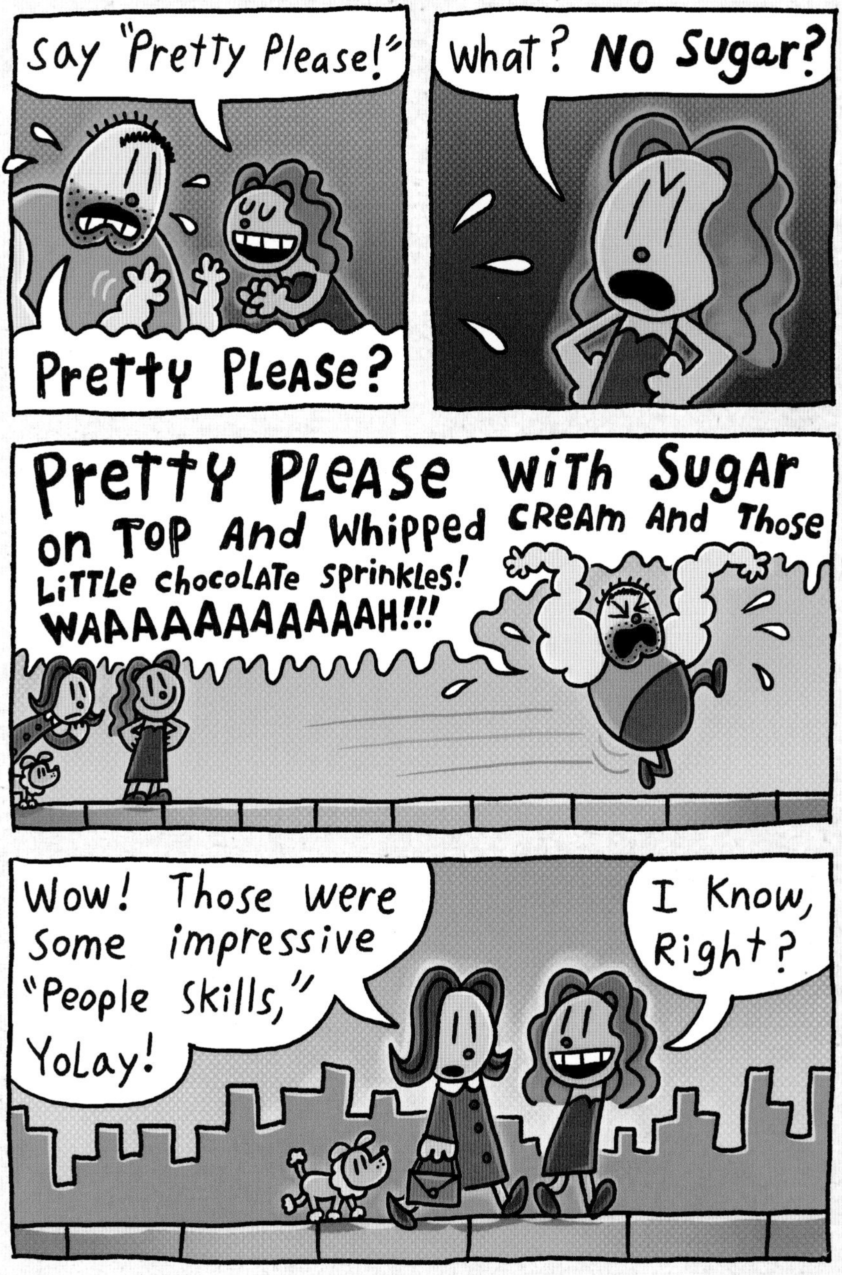
Say "Pretty Please!"
Pretty Please?
What? No Sugar?
Pretty Please with Sugar on Top And Whipped cream And Those Little chocolate sprinkles! WAAAAAAAAAAAH!!!
Wow! Those were some impressive "People Skills," Yolay!
I Know, Right?

Chapter 8
Help is on the Way

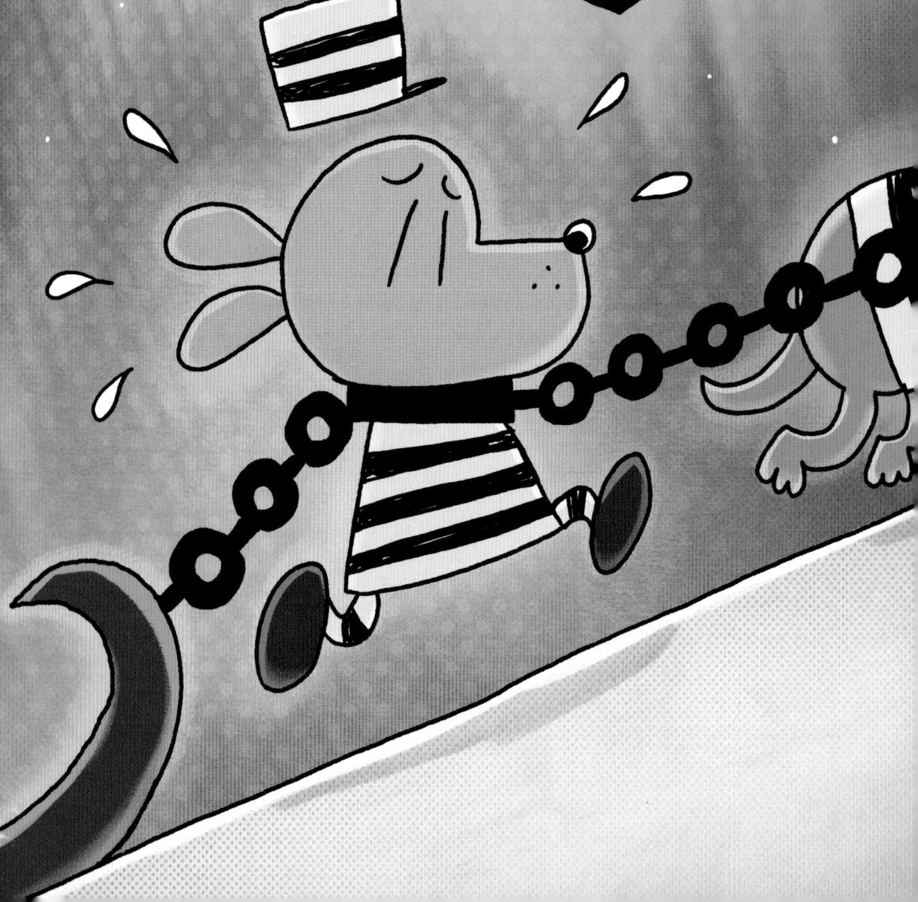

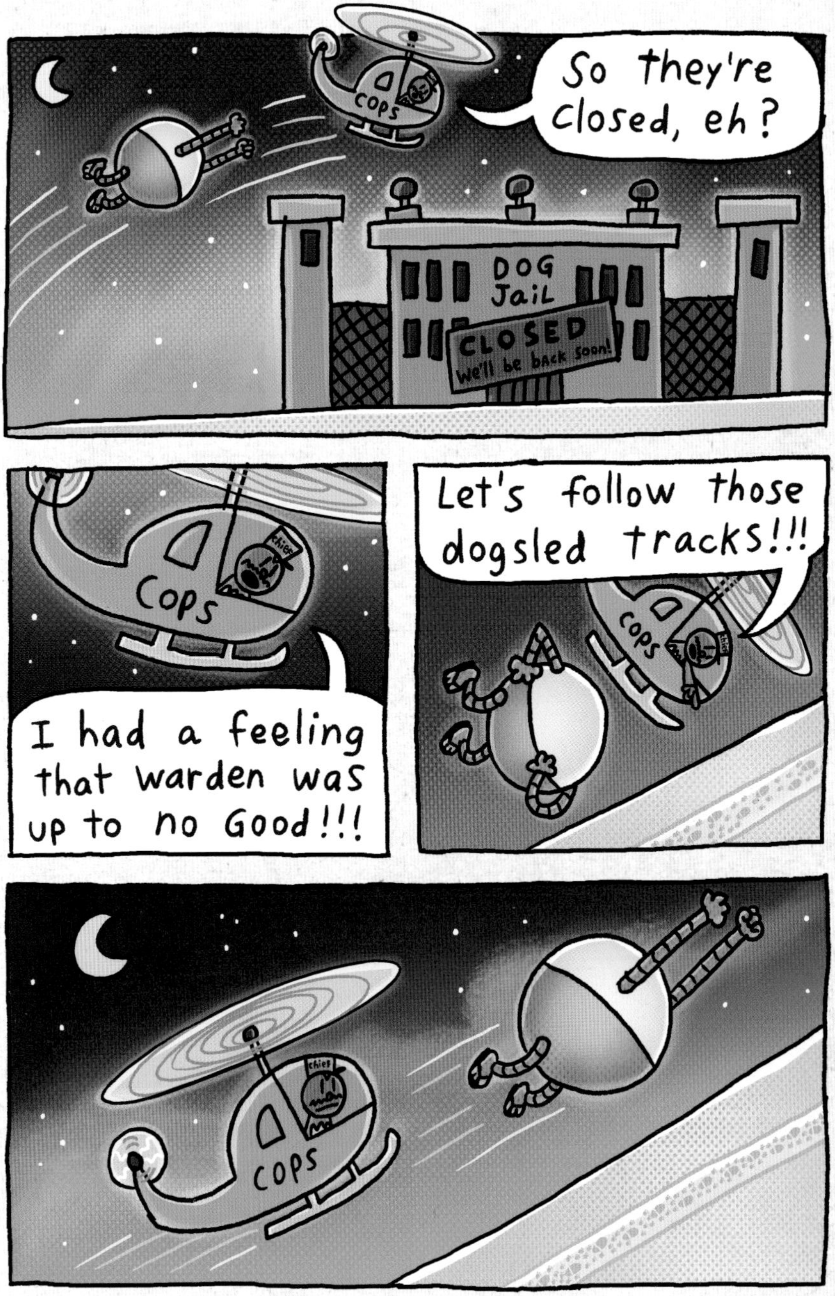
So they're closed, eh?
DOG JaiL
CLOSED
We'll be back soon!
COPS
I had a feeling that warden was up to no Good!!!
COPS
Let's follow those dogsled tracks!!!
COPS
COPS

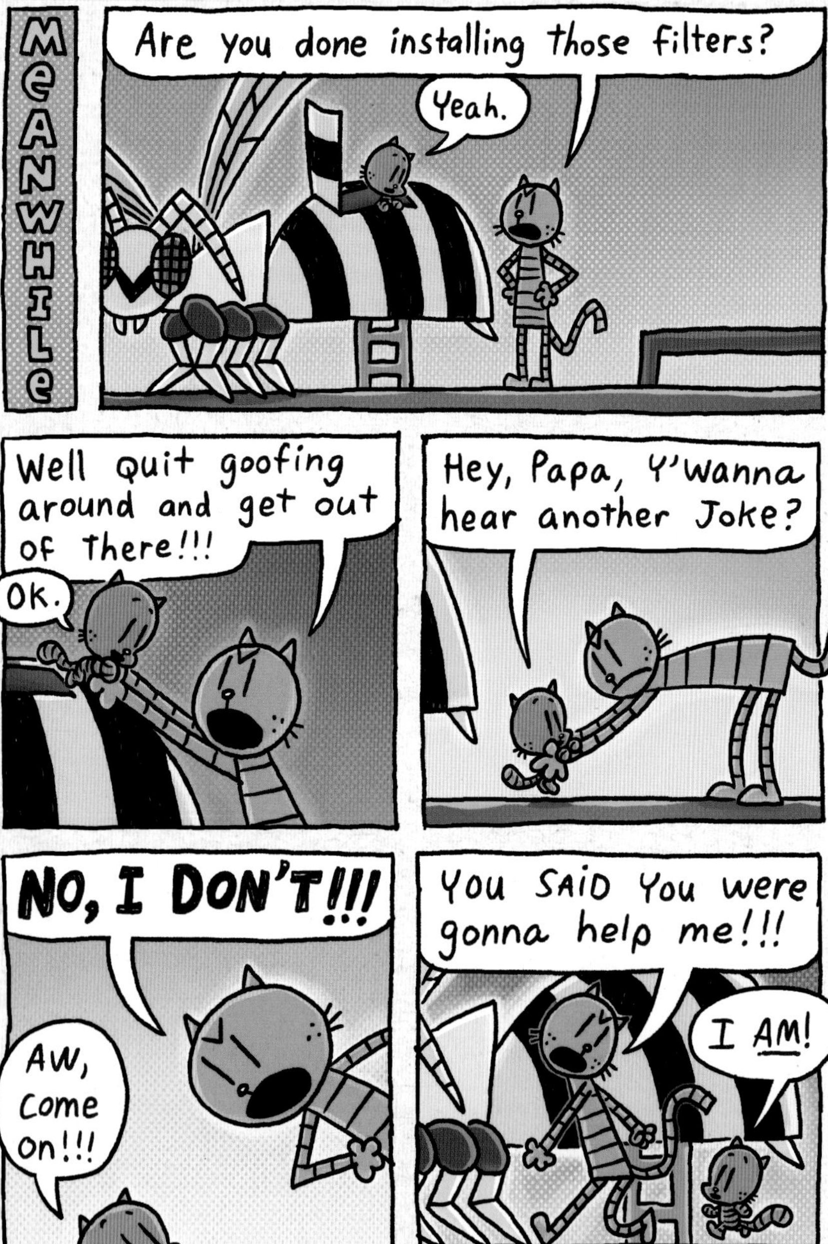
MEANWHILE
Are you done installing those filters?
Yeah.
Well quit goofing around and get out of there!!!
OK.
Hey, Papa, Y'wanna hear another Joke?
NO, I DON'T!!!
AW, come on!!!
You SAID You were gonna help me!!!
I AM!

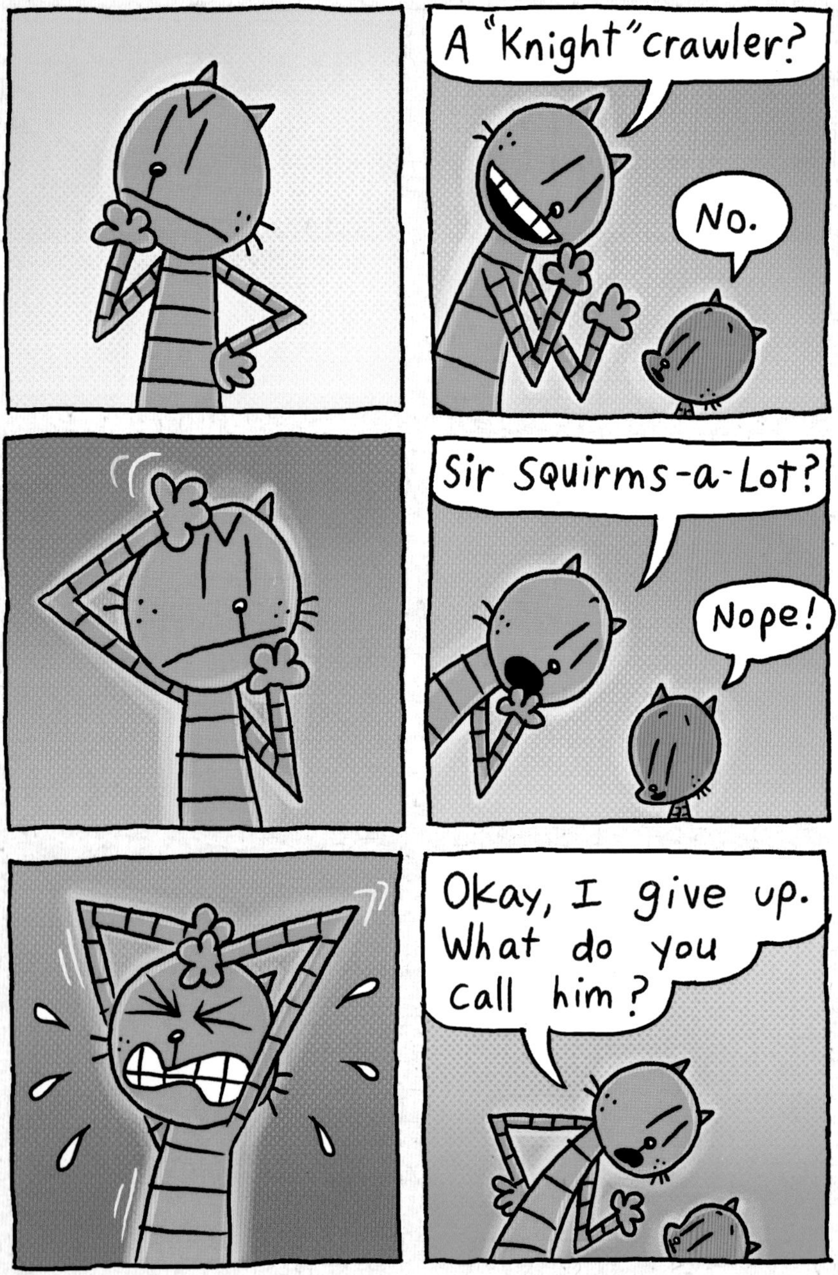
A "Knight" crawler?
No.
Sir Squirms-a-Lot?
Nope!
Okay, I give up. What do you call him?

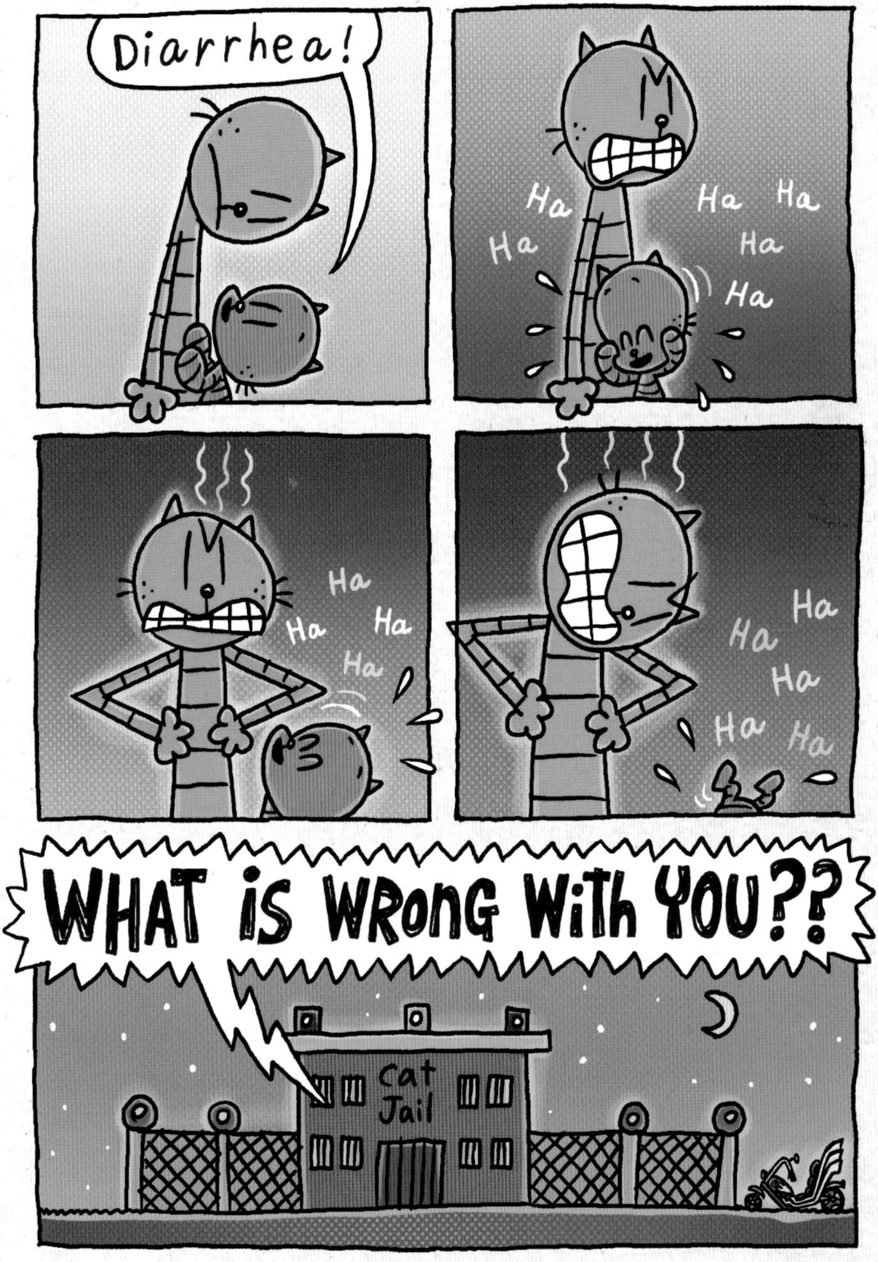
Diarrhea!
Ha Ha Ha Ha Ha Ha
Ha Ha Ha Ha
Ha Ha Ha Ha Ha Ha
WHAT is WRONG With YOU??
Cat Jail

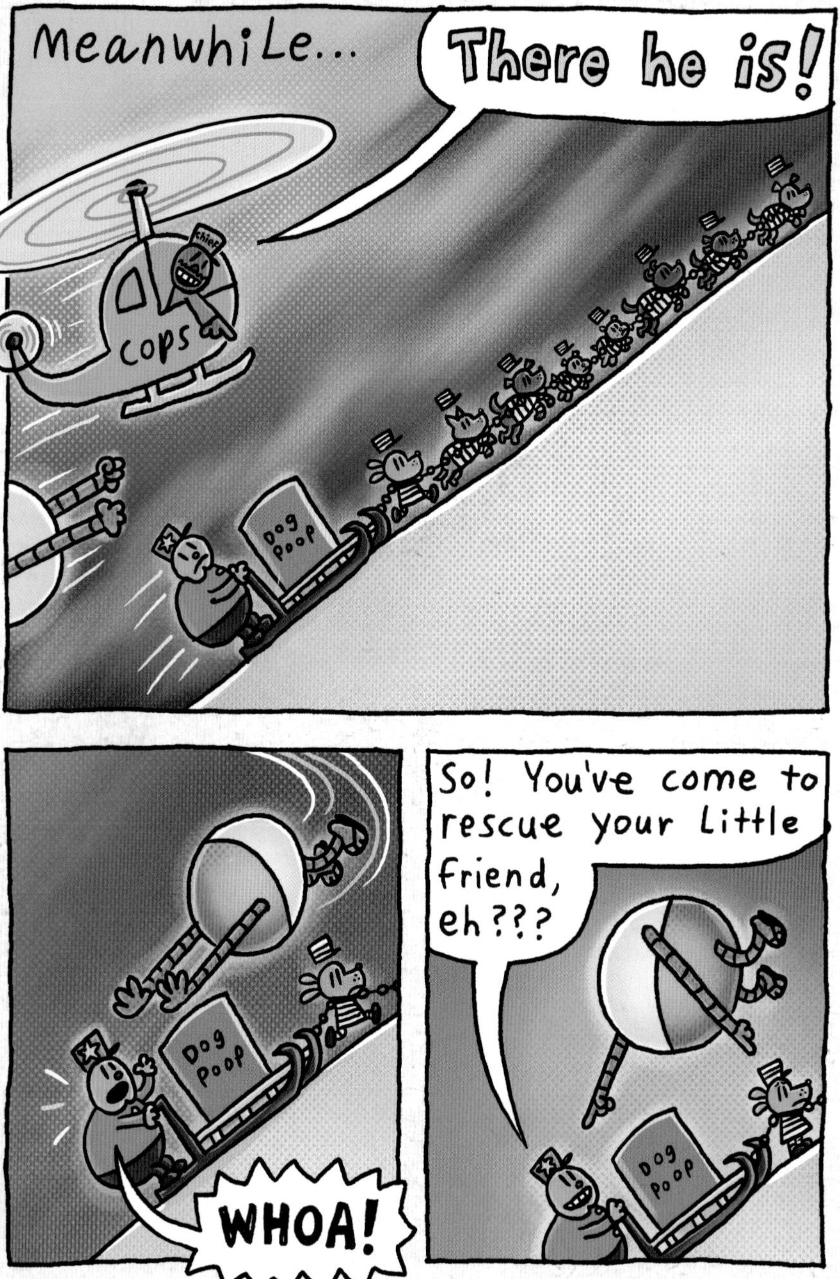
Meanwhile...
There he is!
chief
COPS
Dog Poop
Dog Poop
WHOA!
So! You've come to rescue your little friend, eh???
Dog Poop

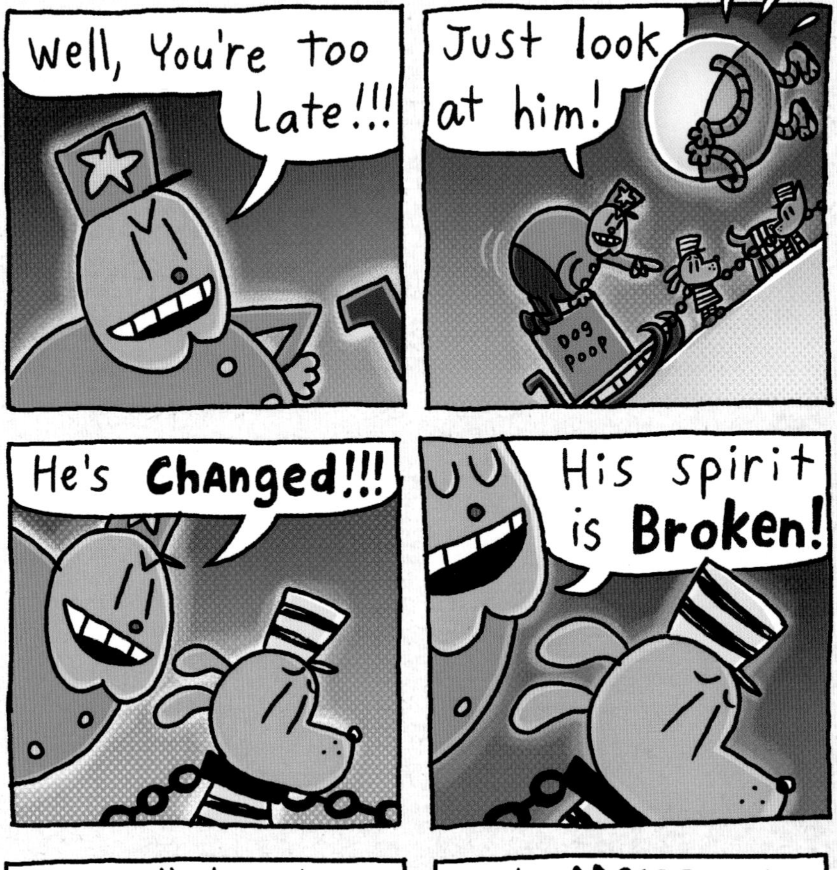
Well, You're too Late!!!
Just look at him!
DOG POOP
He's **Changed!!!**
His spirit is **Broken!**
His will has been **CRUSHED!!!**
He'll **Never** be the **SAME** again!

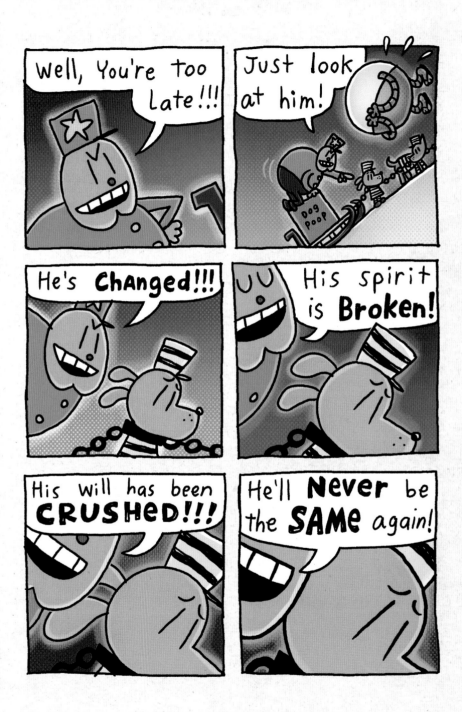

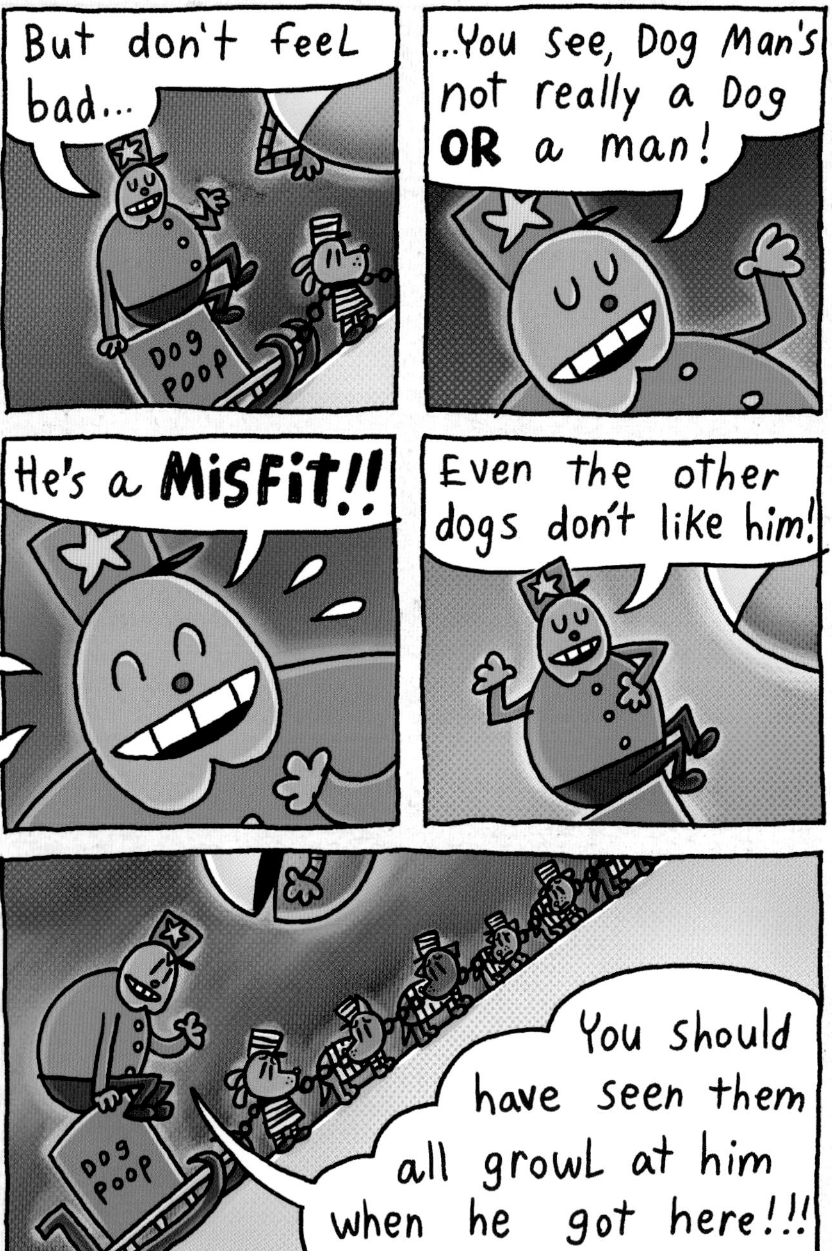
But don't feeL bad...
...You see, Dog Man's not really a Dog OR a man!
DOG POOP
He's a MISFIT!!
Even the other dogs don't like him!
DOG POOP
You should have seen them all growL at him when he got here!!!

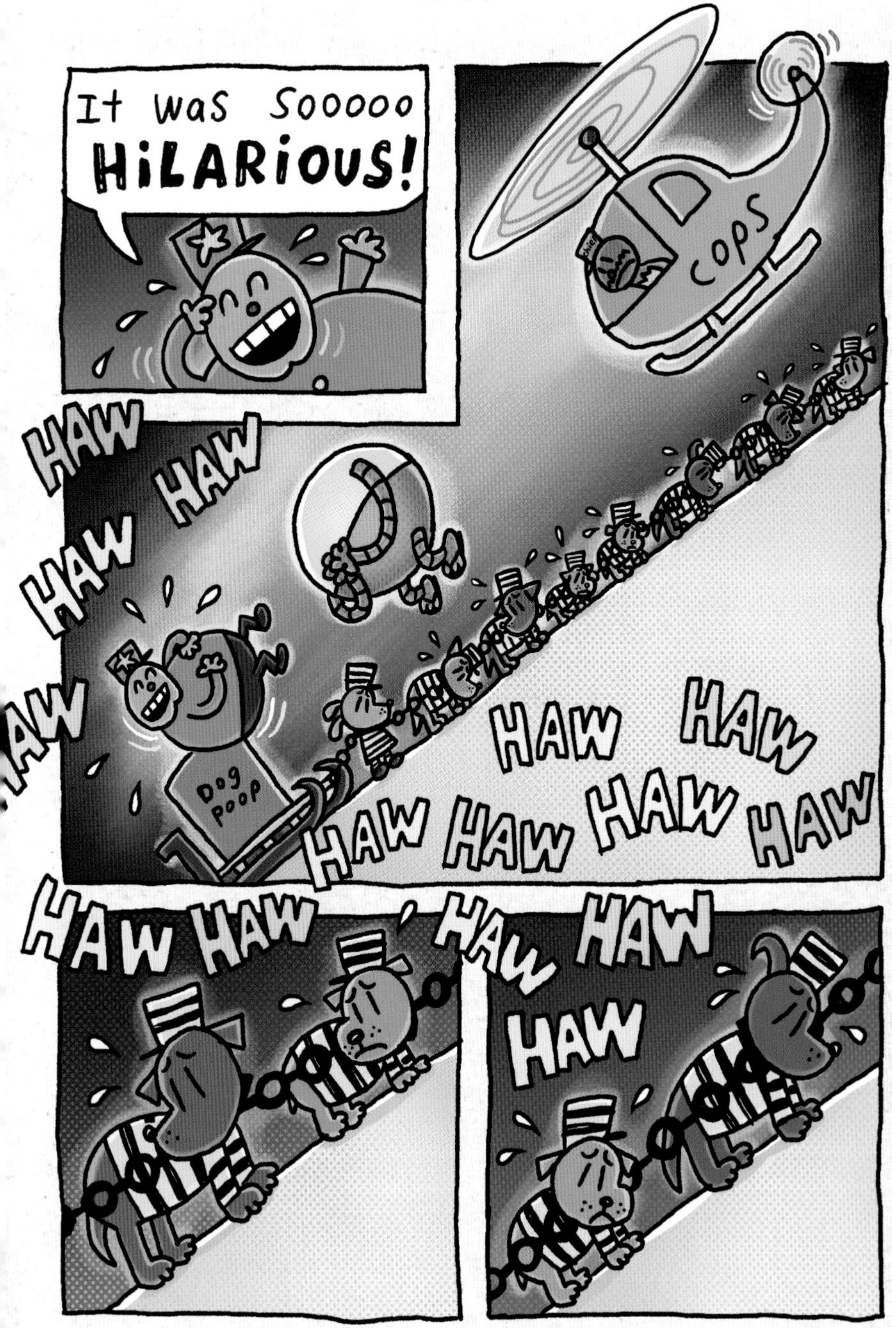
It was Sooooo HiLARIOUS!
COPS
HAW
HAW
HAW
HAW
Dog poop
HAW HAW
HAW HAW HAW HAW
HAW HAW
HAW HAW
HAW

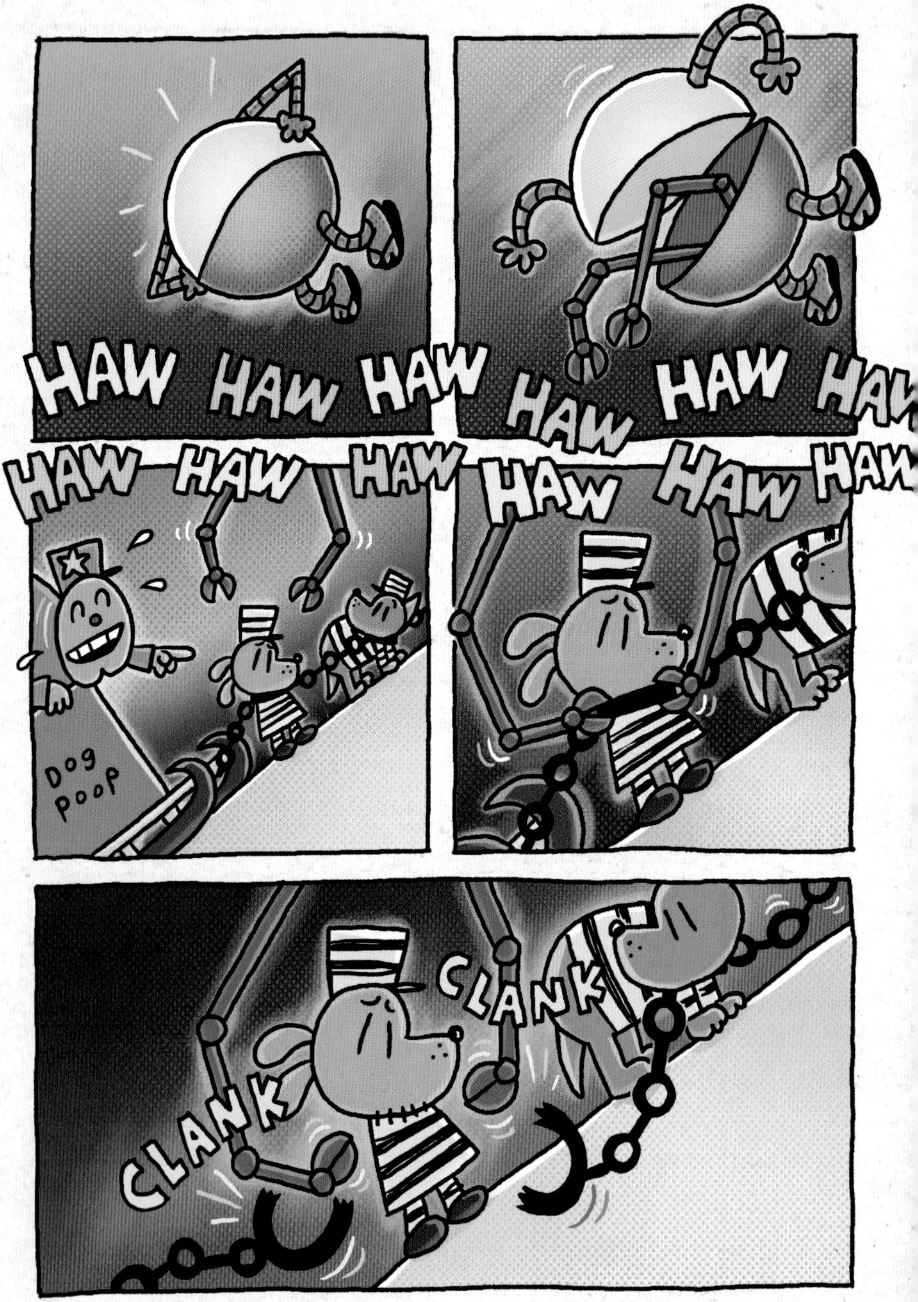
HAW HAW HAW HAW HAW
HAW HAW HAW HAW HAW
Dog poop
CLANK
CLANK

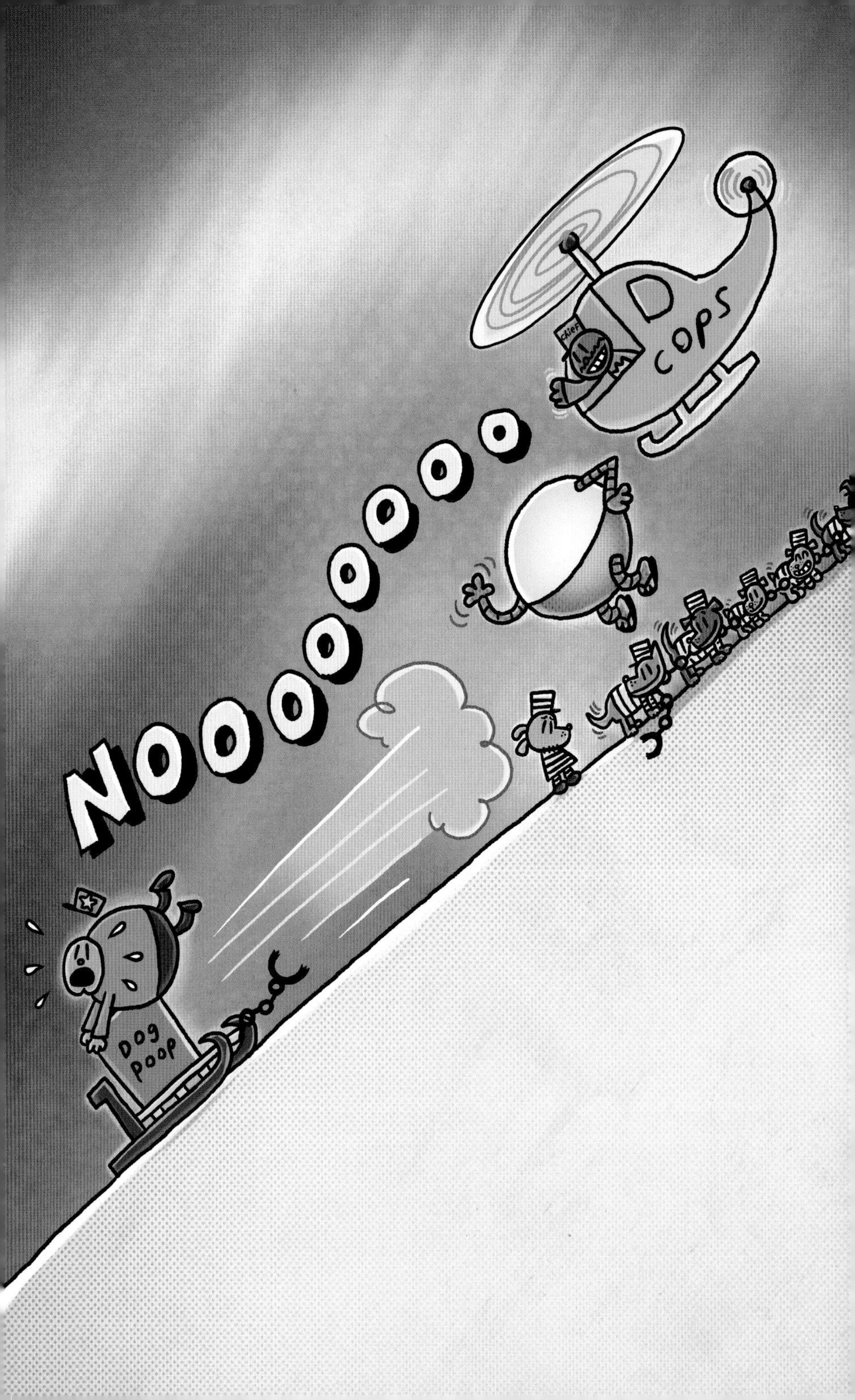

NOOOOOOOOO
CHIEF
COPS
DOG POOP

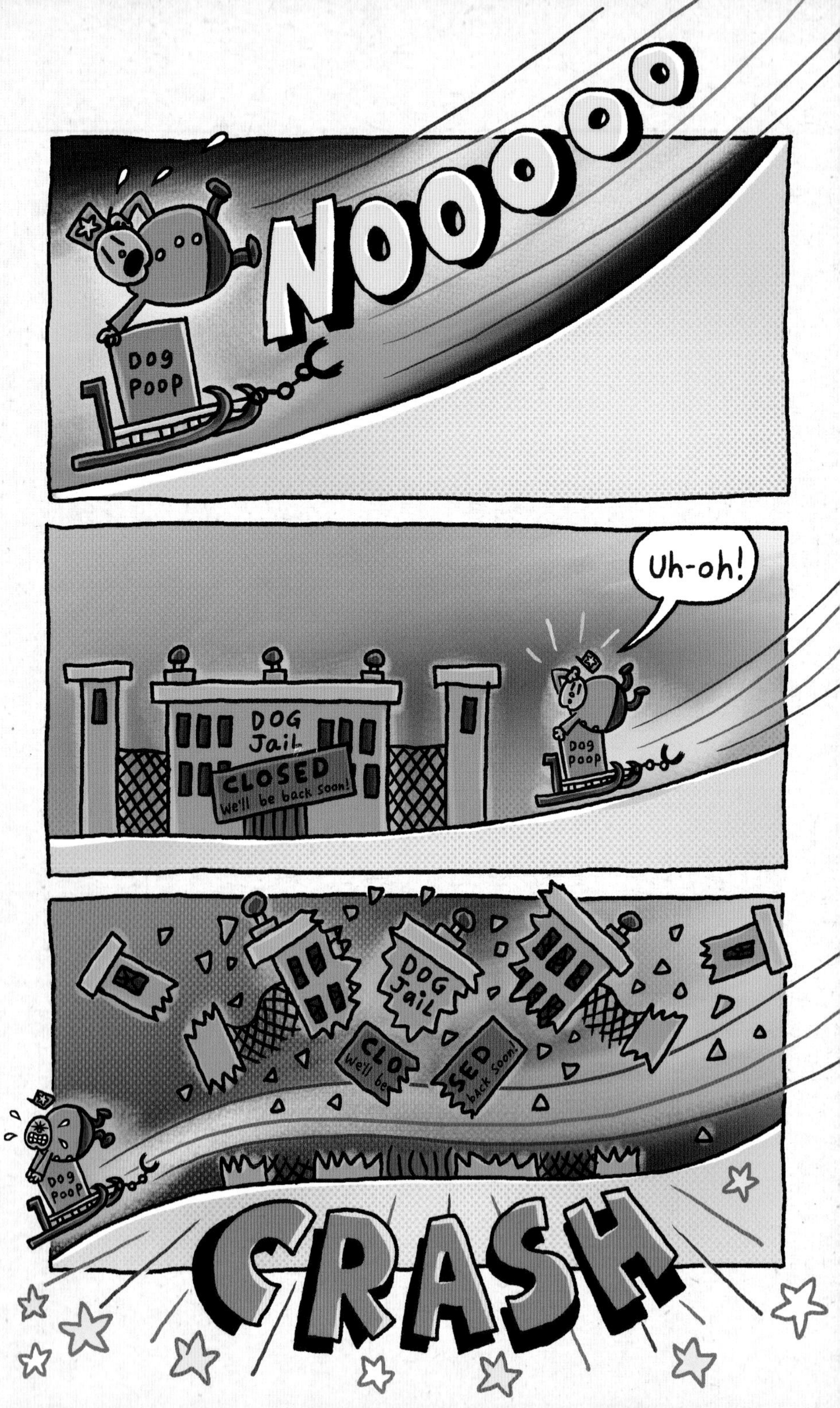

NOOOOOO
DOG POOP
Uh-oh!
DOG Jail
CLOSED
We'll be back Soon!
Dog Poop
DOG Jail
CLO We'll be
SED back Soon!
Dog Poop
CRASH

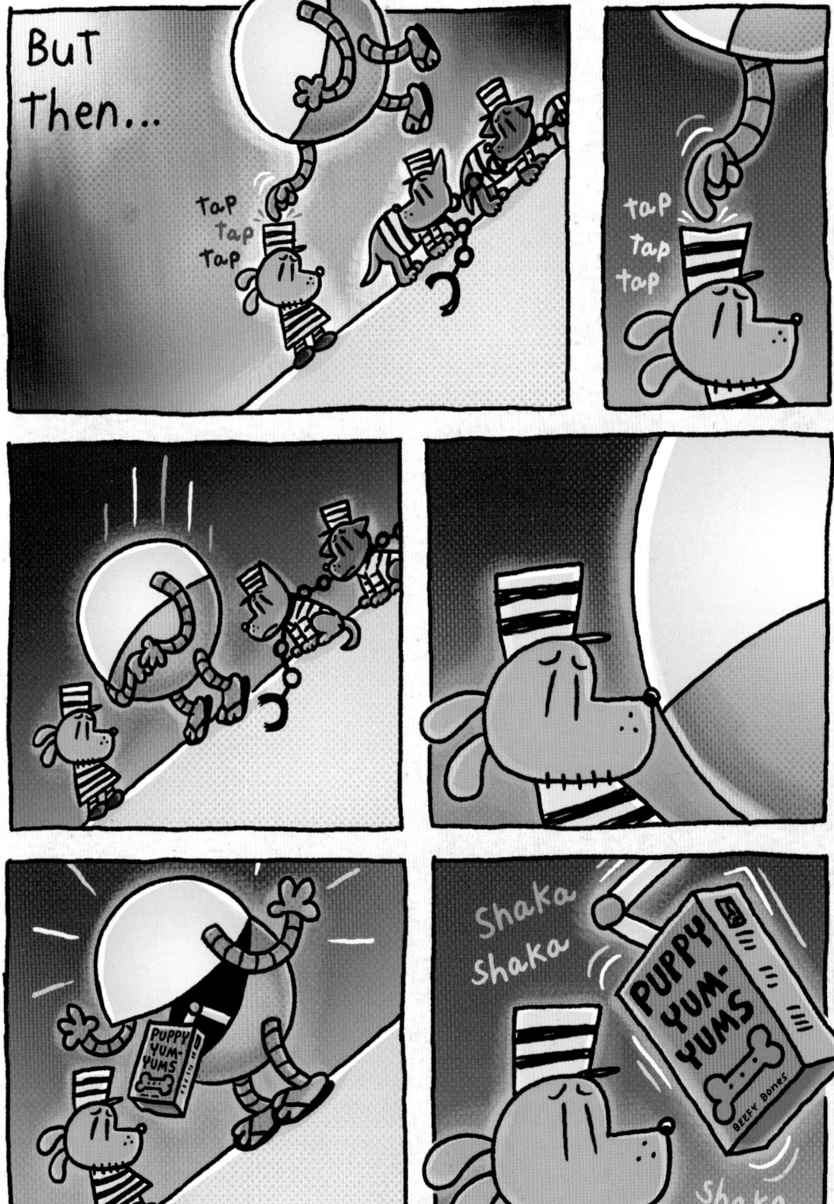
But Then...
Tap
Tap
Tap
Tap
Tap
Tap
PUPPY YUM-YUMS
Shaka
Shaka
PUPPY YUM-YUMS
BEEFY Bones
Shaka
Shaka

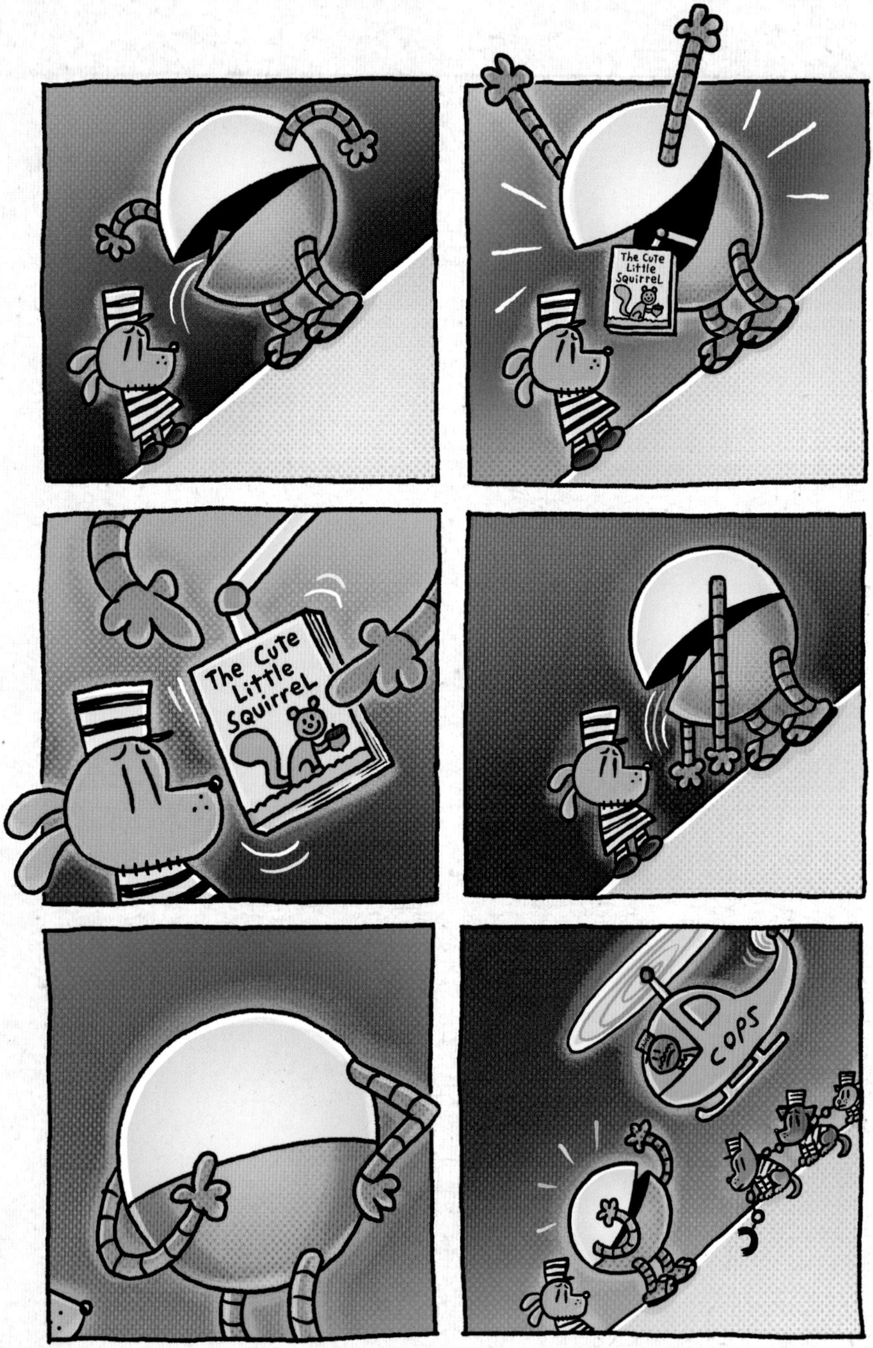
The Cute Little Squirrel
The Cute Little Squirrel
COPS

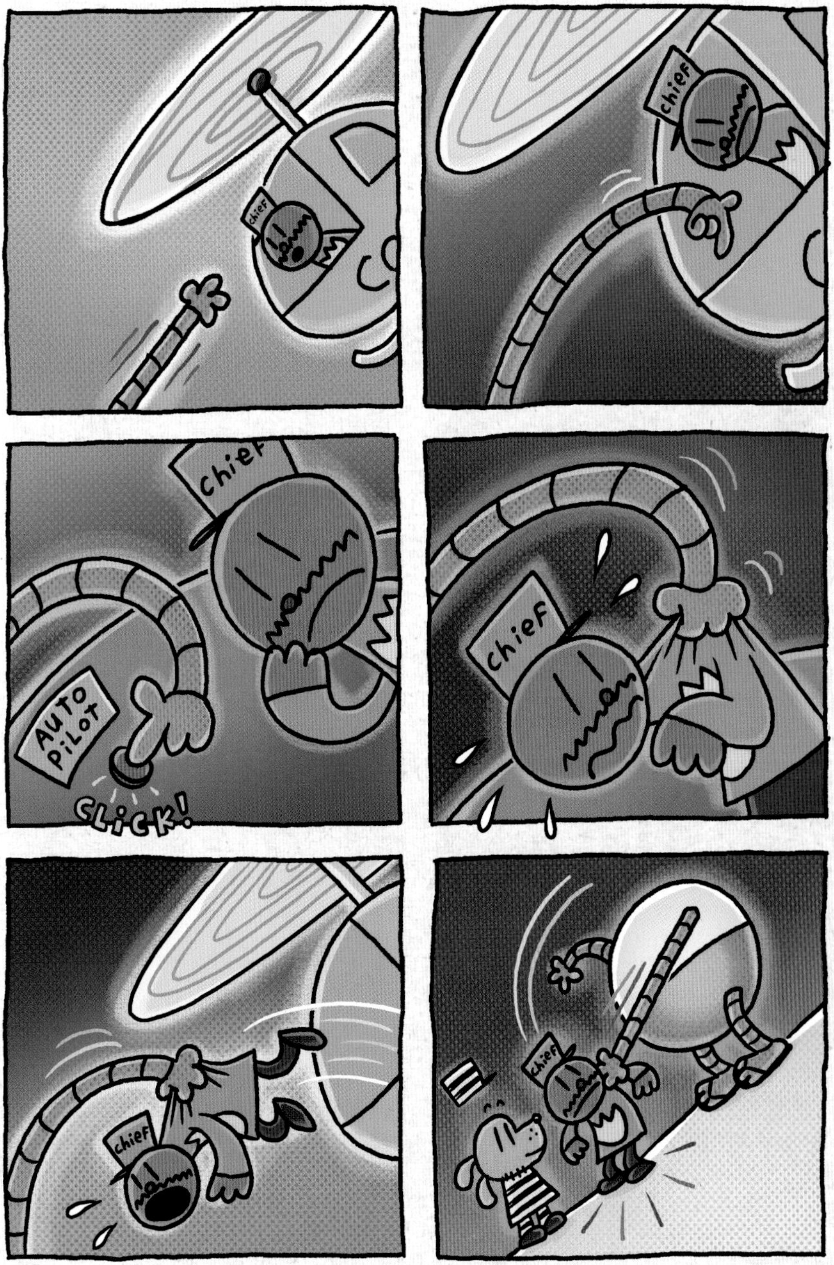
chief
chief
chief
AUTO PILOT
CLICK!
chief
chief
chief

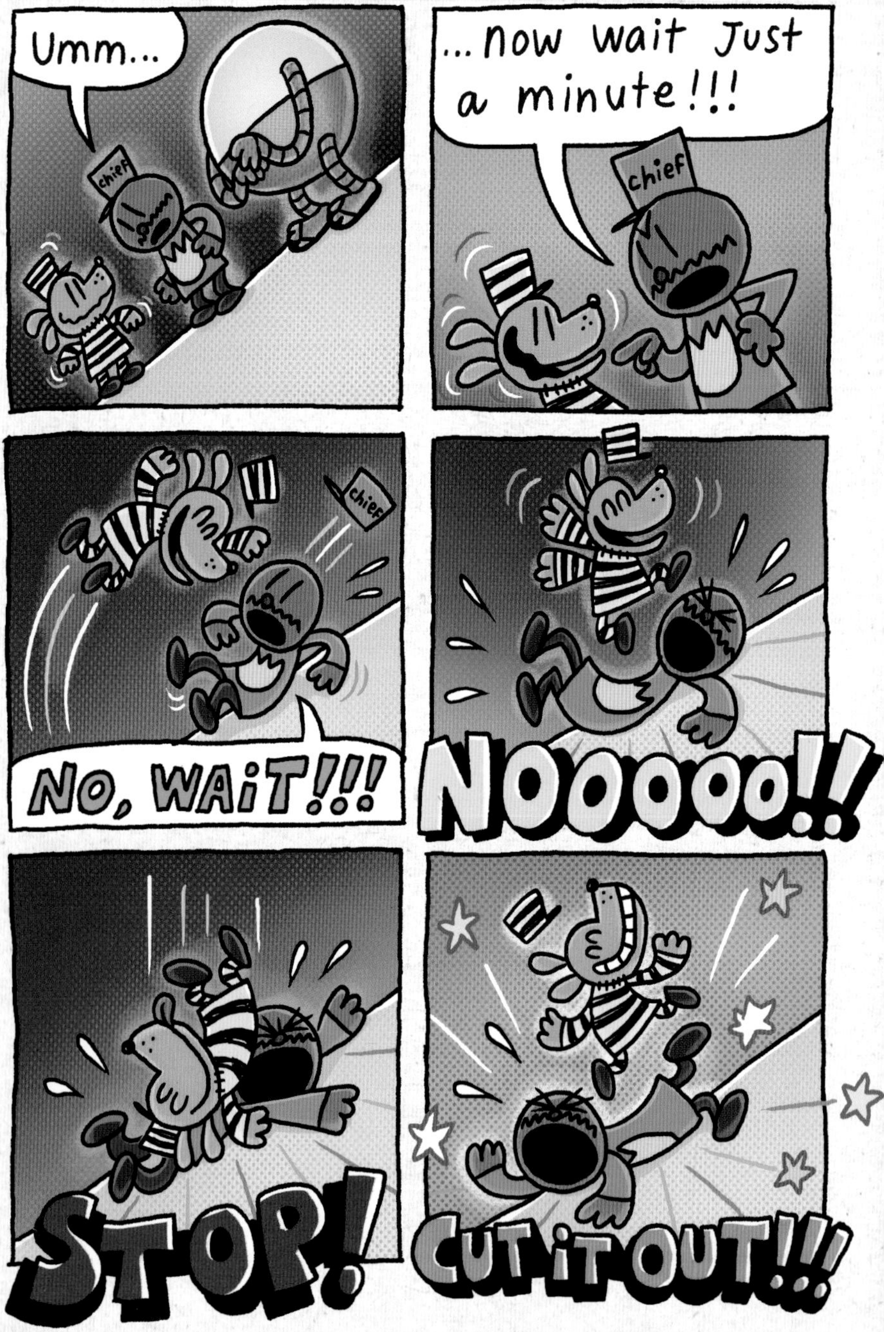
Umm...
...now wait Just a minute!!!
chief
chief
NO, WAiT!!!
NOOOOOO!!
STOP!
CUT iT OUT!!!

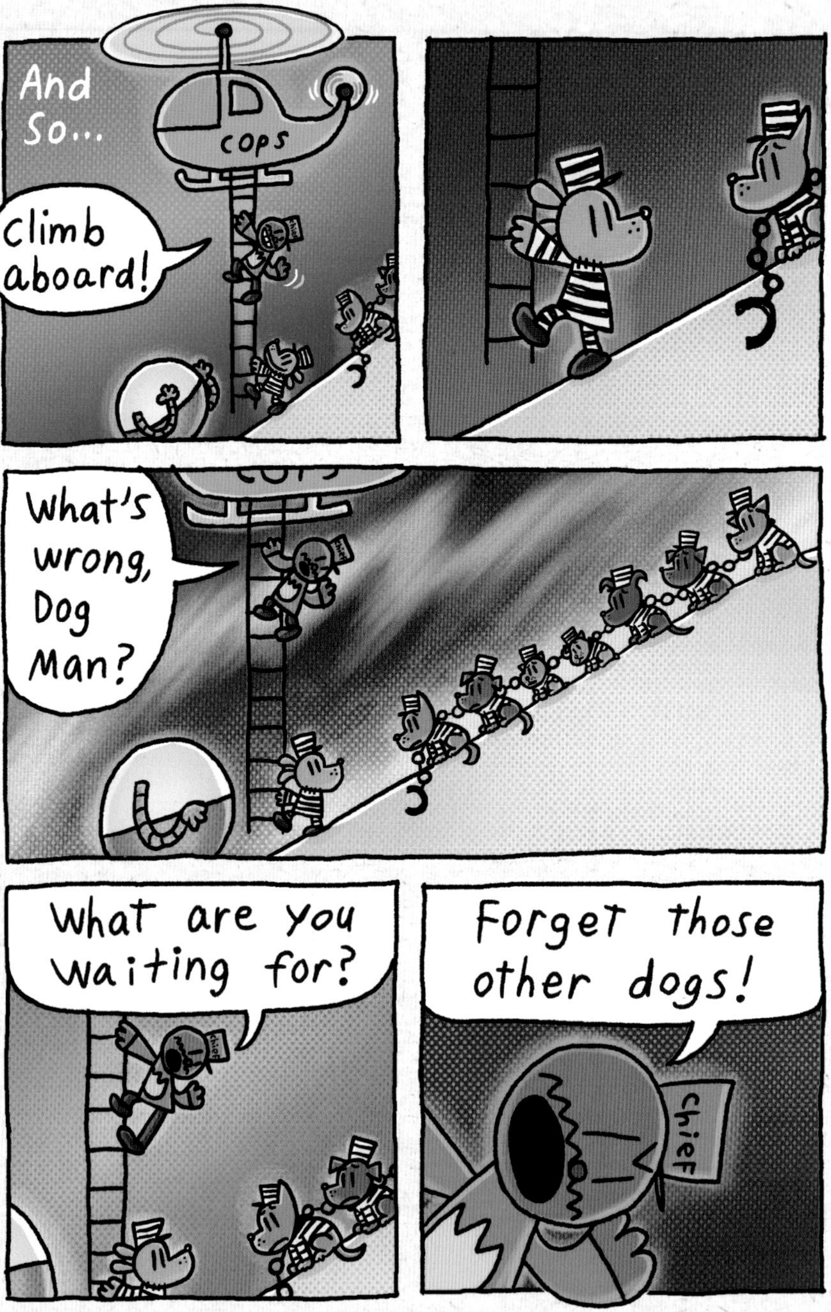
And So...
COPS
Climb aboard!
What's wrong, Dog Man?
What are you waiting for?
Forget those other dogs!
Chief

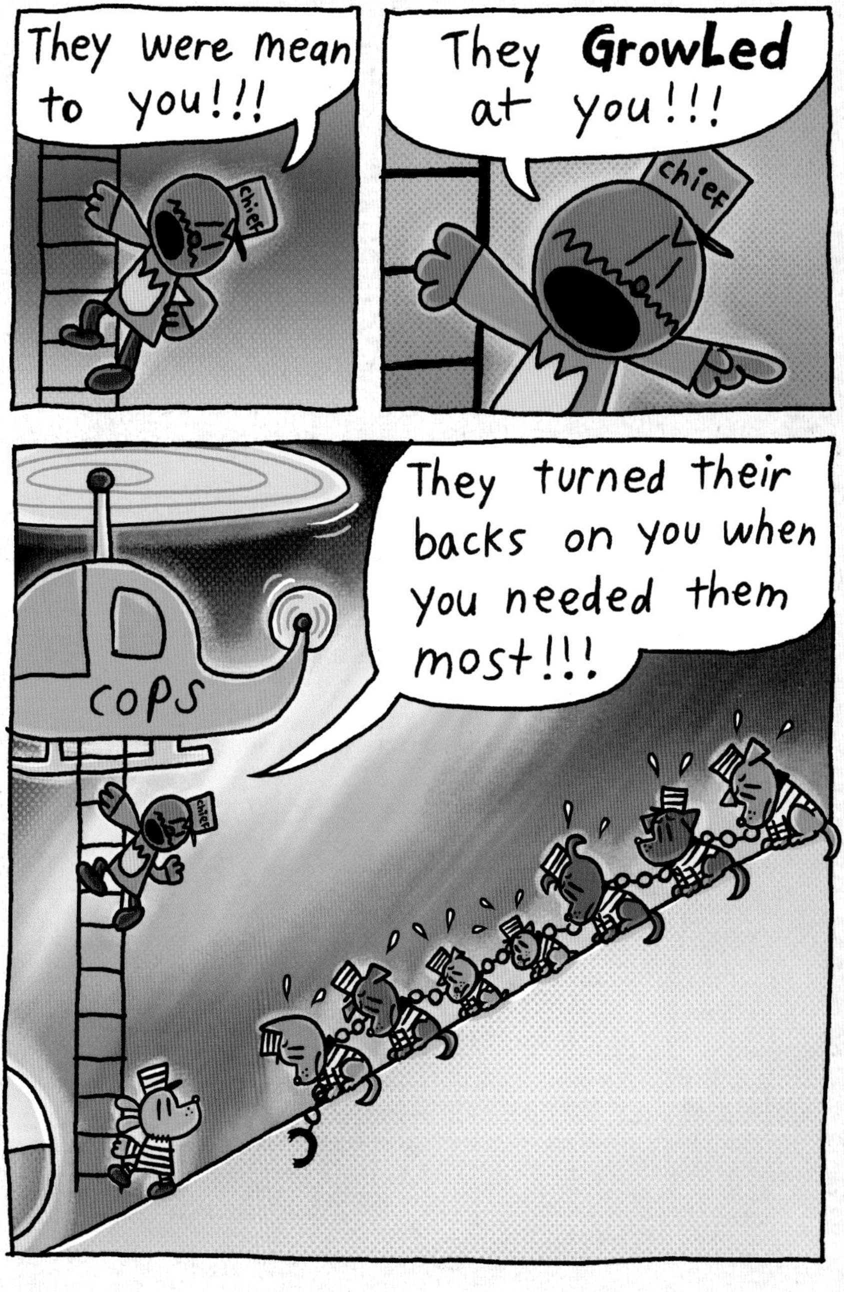
They were mean to you!!!
They GrowLed at you!!!
chief
They turned their backs on you when you needed them most!!!
COPS
chief

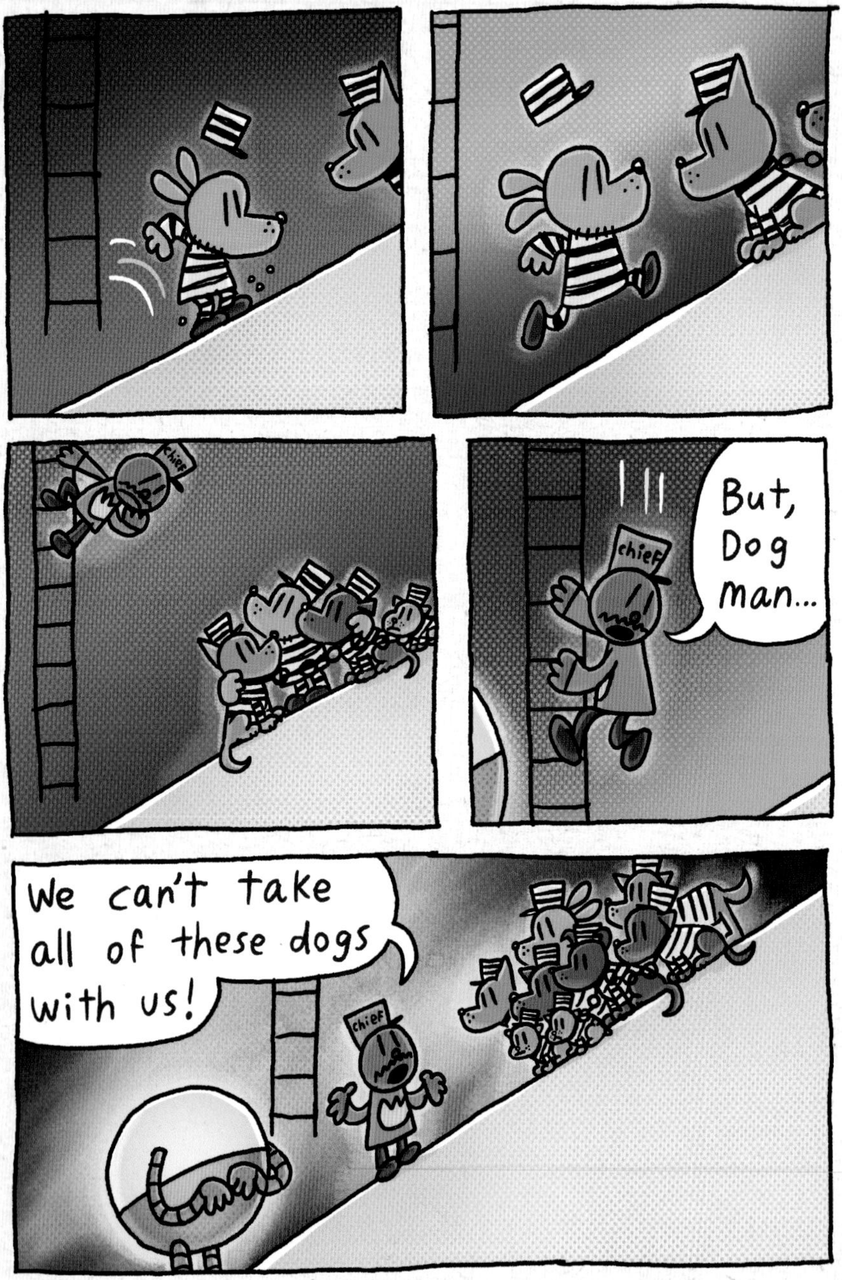
chief
But, Dog man...
We can't take all of these dogs with us!
chief

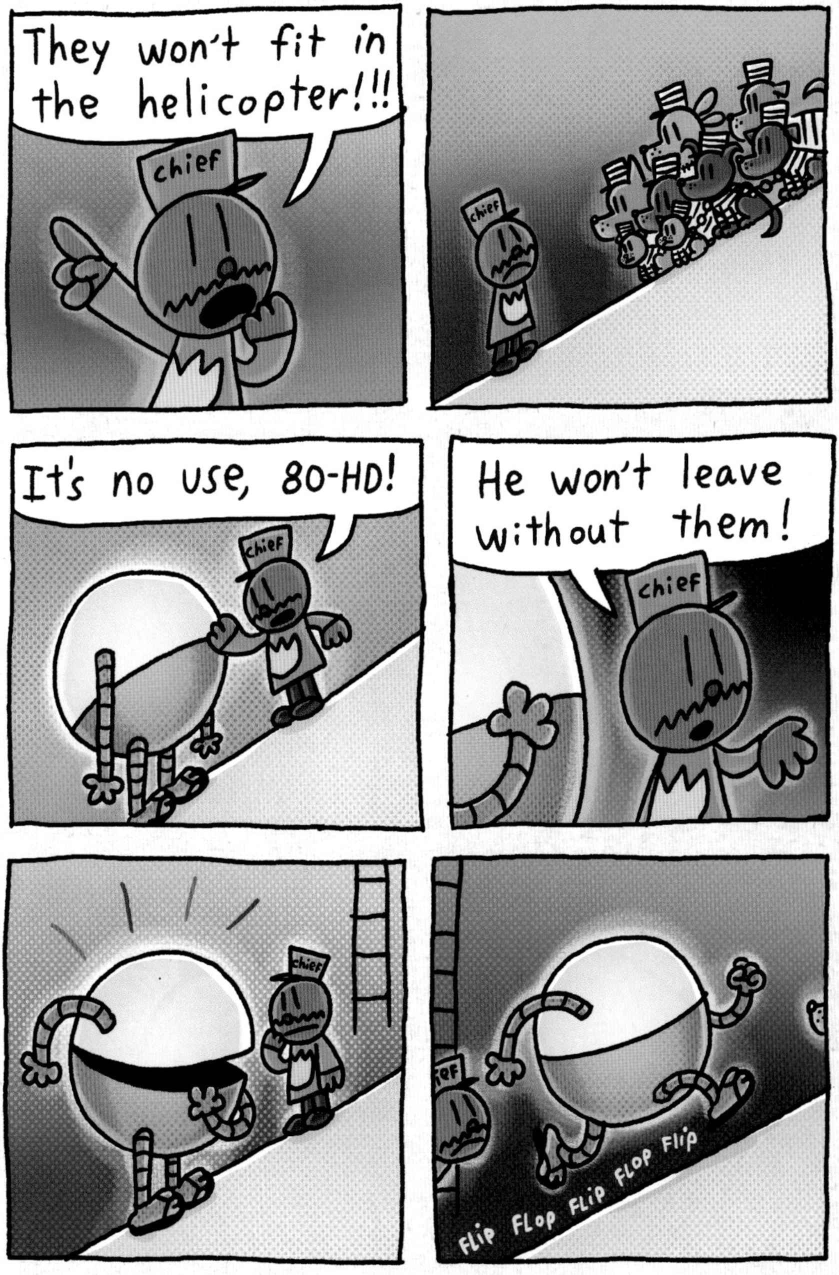
They won't fit in the helicopter!!!
It's no use, 80-HD!
He won't leave without them!
Flip Flop Flip Flop Flip

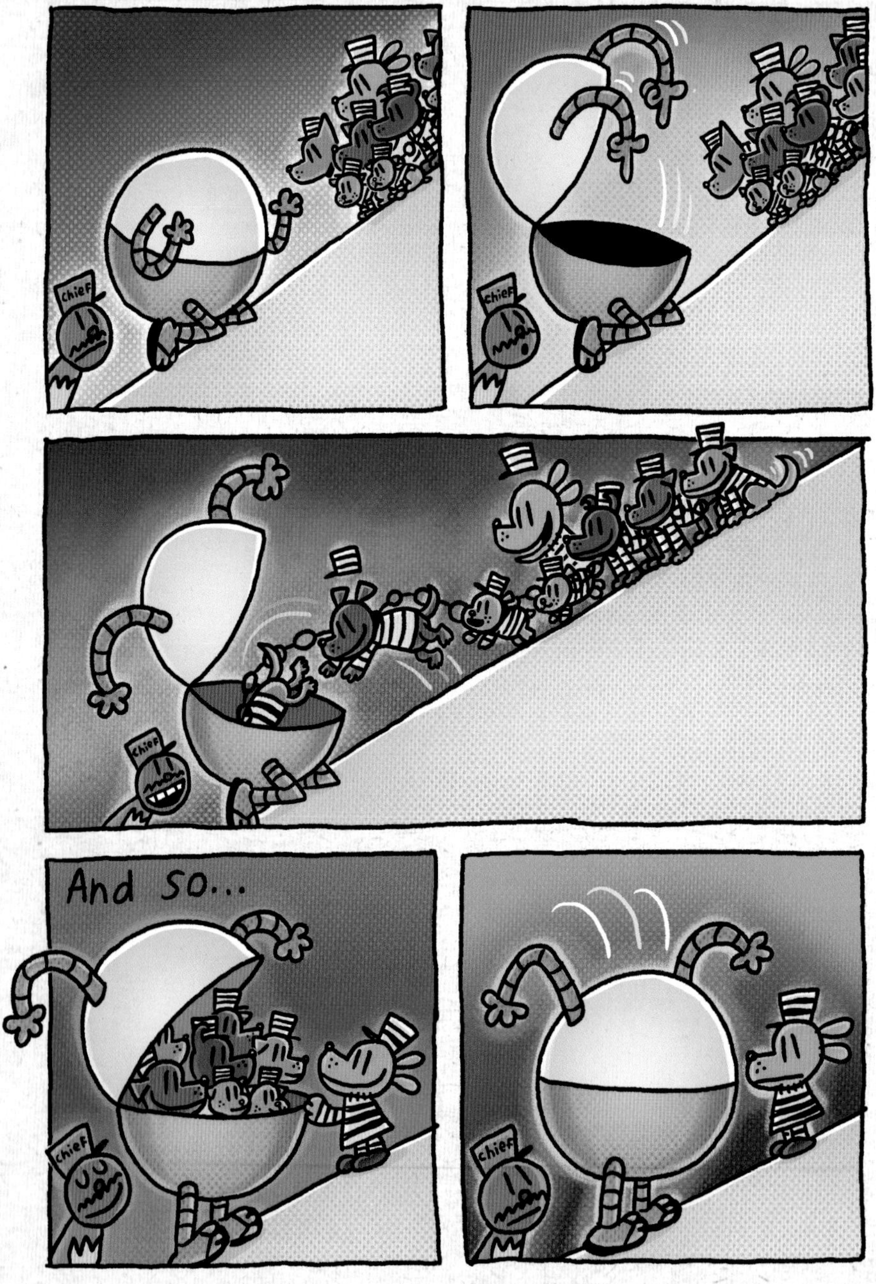
CHIEF
CHIEF
CHIEF
And so...
CHIEF
CHIEF

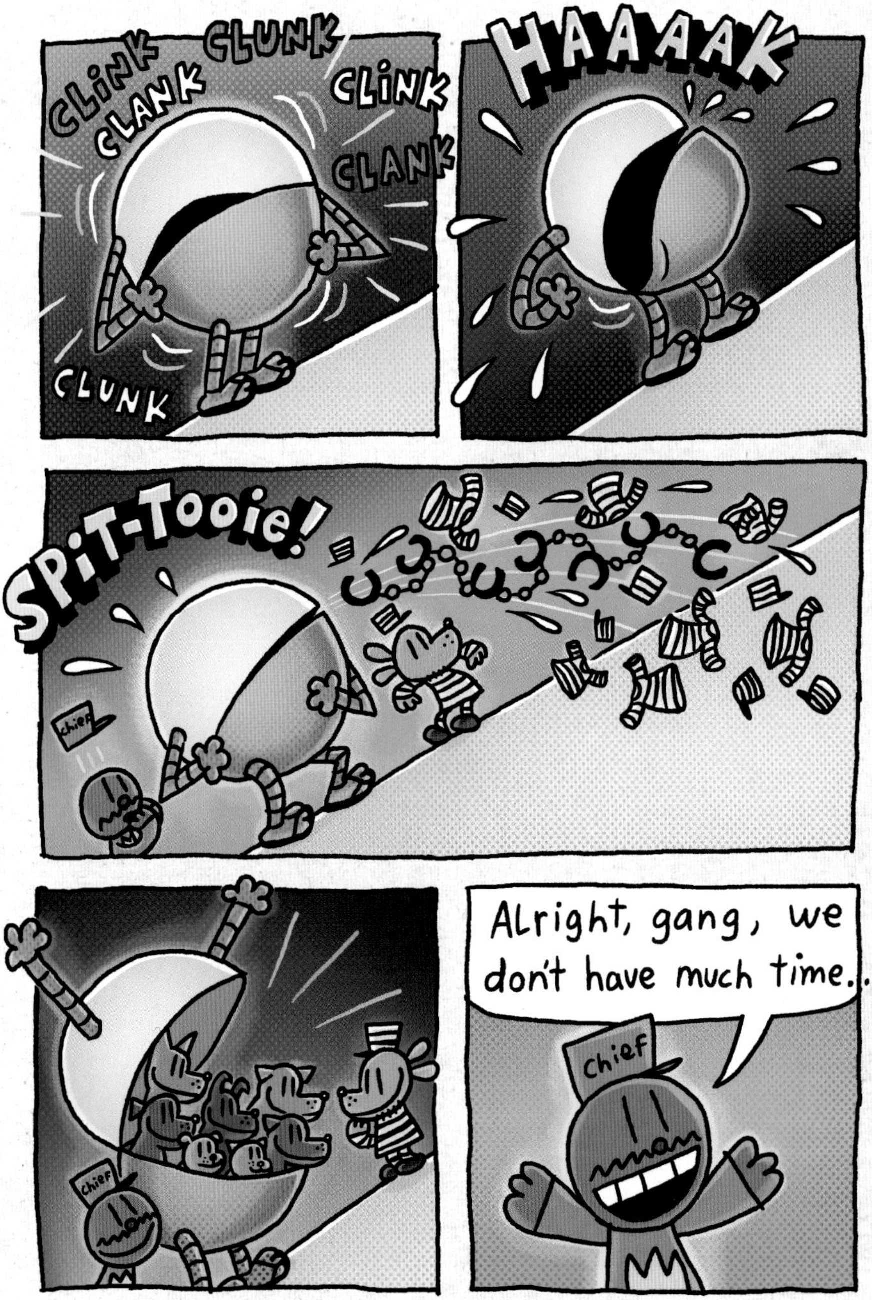
CLINK
CLUNK
CLANK
CLINK
CLANK
CLUNK
HAAAAK
SPIT-TOOIE!
chief
chief
Alright, gang, we don't have much time...
chief

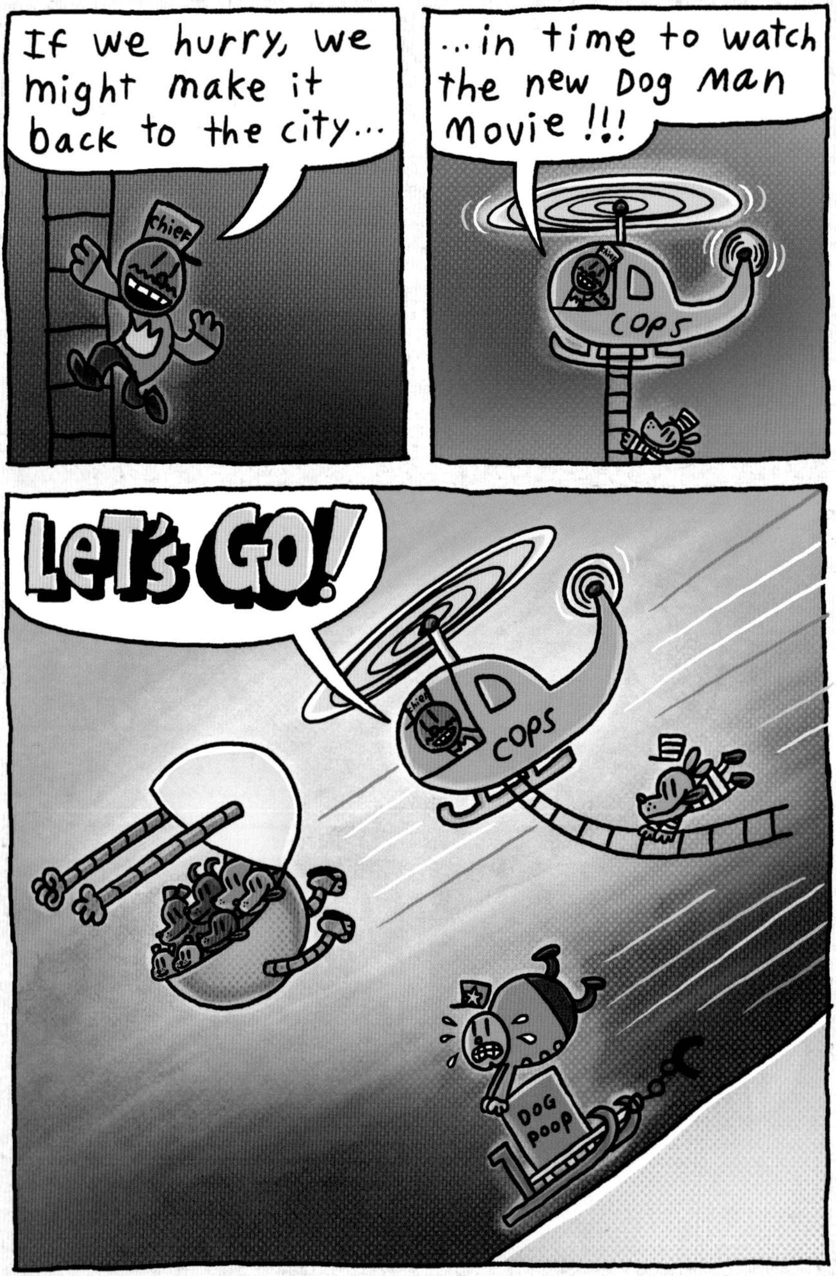
If we hurry, we might make it back to the city...
...in time to watch the new Dog Man movie!!!
Chief
COPS
LET'S GO!
COPS
DOG POOP

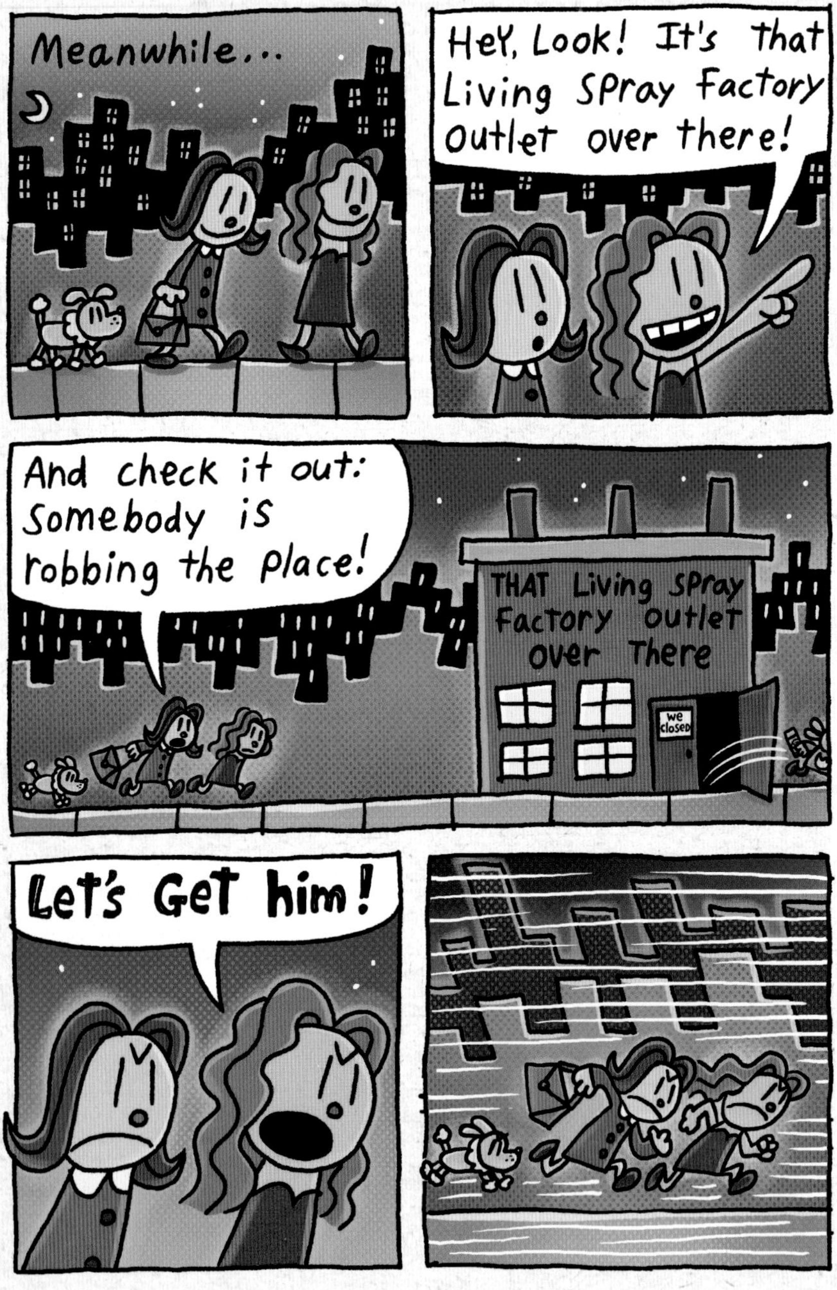

Meanwhile...
HeY, Look! It's that Living SPray Factory Outlet over there!
And check it out: Somebody is robbing the Place!
THAT Living SPray Factory outlet over There
we closed
Let's Get him!

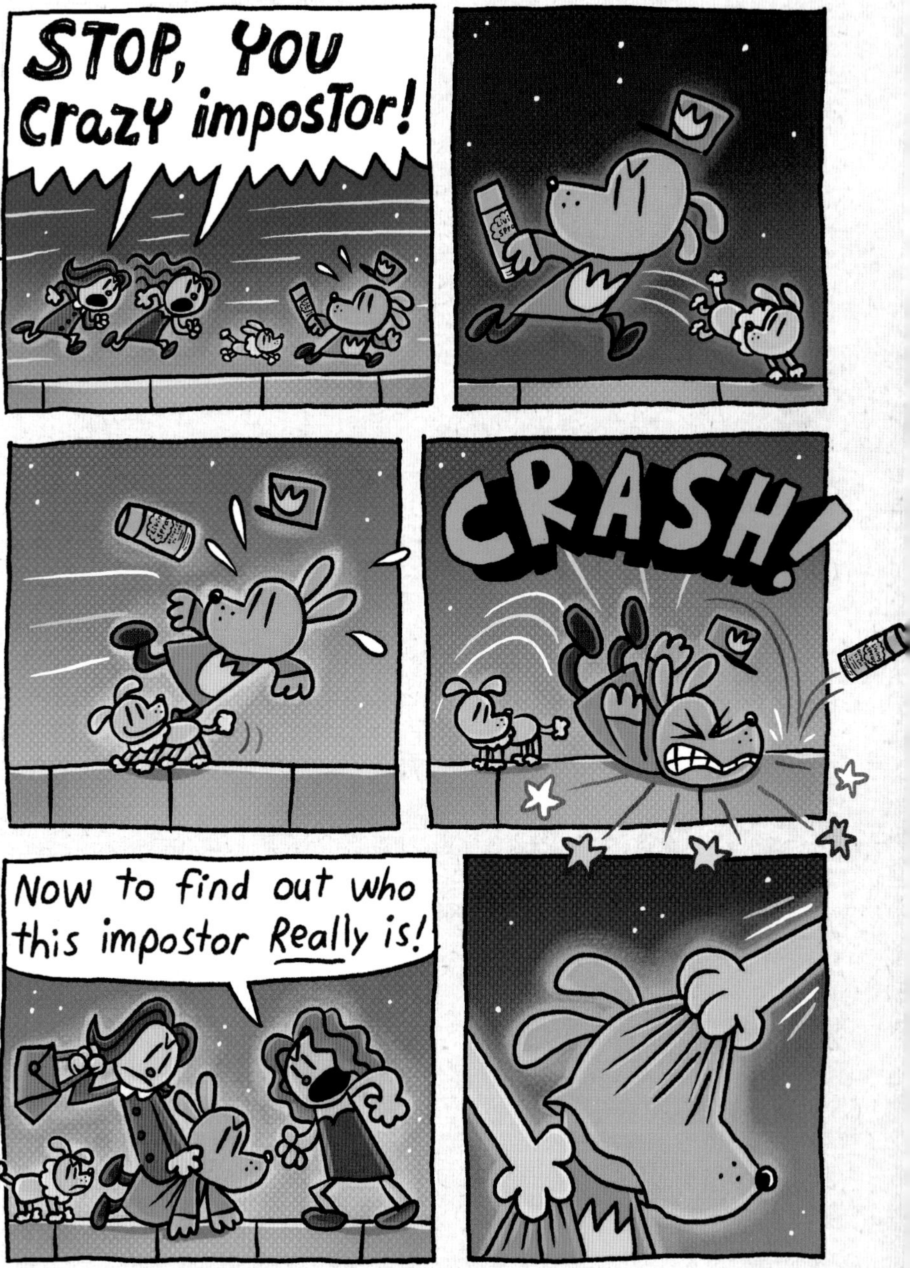
STOP, YOU Crazy impostor!
CRASH!
Now to find out who this impostor Really is!

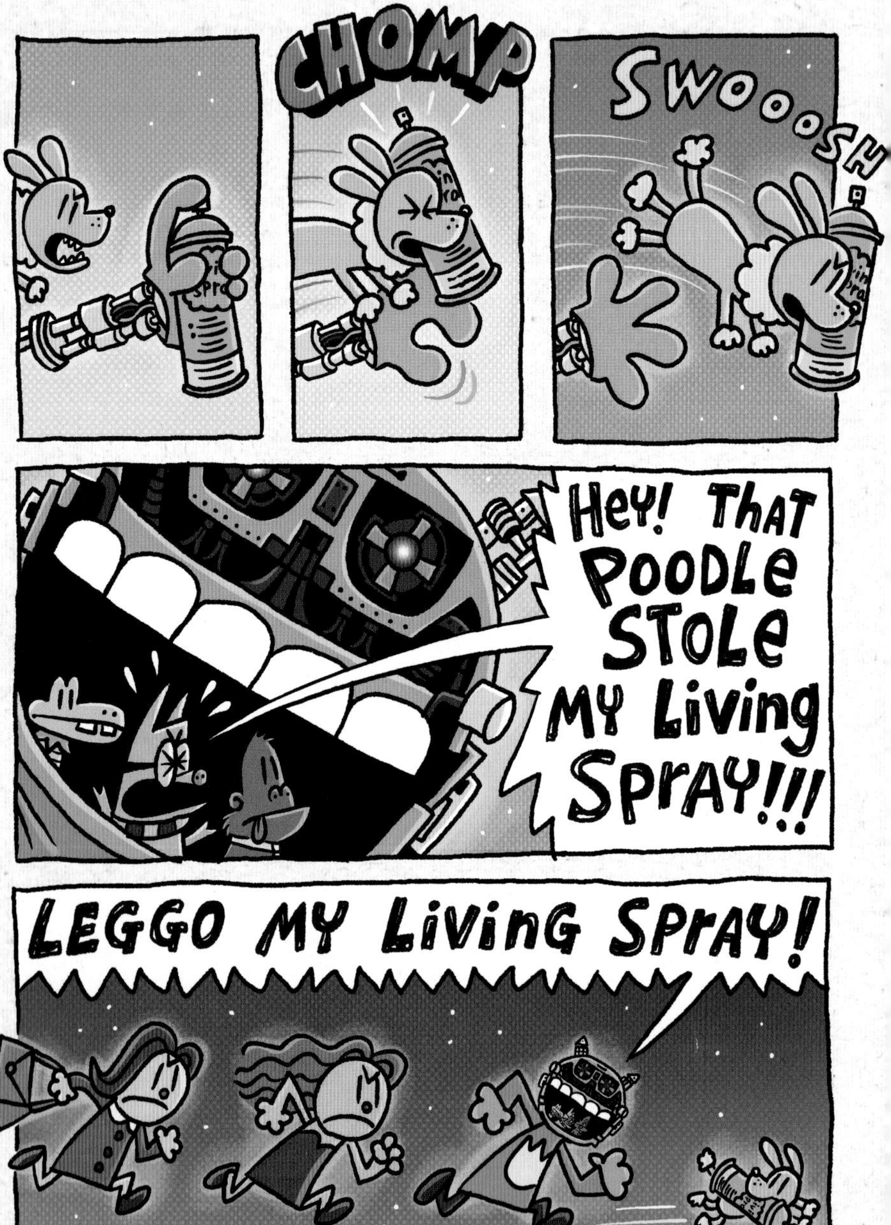
CHOMP
SWOOOSH
HEY! THAT POODLE STOLE MY LIVING SPRAY!!!
LEGGO MY LIVING SPRAY!

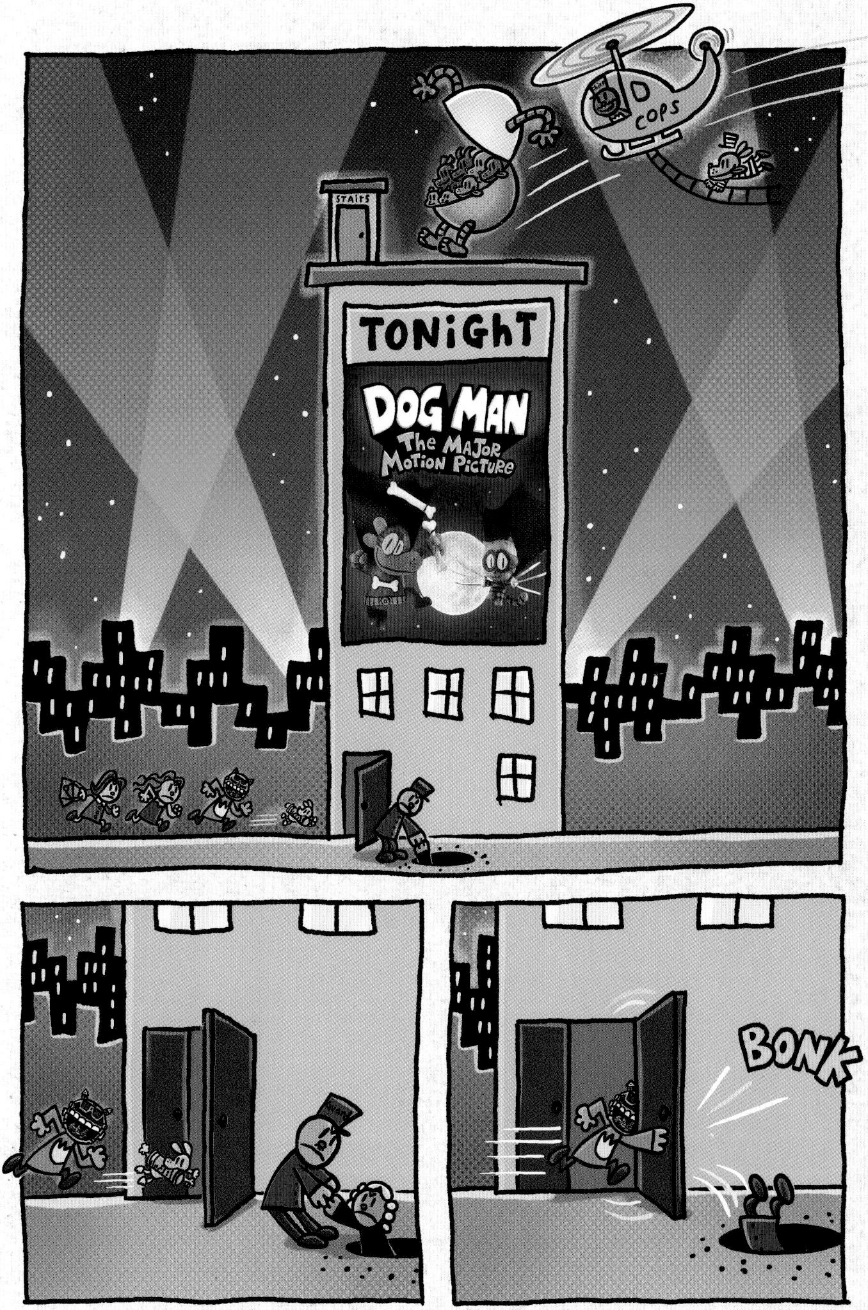
STAIRS
COPS
TONIGHT
DOG MAN
The MAJOR MOTION PICTURE
BONK

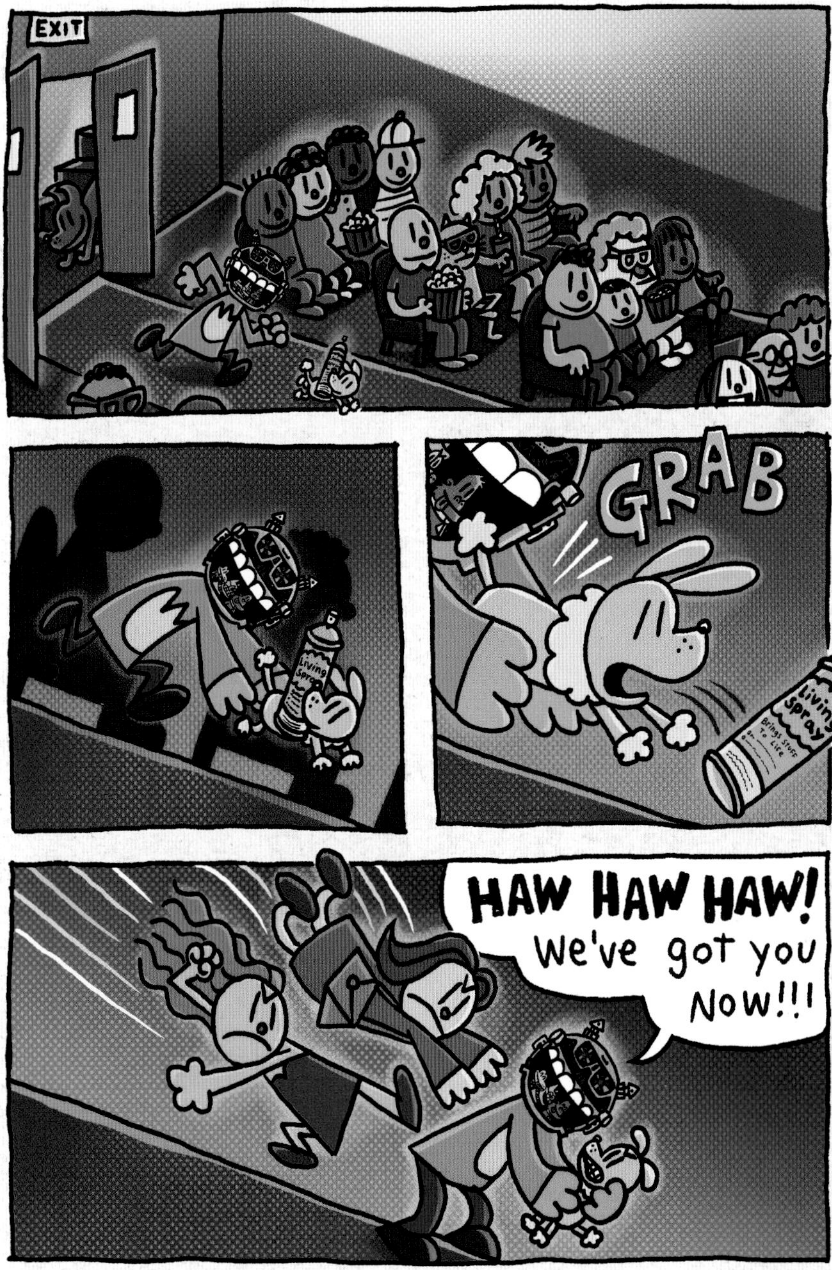
EXIT
Living Spray
GRAB
Living Spray
Brings Stuff To Life
HAW HAW HAW! We've got you NOW!!!

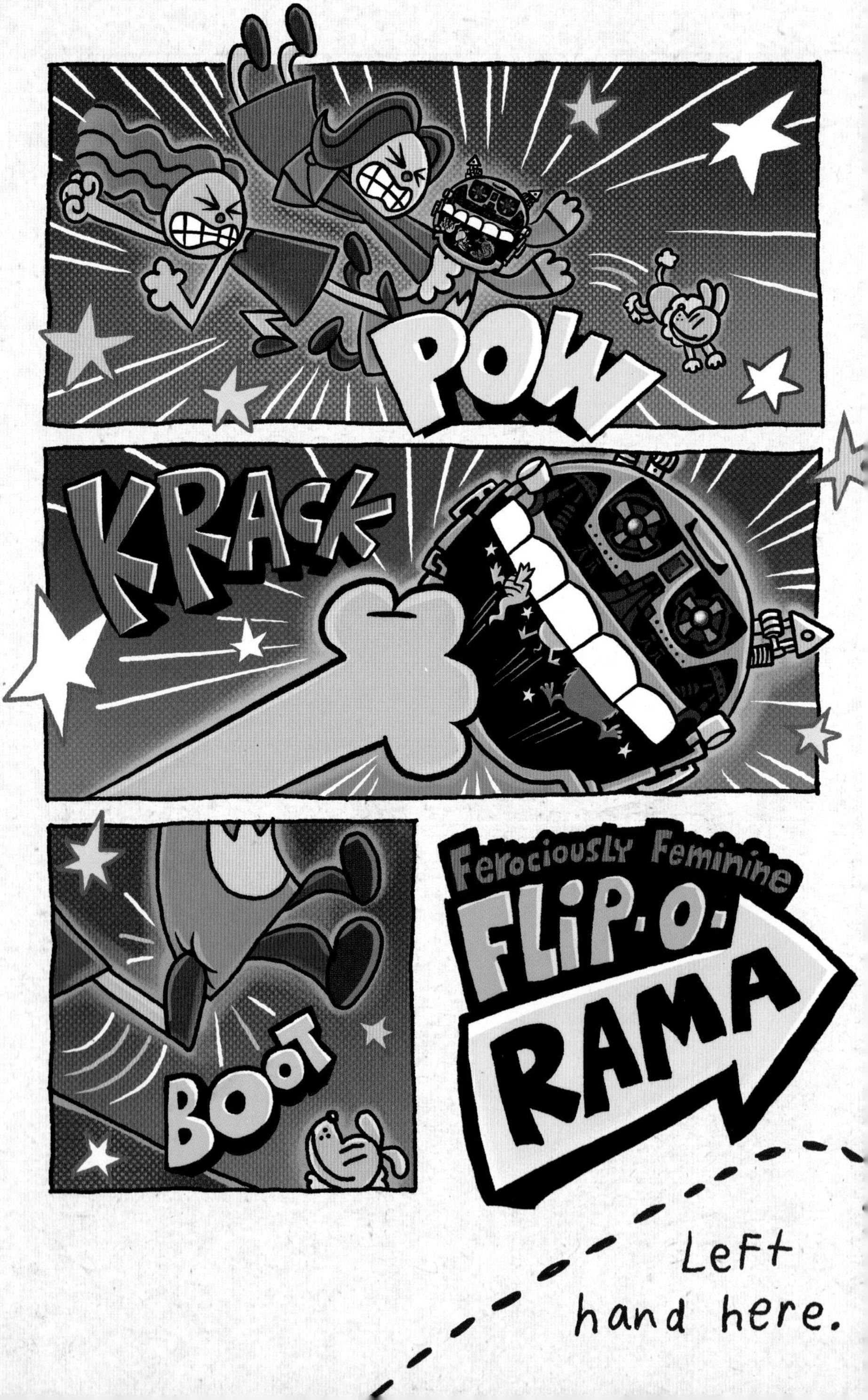
POW
KRACK
BOOT
Ferociously Feminine
FLIP-O-RAMA
Left hand here.

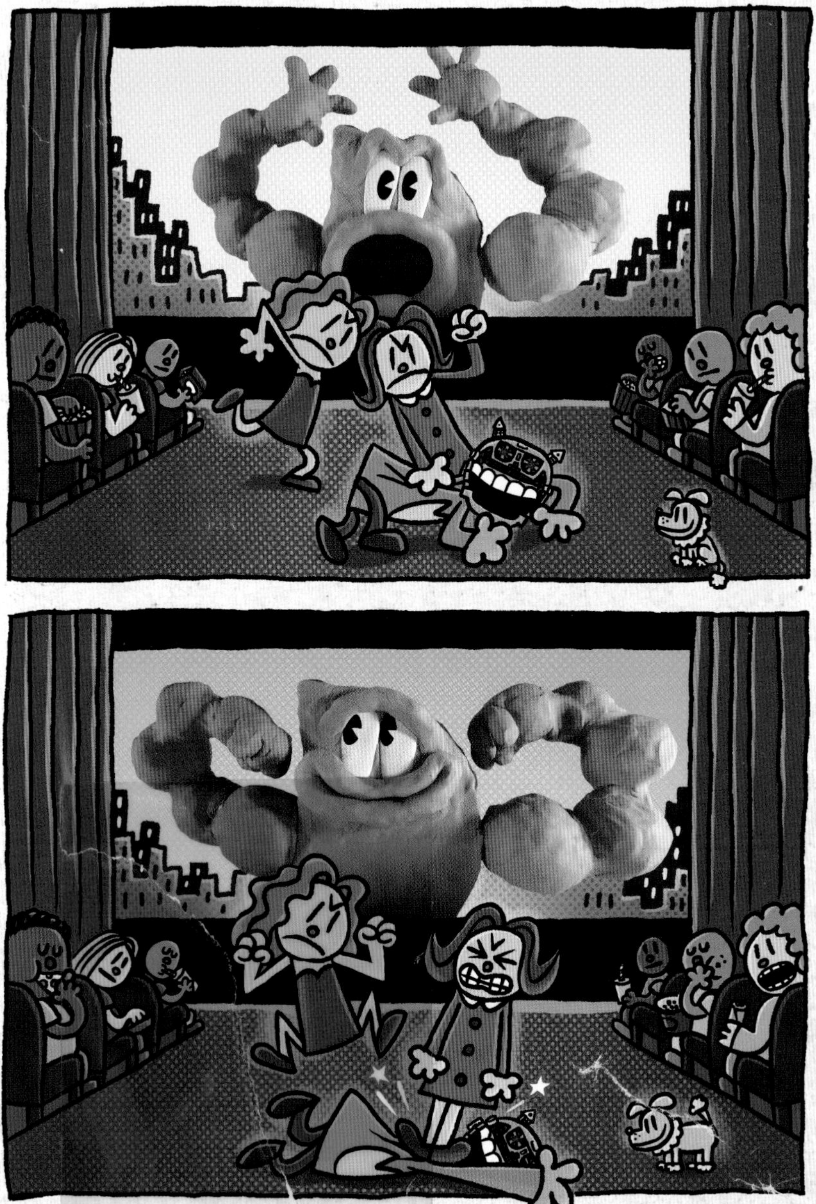

Right
Thumb
here.

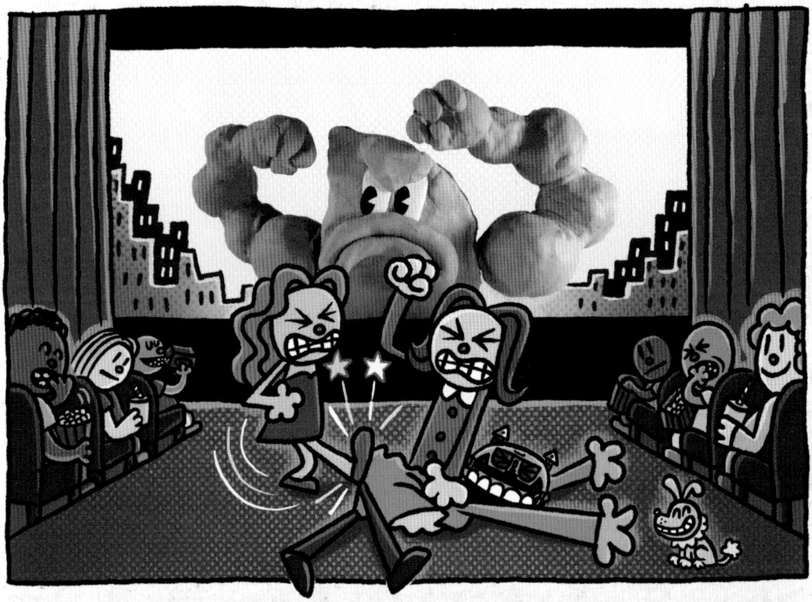

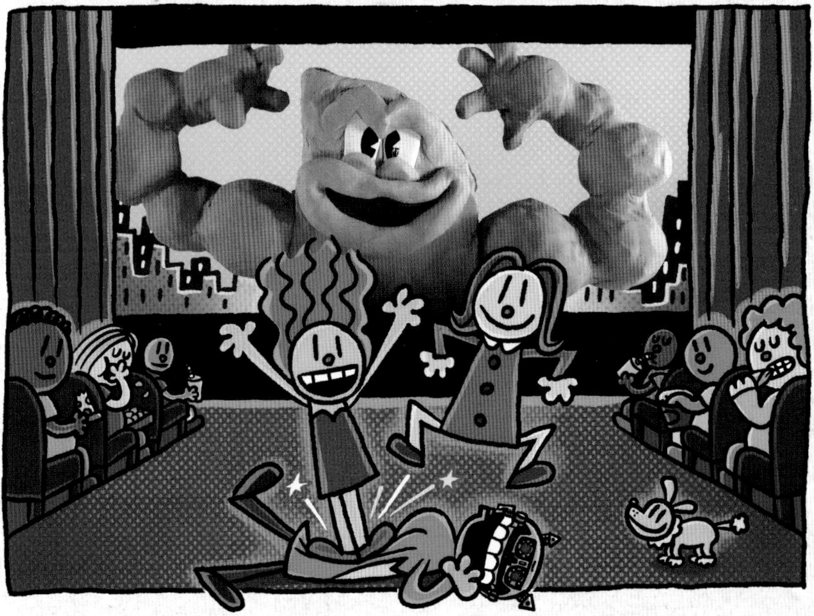

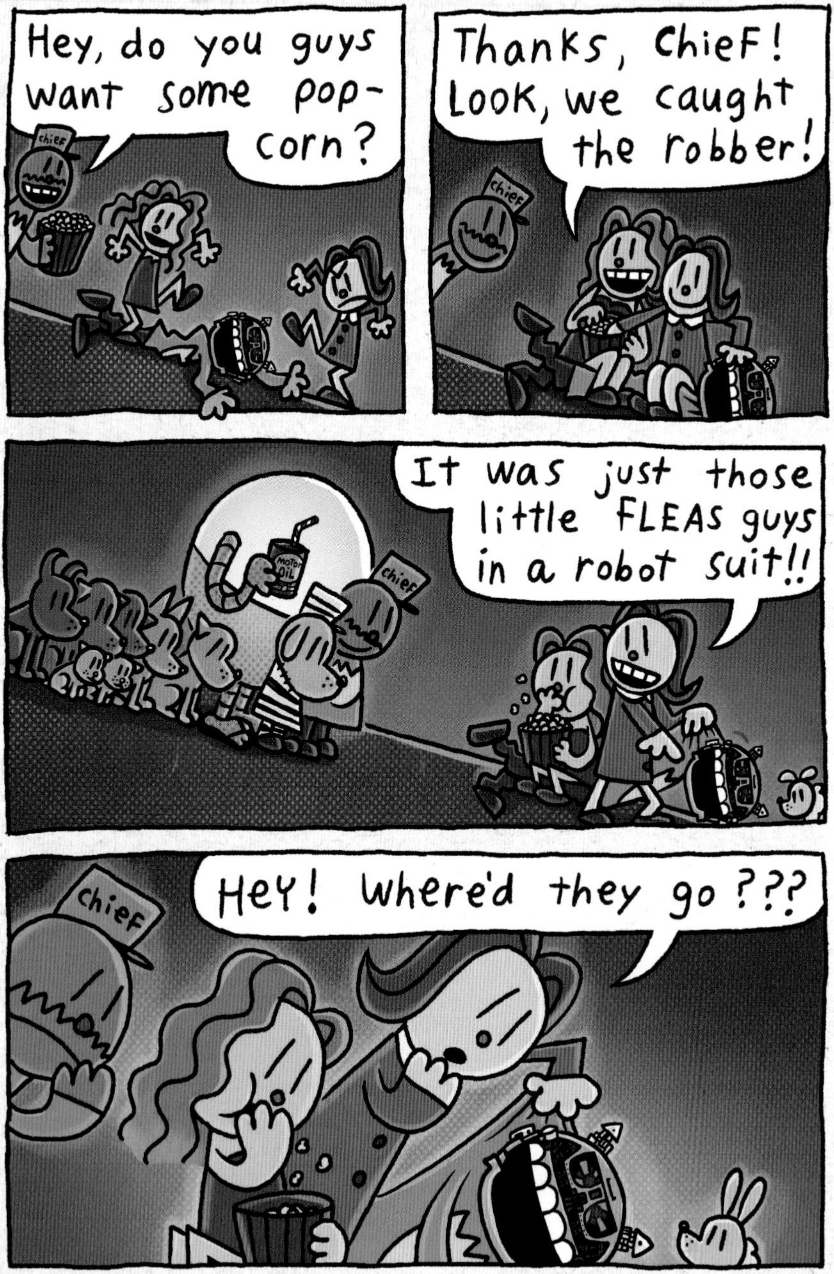
Hey, do you guys want some pop-corn?
Thanks, Chief! Look, we caught the robber!
It was just those little FLEAS guys in a robot suit!!
Hey! Where'd they go???

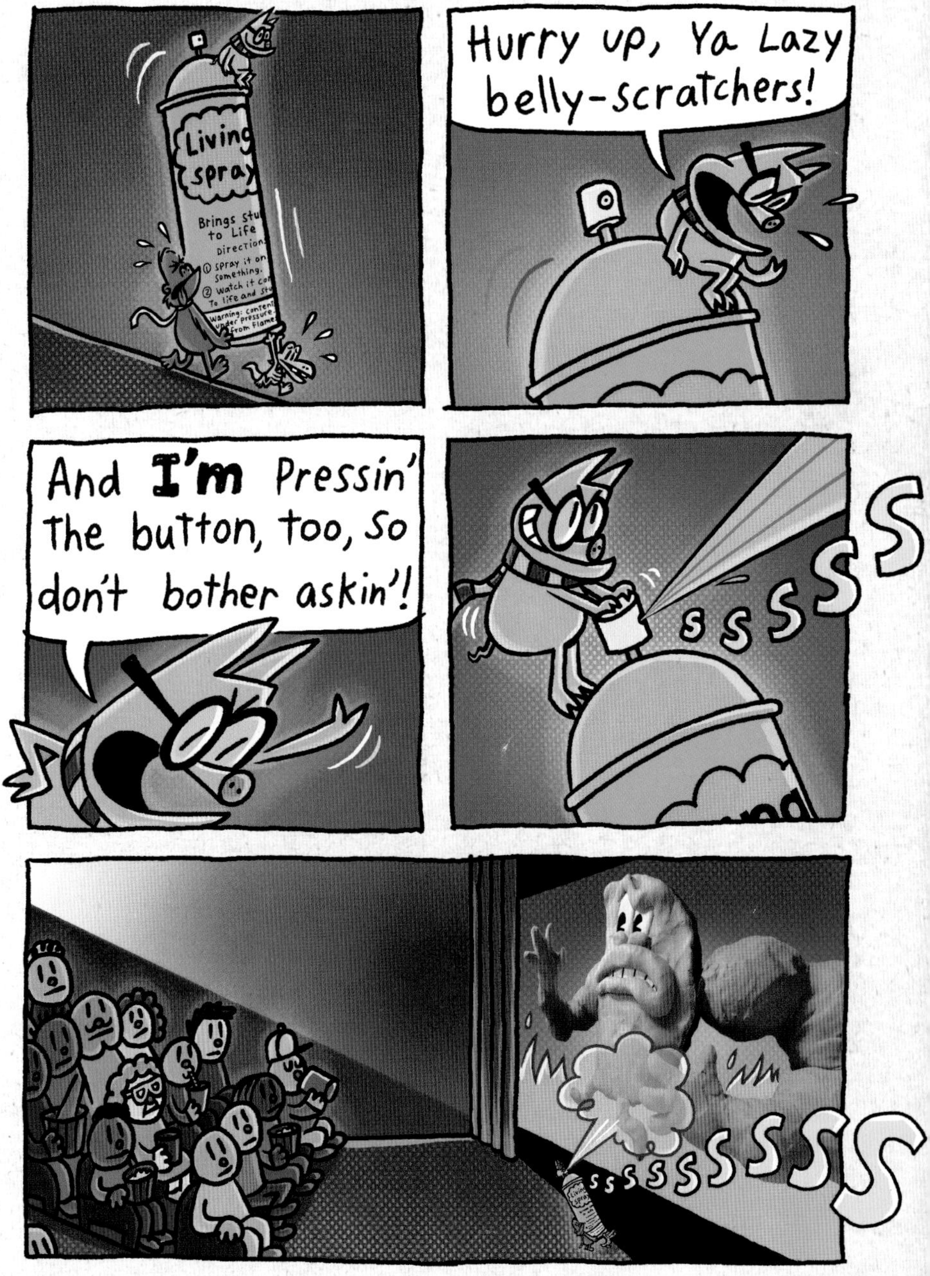
Living spray
Hurry up, Ya Lazy belly-scratchers!
And **I'm** Pressin' The button, too, So don't bother askin'!
sssSSS
sssSSSSSS

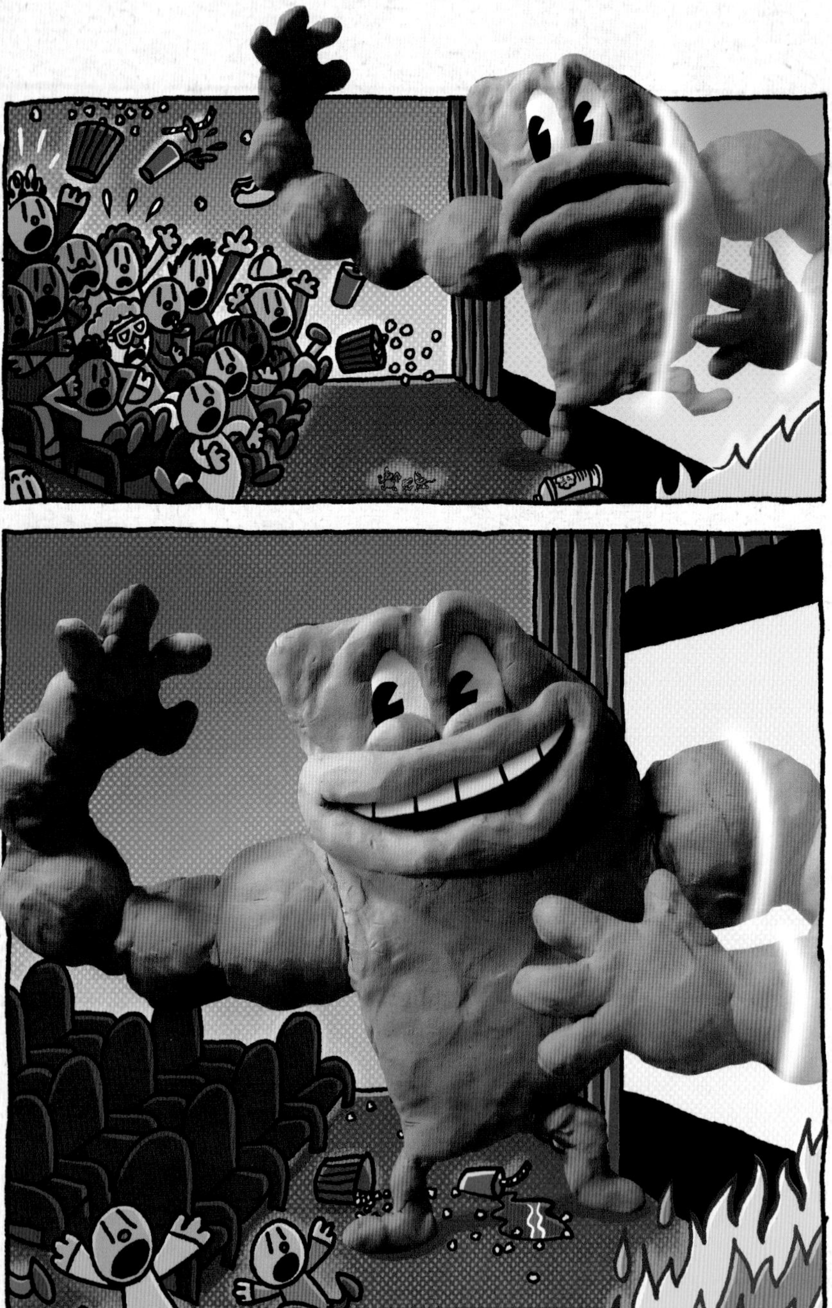

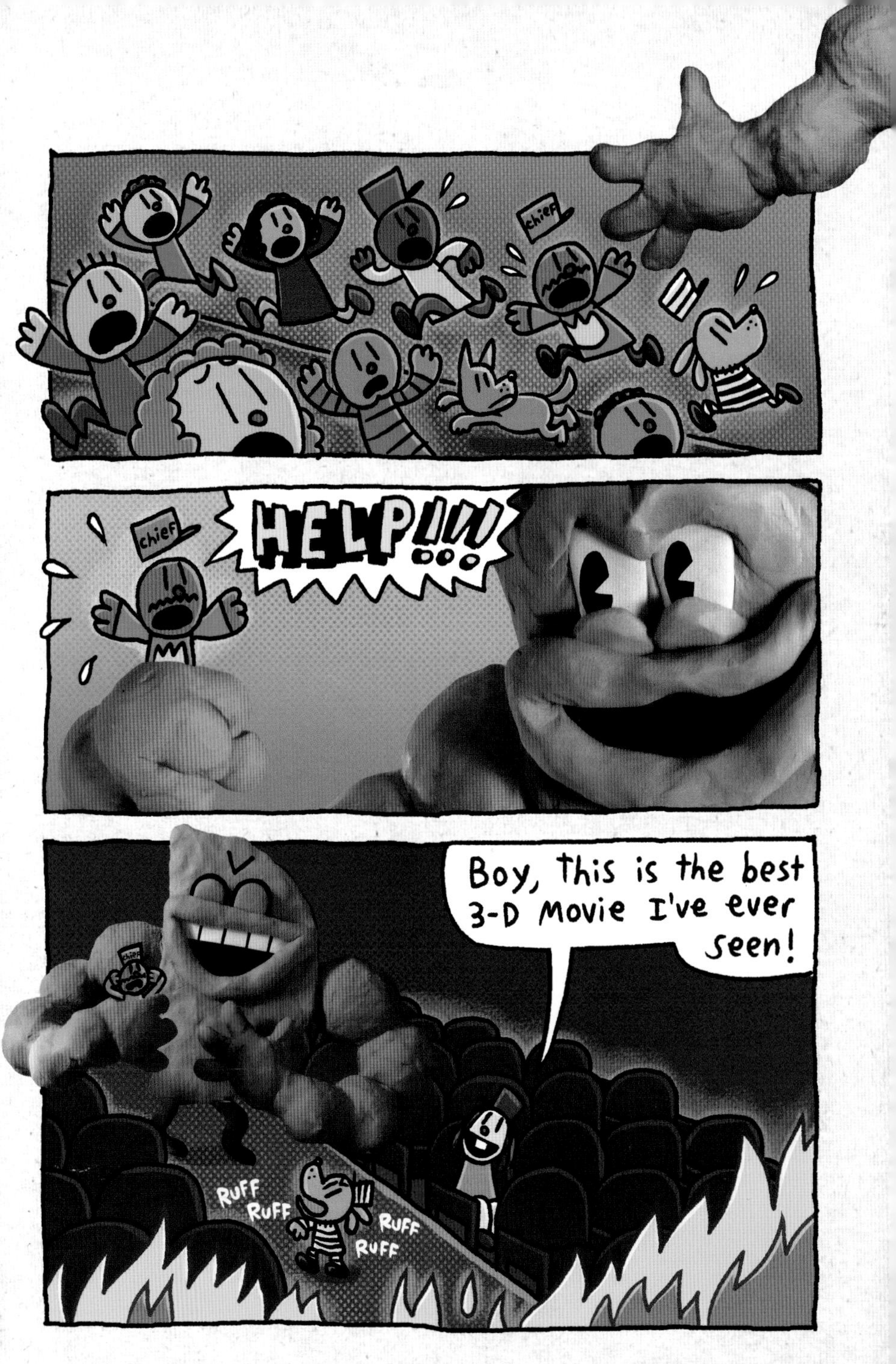
chief
chief
HELP!!!
Boy, This is the best 3-D Movie I've ever seen!
RUFF RUFF
RUFF RUFF

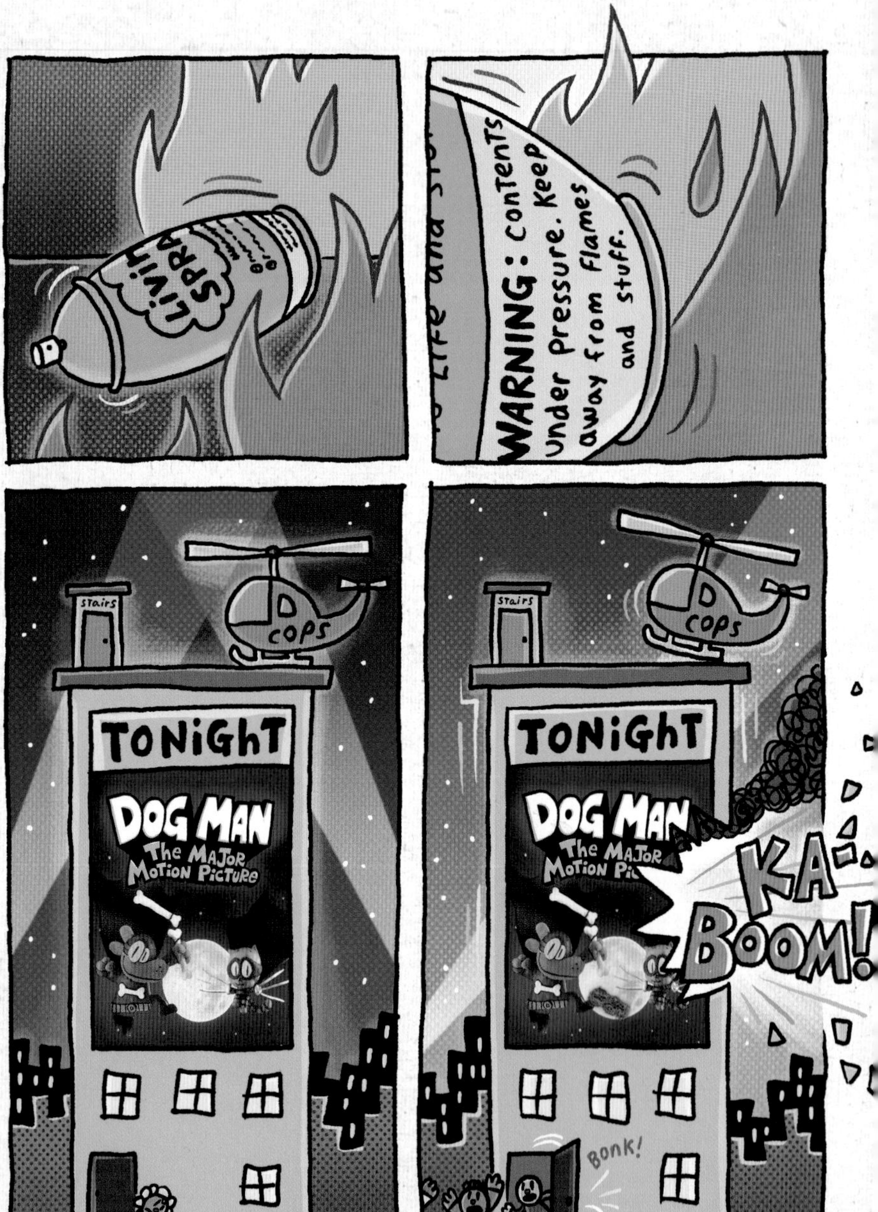

WARNING: contents under pressure. Keep away from flames and stuff.
Stairs
COPS
TONIGhT
DOG MAN
The MAJOR MOTION PICTURE
Stairs
COPS
TONIGhT
DOG MAN
KA-BOOM!
BONK!

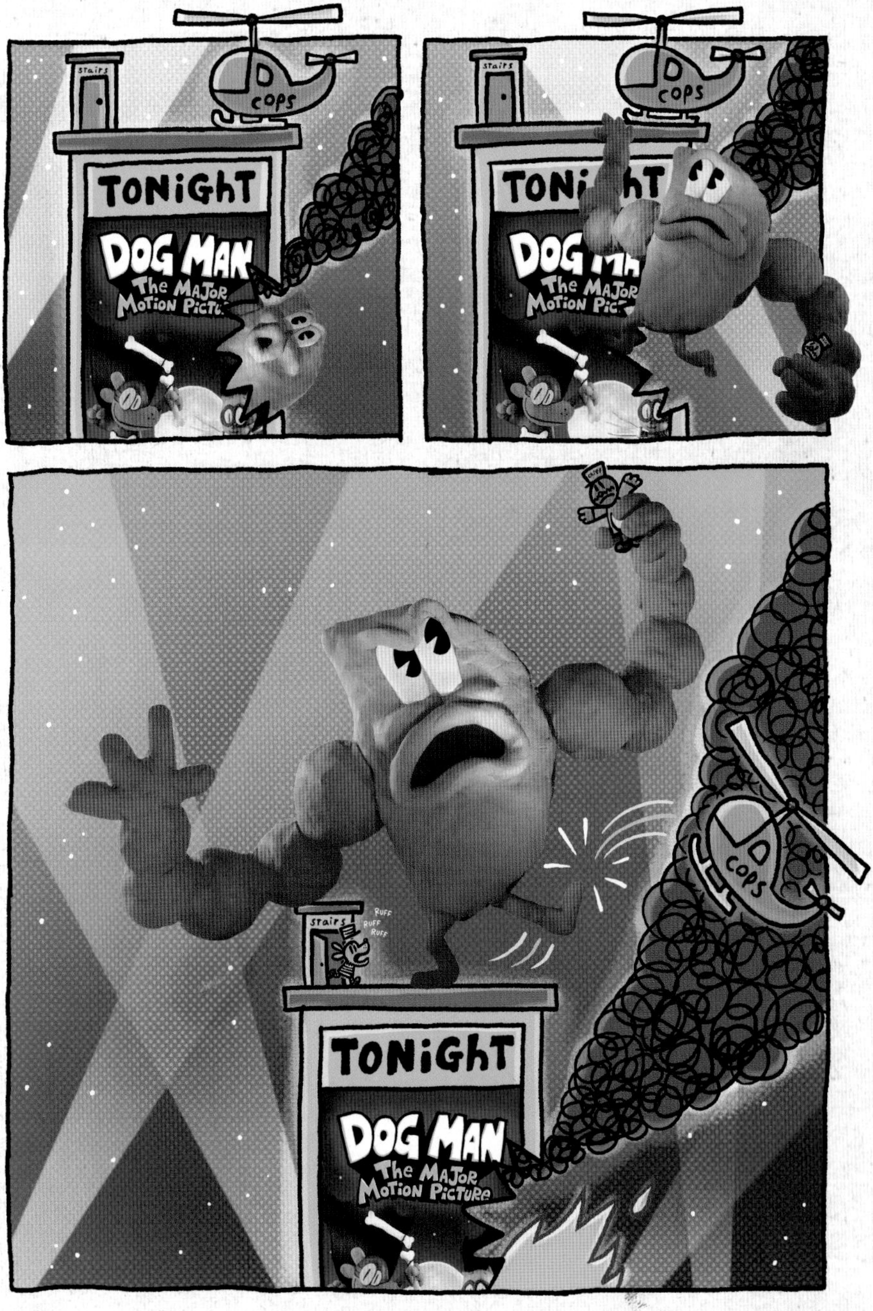
stairs
COPS
TONIGHT
DOG MAN
The MAJOR
stairs
COPS
TONIGHT
The MAJOR
stairs
RUFF
RUFF
RUFF
COPS
TONIGHT
DOG MAN
The MAJOR
MOTION PICTURE

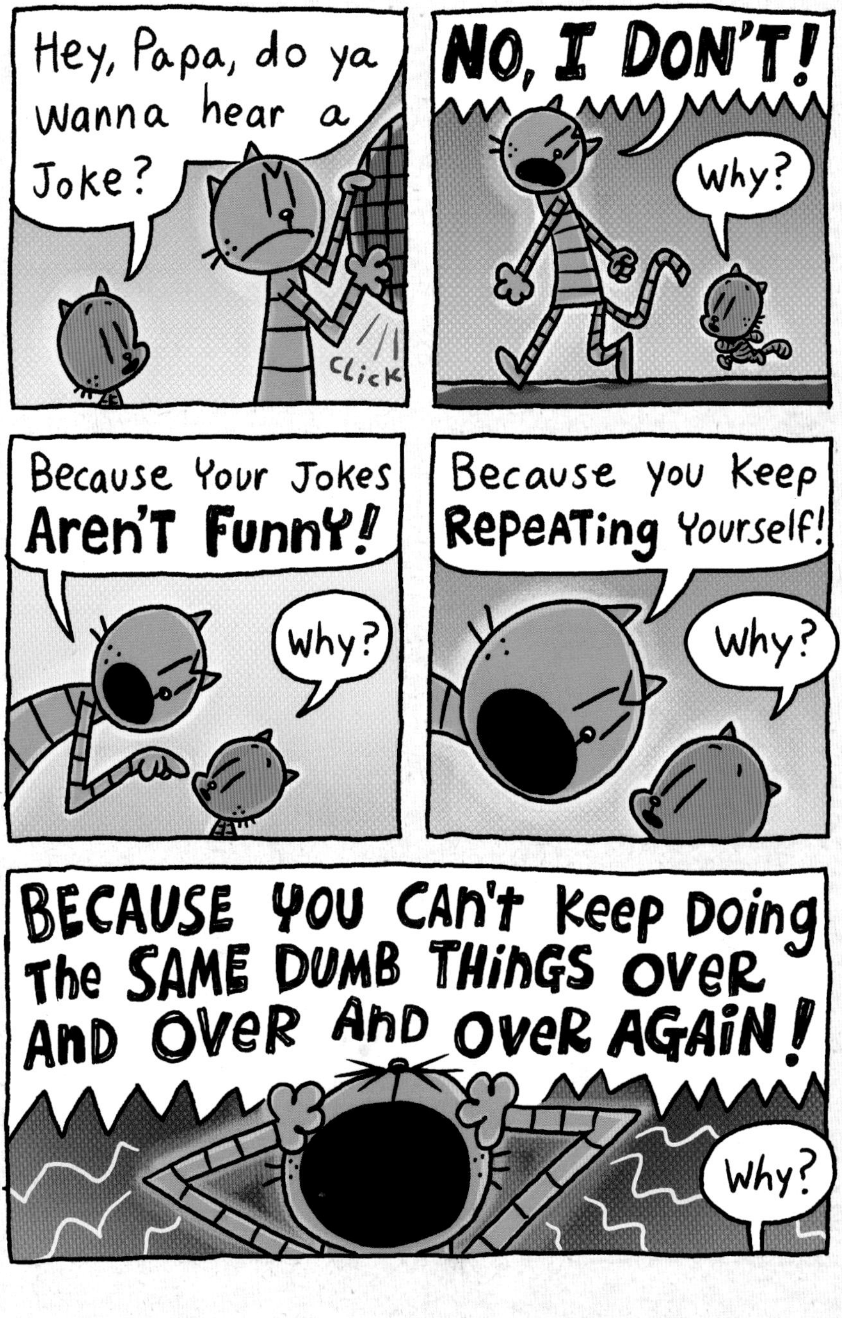

Hey, Papa, do ya wanna hear a Joke?
CLick
NO, I DON'T!
Why?
Because Your Jokes Aren'T FunnY!
Why?
Because you Keep REPEATing Yourself!
Why?
BECAUSE YOU CAN'T Keep Doing The SAME DUMB THINGS OVER AND OVER AND OVER AGAIN!
Why?

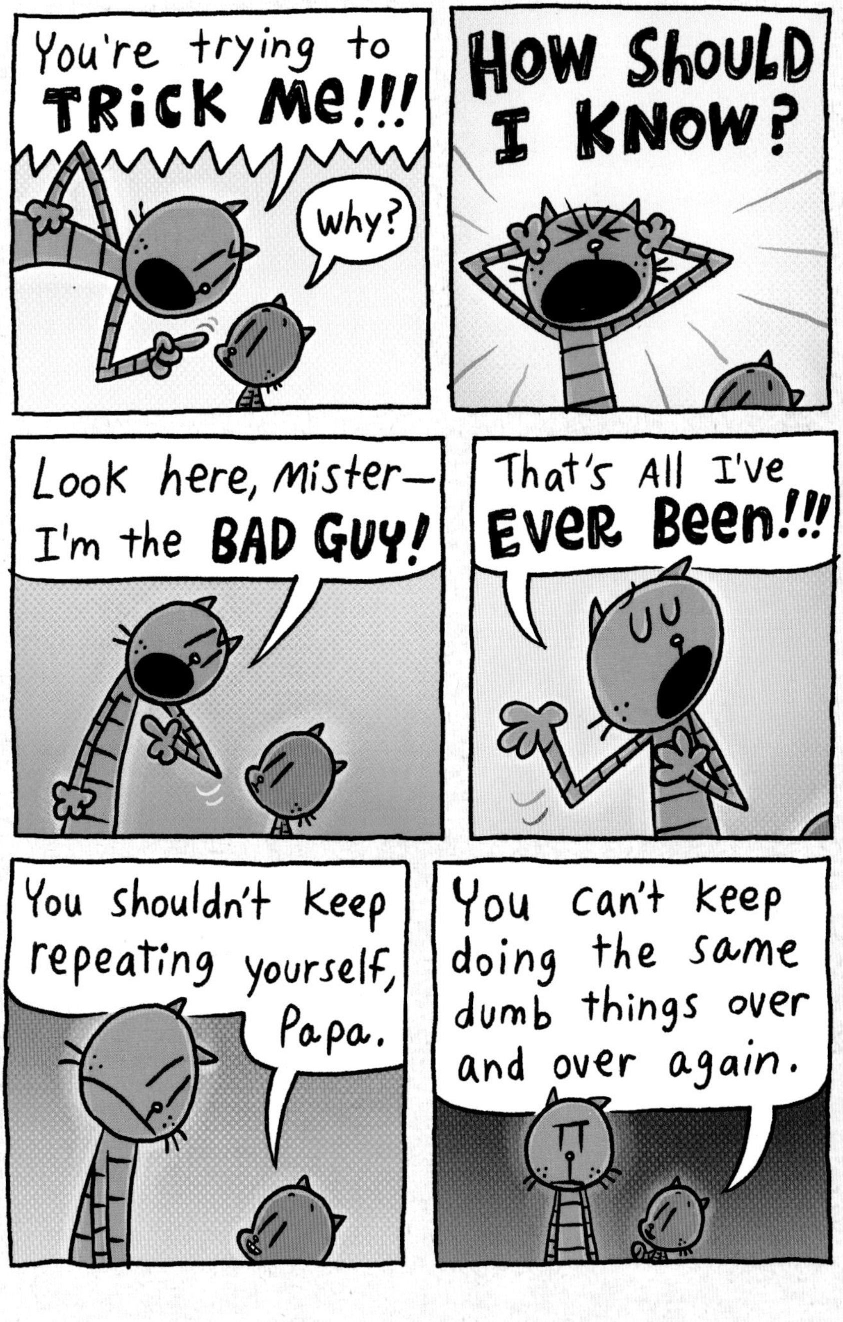
You're trying to TRICK ME!!!
Why?
HOW SHOULD I KNOW?
Look here, Mister— I'm the BAD GUY!
That's All I've EVER Been!!!
You shouldn't keep repeating yourself, Papa.
You can't keep doing the same dumb things over and over again.

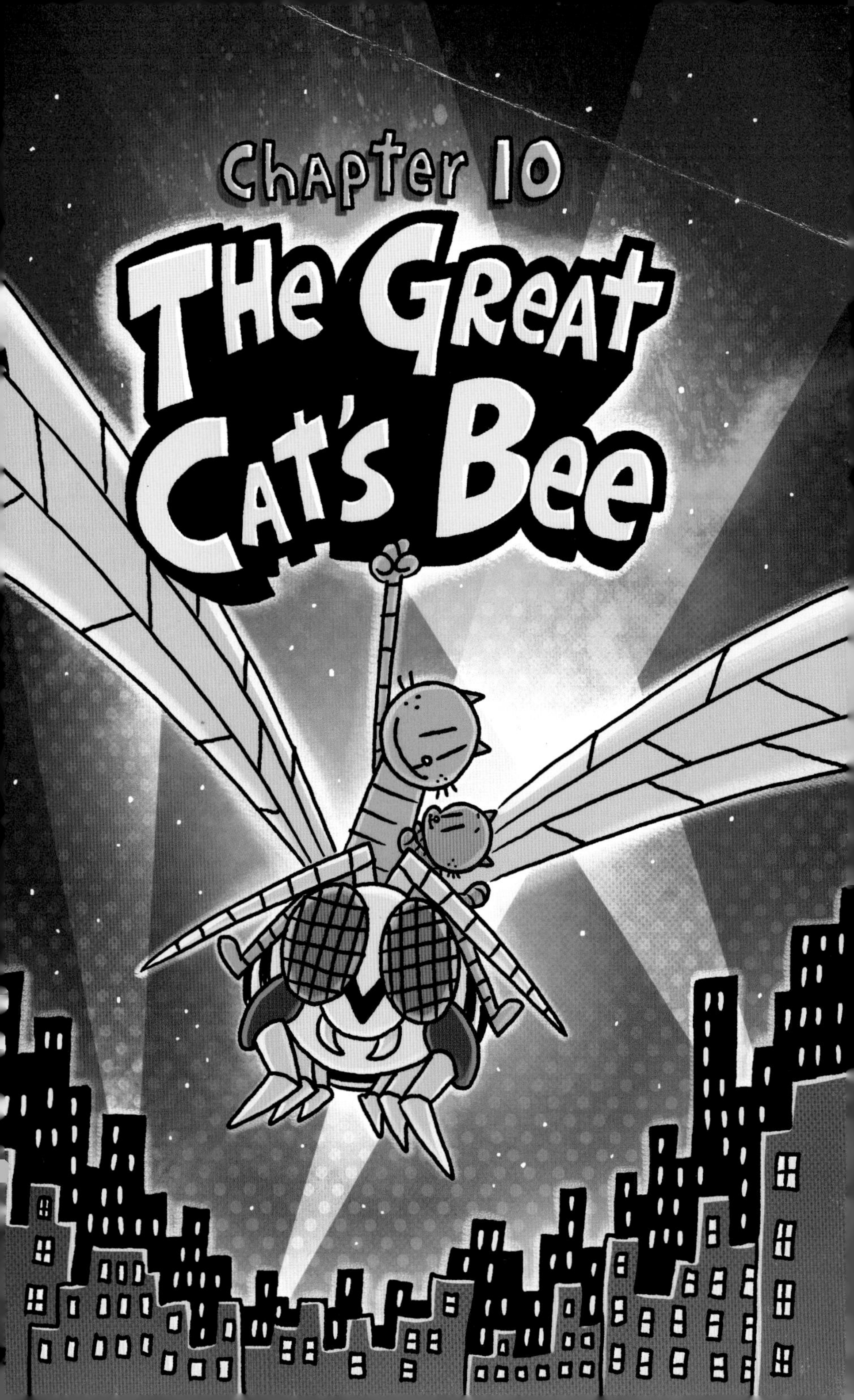
Chapter 10
The Great Cat's Bee

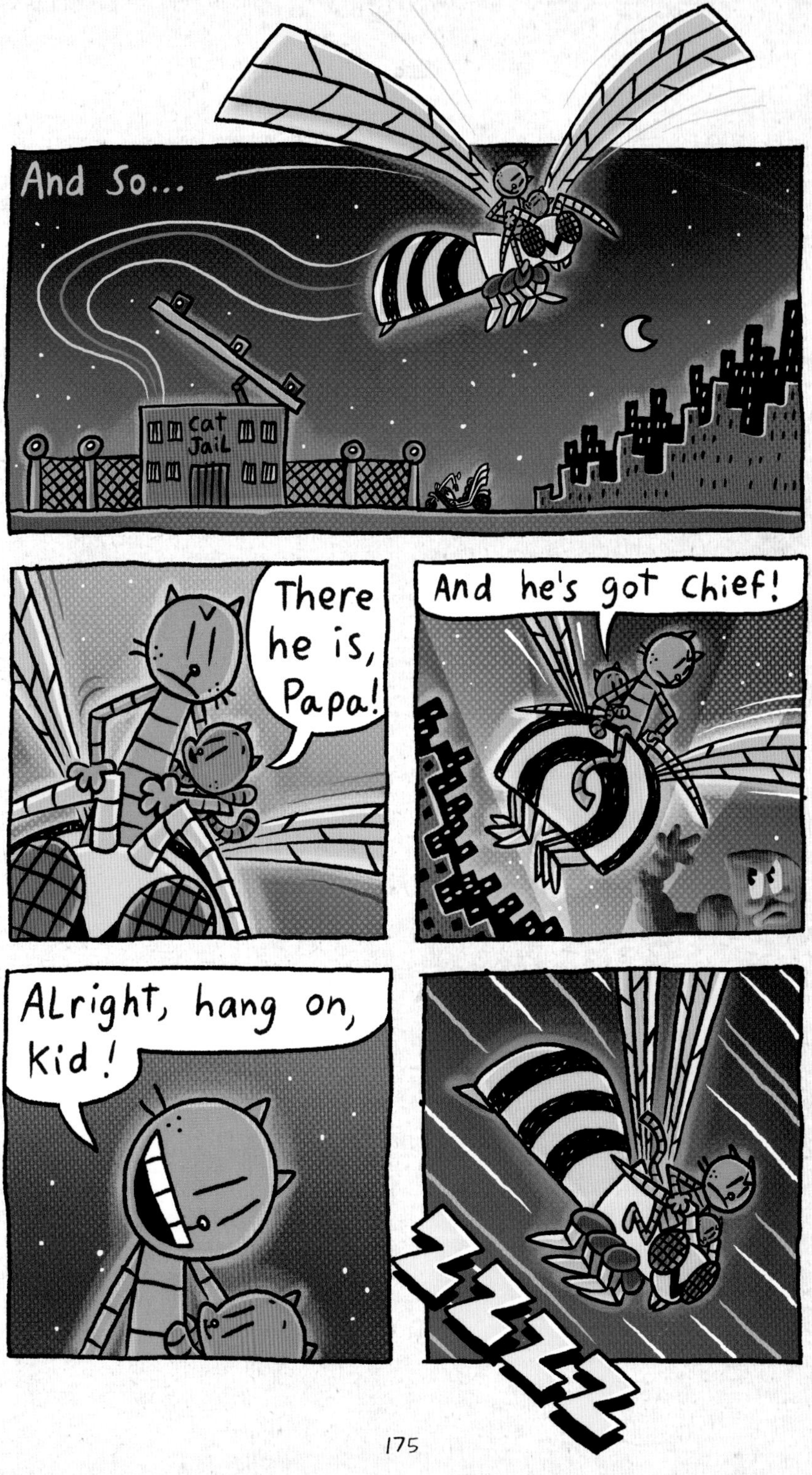
And So...
Cat Jail
There he is, Papa!
And he's got Chief!
ALright, hang on, Kid!

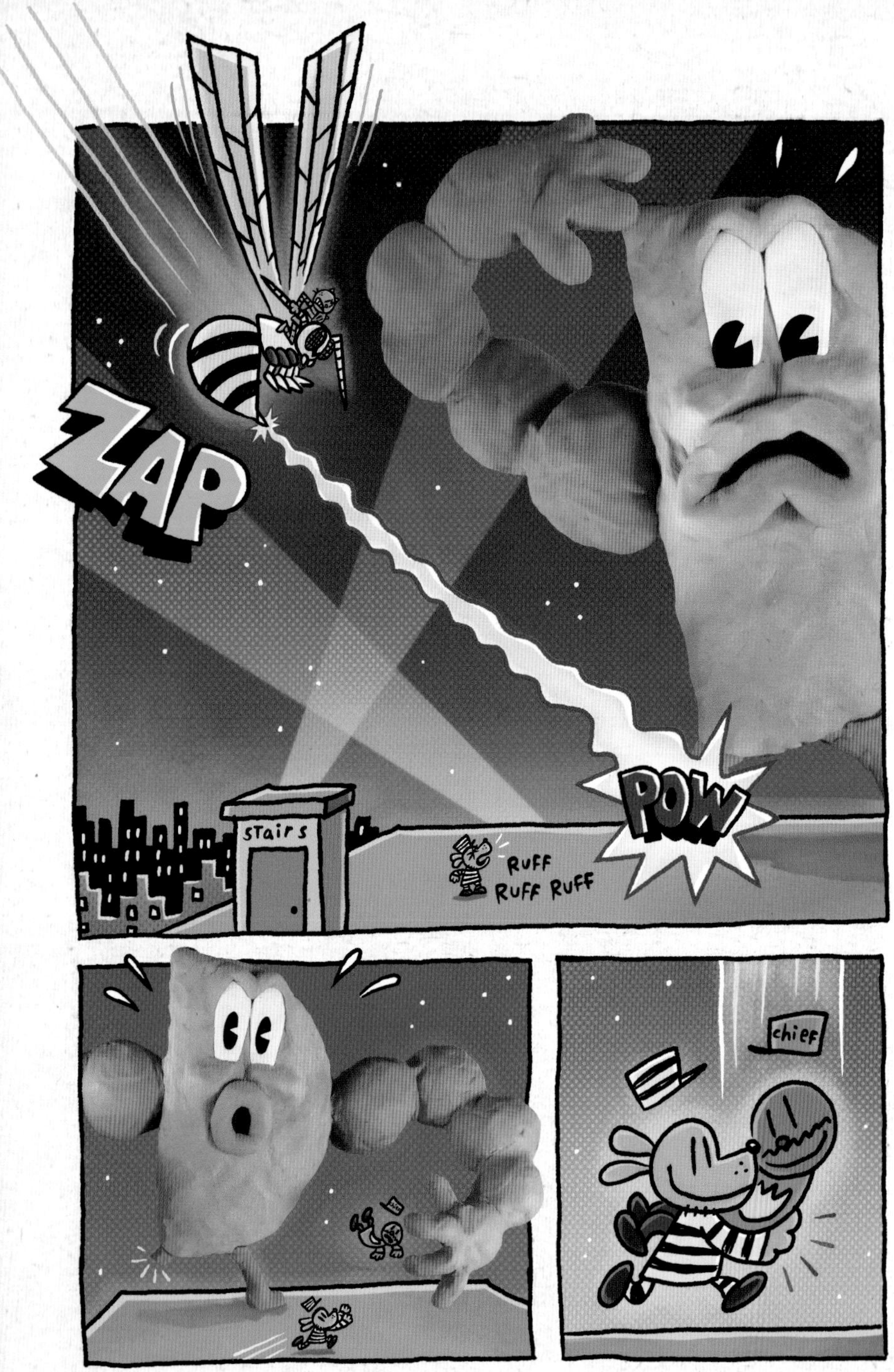
ZAP
POW
stairs
RUFF
RUFF RUFF
chief

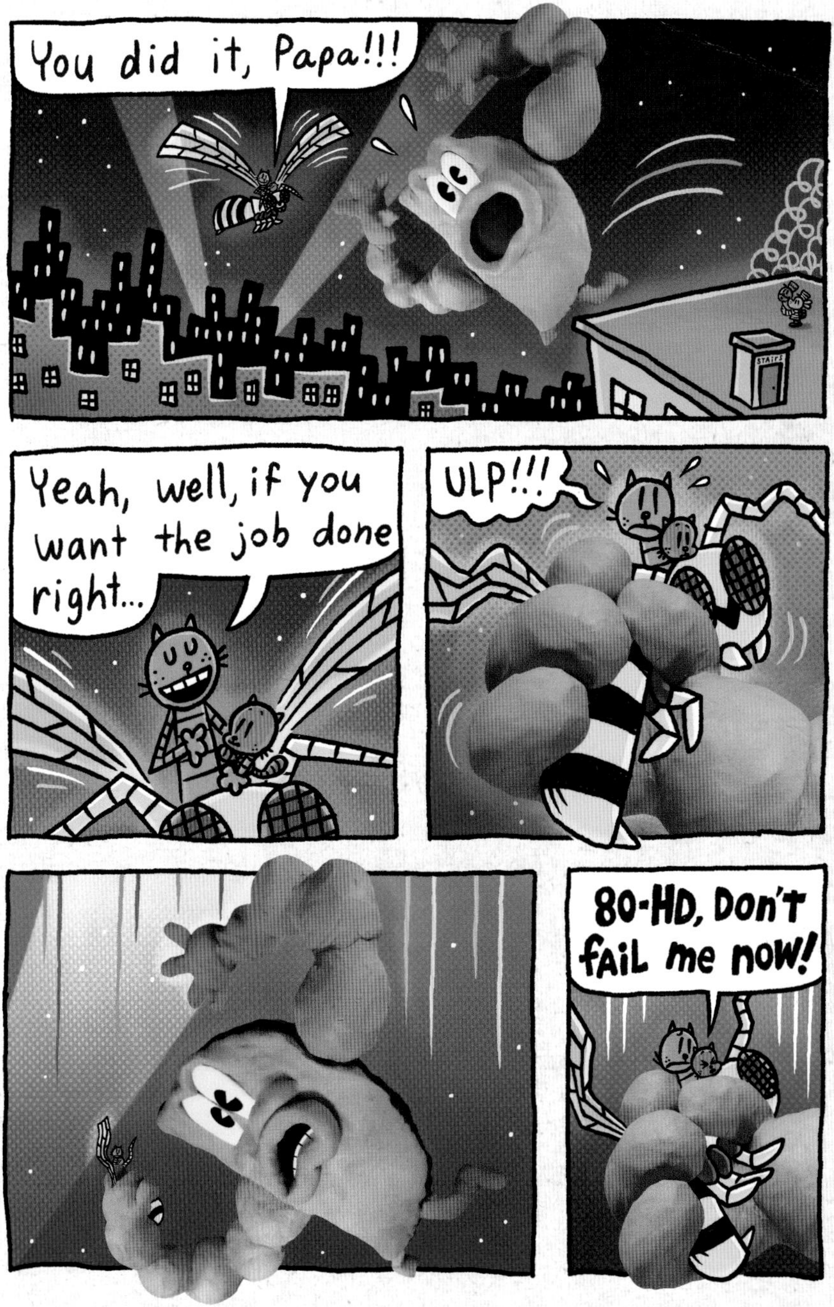
You did it, Papa!!!
Yeah, well, if you want the job done right...
ULP!!!
80-HD, Don't fail me now!

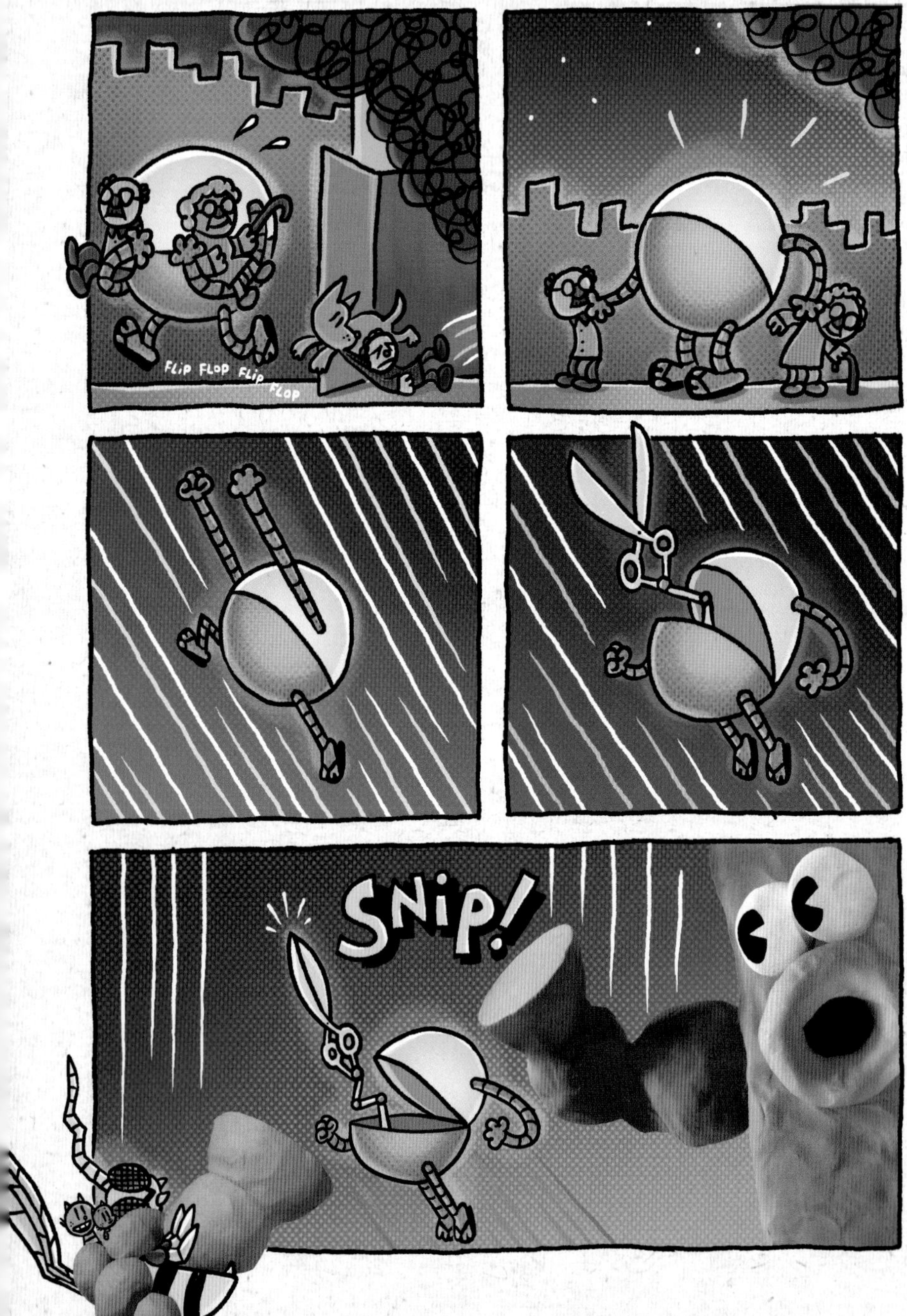
FLIP FLOP FLIP FLOP
SNIP!

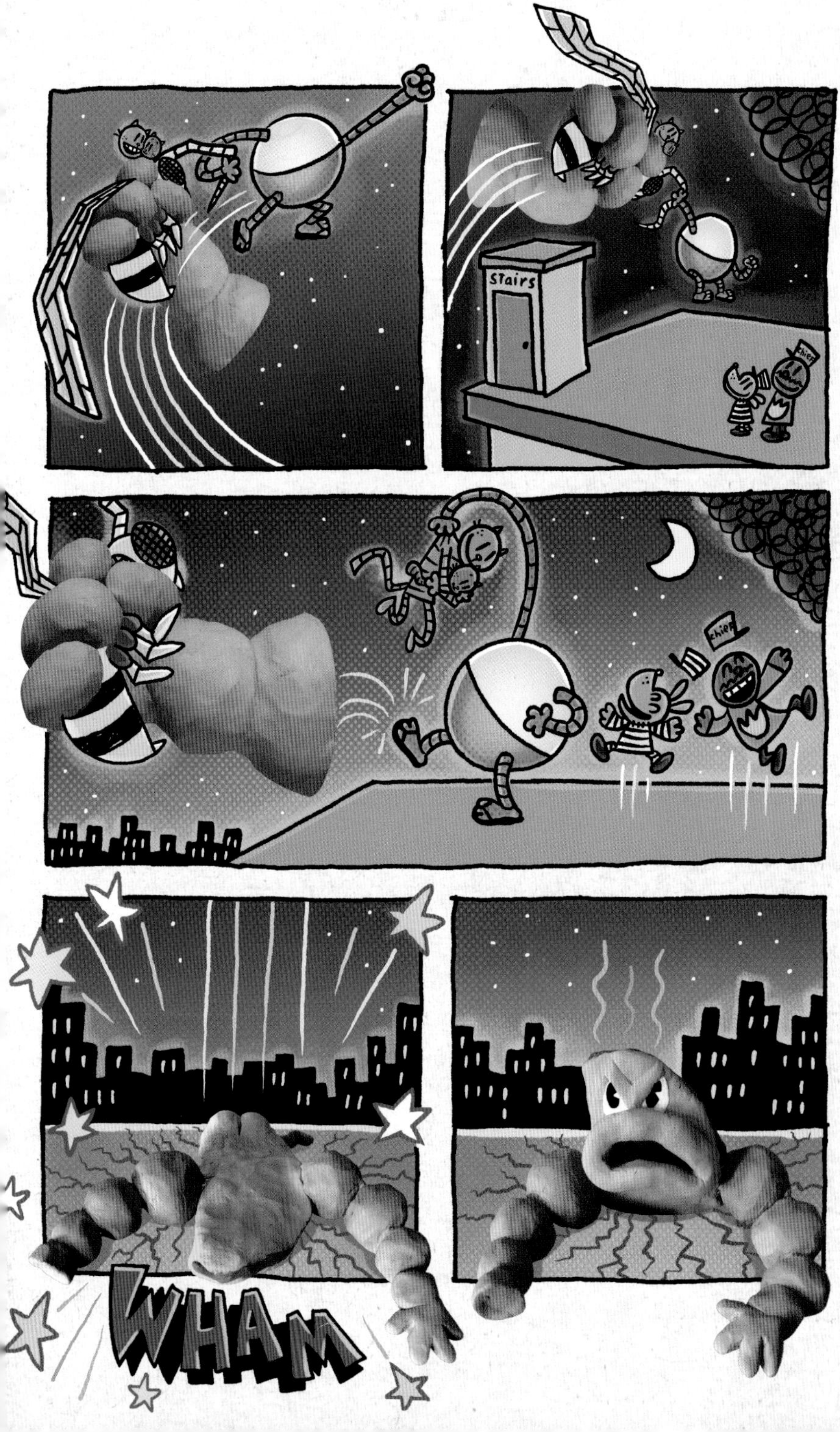
STAIRS
CHIEF
CHIEF
WHAM

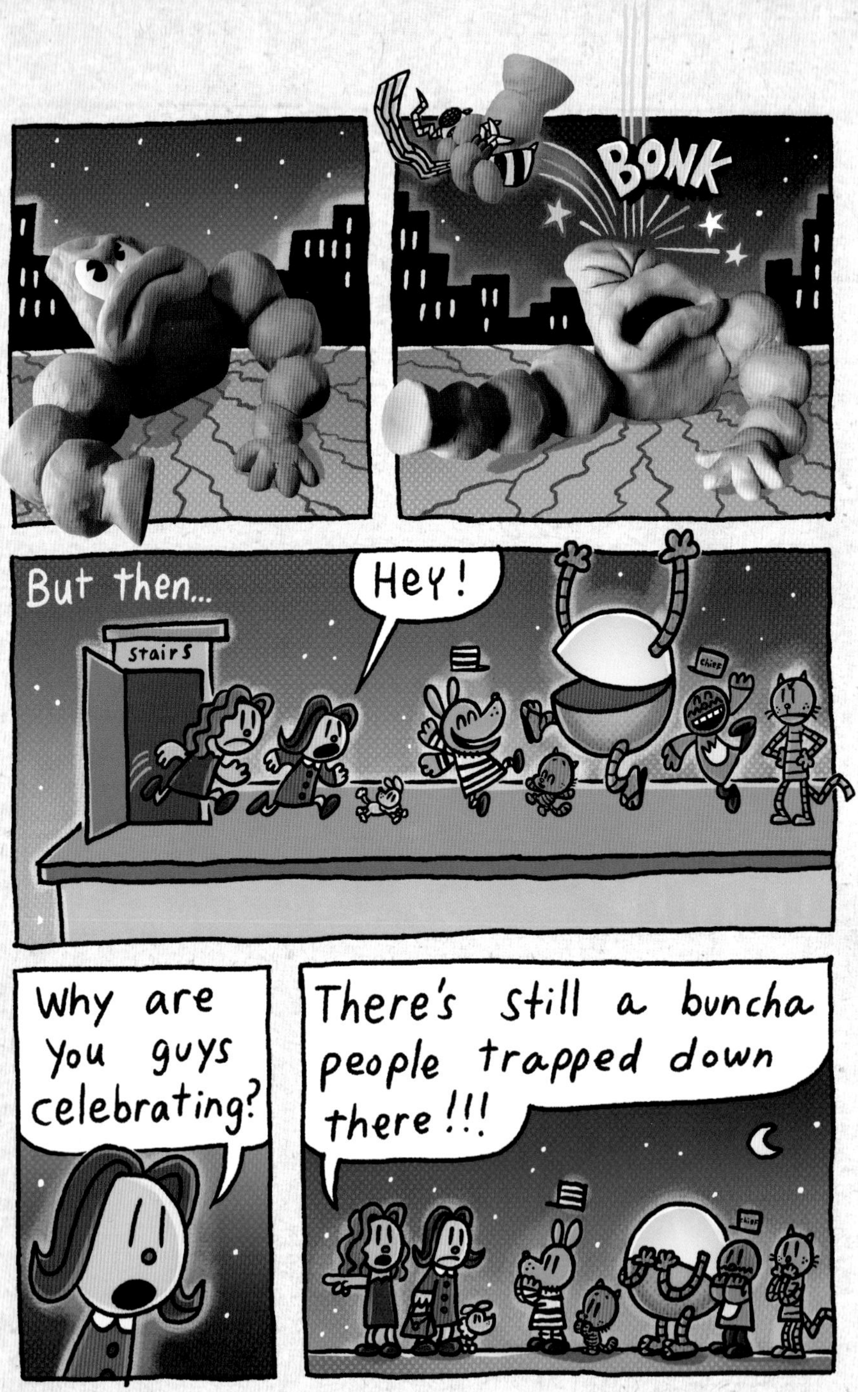
BONK
But then...
Hey!
Stairs
Why are you guys celebrating?
There's still a buncha people trapped down there!!!

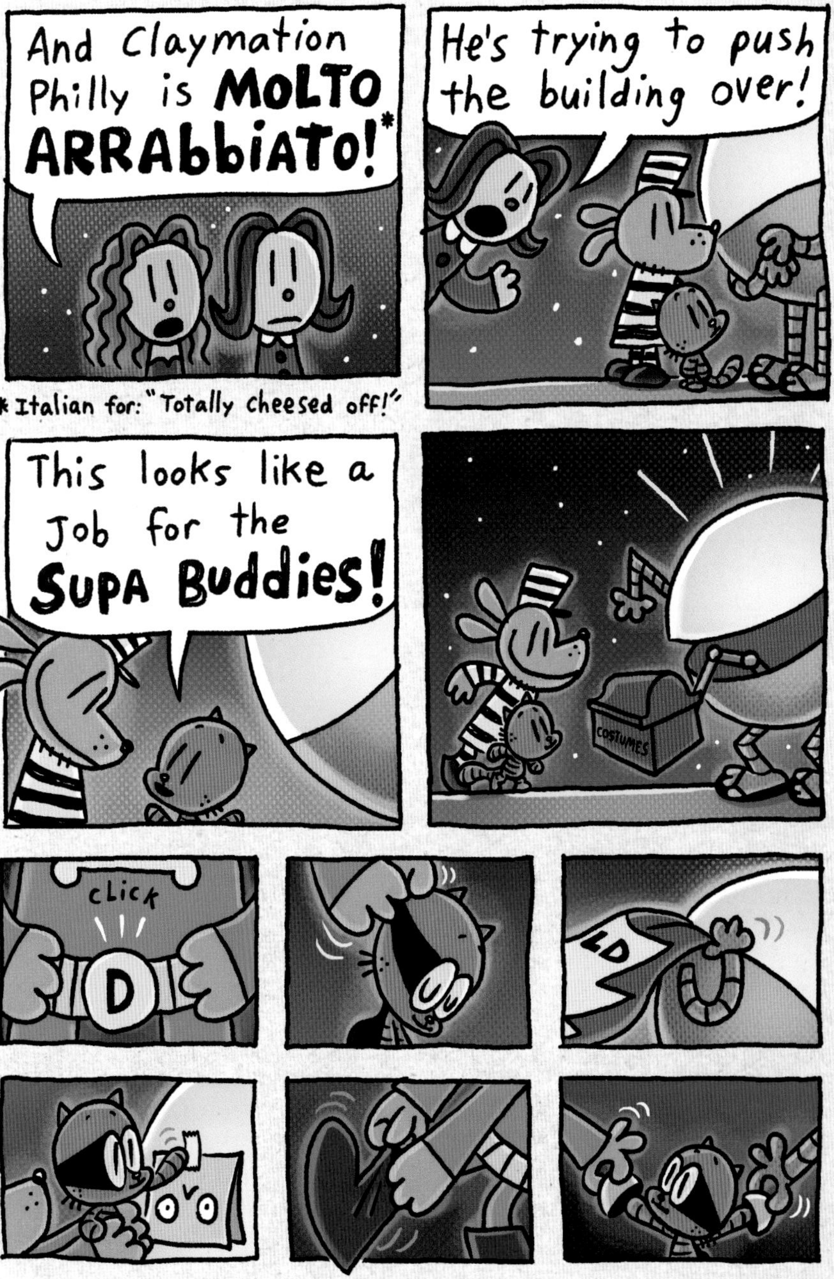
And Claymation Philly is MOLTO ARRABbiATO!*
* Italian for: "Totally cheesed off!"
He's trying to push the building over!
This looks like a Job for the SUPA Buddies!
COSTUMES
CLICK
D

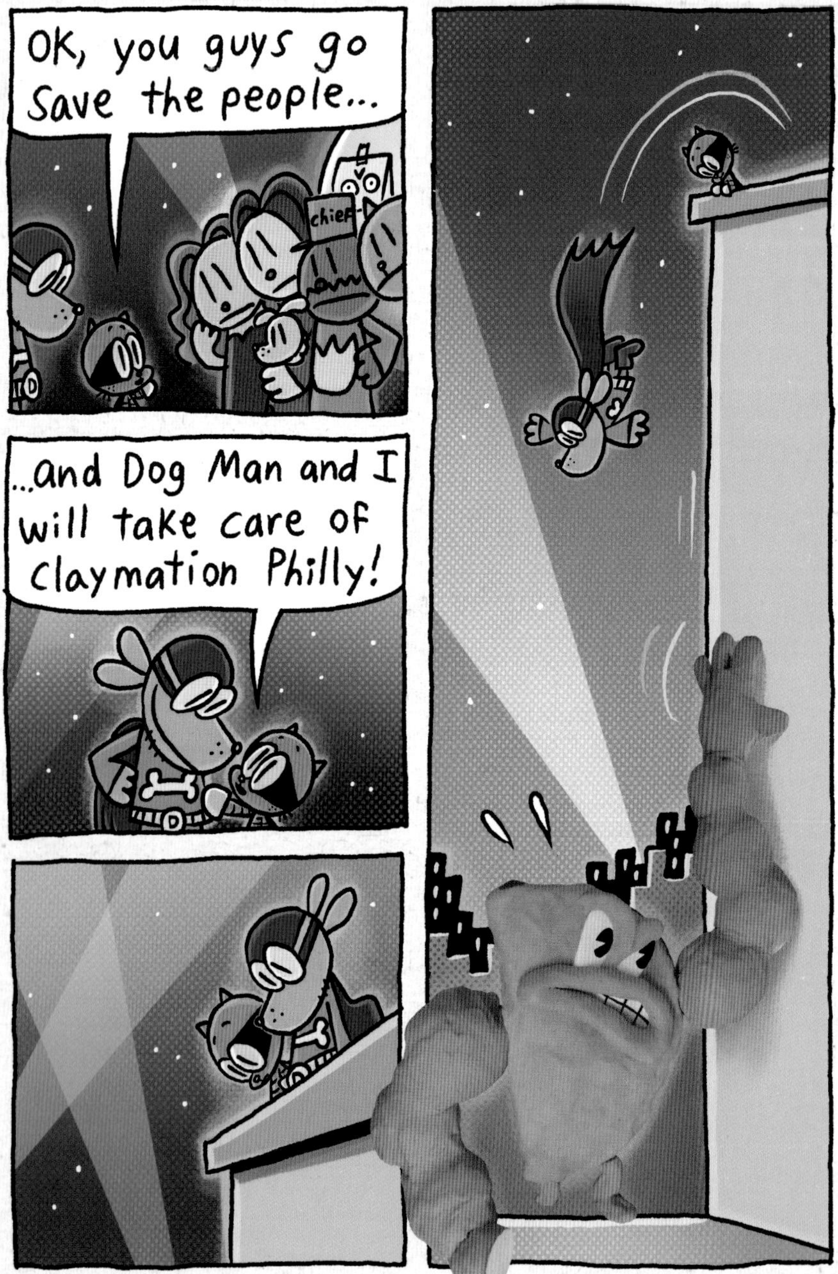
OK, you guys go Save the people...
chief
...and Dog Man and I will take care of Claymation Philly!

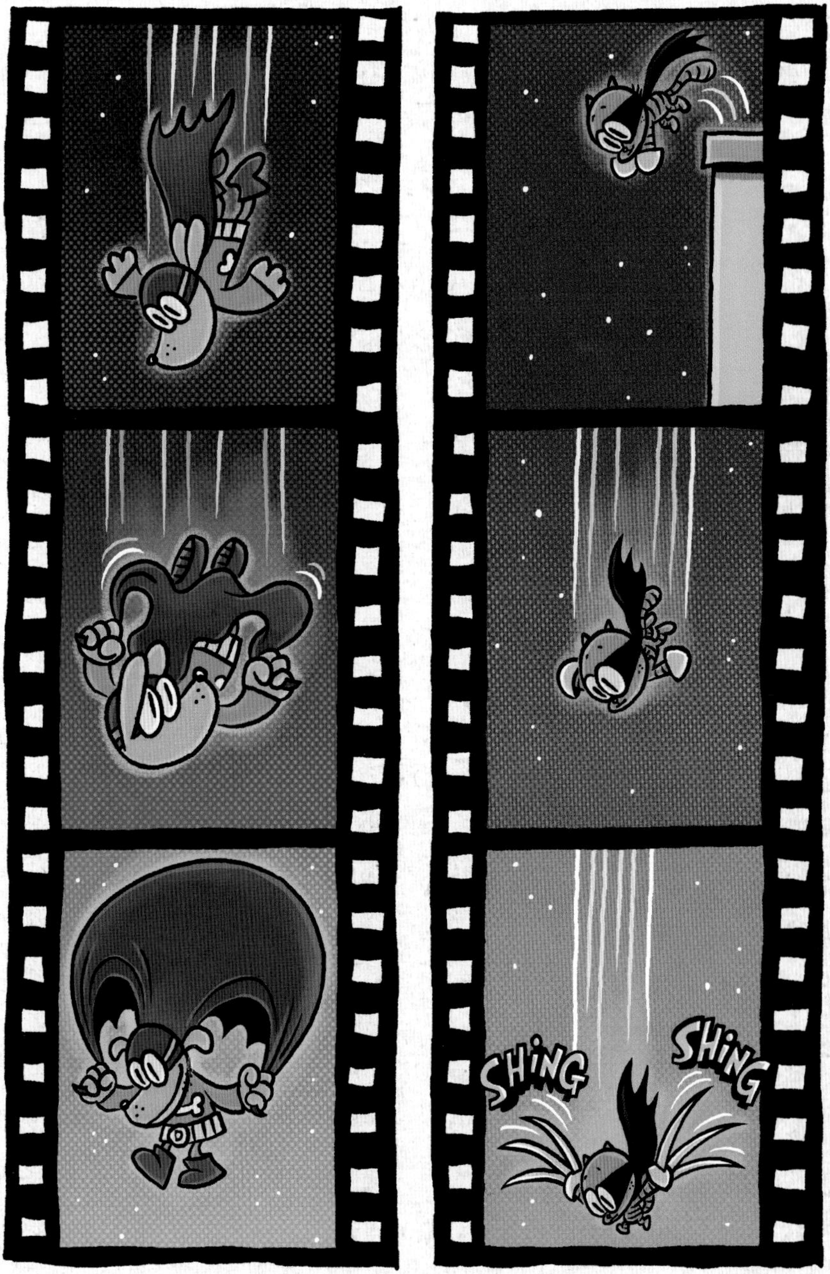
SHING
SHING

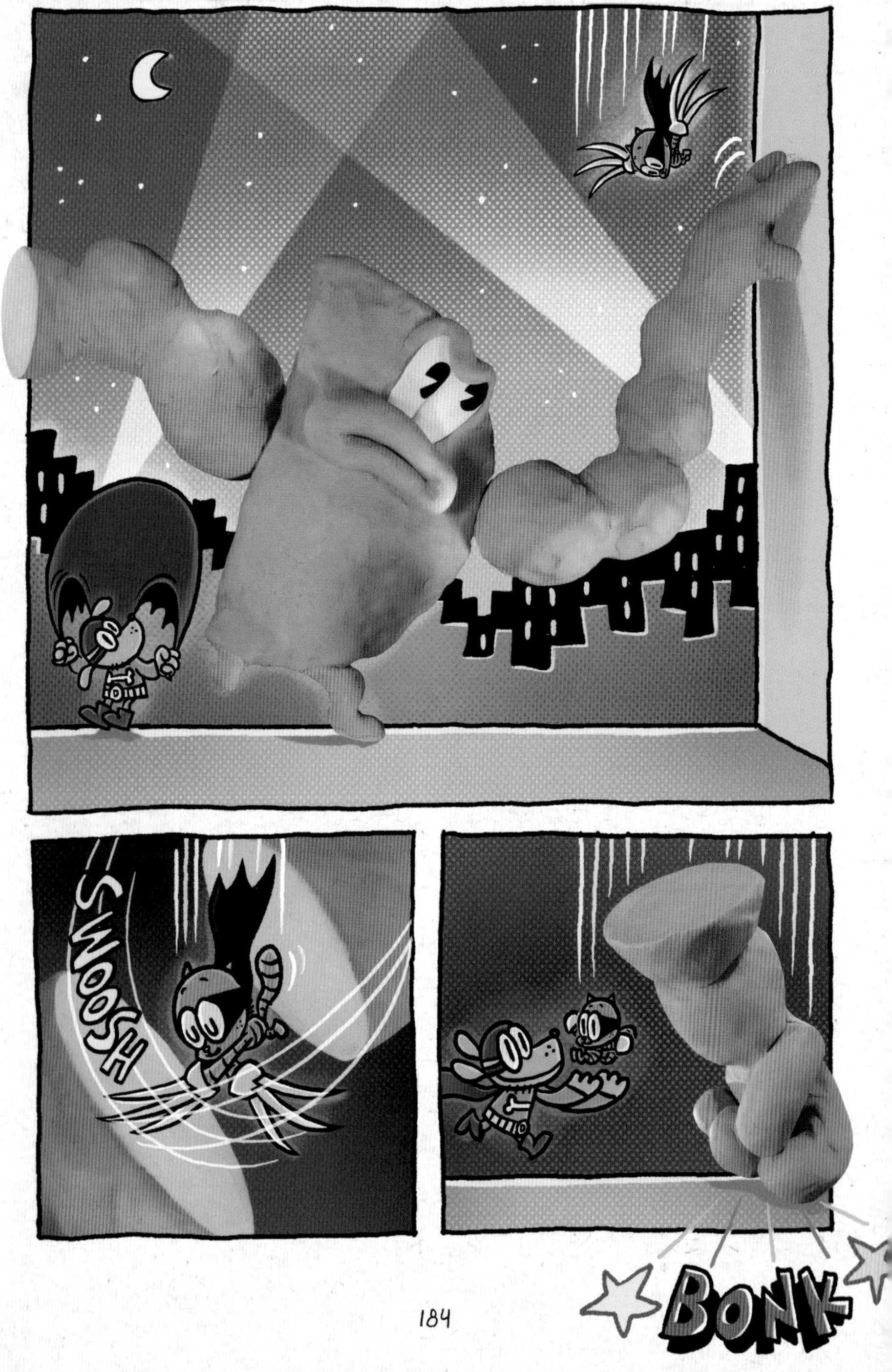
SWOOSH
BONK

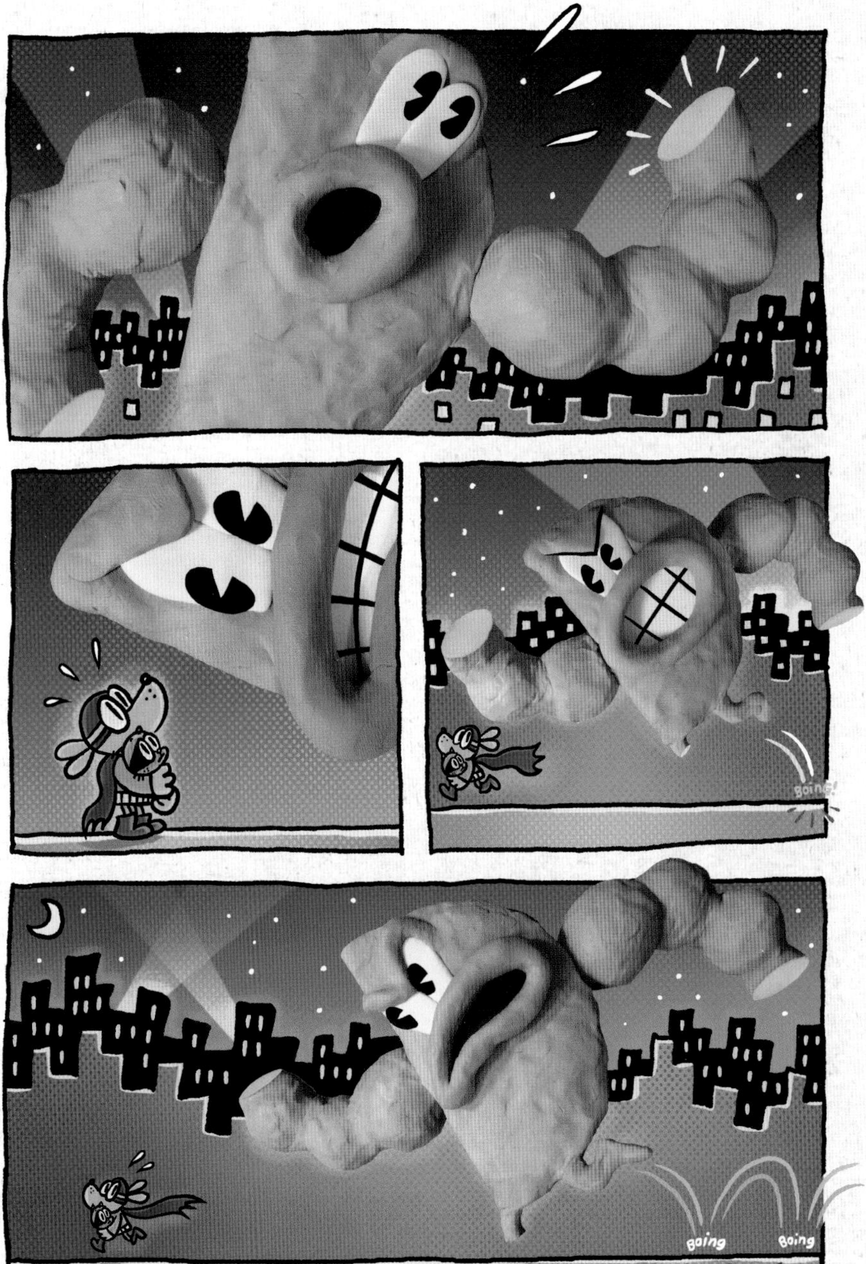
Boing!
Boing
Boing

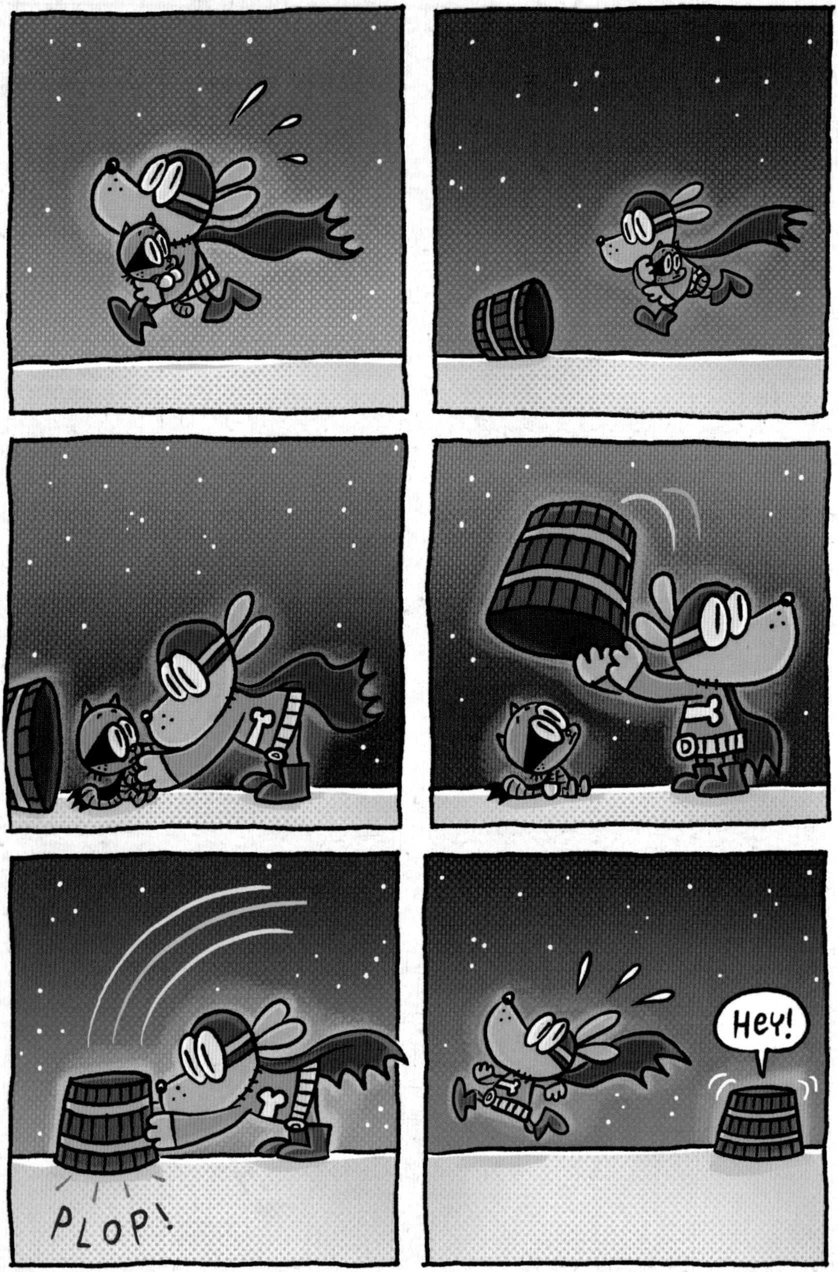
PLOP!
HEY!

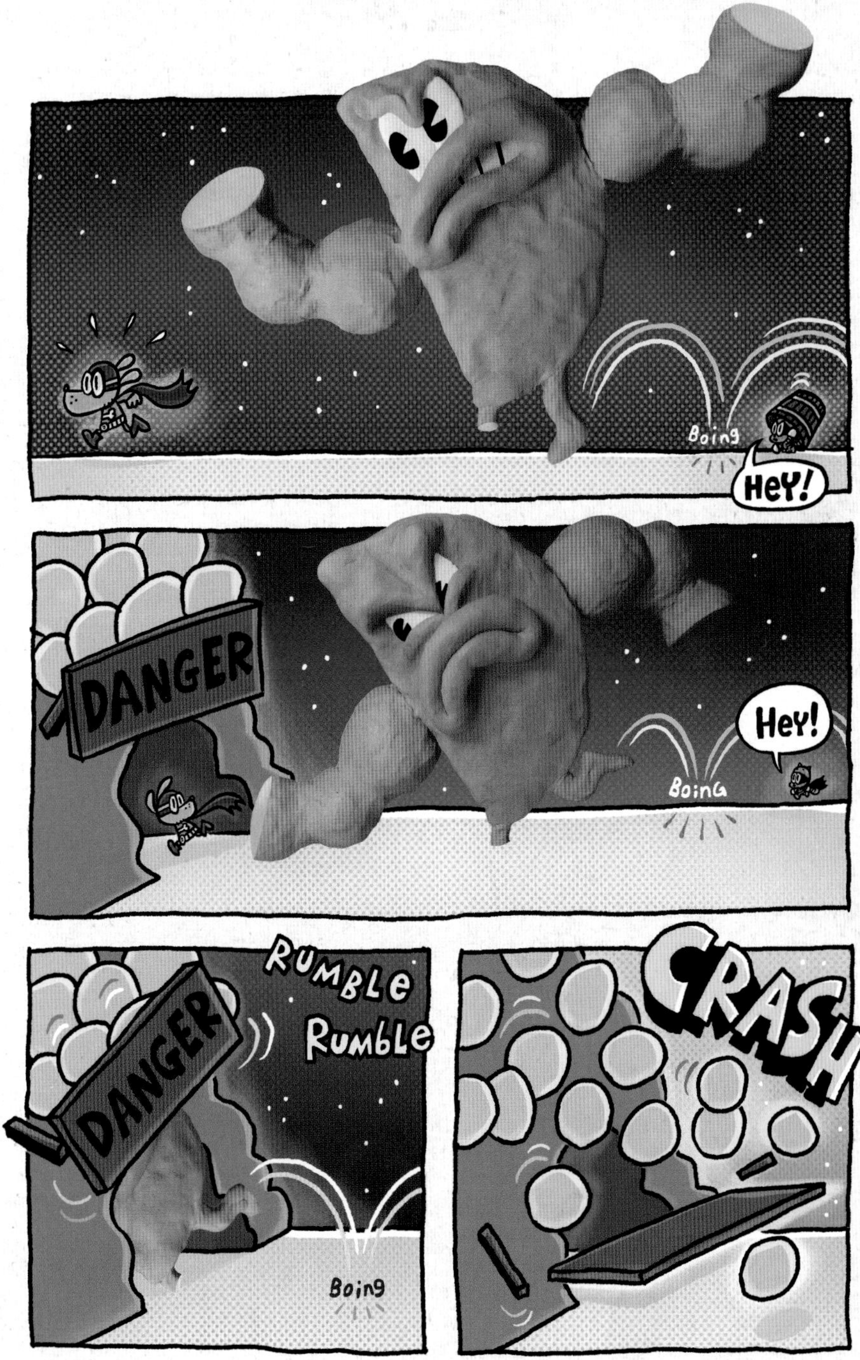
Boing
HEY!
DANGER
Boing
Hey!
DANGER
RUMBLE
Rumble
Boing
CRASH

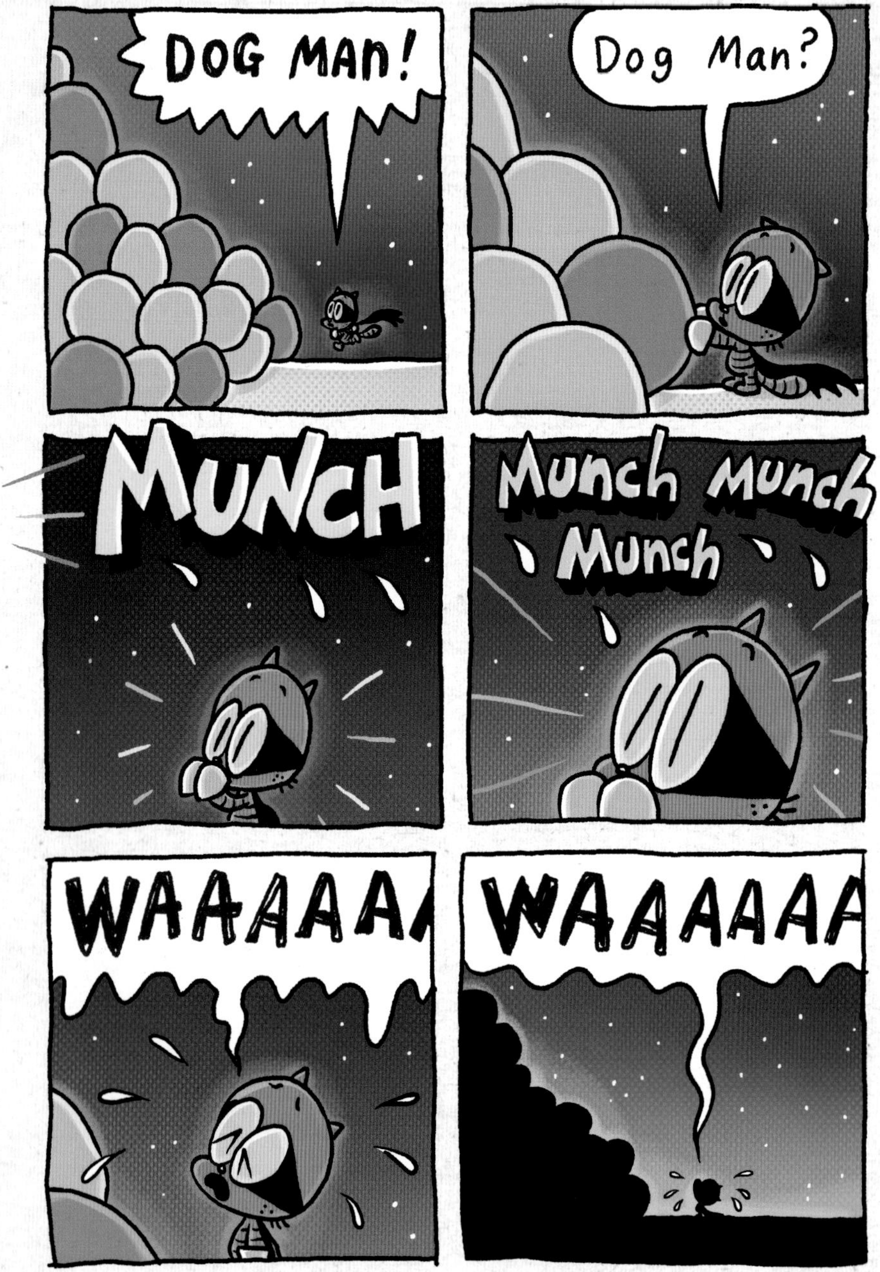
DOG MAN!
Dog Man?
MUNCH
Munch munch
Munch
WAAAAAA
WAAAAAA

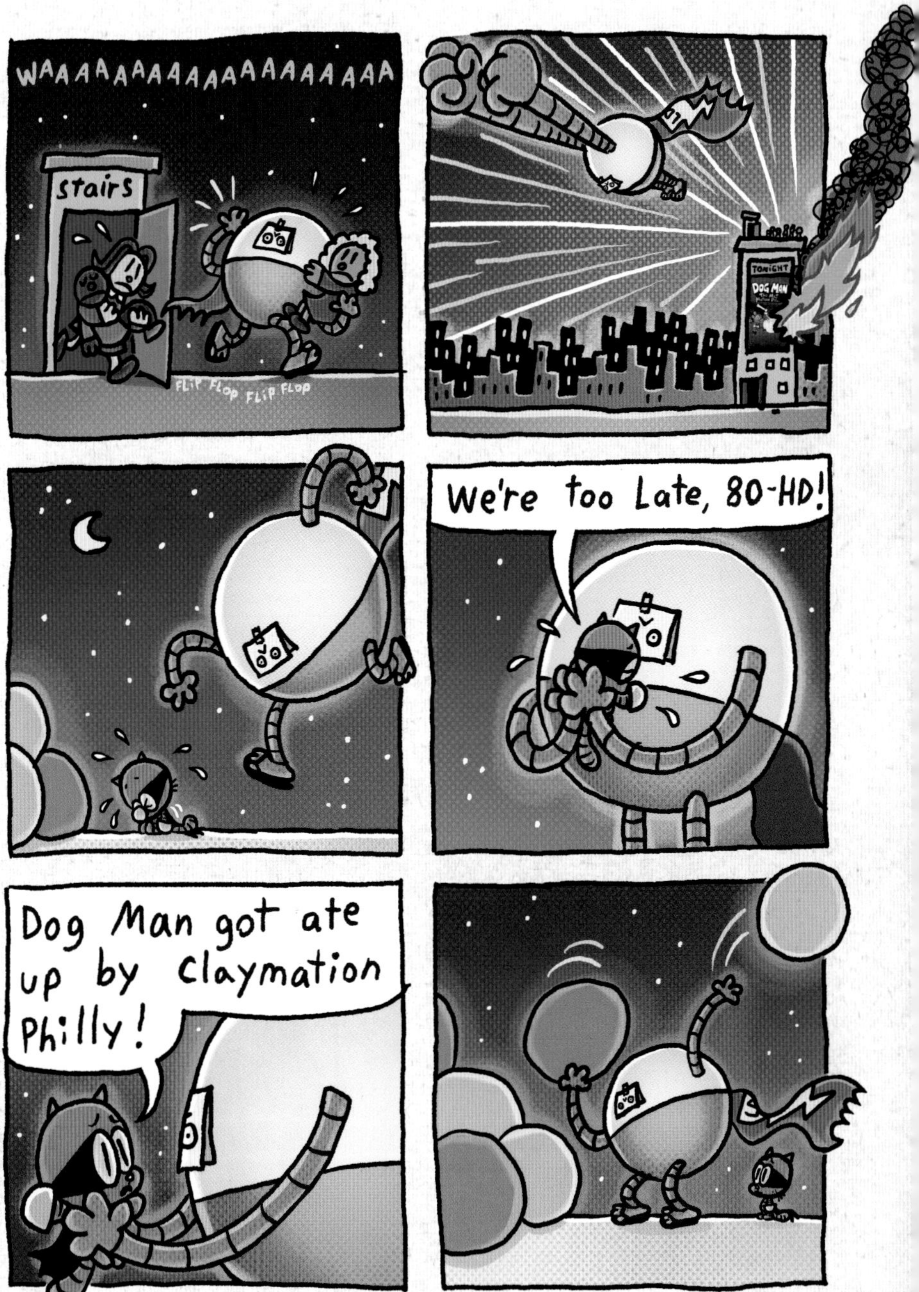
WAAAAAAAAAAAAAAAAA
Stairs
FLIP FLOP FLIP FLOP
TONIGHT
DOG MAN
We're too Late, 80-HD!
Dog Man got ate up by Claymation Philly!

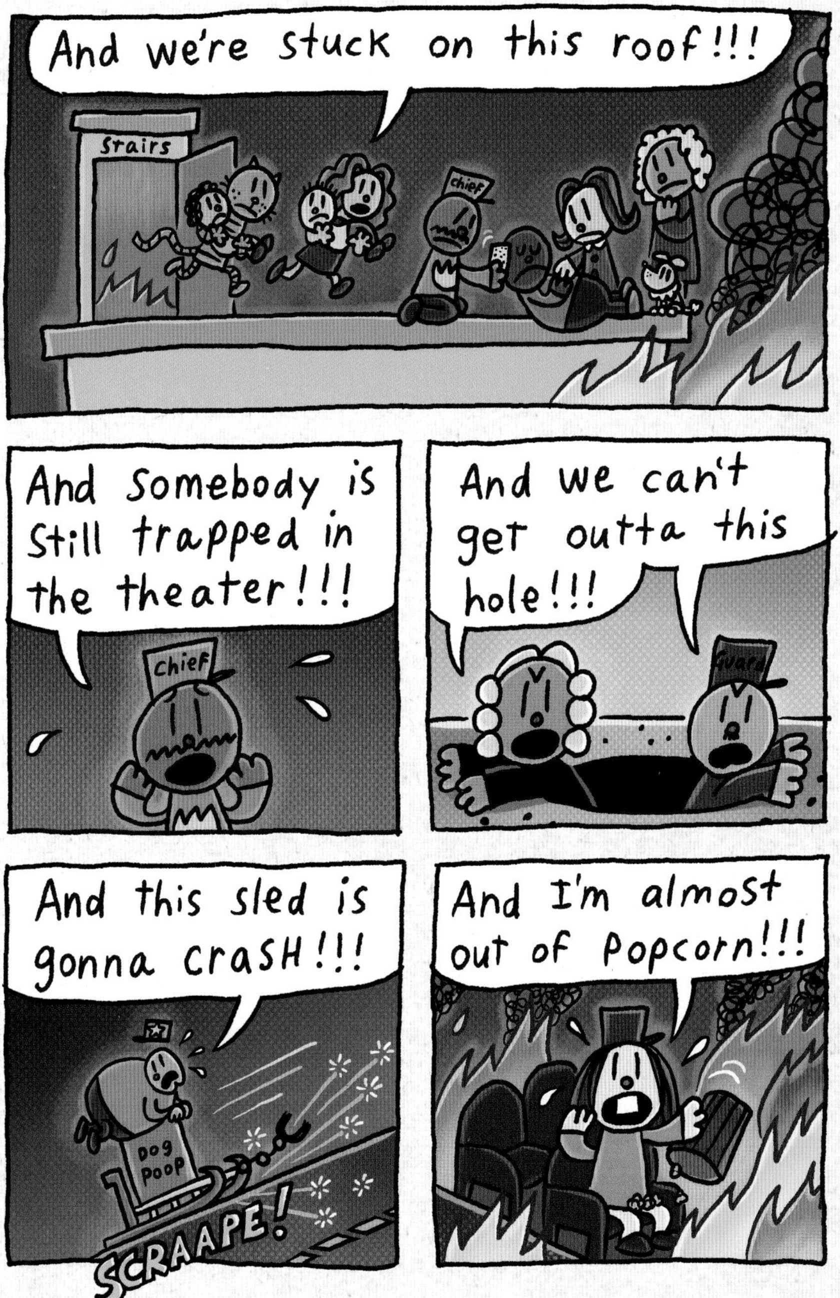
And we're stuck on this roof!!!
Stairs
chief
And somebody is still trapped in the theater!!!
Chief
And we can't get outta this hole!!!
Guard
And this sled is gonna crash!!!
Dog Poop
SCRAAPE!
And I'm almost out of popcorn!!!

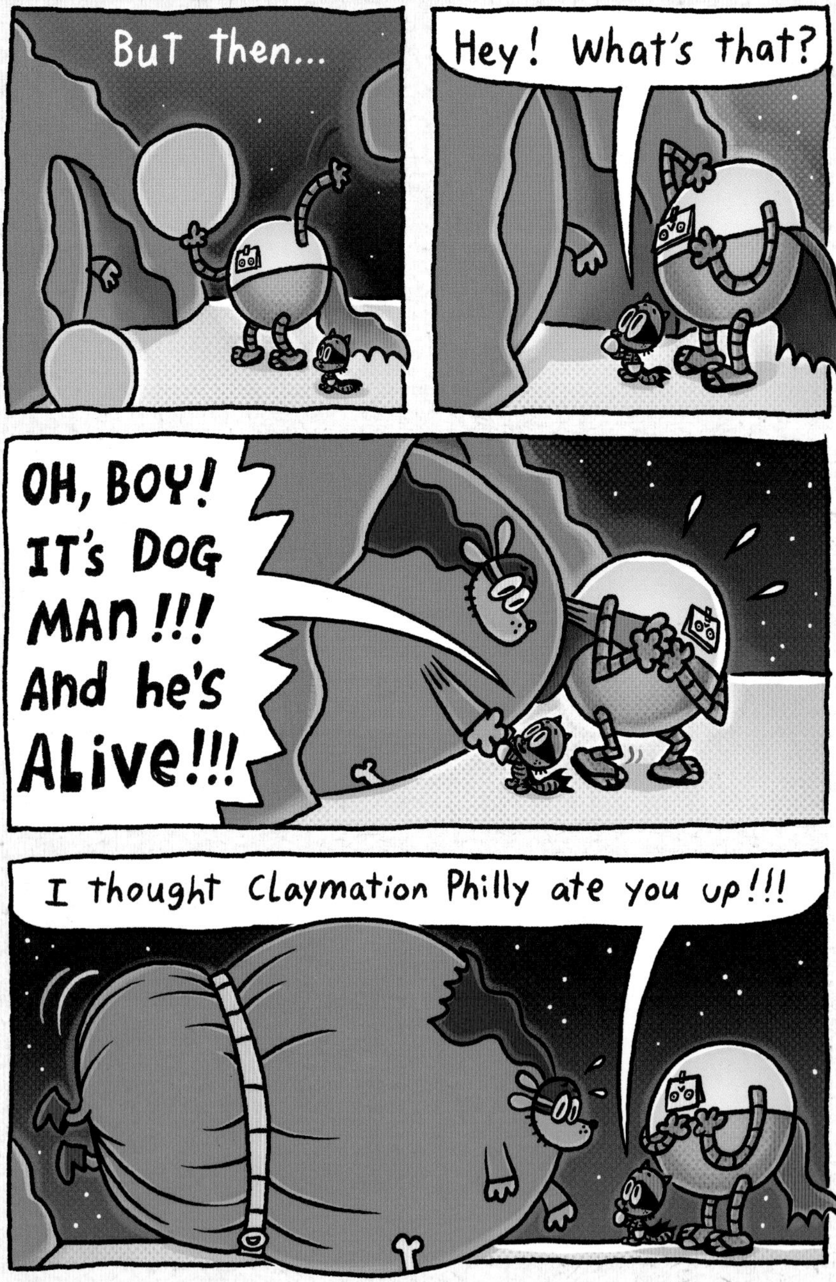
But then...
Hey! What's that?
OH, BOY! IT's DOG MAN!!! And he's ALive!!!
I thought Claymation Philly ate you up!!!

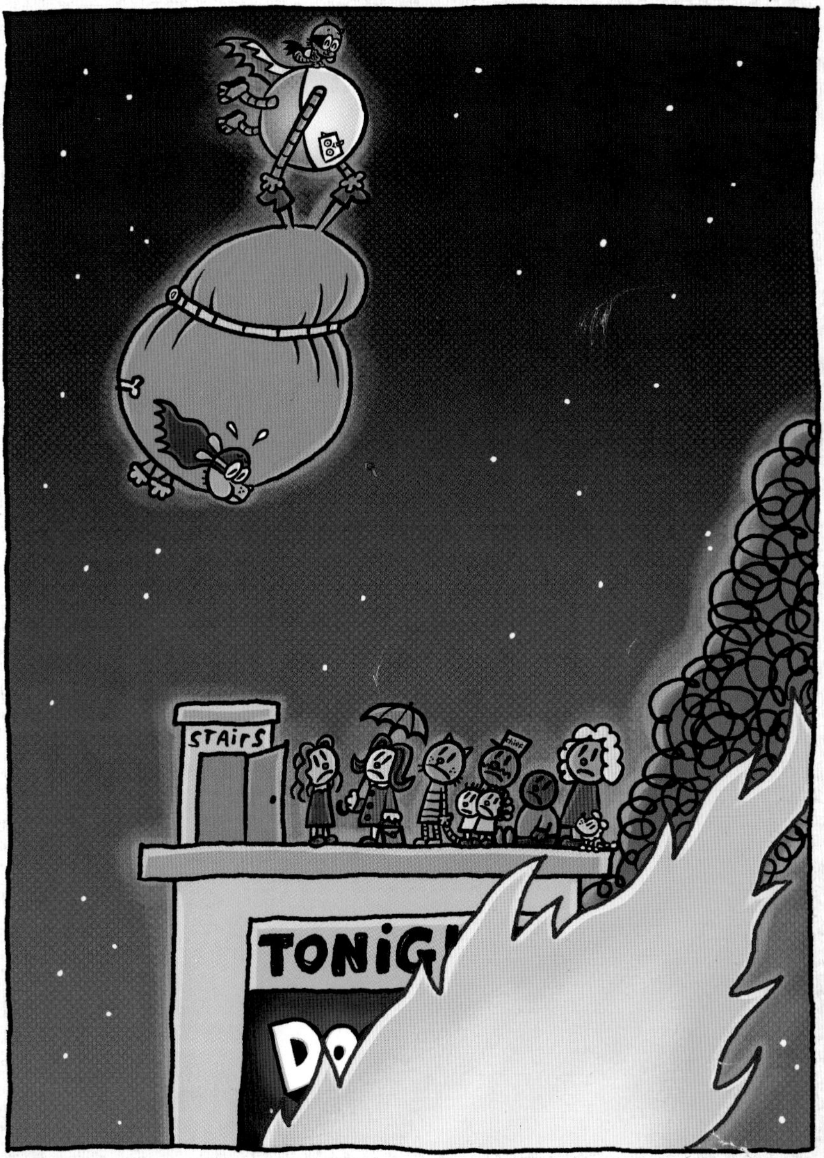
STAIRS
TONIG

Right Thumb here.

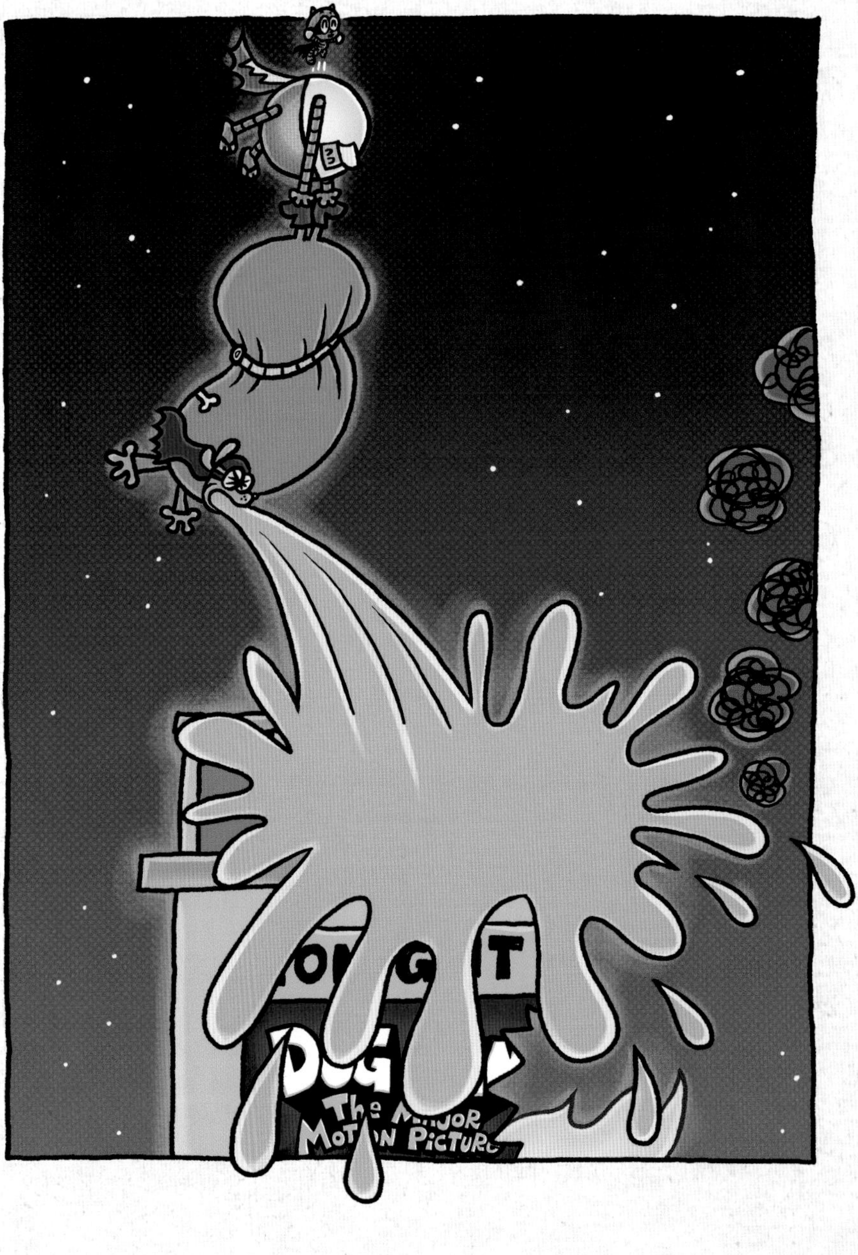
The

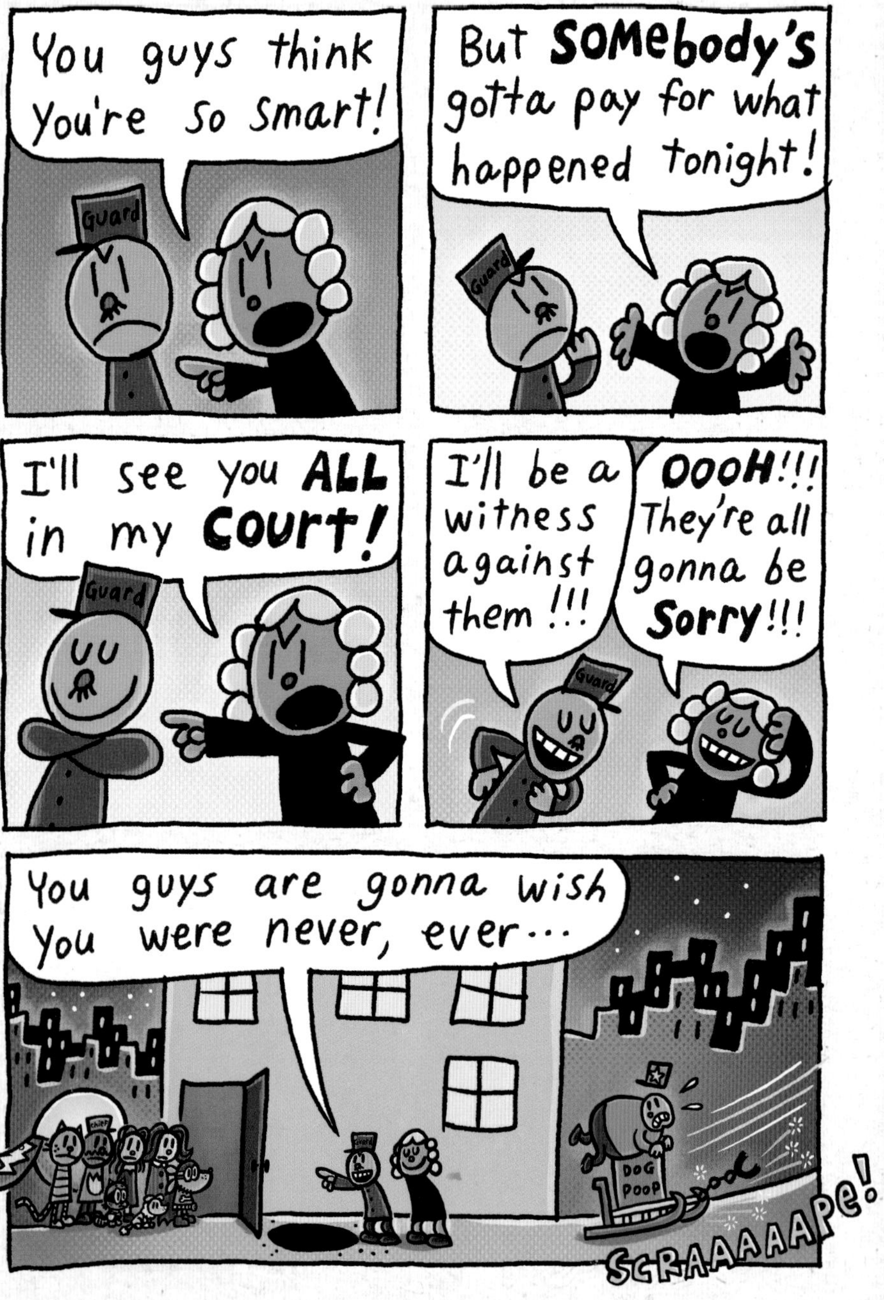
You guys think you're so smart!
But SOMEbody's gotta pay for what happened tonight!
I'll see you ALL in my COURT!
I'll be a witness against them!!!
OOOH!!! They're all gonna be SORRY!!!
You guys are gonna wish you were never, ever...
Guard
DOG POOP
SCRAAAAAPE!

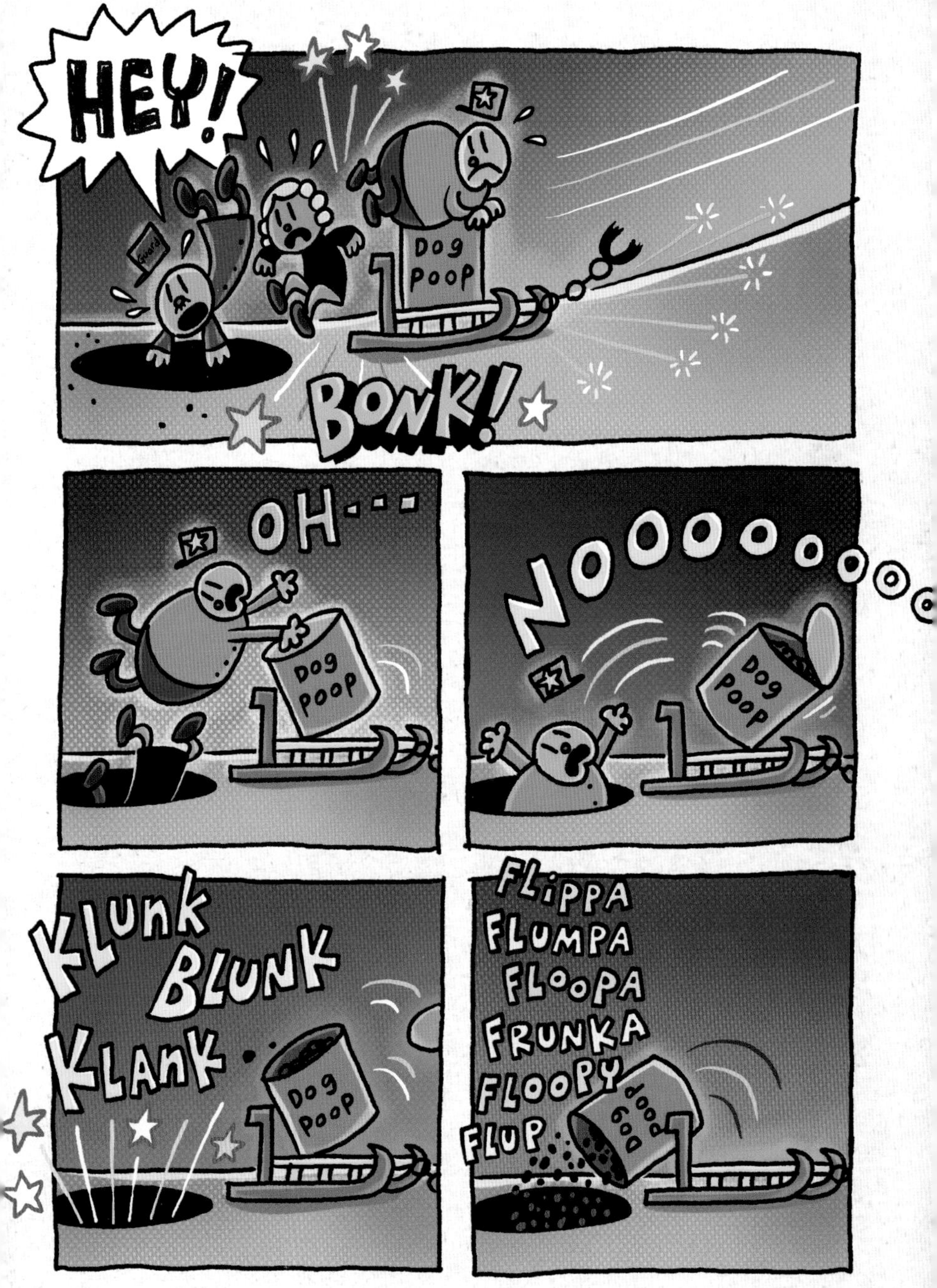
HEY!
Guard
Dog Poop
BONK!
OH...
Dog Poop
NOOOOOOOO
Dog Poop
KLUNK
BLUNK
KLANK
Dog Poop
FLIPPA
FLUMPA
FLOOPA
FRUNKA
FLOOPY
FLUP
Dog Poop

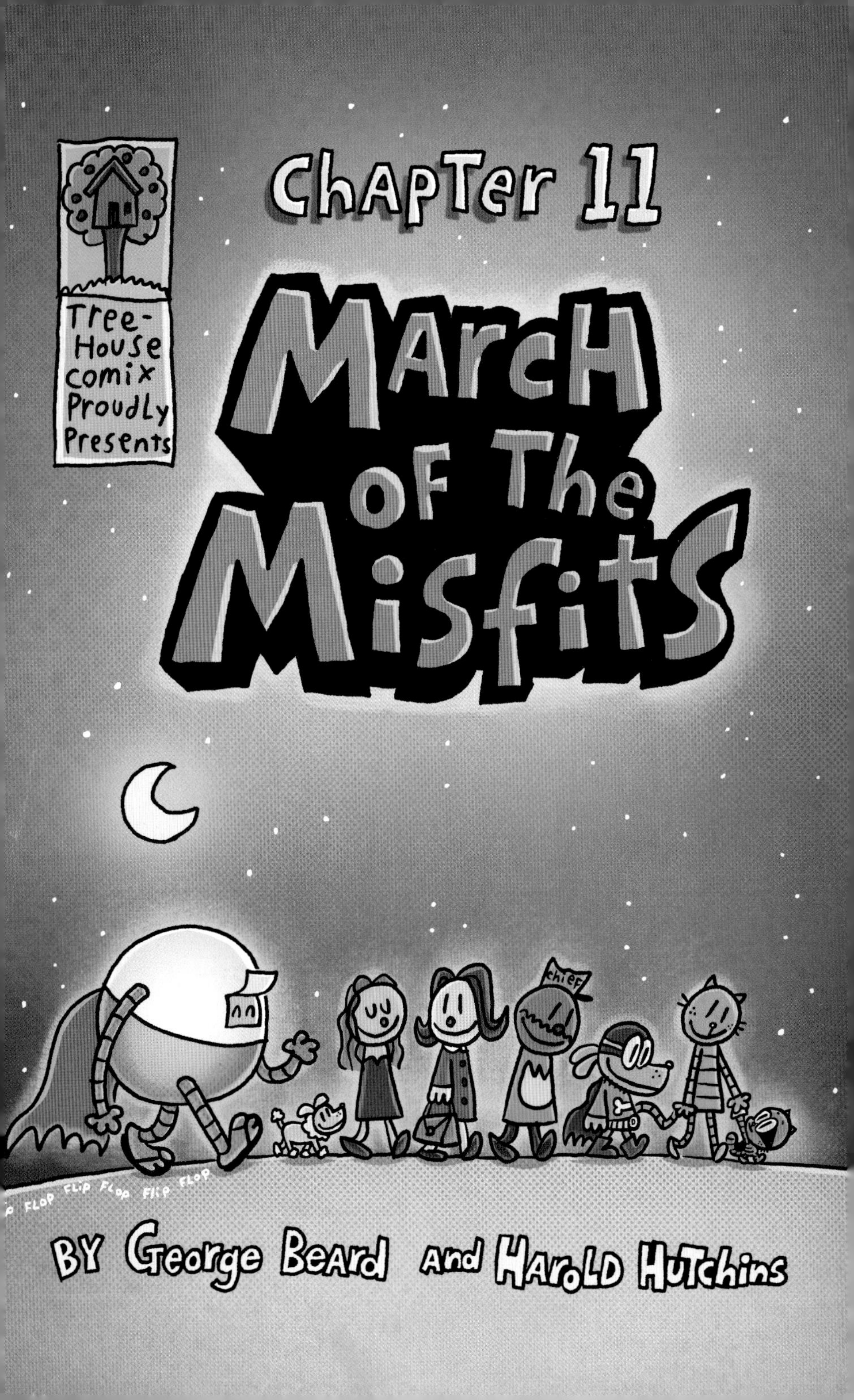

Tree-House comix Proudly Presents
ChapTer 11
March of The Misfits
chief
FLOP FLIP FLOP FLIP FLOP
BY George Beard And Harold Hutchins

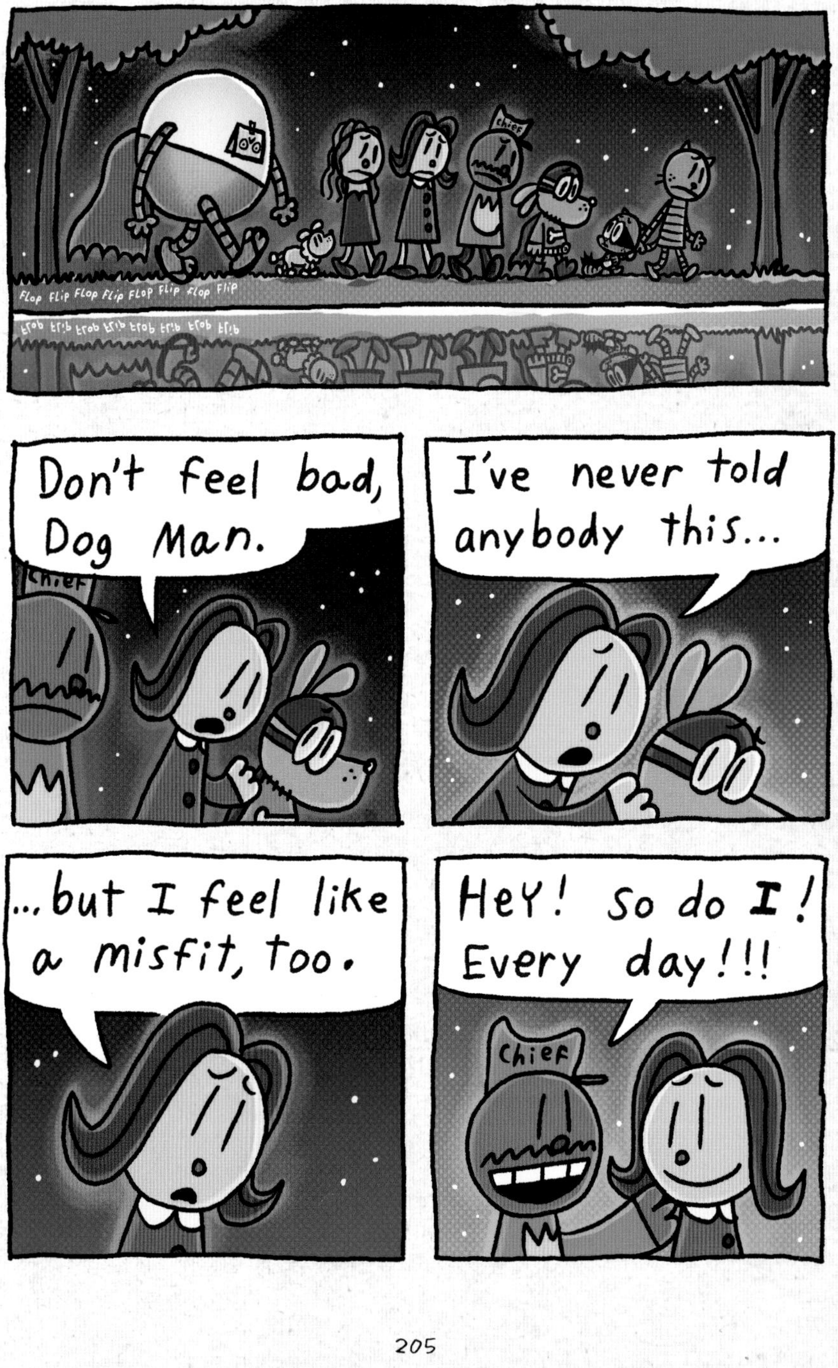
Flop Flip Flop Flip Flop Flip flop Flip
Don't feel bad, Dog Man.
I've never told anybody this...
...but I feel like a misfit, too.
HeY! So do I! Every day!!!

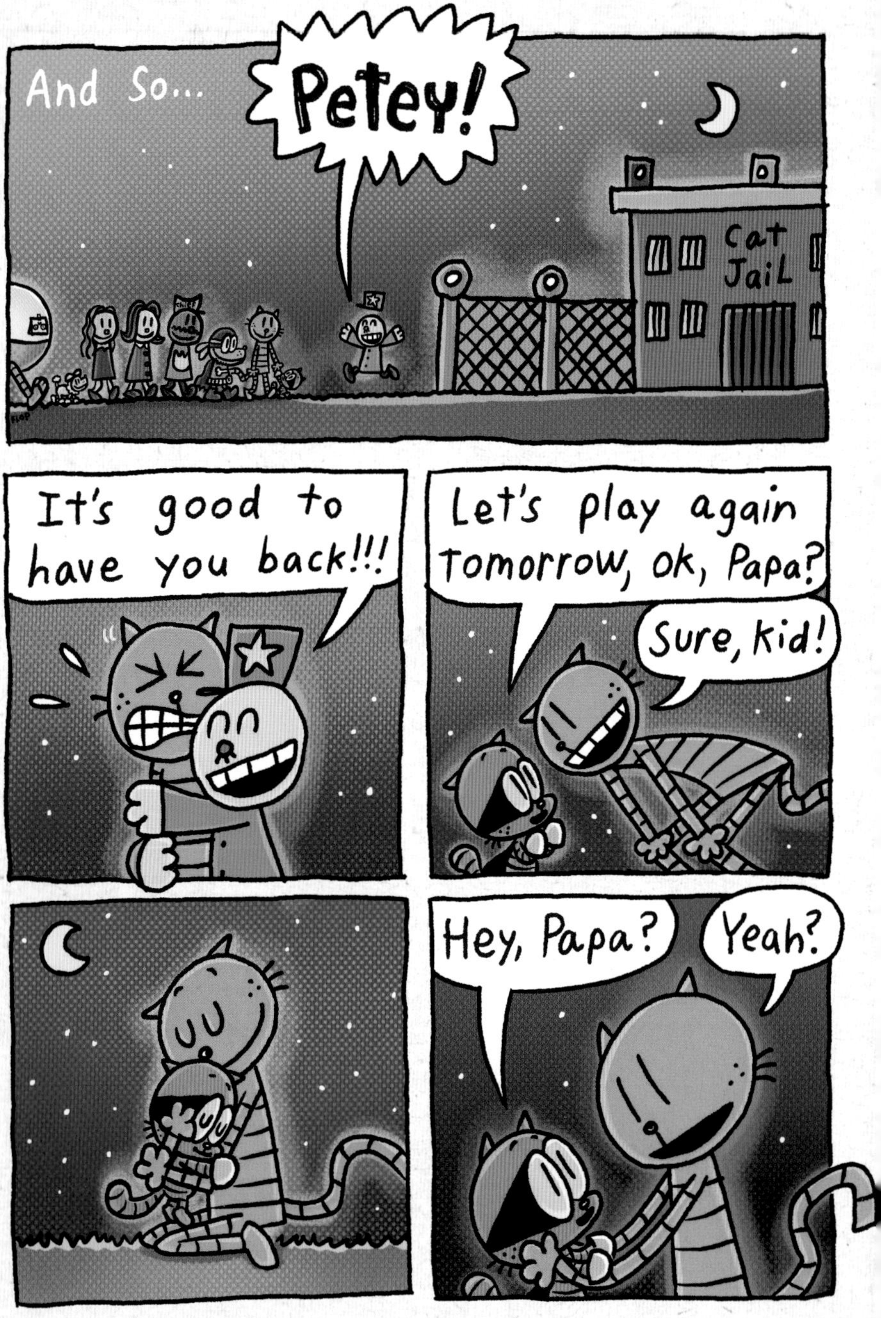
And So...
Petey!
Cat Jail
It's good to have you back!!!
Let's play again tomorrow, ok, Papa?
Sure, kid!
Hey, Papa?
Yeah?

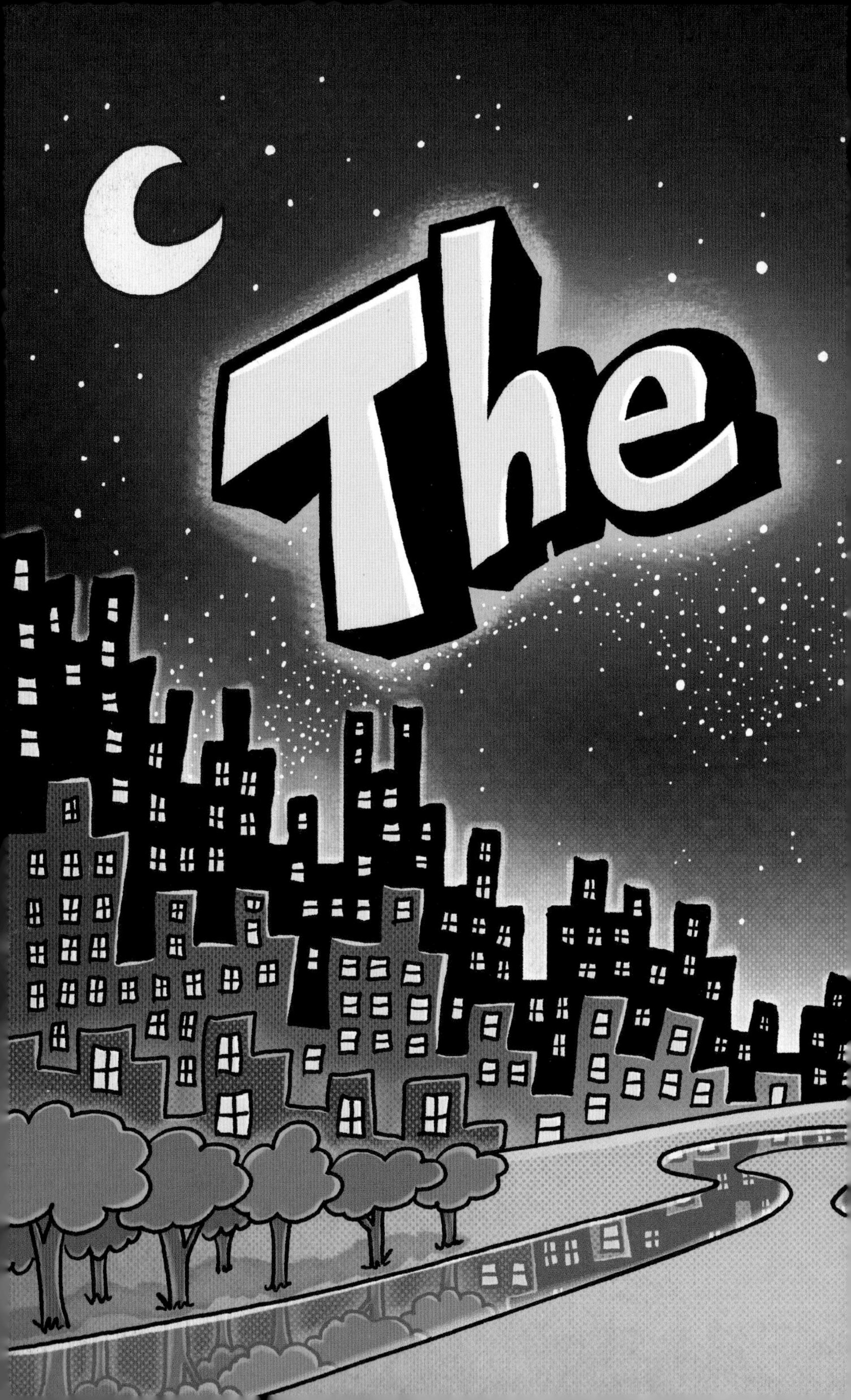
The

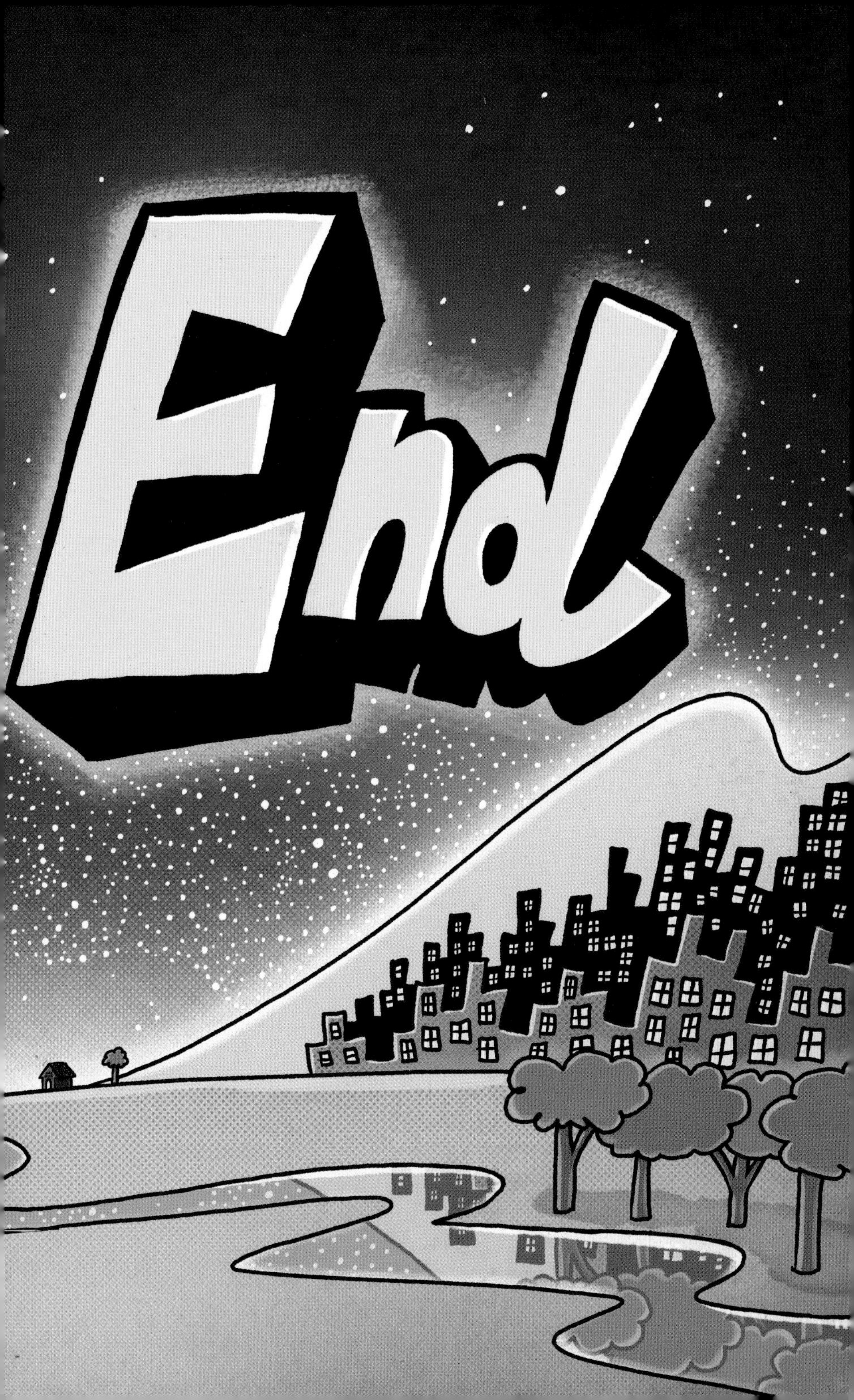
End

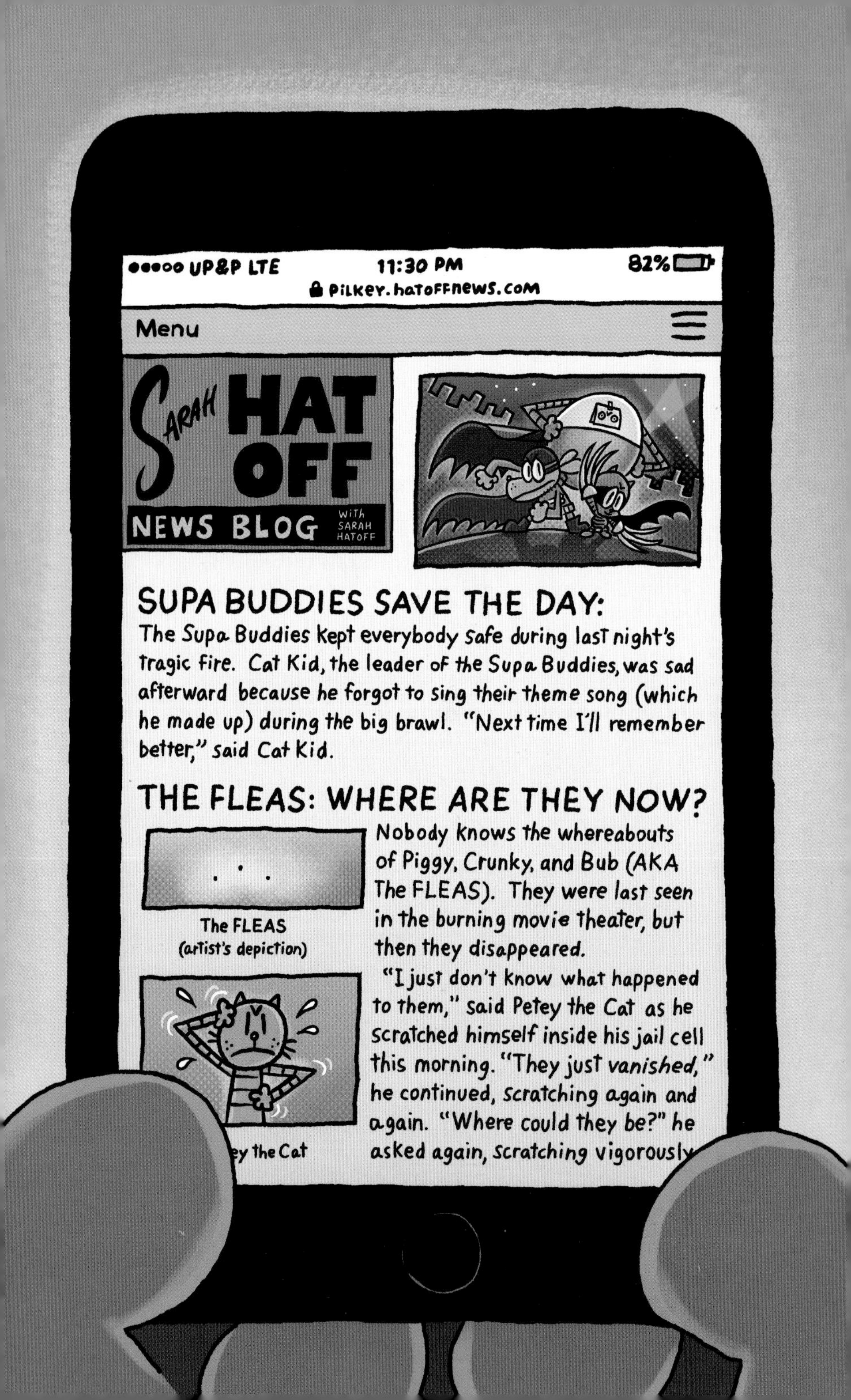

Menu   ☰

SUPA BUDDIES SAVE THE DAY:

The Supa Buddies kept everybody safe during last night's tragic fire. Cat Kid, the leader of the Supa Buddies, was sad afterward because he forgot to sing their theme song (which he made up) during the big brawl. "Next time I'll remember better," said Cat Kid.

THE FLEAS: WHERE ARE THEY NOW?

The FLEAS
(artist's depiction)

ey the Cat

Nobody knows the whereabouts of Piggy, Crunky, and Bub (AKA The FLEAS). They were last seen in the burning movie theater, but then they disappeared.

   "I just don't know what happened to them," said Petey the Cat as he scratched himself inside his jail cell this morning. "They just vanished," he continued, scratching again and again. "Where could they be?" he asked again, scratching vigorously

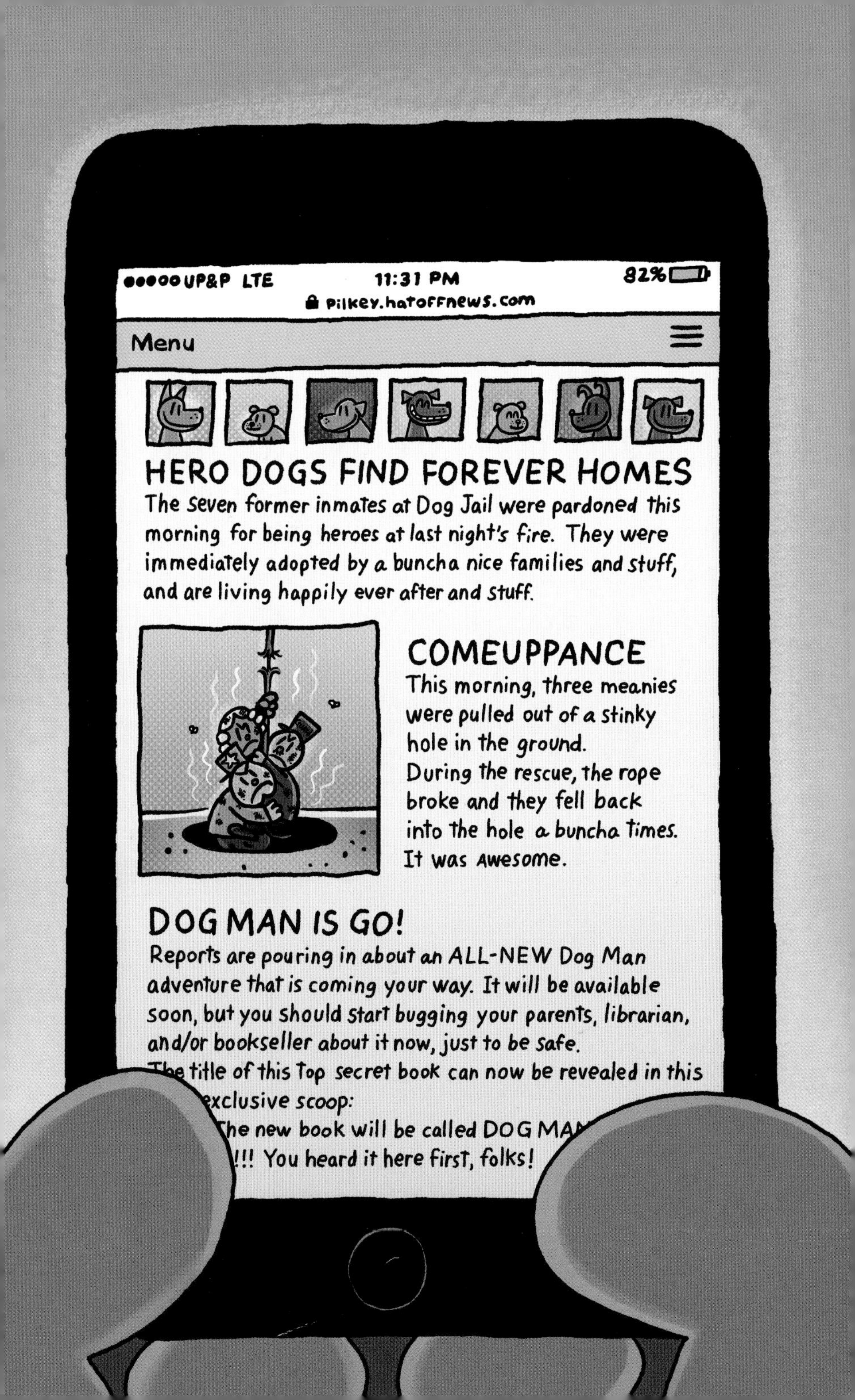

UP&P LTE
11:31 PM
82%
pilkey.hatoffnews.com
Menu
HERO DOGS FIND FOREVER HOMES
The seven former inmates at Dog Jail were pardoned this morning for being heroes at last night's fire. They were immediately adopted by a buncha nice families and stuff, and are living happily ever after and stuff.
COMEUPPANCE
This morning, three meanies were pulled out of a stinky hole in the ground. During the rescue, the rope broke and they fell back into the hole a buncha times. It was awesome.
DOG MAN IS GO!
Reports are pouring in about an ALL-NEW Dog Man adventure that is coming your way. It will be available soon, but you should start bugging your parents, librarian, and/or bookseller about it now, just to be safe.
title of this top secret book can now be revealed in this
exclusive scoop:
new book will be called
!!! You heard it here first, folks!

HOW 2 DRAW CATKiD

in 49 Ridiculously easy Steps!

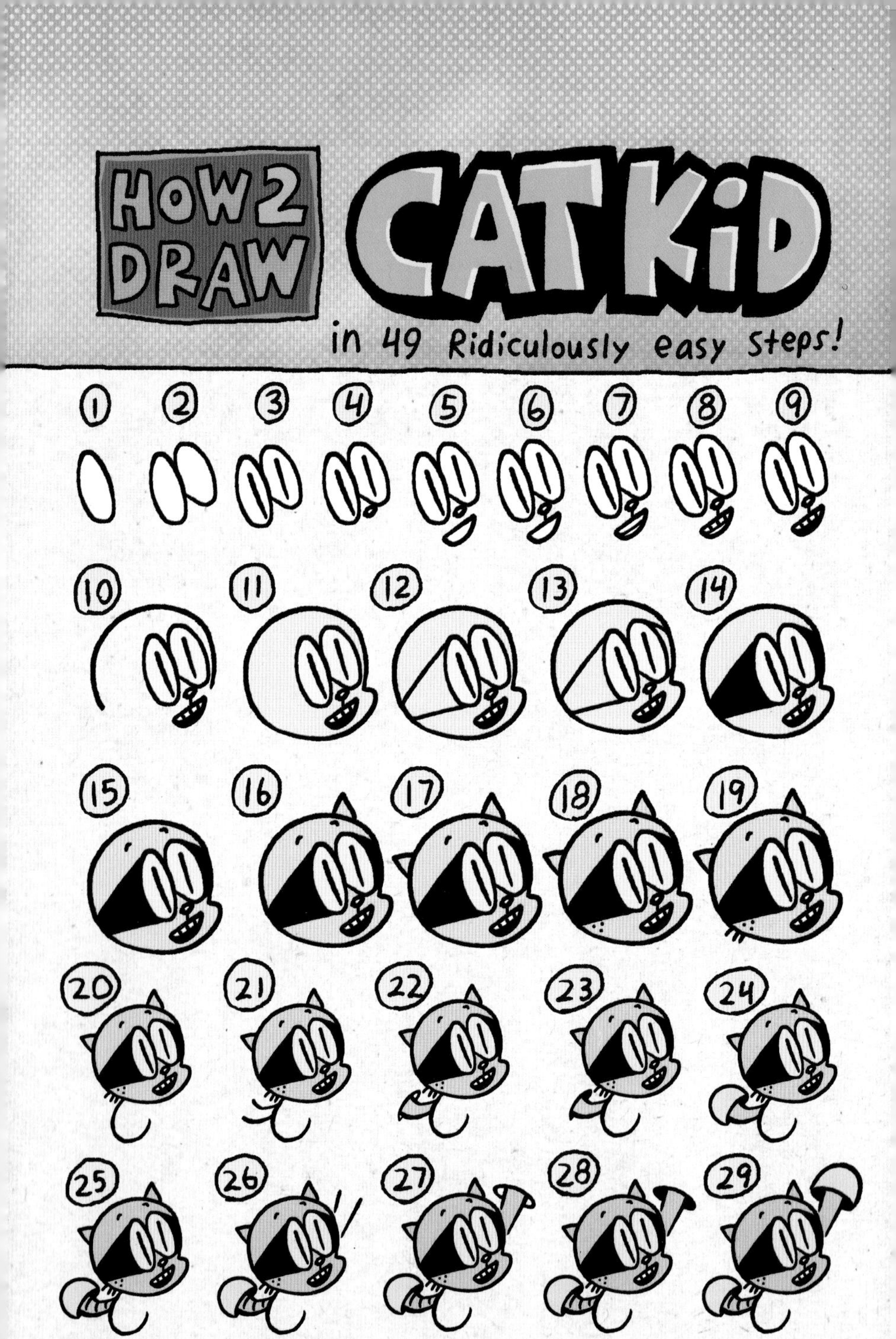
1
2
3
4
5
6
7
8
9
10
11
12
13
14
15
16
17
18
19
20
21
22
23
24
25
26
27
28
29

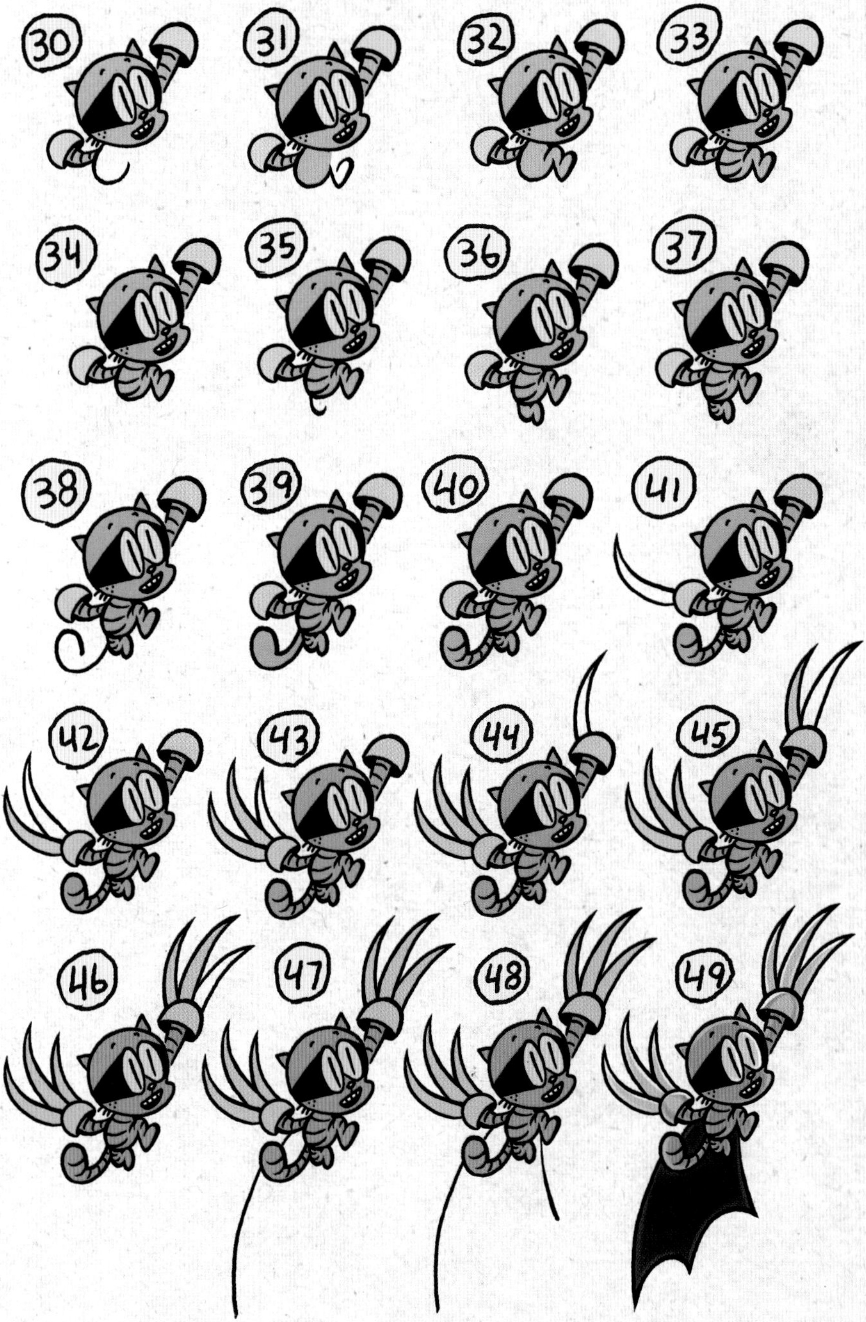
30
31
32
33
34
35
36
37
38
39
40
41
42
43
44
45
46
47
48
49

HOW 2 DRAW LIGHTNING DUDE

in 33 Ridiculously easy steps!

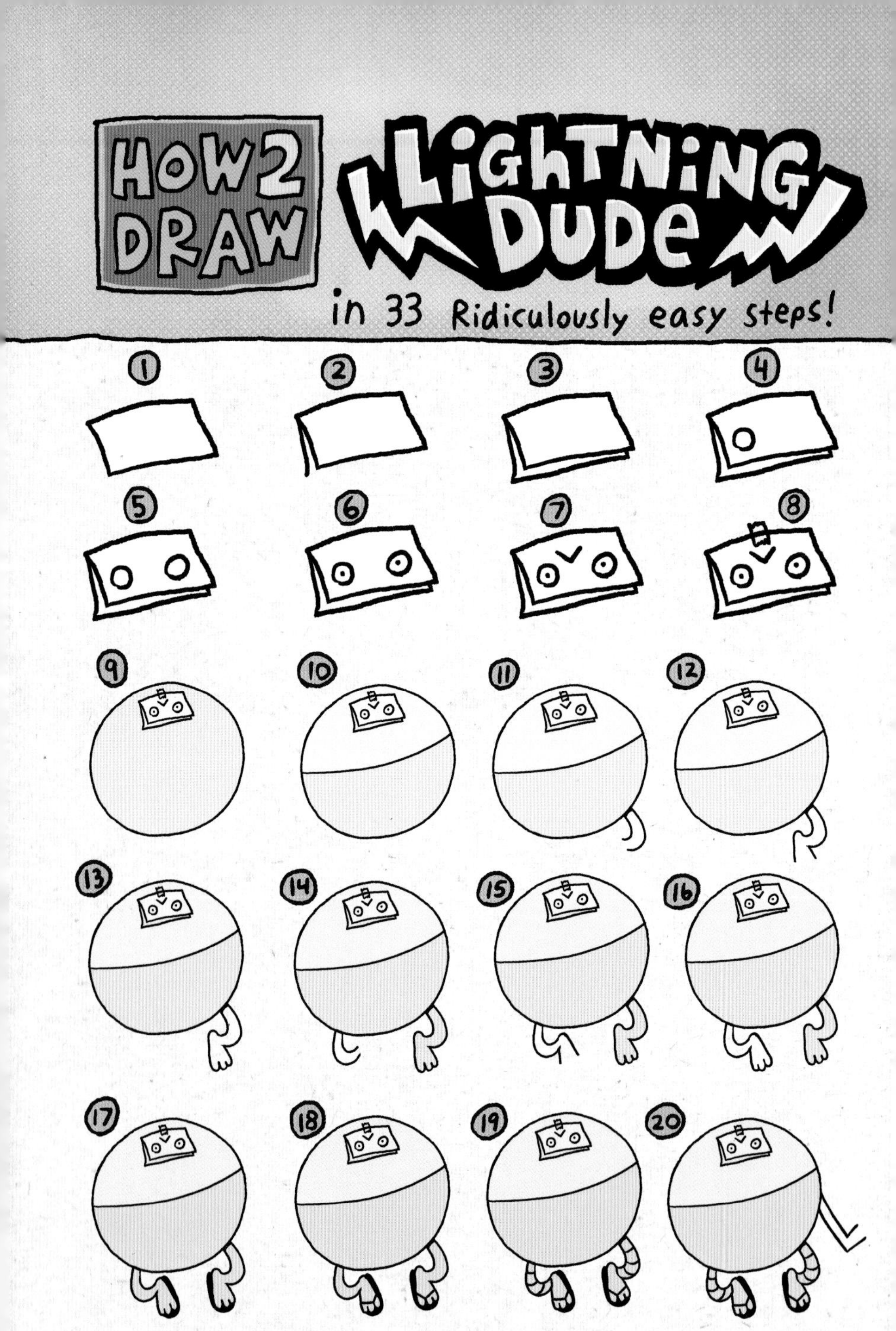
1
2
3
4
5
6
7
8
9
10
11
12
13
14
15
16
17
18
19
20

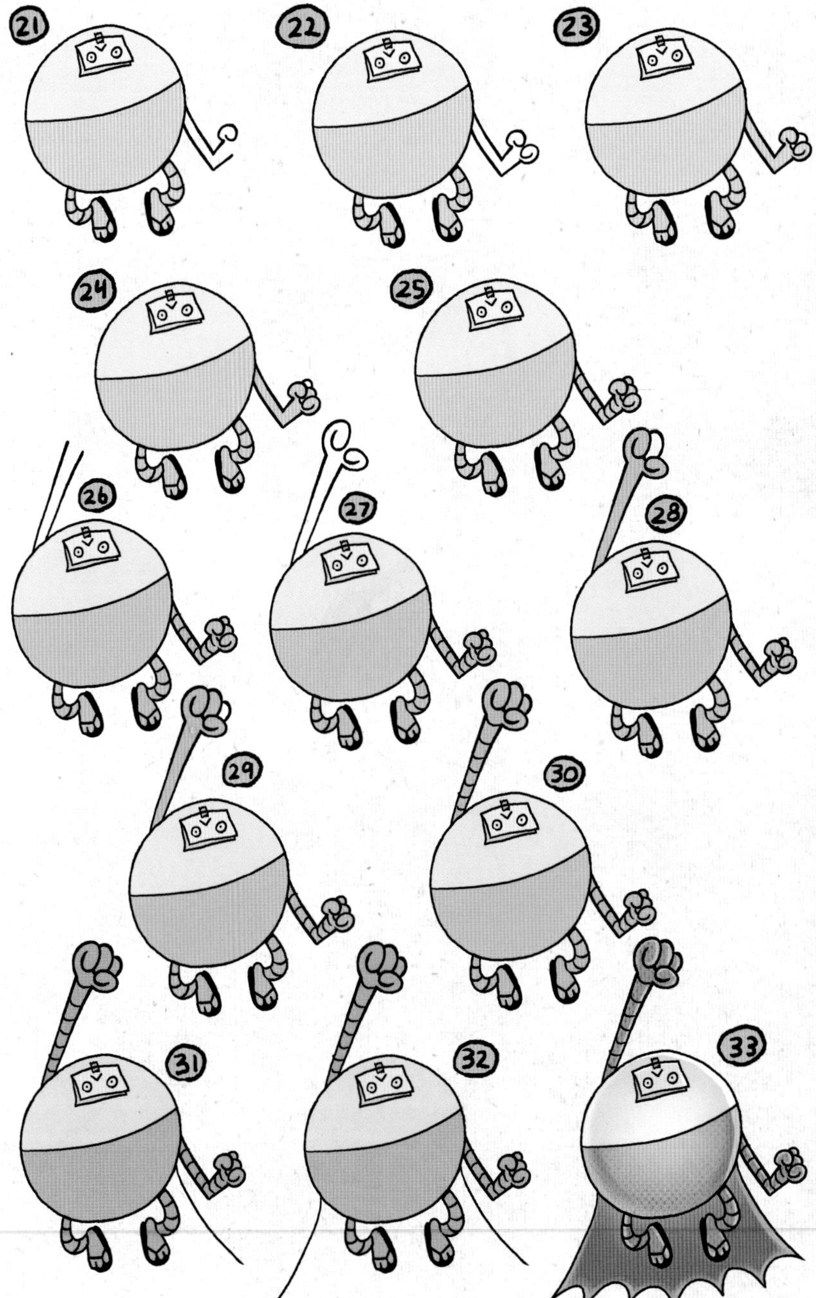
21
22
23
24
25
26
27
28
29
30
31
32
33

HOW 2 DRAW THE BARK KNIGHT

in 46 Ridiculously easy Steps!

1
2
3
4
5
6
7
8
9
10
11
12
13
14
15
16
17

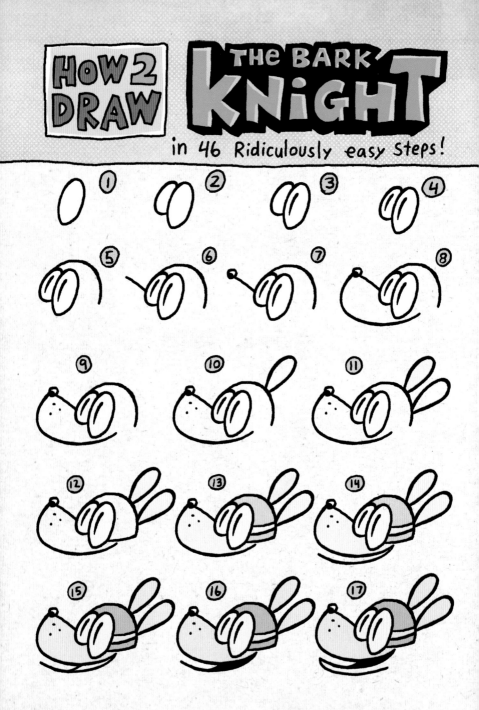

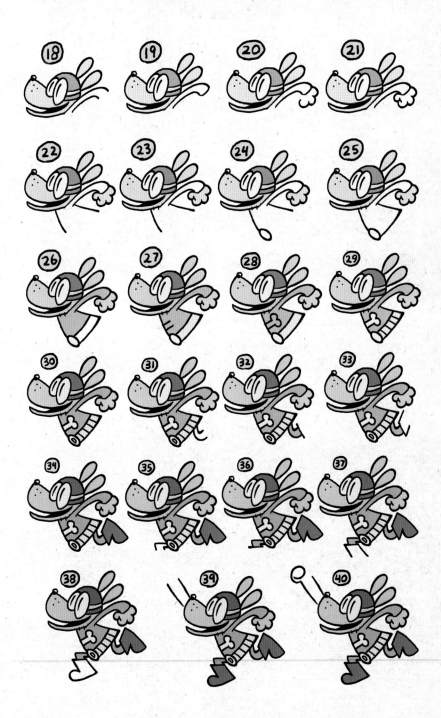

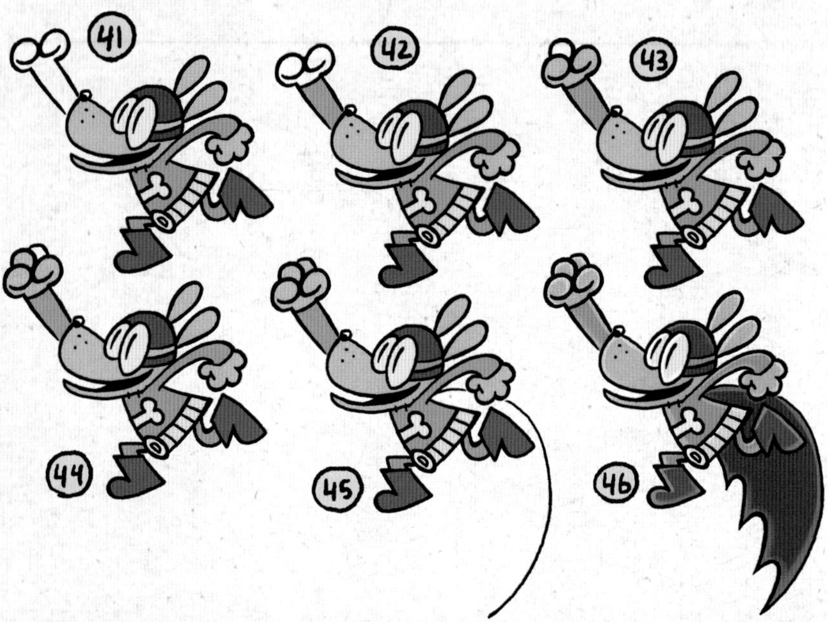
41
42
43
44
45
46

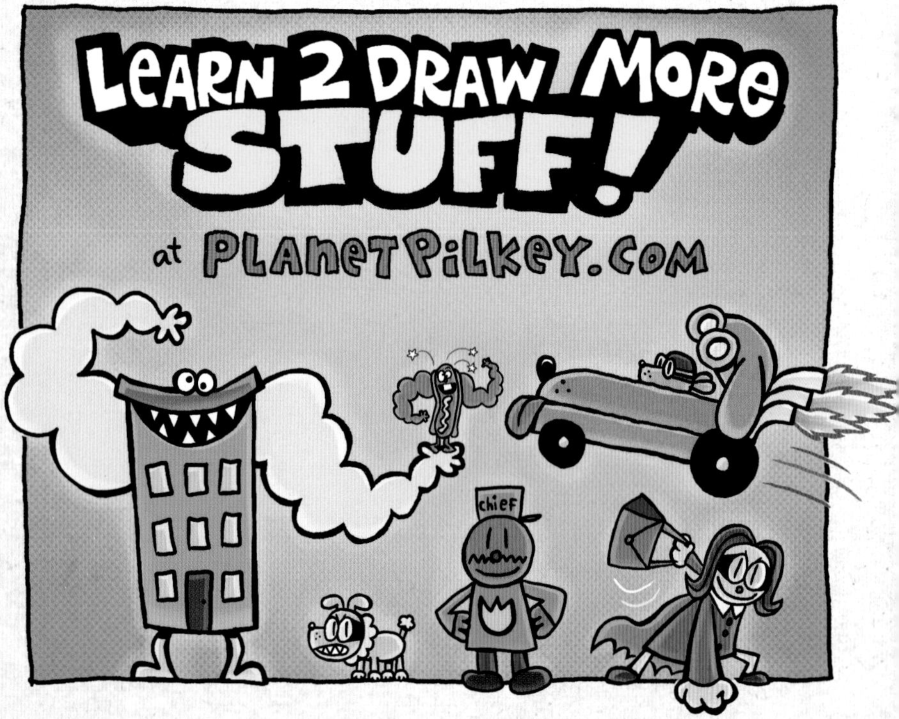
LEARN 2 DRAW MORE
STUFF!
at PLANETPILKEY.COM
chief

GET READING W

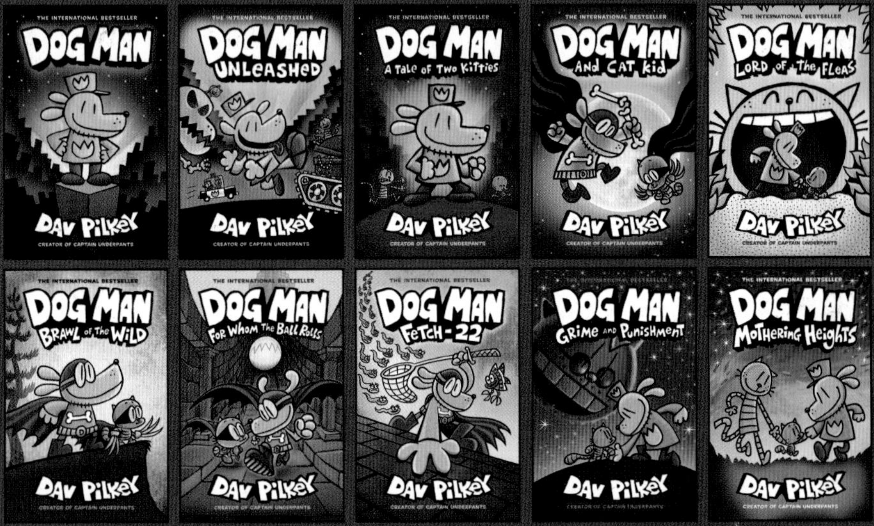
THE INTERNATIONAL BESTSELLER
DOG MAN
DAV PILKEY
CREATOR OF CAPTAIN UNDERPANTS
DOG MAN UNLEASHED
DOG MAN A TALE OF TWO KITTIES
DOG MAN AND CAT KID
DOG MAN LORD OF THE FLEAS
DOG MAN BRAWL OF THE WILD
DOG MAN FOR WHOM THE BALL ROLLS
DOG MAN FETCH-22
DOG MAN GRIME AND PUNISHMENT
DOG MAN MOTHERING HEIGHTS

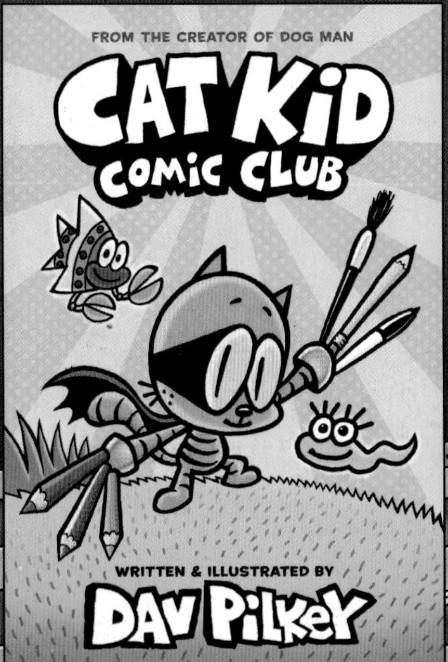
FROM THE CREATOR OF DOG MAN
CAT KID
COMIC CLUB
WRITTEN & ILLUSTRATED BY
DAV PILKEY

★ "Irreverent, laugh-out-loud funny, and . . . downright moving."
— Publishers Weekly, starred review

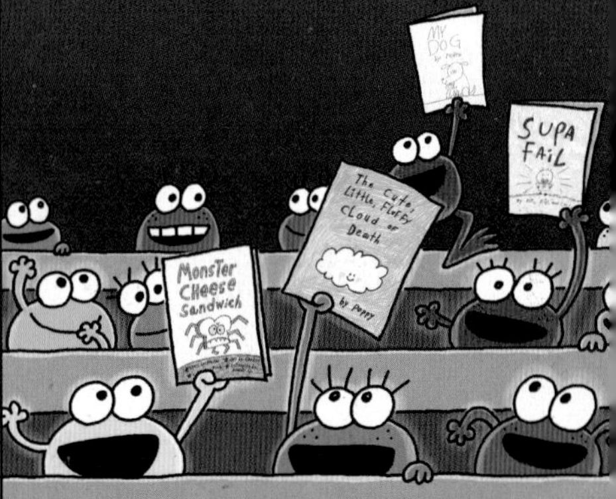
MY DOG
SUPA FAIL
The Cute, Little, Fluffy Cloud of Death
Monster Cheese Sandwich

ABOUT THE
AUTHOR-ILLUSTRATOR

When Dav Pilkey was a kid, he was diagnosed with ADHD and dyslexia. Dav was so disruptive in class that his teachers made him sit out in the hallway every day. Luckily, Dav loved to draw and make up stories. He spent his time in the hallway creating his own original comic books — the very first adventures of Dog Man and Captain Underpants.

In college, Dav met a teacher who encouraged him to illustrate and write. He won a national competition in 1986 and the prize was the publication of his first book, WORLD WAR WON. He made many other books before being awarded the 1998 California Young Reader Medal for DOG BREATH, which was published in 1994, and in 1997 he won the Caldecott Honor for THE PAPERBOY.

THE ADVENTURES OF SUPER DIAPER BABY, published in 2002, was the first complete graphic novel spin-off from the Captain Underpants series and appeared at #6 on the USA Today bestseller list for all books, both adult and children's, and was also a New York Times bestseller. It was followed by THE ADVENTURES OF OOK AND GLUK: KUNG FU CAVEMEN FROM THE FUTURE and SUPER DIAPER BABY 2: THE INVASION OF THE POTTY SNATCHERS, both USA Today bestsellers. The unconventional style of these graphic novels is intended to encourage uninhibited creativity in kids.

His stories are semi-autobiographical and explore universal themes that celebrate friendship, tolerance, and the triumph of the good-hearted.

Dav loves to kayak in the Pacific Northwest with his wife.

Learn more at Pilkey.com.